VIOLENT PEACE

ALSO BY DAVID POYER

Tales of the Modern Navy

Overthrow	*The Threat*
Deep War	*The Command*
Hunter Killer	*Black Storm*
Onslaught	*China Sea*
Tipping Point	*Tomahawk*
The Cruiser	*The Passage*
The Towers	*The Circle*
The Crisis	*The Gulf*
The Weapon	*The Med*
Korea Strait	

Tiller Galloway

Down to a Sunless Sea	*Louisiana Blue*
Bahamas Blue	*Hatteras Blue*

The Civil War at Sea

That Anvil of Our Souls	*Fire on the Waters*
A Country of Our Own	

Hemlock County

Thunder on the Mountain	*As the Wolf Loves Winter*
Winter in the heart	*The Dead of Winter*

Other Books

Heroes of Annapolis	*The Only Thing to Fear*
On War and Politics	*Stepfather Bank*
(with Arnold Punaro)	*The Return of*
The Whiteness of	*Philo T. McGiffin*
the Whale	*Star Seed*
Happier Than This	*The Shiloh Project*
Day and Time	*White Continent*
Ghosting	

VIOLENT
PEACE

THE WAR WITH CHINA—
AFTERMATH OF ARMAGEDDON

DAVID POYER

ST. MARTIN'S
PRESS

NEW YORK

First published in the United States by St. Martin's Press, an imprint of St. Martin's Publishing Group

VIOLENT PEACE. Copyright © 2020 by David Poyer. All rights reserved. Printed in the United States of America. For information, address St. Martin's Publishing Group, 120 Broadway, New York, NY 10271.

www.stmartins.com

The Library of Congress Cataloging-in-Publication Data is available upon request.

ISBN 978-1-250-22058-5 (hardcover)
ISBN 978-1-250-22059-2 (ebook)

Our books may be purchased in bulk for promotional, educational, or business use. Please contact your local bookseller or the Macmillan Corporate and Premium Sales Department at 1-800-221-7945, extension 5442, or by email at MacmillanSpecialMarkets@macmillan.com.

First Edition: 2020

10 9 8 7 6 5 4 3 2 1

To those who seek to heal

The purpose of war is peace.

—Pablo Escobar

I

BOMBLIGHT

1

Beijing

THE huge gray transport shook as it corkscrewed downward, and a barrage of violent bangs rattled the fuselage.

Decoy flares being fired? The slim, fair-haired woman gripping the armrests hoped so. No doubt, to lessen the chance of some rogue commander targeting them as the mission came in to land.

No one was really certain this war was over, after all. And for some elements in China, Iran, and Pakistan, the chairman of the Joint Chiefs had warned, it probably wasn't.

Blair Titus closed her eyes, fighting to avoid losing her cool in front of the other passengers. The C-5 Galaxy capped a huge cargo bay with a low-ceilinged passenger compartment. For this flight, it was occupied by the fourteen civilian and military members of the Allied Advance Mission. The seats were roomy, and the box lunches the flight crew had handed around after their takeoff from Andrews had been adequate to sustain life.

But since one of her previous flights had been cyberjacked by an enemy AI midway through the war, turned into a bomb, and targeted on Los Alamos, flying hadn't been a relaxing interlude for her. Twice so far on this trip she'd had to retreat to the little enclosed restroom, to perch on the toilet and practice her deep breathing.

Blair's family had been active in politics since Francis Preston

Blair had moved to Washington to start a pro–Andrew Jackson newspaper. After being narrowly defeated in a bid for Congress, she'd reluctantly joined the administration, invited aboard to bridge the expertise gap as the country plunged into a world war with China, North Korea, Iran, and the other Opposed Powers.

Now she was the undersecretary for strategy, plans, and forces at Defense, with an office on the third floor of the E wing. And nearly four years of bitter conflict had ironed creases into her forehead and daubed shadows no concealer could hide.

"Four fighters are closing in," a petite African American woman said, sliding back in beside her. Shira Salyers, who looked meek and pliable, was anything but. "Saw them through the little window back there. They're practically wingtip on us."

"Ours or theirs?"

"We should have both," said an Air Force general across the aisle. "F-35s in the air corridor, and J-20s in barrier lanes."

Trying to quell panic, Blair flipped open the order binder. She'd read it three times, festooning it with sticky notes covered with green scribbles, but it was still disturbingly vague on exactly what they were supposed to accomplish here. The official tasking had been outlined in bullet points:

- Establish contacts with interim government and military leaders
- Evaluate that government for support or regime change
- Ensure no rogue military or security elements remain active
- Make sure remaining nuclear, chemical, and biological weapons sites are secure
- Recommend size/constitution of residual self-defense force structure

She rubbed her mouth, considering. The problem was, their goals were contradictory. If no government remained that the Allies could trust, and there were still rogue security elements loose out there, who exactly was going to secure these nuclear sites? The

only Allied troops on the ground were Indonesian and Vietnamese forces, plus a few American support units, fifteen hundred
miles to the south, on Hainan Island; and US Army and Marines a
thousand miles to the east, on Taiwan.

But maybe it wouldn't be that hard. According to StratCom, one
of whose generals was sitting up front, most Chinese nuclear and
missile sites had been wiped out by the massive American retalia-
tion for the attack on the Midwest.

On its way west the C-5 had been forced to dogleg around large
areas of the northern United States. Some of the heavy missiles
from north China had been shot down by a Navy task force based
in the Sea of Okhotsk. Others had been blown from the sky by
ground-based missile defense in Alaska, or smashed out of existence by microsatellites steered to impact. As the survivors of that
gauntlet reached American airspace, more had fallen to shorter-
ranged Patriots and THAAD batteries.

But some had still gotten through. Seattle had been obliterated
by megaton-range airbursts. San Francisco had been struck by a
leaker that detonated over Pacifica. Montana and North Dakota
had been hit hardest, with ground-penetrating warheads eliminat-
ing half of the US ground-based deterrent. Omaha was gone. Colo-
rado and Wyoming had been blasted too, so heavily that no one
really knew yet how many missiles had fallen.

The casualties were still being counted. Both from blast and
radiation; the ground bursts had smeared massive plumes of fallout across the Midwest as far as Ohio and Ontario. Millions were
dead or missing, her husband's daughter among them. She'd never
understood the rationale behind placing America's heaviest deterrent smack in the middle of the United States. Forcing the enemy
to incinerate the very heartland of the country, instead of some
outlying bastion.

But many things looked different now. Illuminated, by the searching rays of bomblight.

Shira Salyers leaned over to say something. But just then the
engines bellowed. Blair grabbed the armrests again as she was

yanked violently forward in her seat. Biting her lips, squeezing her eyes shut, she steeled herself for impact, disaster, fire, death.

But heard only the shriek of tires as the huge aircraft touched down, then the rumble of landing gear over uneven tarmac.

"Ladies and gentlemen, welcome to Shahezhen Military Airbase, Beijing. Our escort is waiting. Our radiation monitors register only slightly above background level. It seems safe to disembark," the pilot announced over the onboard PA.

Knees shaking, she tripped her seat belt, gathered up coat and briefcase and tablet, and got ready to go to work.

SHE craned around as they descended a deplaning ramp toward four blocky black limousines. Barbed wire marked the airfield as military, but except for revetments in the distance it looked deserted. Obviously they were far outside Beijing proper, and she had no idea in which direction the capital lay. Beyond the waiting limos, military vehicles and a cordon of troops circled them, spaced out in a wide perimeter.

Ahead of her, Senator Bankey Talmadge, the senior member of the mission, limped down the stairs very slowly, supporting himself on the handrail. She'd worked for the old man years before, on the Armed Services Committee. Now she hovered behind him as he descended, ready to grab his arm if he made a misstep.

She lifted her face, to a sky blue and clear and somehow . . . rigid. She'd expected smog, but the horizon was only slightly hazy, tinted reddish brown as if with dust or a thin smoke from far away. Low mountains poked up to the north. Contrails, probably from their fighter escorts, were turning back southward. Buildings prickled the sky in that same direction. Temperature, moderate. Early summer, so no need for the wool jacket she'd packed.

At the bottom of the ramp Talmadge paused, looking around, gathering his strength. She heard the effort in his breathing, the rattle in his chest. Two lines of troops in olive drab battle dress lined a path from the ramp to a low combination terminal and control tower in Stalinesque gray concrete. At parade rest, rifles grounded, they faced outward. Motionless. Expressionless. Not one spared the debarking arrivals a glance.

The flight crew stood around a tripodded instrument set up on the pavement near the nose. She flicked them an inquiring look, a raised eyebrow. They nodded slightly, and turned back to their readouts. Four State agents, Diplomatic Security personnel, stood off to the side, ready to accompany the principals. In plain clothes, suits, and dresses, they carried short-barreled submachine guns. But if it came to a shoot-out here, against all these troops, it was perfectly clear who would prevail.

Beyond the soldiery, another line stretched across the tarmac. Seen from close up, the military vehicles she'd noted earlier were tracked machines, green, tanklike, but too small to contain human beings. Their gun turrets, topped and shouldered with strange domed lenses, faced outward as well.

She shivered, looking up at that remorseless sky, then caught her heel on a step and almost pitched headlong down the last flight of stairs off the ramp. A strong hand on one shoulder barely saved her. "Thanks, Adam," she muttered.

Heavyset, chain-smoking, master campaign fund-raiser Adam Ammermann was the deputy chief of staff at the White House. He was close to the president. A fixer. A hatchet man. Whatever they recommended here, he'd carry it up the line.

Or torpedo it, if he disagreed.

SHE had twenty minutes in her hotel room. Just enough time to pee, shower, change, and touch up mascara and lipstick. She'd brought a gray pantsuit that had seen better days, but with a crisp white blouse and her bright blue scarf with the foxes on it, it should suffice.

A tap at the door. Shira's murmur. "Blair? They want us downstairs."

The mission assembled in a worn-looking meeting room that

two security technicians were just finishing scanning. The heat was stifling. The air-conditioning was off, as it had been in the lobby and their rooms. The only light came from the windows, since the overheads were dark. The oversized armchairs seemed to have been built for pro wrestlers. She looked around. Talmadge wasn't there yet. She nodded to Tony Provanzano, from the CIA, and the various generals.

A lanky, klutzy-looking, Lincolnesque man in a civilian suit with too-short sleeves motioned her over. He extended a bony, long-fingered hand. "Blair. Glad you could make it. Good flight from DC?"

"Passable. Admiral, good to see you again. Yours?"

"Jim, please. Direct flight from Hawaii, can't complain. How's Dan?"

"I believe he's headed back to the States. Since you relieved him of command."

Justin Yangerhans was the ranking military member of the delegation. The commander, Indo-Pacific Command, and usually both the ugliest man in any room and the one everyone else looked to for the final say. She found it deeply satisfying and yet somehow totally unexpected that the man in charge of fighting the war in the Pacific was now involved in how it might be ended.

"I'm sorry about having to relieve him. It's become an international issue, apparently." He blinked, and a furrow deepened between his eyes. "Let's discuss that later, all right? We don't have long before the first sit-down."

One of the techs bustled up, holding out an instrument. "Admiral? Room's clear."

"Thanks, Bill." Yangerhans raised his voice to the others. "Folks? Apparently we're secure here, but don't assume that'll be true in any vehicles they may furnish, or anywhere in the Forbidden City. Where's Mr. Ammermann? Hello, Adam. Senator Talmadge, General Naar, Mr. Provanzano, Ms. Salyers—Good, we're all here. Take your seats, please, and let's get this started."

Yangerhans went on as they settled uneasily into the too-wide, too-overstuffed armchairs. "I think you all know me. I'm Justin Yangerhans, and I've been appointed the military envoy. Senator Bankey Talmadge, chair of Senate Armed Services, will be our overall leader. Would you like to say a few words, Senator?"

The old man shook his head, wheezing. "You have the ball, Admiral. Run with it."

Yangerhans inclined his head. "Thank you, sir. Now, you all know each other, I think, except maybe for Mr. Ayala, whom Shira arranged as our official translator." A slight unsmiling man in a black suit, standing against the wall, raised a hand. "No notes, please, and no recordings. I want to be able to lay our cards on the table while we're all together here."

The admiral started with a crisp recap. The enemy premier, and overall leader of the Opposed Powers, Zhang Zurong, was missing. Rumored to be dead, but no one had seen a body yet. Other talk had him fleeing, maybe to Russia. But the bottom line was he was off the map, at least for the moment.

The admiral coughed into a fist. "The North Korean premier's definitely deceased. We found the body in a cave beneath Paektu Mountain. DNA's a match. The provisional president, Jun Min Jung, is in Seoul. Reunification will be complicated, but Korea's not our remit. We can limit ourselves to China."

"Which is going to be quite enough," Salyers put in quietly. "What we fear is the country splitting into warlord-ruled regions again. Also, the Europeans and the UN want to be involved in any postwar process. Plus the International Criminal Court—"

"Could be, Shira. But let me finish before we get into that. All right?"

"Sorry, sir." She folded her hands demurely.

Yangerhans loped back and forth in long strides, fingers locked behind his back. He sounded as if he was thinking out loud. "CNN says Party headquarters throughout the country are being looted. Police stations and domestic surveillance centers trashed and burned. The gates of the prison camps opened as the guards desert. As Shira mentioned, the ICC's indicted Zhang for war crimes, aggressive war, and murder. So even if he's still alive, he's offline, and for the moment the Party's on the defensive too.

"Today we'll be meeting a shadowy bunch that call themselves the Revitalized State Council. Tony?"

The CIA rep uncrossed his legs. "We read them as a truncated and not very representative interim government, mainly dominated by the military, with a few senior Party reps." He nodded at Blair. "Dr. Titus made contact with them last year in Zurich. We'll be counting on you to keep their trust, Blair."

She forced a smile. The Agency had known about her contact with the Chinese? That was . . . unsettling. She'd thought it was between her and the national security advisor. Had Ed Szerenci ratted her out? Or worse yet, had the CIA been watching the whole time?

But Yangerhans was talking again. "We have an armistice, but we don't have a peace. The most dangerous parts of a war are the beginning and the end. We thought we could wrap up this one without a nuclear exchange, despite what the simulations at the War College and Stanford said. Well, we were wrong.

"As Shira said, the shape of any agreement will have major downstream effects. Without a strong central authority, China may split apart again, as it did in the 1920s. And if we don't manage this right, war can resume. We need to proceed delicately. Make sure all the stakeholders are heard from before we advance concrete proposals.

"But first, now, the Allies have to stabilize the environment, and enable civil authority. Help them form a provisional government that's willing to at least consider a move toward democratic rule. And provide enough advice and aid to make that possible."

He turned to the State rep. "What's our desired end state here, Shira? Give me the bullet points."

The tiny woman gestured gracefully. "Our national goals? First, peace. Replace the armistice with a formal treaty, preferably something the other Opposed Powers can sign on to as well. Then, justice. Pave the way to apprehend and try war criminals. Then, a government. A multiparty, representative democracy, if we can get there, to guard against a reversion to authoritarianism. A much smaller military, with perhaps a minimal nuclear deterrent for self-defense. And finally, formal independence for Tibet and Taiwan."

Blair admired how quickly she'd put her finger on the negotiating points, even if they seemed incredibly optimistic. At least, from where she was sitting.

Yangerhans turned to Ammermann next. "So that's the State view. General Naar and I can handle the military side, securing WMD sites and outlining a postwar force structure. Adam, is the White House on the same page?"

Ammermann, who'd been fidgeting while Salyers spoke, jumped in, almost sputtering. "With all due respect, Admiral, you mentioned aid. Advice. Sure, we can advise. But it's not our business to make China some kind of showcase of democracy. We have a terrible record in nation building. Iraq. Afghanistan. Syria. Why throw billions down another rathole? We lost millions of citizens in this war. Five trillion dollars, not counting aid to allies, vets' benefits, interest on debt . . . It'll take decades to rebuild the Midwest. And now there's this epidemic, and a growing rebellion to deal with.

"No, sir." He flicked a hand away, as if shooing a fly. "This administration will *not* support rebuilding former enemies. You can make promises, if you have to. But if there's any money involved, it should come our way. As reparations."

Yangerhans caressed a protuberant jaw. "So you're saying, let 'em stew?"

The senior staffer spread his hands. "I wouldn't put it exactly that way. But let's be realistic. China isn't the only threat, but they were the most dangerous. The longer they take to recover, the better for us."

"Two opposing viewpoints on where we're going," the admiral muttered. "And both possibly equally valid. Okay, let's look at the external power balance. Tony, what's the CIA got for us?"

Provanzano grimaced. He hitched his chair forward, though it barely moved, and tapped a pencil on the table. "Taking the ten-thousand-foot view? China and the US have nearly destroyed each other as first-rate powers. Unfortunately, that leaves a vacuum. Our former allies are already fighting over who'll fill it. The Vietnamese and Indonesians are squaring off over the islands we took in the South China Sea. Moscow's thinking of occupying Manchuria, on the basis of their last-minute declaration of war. And possibly a foothold on the Chinese coast as well." He glanced at Blair. "But there's something Moscow wants even more than land. Repayment of over two trillion dollars' worth of China's war debt. Which they want the US to guarantee."

"Dream on. Not gonna happen," Ammermann snapped. "In this universe or any other."

Yangerhans said, "I agree, but having it on the table for now might strengthen our hand later."

A discreet tap at the door; one of the DSS women leaned in. "The vehicles are waiting, everyone."

"Be finished in a minute," Yangerhans said. "What else, Tony?"

"Moscow's moving again on Ukraine, using hybrid warfare to occupy the rest of the Black Sea coast. Threatening Poland, the Baltic states, and Finland. They restructured the Russian Federation while we were at war; central Asian states, Georgia, Belarus, no longer have independent legislatures. Germany's got a new president, populist sliding toward fascist. He's mustering Hungary, Bulgaria, and the rest of Eastern Europe against Russian adventurism. But they're playing catch-up. If the Russians move west, they'll roll over them."

Blair lifted a finger. "Can I make a point?"

"Blair, sure, go ahead," Yangerhans said.

"Most of what we're discussing here is outside our control. But let's not forget, we're also facing what could be the biggest humanitarian emergency in history. Taiwan's in ruins. Korea's devastated. And China's starving. The famine killed millions, the Central Flower virus millions more, and our nuclear strikes—"

Ammermann cut her off angrily, punching the arm of his chair so hard dust rose. "To hell with them! *They* started this god-damned war—"

Yangerhans held up a hand. "All right. Enough! I see everybody's points. Yours too, Blair—I agree, we have to find some way to feed these people. But first, let's secure peace. Then, outline a Joint Comprehensive Plan of Action we can present to the heads of state meeting in Singapore.

"In fifteen minutes we'll be headed over to meet this state council. For now, let's concentrate on whoever thinks he speaks for the military. General Pei, maybe. He and I met before the war. He may be reasonable.

"If it seems like they have a handle on the security forces, our first priority has to be to work through them to stand the army down and secure the remaining nuclear sites. At least until we can pull in the International Atomic Energy Agency for a freeze in place, and reach some agreement on dismantlement, or some minimal remaining deterrent."

Bankey Talmadge stirred slowly, like an ancient tortoise. Blair didn't like the way his cheeks were purpling. He grunted, "Congress isn't going to approve leaving them with nuclear weapons."

Ammermann twisted in his chair to face him. "That's not up to Congress, Senator. Sorry. The executive will make those decisions."

"And the Hill will fund them. Or not," Talmadge rumbled, and the look in his eye did not bode well for that.

Yangerhans slammed a hand down on the table. Everyone flinched. "United front, people! If we have disagreements, we'll settle them behind closed doors. I do *not* want them to see a divided American mission.

"We've just heard two clear policy options. Door A leads to trying to rebuild a central state along democratic lines while we hold off predators from the carcass. Which leads to decades of China being dependent on us, and, yeah, it'll cost money.

"Door B, we let the country come apart at the seams. Russia and our allies tear off pieces to gorge on. Leading to a new war in twenty years, when China recovers and seeks revenge."

Several people around the table waved their hands, trying to interrupt, but the admiral plowed on. "There're arguments for both sides. But as I see it, the worst course of all is to try to drive down the middle of the road."

Ammermann broke in again. "I say, let 'em fight each other. To the death. Our own country's broke. Millions dead. Why should we pay a nickel more?"

Blair put her hand over Shira's rising one. "I don't agree, Adam. We made a huge mistake, letting Russia revert to authoritarianism when she had a chance to become a normal country. When we win, we have this history of not following through. Let's not miss our chance this time."

Yangerhans raised his palms as shouts broke out again. "Quiet. *Quiet!* I'll present both options to the president. And to the Armed Services Committee, Senator. But the final decision'll be up to the heads of state. They'll provide guidance. But for right now, united front. Adam? Senator? Tony? Shira? Blair?"

They all nodded reluctantly. Yangerhans glared around once more, then snapped his attention back to Salyers. "Shira. Any last-minute diplomatic advice?"

"I can address that, sir," the little man in black said, stepping forward from along the wall. "I have been at many meetings with these same men, during the trade negotiations before the war."

"Fire away, Mr. Ayala," Yangerhans said, looking bemused.

"Sir, it is essential to not humiliate the Chinese. They must save face. Second, resign yourself to a long negotiation. Identify the decision maker. Talk only to him, not underlings. Drink baiju with them if they ask. They are like Russians in that way. It establishes a bond.

"Above all, do not look eager to reach a deal. They will see it as weakness, as desperation, and ask for more."

"Good advice, sounds like," the admiral said after a moment.

He nodded. "Are we ready?" No one spoke. "Then"—and he smiled grimly at the special agent at the door—"tell them we're on our way."

Blair took a deep breath, clawed herself out of the too-soft chair, and followed the others out.

SHE gazed up in wonder at the Hall of Supreme Harmony. The wide timeworn steps, the petal-scarlet tiles of the elegantly pagoda'd roofs, the solemn and absolute emptiness of the far-stretching plazas . . . all were familiar, from one of her favorite films. The forbidding, crabbed Empress Dowager Cixi, who'd doomed China to revolution and chaos. The child emperor Puyi hiding a pet cricket behind his throne. Then, after Mao came to power, becoming a humble gardener at this same walled enclave . . .

She shook off the awe and climbed the steps, catching up with Talmadge, who was toiling upward, leaning heavily on his cane. On impulse, she took the old senator's arm. "We're back together, Bankey."

He squeezed her hand with his free one. "Like old times, Missy."

His pet nickname for her, way back when. Her old employer was one of the few survivors of the age of the titans. He'd served with Barry Goldwater, Bob Dole, Robert Byrd, the other Talmadge, a distant cousin . . . With the passage of decades his offices had grown bigger, his perks greater, his clout colossal. Especially with defense contractors, whose purse strings the Armed Services Committee controlled. The war had only magnified his influence. Others might be bigger names, but in the ways that truly counted, he was the most powerful member of her party.

She said, in the chiding tone that had always made him smile, "I wasn't *gone*, Bankey. Just moved to the executive."

"The other side of the fence," he grumbled.

"Oh, come on, Senator. You're dinging me for joining a wartime coalition government?"

"For fronting for them. Breaking ranks with the party. That's what don't set so good with some of our supporters."

"The White House wanted a hard-line strategy, Bankey. Without me standing on the brakes, this war could've been a lot worse."

"Well," muttered the old man, laboring upward with a huffing groan, "I'm on your side, Missy. Always will be. You know that. But there are other folks out there, they're never gonna forget."

THEY straggled through the palace, then descended another set of broad marble steps. A hundred yards on Bankey halted, panting, cheeks flushed that deep purple she didn't like to see. "Ah can't walk any farther. They're makin' us sweat, Missy. Put up with this crap, we're the ones losin' face here."

She signaled one of the soldiers who walked along with them, and sign-languaged that the old man was done. The trooper murmured into a radio. Within seconds an official came trotting up, pushing a wheelchair.

They caught up with the others in the side courtyard of a smaller, but if possible even more opulent, palace than the first. Its scarlet-and-gold columns stretched up to a roof so lofty it was lost in shadow. The carpet smoothed a floor of hand-set stone flags. In its center, before a divanlike throne, a long table had been set up, with a buffet to one side. Uniformed officers ushered them to more overstuffed seats. Across the table a group of stressed-looking Chinese, all in dark blue suits and bright red ties, stood by their chairs, waiting.

Ammermann took the center seat on the Allied side. Blair hesitated, then grabbed Talmadge's wheelchair and shoved it in between Ammermann and Yangerhans, forcing the staffer to push his own chair over as the wheel slammed into it. Which moved him from the center, off to the side. Where he belonged . . . She headed for a seat at the far end, but was intercepted by two of the Chinese, who'd circled the table to intercept her. After a second glance she recognized them, and inclined her head. "Minister Chen. Good to see you again."

"Good to see you again as well, Dr. Titus." The chubby senior official returned her nod with a partial bow. Deputy Minister Chen

Jialuo was older than she, and to judge by the way his hands trembled as he adjusted his spectacles, extremely nervous. The sopping palm she shook confirmed it.

And no wonder. It was Chen who'd called her "corrupt, untrustworthy, pliable, depraved, and malignant" at their first meeting, under UN auspices, in Dublin. But it was also Chen who'd secretly backchanneled the lower leadership's openness to negotiation. First at Dublin, then again in Zurich.

Beside him stood the young man who'd carried the can on those dangerous covert meetings: the opaque-faced apparatchik Xie Yunlong. "Yun," she murmured, shaking his hand too. His grip was firmer, but only a little less sweaty.

Or maybe the perspiration was actually her own?

Chen beckoned more Chinese over. "Dr. Titus, I would like to introduce you to three of our most distinguished military men. Marshal Chagatai. Admiral Lin. Lieutenant General Pei."

She greeted them formally, trying to ignore the feeling each hand she took had been marinated in blood. Pei had shot hundreds of civilians in Taiwan. The barrel-chested, scowling Dewei Chagatai had crushed a revolt in Hong Kong and gassed whole villages in Xinjiang. And Admiral Lin's fingerprints were on the thermonuclear obliteration of the USS *Roosevelt* strike group at the beginning of the war, killing ten thousand US sailors and fliers.

She murmured through numb lips, "I hope we can make progress together."

"I hope so too. I will trust you to proceed on the basis you agreed to in Zurich." A bead of sweat rolled down Chen's quivering cheek. "The Party must continue to govern. Senior military leaders must be allowed honorable retirement. There can be no prosecutions, no trials. Otherwise we will continue the fight."

She remembered a café near the Place Lenin, deep in the cobblestoned warrens of medieval Zurich. A tense, hostile face-off, with a shadowy Russian sitting in. Trying to profit from ending the war, just as they'd made money from the conflict itself.

Where was that Russian now? Probably not far away.

She retrieved her hand. Gently. Gently. "With all due respect, Minister, those were *your* positions, which you advanced as starting points. As I informed you then, I had no power to negotiate. I made that clear, I believe. But you can certainly present them as your conditions for peace, here, at this table, for our mission to transmit to the Allied heads of state."

Yangerhans coughed into a fist again. He stood waiting, looking bored. *Above all, do not look eager to reach a deal.* Yeah, bored was probably the right tack to start out on. "Uh, Blair? Gentlemen, ladies, we have an armistice. Let's see if we can make a peace."

The Chinese stared at her, then at him. They bowed slightly once more, all together, expressions carefully neutral. Then took their seats, to face their enemies across six feet of lacquered tabletop.

2

California

THERE wasn't much in the way of flights from San Diego north. And nothing, of course, to the Seattle area. The tall officer with the graying hair had deplaned at the Navy terminal in Coronado and inquired at the passenger information desk.

"You're not really headed to Seattle," the Air Force enlisted there said. "You do know it's not there anymore.... That it was hit?"

"My daughter worked at Archipelago," he told her.

"Oh." She blinked rapidly, and looked away. "I'm sorry, sir. The news from there . . . it isn't good."

Dan Lenson was still an admiral. At least so far. The recall message, pulling him from his command after the invasion of Hainan, hadn't taken away the wartime promotion. Not yet.

But he'd have traded it all, promotion, pension, career, hell, his own life—for just one call from Nan.

He had six more days of leave. Eaten one up crossing the Pacific, then gotten a day added back crossing the date line. At the end of the week, he was due in Washington. For what, exactly, the chief of naval operations hadn't specified. But he could guess.

Reversion to his prewar rank of captain, and a desk job entombed so deep in the Pentagon's eighteen miles of corridors he'd never see daylight again. Until the Navy could process him out.

He stood motionless in the empty terminal, stalled like an engine without spark. His brain echoing empty. His soul blank. Daughter gone. Bereft.

And then what?

Home to Arlington, to Blair. He'd have her, at least. But she was a busy woman these days. She'd warned, in the one email exchange they'd managed since his relief, that she might not even be in the country when he got back. Sure, her job.

Their careers had always taken priority. You could call it duty, to put the best spin on it. Especially in wartime. But the word had a bitter sting. He'd given up too much. Spent so little time with the only daughter he'd ever have. But he and her mother had split up, and he'd been so busy since . . .

Water over the dam, Lenson. And it's too late now.

If only you could revise your life. Rewind it. Reformat it. Erase the bad parts, and amp up the good, so that it played the way you should have done it all along . . .

A blue screen near the overhead flickered. Lines of text shifted. He stared blankly up at it. Then jogged over to the window overlooking the airstrip.

A quarter mile away across the concrete, a wheeled train of pallets was being snaked up into a potbellied transport.

He went back to the service desk. "That C-17. Where's it headed?"

The airman looked anxious. "Relief supplies, Admiral. Four flights a day, up to McChord."

"That's near Seattle, right? Where the nukes hit?"

"McChord's south of Tacoma, sir. That's where they're running the relief effort out of. I wouldn't say 'near.' But it's probably as close as you can go without getting lit up."

"Lit up" apparently meant "irradiated" these days. He snapped his ID down on the counter. "I'd be grateful if you'd find me a seat."

She hesitated, then cocked her head and began keystroking. "I . . . guess we might could manifest you, Admiral. Space A.

Bucket seat. Hope you don't mind noise. But are you . . . really *sure* you want to head up there? I mean, I wouldn't advise it. I really wouldn't, sir. Not many people headed that way. Unless they got a damn good reason. Which . . . well, I guess you might."

"Thanks for the warning. I'll be careful." Dan picked up his bag and followed her pointing finger toward the exit.

Then turned back, remembering: The CNO had wanted him to call once he got to CONUS. "Is there a DSN line here?" The defense switched network should still work, if anything did.

The airman opened her mouth as if to object, then glanced at the stars on Dan's collars again. "Certainly, Admiral. The CO's office is right down that hall to the left."

BARRY "Nick" Niles had been Dan's commanding officer years before, at the Cruise Missile Project Office in Crystal City. Afterward he'd become, not exactly an enemy, but definitely not an admirer. After 9/11, though, Niles had turned into a reluctant rabbi. Now the first African American chief of naval operations, he'd fought the war from that position.

The base's commanding officer put Dan through to Niles's main office number. After that, though, Dan got passed up the line. Niles's deputy didn't know what he was calling about, and asked him to hold.

Fully a quarter hour passed before the foghorn tones Dan knew so well tolled in his ear. *"Lenson. You back in town?"*

"Uh, not exactly, Admiral. Just landed in San Diego."

"Uh-huh. Good job in Operation Rupture Plus."

"Thank you, sir."

"Don't thank me, I didn't think you could do it. How soon can you be here?"

Be there? In DC? He frowned. "There must be some misunderstanding, sir. I was authorized leave en route."

"Leave?" Niles sounded as if this were the first time he'd

encountered the concept. Then added, *"Oh—yeah, I forgot. Nancy, right?"*

"Nan. She was in Seattle. I need to find her, Admiral."

"Okay, yeah, I get that. My son's in the Gulf right now. At least I know where he is." A short pause. *"I didn't mean that the way it sounded."*

"No sir."

"Here's the situation. We've got a summons for you from The Hague."

He'd gotten a heads-up on this from Blair, but had hoped it would get overlooked, or die of its own accord. Apparently his luck was running true to form. "The International Criminal Court."

"Uh-huh. For what they call war crimes. Related but not limited to your abandonment of that German tanker."

"Not abandoned, sir. I had to remove the higher-value unit from the threat vicinity."

"Oh, I read your report. And you're not the only poor son of a bitch in this particular barrel. But the thing is, how do we respond? According to the administration, if we send people to trial, it compromises sovereign immunity. But if we don't go, the Chinese will refuse to appear too. We'd have to corral them ourselves, then convene some kind of ad hoc military tribunal, without the UN's blessing. Which the fucking British and Indians are making themselves difficult over."

Dan frowned. *Somebody* had to be held responsible for this war. For the deaths of millions, most of them civilians. Or was Niles saying aggressors like Zhang, and his bloody generals, would get away scot-free? The men who'd sowed first conventional, then nuclear devastation across two continents? He looked around the empty office, and caught the base commander, outside, peering in through the door. He gave the guy a thumbs-up and forced a smile. Said to Niles, "Um . . . So what's the decision, sir?"

"I don't know! I wanted you to stay in China. Take command of relief efforts in the south. But I got overruled. They're still

trying to decide what to do, but they wanted you in pocket back here in the States."

"Uh-huh. Well, what do you think, sir? I'm perfectly happy to go face the music, if it means the Chinese get indicted too. I did the right thing. They didn't."

The heavy voice turned testy, more like the Niles he knew. *"Are you even listening? It's not up to you, Lenson! You just hang loose. Go look for your daughter. But stay in touch, so when they make up their fucking minds we can lay hands on you."*

And with a couple more "Aye aye, sir"'s on Dan's part, and a slammed-down phone on Niles's, the conversation seemed to have reached its end.

McCHORD was a madhouse scramble. It reminded him of Bagram in the first months after 9/11. Trucks, pallet-trains of water and supplies, tent shelters and conexes lining the airfield, National Guard ambulance-modified Oshkoshes rumbling here and there seemingly at random. A dark sky hovered too low for comfort. Lightning flickered, and thunder growled in the distance. He carried his bag toward the terminal as one of the ambulances tore past, nearly running him down. Dan remembered writing the humanitarian relief op order they were probably operating under. He kept trying his phone, but the screen just read NO SIGNAL. Yeah, the airbursts had probably wiped out every cell tower in a hundred-mile radius.

There wasn't much to go on. Seattle had been among the hardest-hit population centers in what the Patriot Network was calling C Day. Much like the old Pearl Harbor slogan, now it was "Remember C Day." Central and north Seattle had essentially been obliterated by megaton-range airbursts. A dud had impacted south of Port Orchard, apparently aimed at the sub base at Kitsap. Neither he nor Blair had been able to get through to Archipelago, where Nan had worked in some kind of biomedical research. Her cell didn't respond, and the electromagnetic pulse had wiped out landlines throughout western Washington State.

And that was all he'd been able to find out.

The line at this service desk was sixteen deep, but eventually he got close enough to ask if there was transportation into the city. A harried-looking sergeant regarded him as if he'd asked for the next bus to Hell. "Sir, ain't nobody going in there without MOPP gear, a full-face respirator, and a damn good reason."

"My daughter worked there. Archipelago Systems."

The guy looked away. "Their campus was in the blast zone, sir."

Dan took a deep breath. Not what he'd hoped to hear. "Well, what happened to the casualties? Is there anything like a central registry? A database of the wounded? The missing? The . . . deceased?"

"Not that I know of, sir. Give us another week, we might have something like that stood up. But not yet. Next?" The sergeant looked past him.

But Dan didn't leave, as he was obviously expected to. "Come on, help me out here. Where would you look? If it was your kid out there."

The sergeant rubbed his nose. "Um . . . I'd probably start with the evacuee camps. Federation, Geyser, Dash Point, Penrose. If your daughter came out still walking, she might be there. If she was a casualty, well . . . you'd want to call the local hospitals. But they're overwhelmed too, what I understand." He shook his head and looked past Dan again. "Sorry I can't help more. Really sorry, sir. Next?"

Outside, Dan stood undecided for a few minutes, looking up. Thunderheads. Anvils in the sky . . . it would rain soon . . . he shivered as a chill wind fluttered a hand-drawn map. It was tacked to a bulletin board with duct tape. It showed Dash Point as the closest of a constellation of evacuee camps scattered to the south and east of the stricken city.

More trucks rumbled past, headed out the gate. McChord seemed to be the arrival point for emergency supplies, which were then distributed to wherever FEMA had gathered survivors and evacuees.

No central list at all? Hard to believe. But then again, not all that incredible, if the computers and electrical power and phones were all down. He didn't envy whoever was in charge of this mess. If anyone was.

So, the camps the sergeant had listed. Check them? One at a time, hoping to catch her face in the welter of tired, frightened people?

Taking charge himself crossed his mind for perhaps a quarter second, but he dismissed the thought. He'd run one tsunami relief effort, in the Maldives. That didn't qualify him to honcho anything this size, with so many federal, military, state, and local authorities to coordinate.

No. She was his daughter. He was her father.

That was his sole and primary mission now. To find her.

Even if she no longer lived, he had to know.

IT was pouring icy rain by the time he caught a ride. First to Millersylvania, in a water truck. The woman driving wore a blue dosimeter badge clipped to her coveralls. She didn't have much to say, other than that she hadn't slept for two days and only got one meal in all that time. "It's fucking hopeless," she muttered, staring through a rain-splattered windscreen as she noodged the heavily loaded deuce-and-a-half up to forty-five. "Nobody knows how many people there are in these camps. We have to get them moved south before the weather changes. It keeps raining like this, they'll be drowning in mud."

Dan bent forward, squinting at the water sleeting down the windshield. Was it . . . *black*? "What about radioactivity? The plume, from the bombing?"

She shook her head. "You're looking at the rain? That's from all the fires. They say the worst stuff mostly blew off to the northeast, but who the fuck knows? We could all be fucking sterile now.

Nobody tells you nothing. That's the worst part. If I believed all the rumors, I'd go nuts. Like, about the rebels."

He massaged his forehead. Apparently he'd missed a lot, or more likely, the controlled media hadn't bothered to cover anything that might sap morale in the war zones. "Uh, rebels?"

"In the Midwest. They declared independence. You believe that? Not that we're not all super pissed out here too. Considering how little help we're getting."

THE evacuee camp lay inland, fronting a freshwater beach, and it was a sea of blue. The same pale blue plastic fly covers he'd seen at other refugee camps; in Ashaara, in the former Yugoslavia, the Maldives, and a dozen other disaster areas around the world. The truck groaned to a stop near a rustic pine picnic shelter. Hundreds of people were already lined up waiting, heads lowered against the rain. They wore tattered ponchos or black plastic trash bags with holes torn for head and arms. They held plastic jugs, coolers, pails, and fishing rods. They seemed orderly, or perhaps simply too tired, frightened, hungry, and overwhelmed to be anything but submissive.

As he swung down out of the cab he wondered briefly what the fishing rods were for, but dismissed it. Much more important to fight his way through the crowd, to where hundreds of scraps of paper, photographs, hand-scrawled notes, were nailed, pinned, stapled, and taped to the wall of the headquarters building, so many they overlapped like leaves, quickly growing sodden in the rain.

WHERE ARE YOU HOLLY CAPOLLONE WE ARE AT KANASKAT MOM AND DAD

SAKURA FAMILY MEET JUNE 19 AT NOON AT TOLMIE STATE PARK

LUKAS—SANDY, WILLIAM, AND FEY HAVE GONE TO STAY WITH AUNT BARB IN EUGENE. POP POP PLEASE CALL US AND LET US KNOW YOU ARE ALRITE

A ranger at a picnic table was handing out index cards and pencil stubs. Clipped to his lapel was the same type of blue dosimeter badge the water truck driver had worn. Dan stood in line again, hair dripping, rain in his eyes, fighting a growing rage at the disorder and futility all around. He got a card and a pencil at last, and positioned himself against a tree trunk to write.

Once upon a time, he was old enough to remember, the country had been prepared for a catastrophe like this. There'd been civil defense drills. Shelters. Procedures. Duck and cover. Not that a school desk would have been much protection. But still . . . when had the country lost the will, or the wisdom, to prepare for the worst? Even as the threat had grown, as weaponry on both sides had assumed fearsome proportions, the government had ignored the basics: protection of the civil population, public health, disease control, infrastructure resiliency. Instead, both sides had wrestled in the mire. Shrill, endless, pointless fights over identity and abortion and guns and tax rates. While underwriting enormous expenditures, on a defense that had largely crumpled when an enemy actually attacked.

He snarled, pressing the pencil hard into the paper.

The point snapped off. When he inspected it the small print stamped into the cheerful yellow paint read MADE IN CHINA.

No, this was futile. Nan would never see this. He balled up the card and threw it into an overflowing trash can and retraced his steps toward the road.

Then halted, appalled.

A weeping child huddled beneath a bush. A sign hung around her neck, but it was wet, torn, unreadable. She was perhaps eight, and her hair had been burned away down to the scalp. Her bare arms were erupting with what looked like flash burns. The skin was peeling. Straw-yellow plasma stained her pajama pants.

He nearly stopped, but his next step forward revealed four more children lying on the ground. Outside a trimly painted outdoor lavatory people were openly relieving themselves, adding to brown piles that stained their broken shoes or bare feet. Dozens of sick lay tossing uneasily on the concrete pad beneath a picnic shelter. A ceaseless drone of groans and weeping and screams floated on the stinking air. A lone woman in a Salvation Army uniform moved among them with a bucket of water and a soup ladle, but there was no sign of any medical attendance.

And behind him, down a trail from the north, stumbled more wounded. An unending line, like the damned in a medieval painting. The bent figures carried suitcases, backpacks, computers. Their clothing hung in rags, and they shambled as if hypnotized, mouths slack, gazes fixed. They infected the breeze with a stench of rot and burned meat. They passed nearly in silence in the pelting rain, with only faint whimpers and a harsh panting, as if they couldn't quite catch their breaths. Some stumbled blindly, hands outstretched for the backs of those they followed. Some were completely naked, with bloated arms and faces, contorted and horrible. Raw burns glistened on their cheeks and foreheads and arms. Blood and yellow fluid ran down their arms, mingling with the pouring rain. Which they didn't seem even to register, except for one gray-haired Asian-looking man, who carefully held a shredded, useless umbrella to shield a short woman with a floral scarf tied tightly over her eyes.

A middle-aged woman stumbled and fell, sprawling. The red plastic bucket she'd carried tumbled away. The others did not pause. They stepped around her, or on her hands and feet as she groped. No one stopped to help her. At last, moaning, she stirred, rolled over, and laboriously pushed herself up to all fours. She searched anxiously about, patting the ground for the bucket, which had rolled a few feet away, into a patch of dripping weeds. When she found it she reached in to cradle something inside, kissing the limp thing fervently.

Then she crept on, after the others.

He stared, not wanting to believe his eyes. It had been days since the attack. Had these victims walked all the way from the city?

He trotted back to the ranger. "Can't we do anything for these people? They're wounded, still coming in. They need food. Water. Shelter. Medical care. Bandages, at least."

The ranger's face closed. "These are the lucky ones."

Dan stared at him. "What are you talking about?"

"They made it out alive. The Army brings food in the evening. They truck in water. And we're boiling more, from the lake, on those wood fires over there. But without power, pumps, lighting, internet . . . it's nearly impossible to get anything done."

"What about medical care? There are children dying here."

"You think I don't know that?" The ranger's face reddened. He slammed a fist down. "You think we haven't been *trying*, is that it?"

"No, not exactly, it's just that—"

"I don't know who the fuck you are, mister, but we're doing the best we can. There *aren't* any supplies. The worst-off ones come in on the trucks. The medics triage them. The ones who won't make it, they tell me to make them as comfortable as I can. And that's it. The ones that're burned, well . . . they're dead already. They took so much radiation in the initial pulse that even if you dress the burns, they die in a few days anyway." The ranger's gaze suddenly fastened to the collar of Dan's khakis. To the stars pinned there . . . "What are you, anyway? A general? Why don't *you* get some of *your* fucking troops in here? Get us some fucking help!"

Dan felt sick. "Sorry," he muttered, and turned away. Suddenly his own loss didn't seem so great. Or, more accurately, seemed now to be only one fragment of a much greater failure, a mere splinter in a great running sore on the body of the country he'd tried to defend.

Maybe if he'd done his job better somehow, fought harder, made other choices, this wouldn't have happened.

Yeah, that probably wasn't really true. But it was how he felt. That he should have done more.

He retraced his steps, and found the little girl who crouched beneath the bushes. He carried a tin cup of water to her, and washed out her burns. Bound them as best he could with clean leaves from the woods and the laces from his shoes. She didn't cry. Just stared into the distance. Then he sat with her. Until, gradually, she slumped against him. The next time he looked down, her eyes were closed.

It wasn't military people who started wars. They only went out to do the fighting, when the politicians failed.

But they weren't the only ones who suffered, either.

THE girl died two hours later, never speaking a word. He didn't even know her name. He sat with her until the end. Then picked her up, gently as he'd once held his own daughter, years before. He carried her behind the picnic shelter, where other bodies had been laid out. Scores. No, hundreds . . . a few yards away a Ditch Witch was chugging away, scooping out a long trench in the soil by the edge of the woods. He told a black woman in coveralls by the ditch, who made a note on a yellow tablet. There were lots of other notes on that page.

As dark fell, shooting broke out. A popping of small-arms fire, some distance away. No one seemed to remark on it, nor did they look disturbed. As if this happened often. The firing went on for some minutes, then gradually died away.

He left the camp with the ration truck, which took him back to McChord. He couldn't do anything useful at the camps. Just add to the burden, exacerbate the chaos.

And he still didn't have a clue what had happened to his own daughter.

Which really meant . . . cold logic here, Lenson . . . starting at the last place he knew she'd worked, and tracing what had happened there. Discovering how close to the zone of utter destruction she'd been during the attack, and, if she'd survived, where she might have gone from there.

It was all he could think of to do. And he owed her mother some kind of resolution, at least. Even if the news was bad, even if it was final, he should tell Susan.

That night he dozed on the floor in the passenger terminal. A restless sleep, disturbed by nearby coughing, loud snoring, muffled sobbing, and more of the distant shots. The waiting area was carpeted by recumbent bodies. The first responders, firefighters, truckers, supply people, guards, Red Cross and other volunteers. He'd seen pictures of Russian train stations during the Revolution, and the subways in London during the Blitz. This looked much the same.

When dawn came the bodies stirred. He lined up with the others for weak coffee and limp white bread and withered apples. No one asked what he was doing there. Everyone had a job. Except him.

When he went outside again a fire truck stood idling a hundred yards away, shining wet with streaks of foam, freshly emerged from the decontamination line. Helmeted and suited-up figures were restowing equipment. Respirator masks hung from their belts or around their necks. The dawn sky was still overcast, the wind was still damp, but at least it wasn't raining.

Masks . . . in IndoPac you carried yours with you wherever you went. And his was still in his duffel.

He found his bag undisturbed in the DV lounge, where he'd dropped it off before heading to Millersylvania. He pulled out his jacket and soft cap. Slung the mask, in its carrier, around his waist. Unpinned his stars and dropped them into a pocket. Then headed out of the terminal, to see whom he could talk into giving him a ride.

FOUR hours later he stood panting amid blasted and twisted cars in the Archipelago parking lot, looking up. The immense circular building had been smashed and torched. He caught the carbonized whiff of burning and char even through the charcoal filters of the mask. And mixed with it, disquieting and ominous smells of rotting flesh.

Nan had been developing a flu drug for Archipelago. That much she'd told him on their infrequent phone calls during the war. The main research campus, here in Seattle, had been within the blast radius of the southern burst. The firefighters who'd given him a lift here had told him he wouldn't find much. That everyone would be either evacked or dead. But Nan had once mentioned the name of her team leader.

A Dr. Anton Lukajs, who'd apparently relocated to a satellite facility in Yakima.

And, fortunately, the fire truck could patch its radio into an operational landline back at the station.

"Yes, Doctor Lenson worked for me," an ancient, quavery, Middle European–accented voice informed him. *"She is your daughter? I too have one. A daughter. In Albania."*

Dan pushed the mask higher on his face. He could risk a few minutes' exposure. He said into the phone, "Is she with you? Do you know where she is?"

"I have not seen her since I left Albania. She was working for the government there, and then afterward I heard—"

Dan clutched his head. "No. Sorry. I meant *my* daughter, sir. Doctor Nan Lenson. When did you see her last?"

"Oh. The disaster. You are the hero, right? The naval officer?"

"Right now I'm just Nan Lenson's dad. Please . . . can you tell me anything? Where is she? When was the last time you saw her?"

"No, no, she is not here. A very competent researcher, though she had independent ideas. She and some of the younger faculty had their doubts about security of formulary information. I had to agree with them, they had a good point—"

Dan took a deep breath, forcing himself to calm down. The guy was old, he'd been through a lot. He said again, mastering his impatience, "I'm sorry, Doctor, but I only have a few minutes to use this line. Can you tell me the last time you saw Nan Lenson, and where that was?"

"When did I see her? Just before the attack. At the campus. But . . . wait a moment. Yes. I remember. A woman who was in the bunker with her came to Yakima with us," the quavering regretful voice muttered. *"She said Doctor Lenson left just before the first warhead hit."*

Dan fought a sinking feeling. "She left the bunker, you mean? *Before* the burst? Why in hell would she—"

"Well, perhaps not. Just before, or just during—she was not sure. Just that she, Doctor Lenson, your daughter, yes, forced the shelter manager to open the door, and left. Saying she had something important to do."

Dan nodded grimly, as if that could encourage the guy to remember. "Something important. Okay. What could that have been, sir? Where would she have gone, to check on something so important she'd leave a bomb shelter during an alert?"

"Well, that I do not know. My guess is that it had to do with Qwent."

"Qwent. And that is—?"

Lukajs explained that Qwent, or perhaps he was saying Quant, had a pharmaceutical plant not far from Lake Washington. Manufacture of the new drug had been subcontracted to them. Nan had been in charge of overseeing that effort, both hitting the production milestones and maintaining quality control. *"They had just finished the first production run. Preliminary bulk production. She went there every day to check on it. It may be she felt she must find out if it was protected, or had survived the blast. She was very much involved. Very concerned the compound, it is called LJL, would be properly manufactured, properly packaged. Since Qwent also manufactured a pesticide at the same factory, you know. She was—she is—a good girl. I mean, a good scientist. You are her father? I should tell you that."*

"Thank you." Okay, he had to admit that sounded like her, to put her project ahead of her own safety. "But you, or this woman from the shelter, never heard from her after that. After she left the bunker."

"No one. Not a word. I am sorry, Admiral."

Dan wondered how he knew his rank, then realized Nan must have told him. For some obscure reason, this buoyed him up a little. She'd been proud of him. Just as he had been so very proud of her.

He thanked the old man quietly, and signed off.

THE Qwent facility, the pharmaceutical plant, lay at the top of a modest crest, looking out over the lake. He could see, now, where all the soot-stained rain was coming from. Beyond the water, which was like a pool of ink dotted with patches of floating ash, the city was still burning. A heavy smoke shrouded its broken remains. Small twisted forms lay scattered along the lake's near shore. After a moment he recognized them as ducks, or maybe geese.

The hand-laid brickwork told him the shell of this building was old. Converted from some earlier industrial structure, an old factory, probably. Now it was all just twisted wreckage. Shattered rubble—bricks, pieces of gray mortar, glass, twisted iron beams—littered the ground outside a chain-link fence. Looters had already been at work; broken computers and the spilled guts of process equipment, more glass, stainless tubing, wrecked motors, the debris lay scattered across the grass, which still showed signs of flash scorching, although a few fresh, pale green shoots were pushing through. A corkscrewed-off section of metal roof, complete with blasted and wrecked solar panels, lay canted across the chain link.

He skirted it to a gap and walked up to the building, following the whine of chain saws and yelling voices.

A crew in face masks, rubber boots, and heavy gloves, but without protective suits, was digging at one corner of the building. Dan couldn't see why and didn't care. When he trudged up, one of the men halted and looked at him quizzically. Dan lifted his mask. "Where's your supervisor?"

"See Jimmy," the guy said, and pointed.

Dan found Jimmy, who wore a green-and-yellow shirt with *Qwent* embroidered on the breast pocket, and asked his questions. To his surprise, the super nodded. He lifted his mask and palmed sweat from his face. "Sure. I seen her. Long dark hair, young, Archipelago tag? White coat? Yeah, she was here."

"You mean, the day of the attack? Before or after the hit?"

The supervisor nodded. "On C Day, but after the burst. Definitely after. We were still getting the building evacuated, computers and process equipment loaded on trucks. She came in with a motor-cycle gang."

Dan furrowed his brow, not sure he'd heard that right. "A . . . motorcycle gang?"

"Yeah. The Berzerkers. I recognized their colors. No idea how she picked those dudes up. Not a bunch you want to get in their face, know what I mean? But she seemed tight with them. They had their guns on Heremy, he's the manager? Or was—he hasn't been back since. I heard 'em arguing. He didn't want to let the shipment go. She persuaded him otherwise. With them pointing rifles at him."

"Hm," Dan muttered. Not sure what to make of what he was hearing.

"Next thing we know, she's hijacked a reefer truck. You know, a refrigerator truck? And they forced us to load up all million doses. Then they all took off. The Berzerkers, her, the truck, everybody."

"And I ain't seen them since." He looked Dan's uniform up and down. "Where'd you serve?"

"Navy. Taiwan Strait, central Pacific, then the invasion of China."

"Oh yeah? What's it like there?"

"A disaster," Dan said. "Famine. Disease. Fallout. We hit them hard."

Jimmy gazed out over the ruins of the city. "As bad as here?"

"At least. In fact, probably a lot worse."

"Good," the guy said, satisfaction clear in his voice. "Serve the fucking slants right. I hope they all died screaming. Thanks for your service."

Dan digested this in silence, he too looking out to the north, over the ruins of what had once been Seattle. Now it was a plain of radioactive rubble. Still smoking, still burning, though it had been days since the strikes. Just miles of level destruction, stretching away until it was lost to the eye in a dark reddish haze, through which the sun shone like a distant ruby. There had to be thousands of bodies down there still. Charred. Buried. Burned.

He looked back at the lake, blinking sweat from his eyes. Now he understood. The dark lumps floating on its far side weren't clumps of ash. Or, not just ash. He hadn't been able to see them well through the blurred, fogged, single-element lens of the mask.

They were bodies. Corpses. Floating on the lake they'd taken refuge in, when the searing heat had become too hellish to withstand. Cooked like chickens on a grill. But still alive, while they roasted.

He shook his head, and tore his fugitive mind back as Jimmy held out a bottle of water. Dan poured some into his hand, washed his face, drank two swallows, and handed it back. He wanted more, but drinkable water seemed to be in short supply. "Thanks. Thanks a lot. Where do you think they might've been headed?"

"Couldn't tell you. We just wanted them out of here before the wind changed and brought that fucking plume back over us. Or before that mob decided to start shooting. We were all in shock. Half the people on the line that day . . . God, it was bad. And they kept walking past, from the city. Burned, blinded, arms missing, carrying dead kids, their skin hanging off them . . . they'd just stop, looking at nothing, if they still had eyes . . . then fall down dead." He swallowed. "We cleaned up most of the bodies, put them on the trucks, but they were layin' all over the grass here."

Dan squeezed his eyes shut for a moment. "Yeah, I can imagine."

"My best guess . . . your daughter . . . maybe they'd head inland.

You know, east? Maybe toward Yakima? Seems like I heard one of them mention that."

Yakima, where Dr. Lukajs was. Where Archipelago had relocated to. But Lukajs had said Nan wasn't there.

But her team leader hadn't exactly come across as on top of things, and there might be enough confusion that she *could* be there and her boss didn't know it. A possibility, anyway. But how was he going to get to Yakima? He was turning away again when the guy said, "You got transportation?"

"Uh—no." This would be a problem. He had no car, and from everything he'd heard, gasoline was scarce and all the public charging stations for EVs had gone down in the Cloudburst. Bus, train? They'd be packed, if they still ran. He could maybe pull rank and get aboard, but even as he thought it, knew he wouldn't.

Plus, if she *wasn't* in Yakima, he might need to follow her trail somewhere else. Nan, and this . . . gang . . . had apparently showed up here to get the drug. He still hadn't figured that partnership out. Unless this Jimmy was feeding him some kind of bizarre confabulation.

The supervisor was walking away, back toward the building. He called over his shoulder, "Well, hey . . . it may not be what you want. But one of the guys, he left this here."

Dan followed him around the corner, and halted.

It lay canted against a dumpster. Scorched on one side, and dented, probably by the bricks that lay scattered around it. But by some miracle, the gas tank hadn't exploded.

He contemplated a battered black Honda Gold Wing. The windshield was cracked. Deep scuff marks along the side showed where it had been laid down, maybe several times. Or maybe that was from the bricks and debris kicked up by the shock wave.

Jimmy reached into the leather saddlebag and came up with a key. When he turned it the headlight came on, though not very brightly. A hollow click evidenced signs of life in the battery, though not enough charge to turn the starter over.

Nan had left with a motorcycle gang. Was this the way to find her, to literally follow in her tracks?

Magical thinking? Maybe. But if this was a straw, he was ready to grasp at it. At the very least, today he'd learned one shining, intoxicating fact. *She'd been alive.* Alive and kicking, making things happen, *after* the attack.

Which lifted an immense weight from his heart, though a sickening anxiety remained.

"This is yours, Jimmy?" Dan asked the guy. "This bike?"

"Mine? No. A guy left it last year, after they laid him off. Said I could sell it if I wanted to. But the market's been kind of . . . anyway, I never got any takers. So if you want it, I'll let 'er go. Cheap."

Dan didn't have much cash. A skimpy roll of the new-issue, tissue-paper-thin hundred-dollar bills. If you needed something out in the war zone, either the Navy supplied it or you did without. He had most of his pay socked away, a nice chunk of change by now, but no way to access it. And if he did what he was contemplating, he'd need every dollar left in his wallet.

At last he slipped off his Academy ring. Over an ounce of massive fourteen-carat gold. It had accompanied him for thirty years. Gone around the world, accumulated dents and dings from ships and subs and planes. He valued it, sure. But a ring could be replaced, while Nan . . .

He held it out, the carved facets of his class crest glittering in the dull reddish sunlight. "How about this?"

"Whoa. I can't take that from . . . is that gold?" Sudden avarice glittered in the man's eyes. Yeah, that age-old shiny yellow metal never lost its appeal. The worse things got, the more valuable it became.

"Give me your full name and I'll buy it back later. So, no worries. And if you never hear from me again, well, then, it's yours. Deal?"

Jimmy hefted the ring in his palm. "Uh . . . sure. If that's really how you want to do it."

"Deal, then."

Suddenly enthusiastic, Jimmy rushed about, helping him siphon fuel from a wrecked car. Dan checked the oil on the bike.
The level seemed adequate, though it was dirty, obviously overdue for a change. The other workers gathered around, interested. They jumpered the bike into a hesitant grumble. One man
checked his tires and pronounced them "Worn, but okay if ya
don't push it in the rain." Another briefed him on how to change
gears. A third sketched out directions to Yakima. Yet another
broke out a sandwich and handed half of it over. "For the road,"
he said.

Dan was gifted bottled water, a ragged blanket, a rusty mul-
titool, a small tarp. He thanked them, and stuffed it all into the
saddlebags. Sailing a small boat taught you one thing: it was
better to have a thing and not need it, than to need it and not
have it. They all agreed Yakima was only 150, 160 miles away.
One tank would probably get him there. "Down Route 90, then
head across the mountains. Keep Mount Rainier on your right,"
Jimmy said. "And you can ask along the way if anybody's seen a
shitload of Berzerkers convoying a reefer truck. That'd be hard
to miss."

"And watch for zombies and cannibals," another worker added.

Dan shook hands all around, zipped his jacket, and climbed
aboard. No helmet, but considering this was the long-awaited Nuclear Apocalypse, he wasn't going to worry about a lid. He blipped
the throttle experimentally, put it in first, and let up cautiously
on the clutch. The bike jerked forward and stalled. He got off,
kick-started it again, and climbed back on. He wobbled around
the building, nearly running into a toppled section of fence, but
straightened out on the scorched grass and headed down the hill.

Second gear . . . third.

But as he rode, gradually pushing up his speed as he got used
to the machine, the heartsickness returned. Why had anyone ever
thought war solved anything? It only traded old dilemmas for new,
far more terrible problems.

Someone needed to pay. For that dead girl-child. For the men and women who'd died beside him, out in the far Pacific. For this murdered city, through whose abandoned, smashed, radioactive streets he slowly rode.

But who could bring charges, assign blame, pass judgment, hand down punishment? He could think of only one court, at least on this earth.

But if the US wouldn't submit to its jurisdiction, neither would the Chinese.

The ICC inquiry . . . Maybe he should respond. Offer himself, as a sacrifice to justice. Whether or not the administration thought it was a good idea.

He shook his head angrily. That could wait for later. For now, he'd better concentrate on what he was doing.

At first the asphalt pavement was buckled, warped, melted in the higher spots, the hills, where the heat from the fireball had struck most directly. But as he rolled south, gradually picking up speed, buildings no longer slumped across the pavement like toppled giants. Fewer wrecks littered the road. Wires no longer trailed across his path, and power poles and lampposts and sometimes even road signs still stood. The sky brightened as the smoking city fell behind. The mingled stenches of burning and death grew fainter, though those of uncollected garbage remained, giving off a rank, vegetable rot, and here and there his wheels splashed through backed-up sewage.

But town after town he rolled through lay deserted. Storefronts were shuttered, or their plate glass lay sparkling on the sidewalks. No one was out on the streets. The roads stretched empty, the gas stations and recharge stations dark, the traffic lights unlit. He didn't even see any birds or stray dogs. Hadn't there been a dog in every movie about the apocalypse?

His disquiet grew. What had happened to the country? He'd been away so long. Years, in fact. Things had changed. Even beyond the impact of a nuclear war.

He hesitated. Steered around a wrecked and abandoned cop car, its windows smashed out, its interior still smoldering tendrils of plasticky-smelling white smoke. Then inhaled, deep, and gunned the throttle as clear highway opened ahead.

A reluctant pilgrim, he set out to cross a ruined land.

3

USS *Savo Island*
Wakkanai Bay, Japan

T HE enemy missiles kept coming, rapidly emptying *Savo*'s defensive magazines. Until at last the fatal zeros glowed on the ordnance tally readouts. Yet the cuing note bonged on and on, while Chief Terranova screamed at her from her console. And the missiles climbed. Pitched over. Headed straight for America . . .

Captain Cheryl Staurulakis, USN, came awake unwillingly, heart pounding and with a splitting headache. She rolled out of the bunk, hands thrust out as if to ward off a knife. Stood swaying in a darkened stateroom, panting.

The snug little sea cabin seemed suddenly immense. Then it shrank, and dwindled again, until it barely held space for air. Sudden apprehension palpitated her chest and turned her muscles to stone. Why were they *not moving*? Why did the knotmeter remote on her cabin bulkhead register *zero*? Were they dead in the water again, without power, without *defenses*—

Then she remembered, and reality flooded back in a reassuring tide. Her ship was *safe*. Not on fire. In port, not adrift and under attack.

But she was still guilty. Of sending American sailors to their deaths.

She scratched viciously at her neck, at her crotch, at her calves, until the warm blood trickled. It would stain her sheets. Her uniform. The fucking itching, that would only let her sleep in snatches.

She'd ordered *Sioux City* to shield *Savo*'s stern off Korea. The wake-homing torpedoes had mangled the smaller ship, wrecking it so badly she had to be towed to Sasebo. With thirty-two dead, and dozens more injured or burned.

And still she'd failed to intercept the Chinese missiles aimed at the homeland.

Millions dead. Because Cheryl Morehead Staurulakis hadn't measured up.

The relief ebbed. She staggered into the little attached head. Pulled down her panties and squatted, squeezing her eyes shut as urine hissed into the stainless steel bowl.

Got to get a grip, Cheryl.

You did your best. There were just too many enemy ICBMs. Too many decoys along with the live warheads, and not enough of your own weapons to take them all out.

You're in port now. The war's over, and your crew's safe. You brought them back.

Most of them, at least.

Hands over her face, she told herself this over and over and at last her lungs stopped heaving and the dancing glowing specks of broken light at the edges of her vision dimmed. She slumped, breathing deep, eyes closed. Then forced herself up, wiped, flushed, and snapped the light on.

She turned from the mirror, shuddering. Unable to meet the dead gaze that stared back from that haggard visage. The bleached-pale cheeks, the reddened, scabbed lids, the thinning, washed-out hair.

She dry-gulped an antihistamine, and rubbed cortisone cream into her hands. The doc had said that once she wasn't under so much stress, the itching and eruptions should back off. But they seemed just as bad as ever, if not worse. Red oozing pustules from which the skin peeled. Unsightly. Maddening. Like she was under some kind of sorcerous curse.

Maybe it was for the best that Eddie was dead. That he'd been shot down, and would never see her again.

Would never see her like this.

SAVO ISLAND was the third ship named to commemorate a deadly battle fought north of Guadalcanal. The first had been an escort carrier commissioned in 1944. The second, a Ticonderoga-class cruiser, had fought in the opening phases of the war just ended. Cheryl had been her operations officer, then exec, and finally skipper. After action in the Taiwan Strait, the Battle of the Central Pacific, and the East China Sea, that second *Savo* had been sunk in the nuclear attack on Honolulu.

Some of the crew manning this third namesake had served aboard her as well.

The current *Savo*'s primary mission was antimissile defense. Its Alliance interceptors were AI-enabled to discriminate between the decoys and warheads of heavy ICBMs. Displacing close to twenty thousand tons on a modified Zumwalt hull, it carried railguns and beam weapons to defend the task forces it had accompanied to war. The cruiser was armored, compartmented, and sealed from the outside air. A dynamic access network provided high-bandwidth exchange among air-, surface-, subsurface-, and ground-based tactical data systems. Instead of shafts and reduction gears, it was propelled by podded Tesla truck motors, powered by gas turbines looted from commercial airliners.

Following commissioning, and weeks of exhausting training, they'd transited to the western Pacific to stand guard as Allied forces landed in Korea. Then moved north to block a possible Chinese strike over the Sea of Okhotsk, Siberia, and the Arctic. When the war had ended with a nuclear exchange, Cheryl had fought to intercept the enemy's heaviest missiles.

And mostly, she had. But a few had gotten through, sending megaton-range nukes plunging down on the western and central United States.

With the news of the armistice, her task group had been recalled to port. She was still technically in tactical command, but her units were scattered about the northwestern Pacific: Japan, Korea, Taiwan, a few in China itself, providing humanitarian aid, electrical power, potable water, and medical care. The frantic tempo of wartime operations had abruptly dropped to a sluggish crawl.

Of course, that didn't mean she had nothing to do.

In its inimitable wisdom, the Navy had protected them all against that hideous fate.

THE wardroom. The homely smells of coffee and eggs and grits and ham. Matt Mills, her executive officer, was elbows down at the table. Even frowning and rubbing his forehead, he was easy on the eyes, blond and chiseled as any romantic lead on a Netflix series. "Morning, Skipper," he said, starting to get up. The others rose as well.

She waved them back down and drew herself a cup from the urn, black. "Take it easy, everyone. Any progress?"

"A little." Her second-in-command glanced at his phone. "But it's more like death from a thousand paper cuts. We're going to reconvene here shortly, and hit it again."

In any sane organization, training would have started from a blank sheet with war's end. Or even—though no one aboard was naive enough to expect this—with a month off to recover, catch up on sleep, and do planned maintenance instead of voyage repairs.

But with the abeyance of hostilities, a flood of pent-up demands had poured in. Fleet had promulgated a new and rigorous certification instruction. It increased requirements for training on Information Assurance, Antiharassment, Antidiscrimination, Sexual Assault Prevention, Cyber Awareness, Counterintelligence Awareness and Reporting, and Suicide Prevention. Personnel with less than three years of time in service had to complete Antiterrorism Level 1 training, with mandatory triennial periodicity for all others. Cheryl could exercise command discretion on Alcohol, Drugs, and Tobacco Awareness, Combating Trafficking in Persons, Domestic Violence Prevention and Reporting, Electromagnetic Warfare, Equal Opportunity, Hazing Policy, Operational Risk Management, Operations Security, Personal Financial Management, Records Management, Sexual Health and Responsibility, Stress Management, Traumatic Brain Injury Awareness, and a dozen more programs that had been suspended for the duration, but that now required backdated reports covering the period of suspension.

So for the last three days, she, Mills, and her operations officer, Dave Branscombe, along with the division officers and senior enlisted, had been locked in a massive paperwork drill. They were trying to document certifiable training events from wartime logs while at the same time building a training regimen for the next quarter from scratch.

Piecing together the past was an opportunity for creativity. But also a chance to shoot herself in the foot. If they got too fast and loose, some staff lieutenant back in Hawaii would be sure to drop a dime on them. So she was torn between encouraging her people to fudge, which would save the crew time and work that could be spent instead on actual maintenance, and reining them in, which would eat more work hours but protect her own heinie.

The choice here was clear, since that very heinie had been put at risk quite a lot lately, and theirs too along with it, all too literally. They all deserved whatever slack she could cut them.

A tap at the door, and the chiefs filed in. She pointed a chin at the urn. "Help yourself," she said. "Chief Zotcher. Chief Terranova. Chief Van Gogh.

"Okay, to say it once more: we're going to stretch those guidelines to the limit," she told them when everyone was finally settled around the table with tablets and binders. "Don't make anything up. But count every action, every actual operation we participated in, as a training opportunity. And we put in a shitlot of hours at Condition One ABM. Don't lie, but use your imagination."

"Copy all. Where will you be, Captain?" Zotcher asked. The sonar chief, she suddenly noticed, had gone completely bald during the war. "In case we have any questions?"

"Any gray areas, Commander Mills will decide."

Her exec said mildly, "I have a zone inspection today, Captain. I'll need to break for that."

Cheryl finished her coffee and stood. "I'll take your inspection, XO. About time I got a good look around again."

"Thanks, ma'am," Mills said, but he didn't sound especially glad to be relieved of that duty. He rubbed his forehead again, narrowing his eyes as he studied a tablet. "Fuck," he muttered under his breath.

SHE left them complaining and fabricating and commenced her inspection at the boatswain's locker, in the very nook of the bow. A note taker, one of the ship's yeomen, followed her.

It had been some months since she'd had time for a detailed reading on *Savo*'s material condition. Being at Condition One tended to keep a skipper glued close to CIC. This morning, as petty officer after compartment petty officer reported, "Ready for inspection, ma'am," she snooped and pried. First, to emphasize ownership, she asked each responsible man or woman for a look at the compartment deficiency report. To emphasize responsibility, what they'd done to remedy the problems. To highlight follow-through, what the result had been. Only then did she click her flashlight on.

Working her way slowly aft through the storerooms and offices, she touched her augmented-reality glasses to match the data and documentation overlay against the ground truth of what years of experience told her at a glance. She called up compartment pressure testing reports, bent to read the tags on firefighting equipment, and pressed a finger into the rubber seals on the watertight doors. She checked fire hose discharge fittings, classification, and numbering against the records in the ship's computers. She rattled each fuse panel looking for loose cover bolts, and inspected each individual fuse and breaker to make sure it hadn't been replaced with one of a higher amperage rating. She uncoiled, laid out, and inspected the casualty power cables and risers for cracks, frayed insulation, and damage.

In forward berthing, she sniffed the air. Bent close to the deck, checking cleanliness in the corners with the aid of the flashlight. Then asked the presenter to turn off the overheads.

Seaman Downie bobbed his head, smirking, and went to comply. She ignored the smirk. The diminutive, eccentric Downie, long ago nicknamed "the Troll" by his shipmates, was about the only person aboard who'd gone through the entire war without a single promotion. A career seaman, as the saying went. She'd tried to transfer him out, but NavPers had decided, in its infinite wisdom, that once aboard, he would stay.

A snap, and darkness flooded the compartment. It brought back the panicky terror she'd felt waking up. She pushed it off like a too-heavy quilt and groped her way around the space, craning her neck this way and that, alert for any holes in the bulkhead or overhead or gaps in the cable penetrations. Any chink that would admit light from adjacent spaces would also compromise its watertightness, defeating the whole point of compartmentation.

But she didn't see any. "You can turn them back on now," she yelled.

When they came on Downie was staring into her face from four inches away. Sneaking up on her like some knife-wielding psycho in a dark alley, wearing that unsettling pixie grin. "Skipper?" he smirked. "Hey, got a question for you."

She placed a hand on his skivvy-shirted chest, suppressing a shudder at its stiff clamminess. How long had he been *wearing* it? "Back off, Seaman Downie. What is it?"

"The guys are saying, I got to plan how to rig extra bunks down here. That so?"

She frowned. "First I've heard of it. What for?"

Downie twirled in place, a ballerina-like pirouette but without grace. "They say we're gonna take the Army back home. Demob, they call it. Ship everybody back from the war. And we go back too."

Scuttlebutt was amazing. And Downie, who dated from the old *Savo*, always seemed to have the latest and greatest. Or maybe he made it up himself. "I don't think so," she told him gently. "At least, not that I've heard. Maybe you're just ahead of me, though. If you get any updates on that? . . ."

He smirked and bobbed his head. "I'll keep you posted, Skipper."

SHE proceeded from the office and berthing spaces to inspect the forward missile magazines. Then, to the far-belowdecks spaces where the pumps, motors, cooling equipment, pressurized gas and capacitor banks for the lasers and railgun batteries were located. Here she checked insulating matting, warning and precaution signs, deck drains, overpressure inspection and test certifications, and safety and escape gear. She made sure the alarms were live, that safety nets were rigged in the trunks, ventilation closures and controls were operational, and the emergency lighting worked.

It was 0900 when she reached the mess decks. Breakfast had been cleared. Here she doubled down on deck drains, cleanliness, fixtures, and firefighting readiness. But as she'd expected, word had percolated back that the skipper was on a tear. Chief Lubkeman had his men and women turned out in spotless serving aprons and paper hats. The food prep and serving areas smelled of bleach and the decks gleamed with fresh wax. She gave these areas a quick once-over, snapped the UV disinfection lights on and off, and checked the tags on the fire-extinguishing system. "Looking good, everyone," she complimented them, and moved on.

She clattered down two decks on metal ladders to the engineering spaces. The old *Savo*'s engine compartments had been a howl of noise and dry heat. Gas turbines and pumps had fattened the air with sound. But pierside now, "cold iron," this cruiser's spaces were capacious, quiet, and cool. Here Cheryl concentrated on valve condition, labeling, and classification. She asked for gauge and tool calibration dates, checked them against the maintenance requirements, and looked behind every console and pump for flammable consumables. Master Chief McMottie accompanied her, never more than a step behind. Each time she turned to ask a question he had his tablet out and the relevant graph or checklist ready on the screen.

The third time this happened she grimaced, torn between pleasure and annoyance. "Maybe I don't actually need to inspect down here, Master Chief?"

McMottie half grinned. "Maybe not, ma'am. But it's always nice to see you in coveralls."

She squinted, but his open frank smile didn't seem to mask a double entendre. Maybe he just meant . . . oh, never mind. "All right," she snapped. "How about the overheating issue on number three drive motor?"

"Sensor fault, ma'am. Easy fix. Replaced that and CASREP'd issue's resolved."

"Fluctuations in the low-voltage distribution system after switching to manual control?"

"Did a root-cause analysis and found it in that new software drop. Bad response logic from the SDC when it translated the manual control order. Patched it with code from the previous flight. Ran it fifteen times. No recurrence, smooth output."

"Give it fifty more cycles before you report it fixed."

He nodded gravely. "Aye aye, Skipper."

"And all those spare parts back here, still in their boxes?"

Another grave nod. "You know what they say, ma'am. 'Engineer''s just another word for 'hoarder.'"

Up two platforms and aft again, this time to the after mounts. She took her time and did just as thorough a job, though her legs ached now and her headache was forming up for a new assault. She inspected for proper stowage and cycled the safety interlocks. Then looked for missile hazards, fire hazards, and hygiene and safety violations.

A bustle of activity rose behind her as the divisions mustered to clean, restow, and repaint. Unfortunately the hands she could call on were all too few. Her first command had manned a ten-thousand-ton hull with nearly 380 officers and enlisted, when you included the helicopter flight crews. The new cruisers displaced nearly double that, but with half the personnel. The railguns and lasers had further strained the manning situation, since the ship retained PVLS and conventional weapons. There'd been savings in admin and engineering, but even with a wartime plus-up to complement the baseline manning, she had fewer than two hundred warm bodies.

In the aft magazine a petty officer objected mildly. "Ma'am, the war's over. We really got to worry about handling placards for HVAP projectiles?"

"The war *may* be over. Right now all we have is an armistice."

His face changed. "So we could go back out."

She considered her answer carefully. Anything the CO said would carom around the ship like a rubber bullet. "I don't *think* we will, but sure . . . we *could*. This peace might not hold. And even if it does, we still have the Russians up there looking to tear off tasty pieces wherever they can."

"Pieces. Off of China, you mean?"

"Exactly. They're already occupying part of Manchuria, on the basis of their last-minute declaration of war. And the trouble with feeding a bear one cookie . . . well, you know where I'm going with that."

He made a wry face. "I don't want to seem . . . uh, contrary, Skipper . . . but why should we care about what happens to the slants?"

She couldn't help letting a quarter-smile slip. But then the itch flared. She scratched at her neck, then jerked her nails away. "Whether you or I care or not doesn't really matter. If we get tasked, we'd better be ready." She pointed at the placard she'd found lying on the deck behind a control console. "So let's get that glued back on, and make sure the battle lantern's angled to illuminate it."

SHE was actually enjoying herself by the time she got to CIC. Petty Officer Eastwood was running an intercept scenario, but paused it for the inspection. Cheryl moved through here quickly, since she didn't want to hold up the drill. After nearly a year at war the space seemed worn already. The seat covers were faded. The decks were scuffed, especially beneath the consoles, where booted feet had rested 24/7. But everything seemed to have been freshly swept and free of dust. The low hum of ventilating fans crooned like a lullaby.

She'd fought her war from here. She paused at the command desk, where her ass had been planted for so many weary hours, interspersed with minutes of pure terror. Hard to believe the second Pacific war, the Third World War, whatever they were going to call it in the history books, might really be over, despite the caveats she'd given the crew.

One large screen display had the current fused picture up. She glanced at the VR helmet in its rack, and shuddered. She'd spent enough time with her head stuck in that thing, thank you.

The screen showed Russia to the west: the rugged, mountainous Asian coastline the tsars had wrested from the Manchu emperors two centuries before. Sparsely populated, and economically nearly worthless, but somehow that never stopped the Russians from wanting more. To the south stretched Hokkaido, northernmost of the main islands of Japan.

Again, staring at the screen and scratching absently at her neck, she pondered what Downie, the compartment cleaner, had said. A daydream, probably, made up from the crew's homesick longings. But sometimes scuttlebutt was more like foresight than fantasy.

If this really did turn out to be a lasting peace . . .

Then a massive demobilization was certainly in the cards. Back home, Congress was debating the future. Of the Pacific, and thus, the future of the Navy. With Europe's revitalization, the country now maintained only a token presence in the Atlantic and Med, except for the battle groups maintaining the chokehold on Iran, the sole remaining holdout of the Opposed Powers.

Fleet had sounded her out about participating in a congressionally mandated force-structure study. Someone had to decide what fleet units would be kept on, and which would be returned to mothballs or even scrapped. Getting the Navy's views on record, at least, before Congress tied on a blindfold and started wielding a blunt machete.

Postwar cuts tended to be murderous. The reactivated units, Spruances, Perrys, Los Angeleses, and Ticonderogas pulled from mothballs to pad out numbers at the low end of the warfighting spectrum, would go first, scrapped or sold off to allies. Ditto the converted merchantmen that had served as jeep carriers and missile barges. They'd either be sold or returned to their peacetime roles. *Savo* and the others of her class would probably survive. But the *Early Bird* had reported a proposal to shrink the fleet from wartime's 670 active units down to fewer than 200, not counting the autonomous Hunters. And there were already questions about whether the carriers had paid their way in this war.

But you couldn't design a fleet in a strategic or budgetary vacuum. They'd have to examine cost, tactical doctrine, forward-presence models, and national strategy to see what the Navy would look like going forward.

"Resume the drill, Captain?" Eastwood murmured, at her side.

Cheryl masked a yawn with a gloved hand, and nodded.

SHE ended her inspection on the bridge. Here, so many decks up she'd taken an elevator to reach it, the untenanted air lay quiet. These days a warship was conned from a citadel far belowdecks. The remaining humans were sealed from the outside air, cocooned like fragile Delftware in armor and shock mounting. The pilothouse was only manned up leaving or returning to port.

The next class of ships might not have a bridge at all. The space was becoming a vestigial appendage, like the cockpit on a submarine sail. Eventually it might pass out of physical existence entirely. Like the "quarterdeck," which had been a real location in the age of sail, but now existed only as a ceremonial fiction, floating wherever the officer of the deck was stationed.

All was change. Everything remained in flux. And never more so than in the afterlight of a disastrous war.

Musing on that, she let herself out onto the little balconylike wing. Opened her arms wide and stretched, welcoming the cool of the open air after a whole morning spent inside. Far below, four Hunter autonomous drones were rafted alongside. Two autonomous Orca submarines were moored outboard of them. A few technicians in blue coveralls clambered about them, and umbilicals snaked down, feeding them shoreside power and updating their artificial brains.

Yeah, that might be the future.

The next generation of warships might go to sea without berthing areas, mess decks, crew's lounges, barbershops, ship's stores, laundries, sick bays . . . Without any humans aboard at all, fighting units could be a lot smaller. Probably cheaper, too. And if the worst happened, no one would need to explain things to grieving families . . .

Past the black whalelike Orcas, Soya Bay opened out, blue and wind-ruffled, barriered only by a breakwater. A saucer-shaped security drone skated slowly along the horizon, scanning down to the seabed with magnetic sensors and radar. A low sun glittered to the east. Past that lay thirty miles of dark sapphire sea, then Sakhalin . . . Russian territory.

During the war the Japanese had hastily built and dredged Wakkanai, originally a small commercial port, into a modest naval base and logistics hub. Right now it mainly supported her own task force, plus the Japanese northern squadron. The base was strategically located, though requiring a difficult sea detail, and there wasn't really enough pier space to accommodate more than two cruiser/destroyer-size units at a time. A military airstrip ten miles to the south accommodated fifteen JSDF fighters and a Patriot battery.

She wandered back into what was still called the chartroom, though there were no longer paper charts. Well, only a few as final backup, rolled tightly and stowed in a rack in the overhead. As she filched one down and unscrolled it, smoothing it out on the table, a few dust motes sprang free, sparkling in the sunlight. The chart they'd used for Operation Chromite, the decapitation strike on North Korea.

Her note taker cleared his throat behind her. Cheryl flinched; she'd forgotten he was still following her. "Yeoman. What is it?"

"Are we done, ma'am? Want me to clean up these notes, put 'em up on the LAN?"

"Sure. Yes, thank you. We're done."

He started to turn away, but lingered. "So . . . what happens next, Skipper?"

Apparently she and Downie weren't the only ones pondering possible futures. "Next? We transition to peacetime steaming, I guess."

"Um, well, I heard we're headed back. To Guam, then San Diego. Ma'am."

"I heard that too. But it's just a rumor, Yeoman. I haven't gotten anything official."

He looked quickly away, as if he knew better, and she felt a flash of annoyance. No; anger. Did they think she was *hiding* things from them? "I have the same questions as everyone else, believe me," she said, trying to keep her voice level, casual, workaday. "As soon as I know something concrete, I'll pass it to everyone over the 1MC."

Trying not to show what she felt . . . as she so often had to do. Smiling when she didn't want to smile. Feigning confidence when she was scared shitless. Acting as if she knew what she was doing, when she was really making it all up as she went along half the time. Finding a secluded corner to scratch furiously at her butt crack, when the spreading itch threatened to drive her crazy.

Well, now that the war was over, maybe there'd be less of all of that. If the fucking itching, "psychogenic pruritus," as one shoreside doctor had called it, really *was* her body's response to sleeplessness, stress, anxiety, terror—

The 1MC snapped on. *"Commanding officer, please contact the XO in the wardroom,"* it stated.

Her hand went to her belt, for her radio. But no. Maybe it would be better to . . . She crossed with swift strides to her command chair. Hit the 21MC. "This is the captain. XO there?"

"Wait one, ma'am . . . Here he is."

"Commander?"

"Skipper? Where are you?" Mills's voice.

"Bridge. Finishing the inspection. What's going on?"

"Flash message. I'll send a runner, but can you log on up there, come up on high side nanochat, Fleet command?"

"On it." She told her terminal, "This is Captain Staurulakis. Alice, log me on."

"Logging on, Skipper," said AALIS, the ship's command computer.

Task Force satellite chat unscrolled on the screen. She found the latest message. From Fleet.

```
Bootstrap: To Tangler
    FLASH FLASH FLASH
    Forces from Russian Federation EMD preparing to occupy
portions of eastern Heilongjiang and possibly port of
Dalian. Russian Pacific Fleet at enhanced readiness for
sortie en route Sea of Japan. Commence reconstitute Sea
of Okhotsk task force 73.3 rdvu ASAP PIM as per TG Cdr
directs. Prepare to intercept. Dirlauth. Enders
```

A chill harrowed her spine. "Bootstrap," the message initiator, was Seventh Fleet. Dick Enders was its J-3, the operations deputy.

Shorn of its acronyms, and supplied with what she could infer, the message directed her to reassemble her scattered task force and prepare for battle forthwith. So much for a lasting peace . . . She dictated a quick acknowledgment, then signed off.

"Heilongjiang," she muttered. "Alice, where's that? Heilongjiang? And where and what is Dalian?"

The map the AI brought up on the screen outlined an awkwardly shaped tongue of China stuck out tauntingly into Russian territory north of Vladivostok. When she toggled to overhead imagery, the terrain looked mountainous and barren in the west, flatter and probably more productive toward the coast. But Russia cupped it, and had stationed heavy forces in eastern Siberia throughout the war, despite Moscow's role supplying Zhang's regime with weaponry, energy, and diplomatic cover.

The information that came up on the other name froze her to ice where she stood. Dalian was a port city with an excellent harbor. It lay at the north end of the Yellow Sea, west of the Korean Peninsula. The city had been Russia's before, as Port Arthur, the eastern terminus of the Manchurian Railway. The Russians had administered it again, briefly, after World War II.

As a forward base in north China once again, and as an ice-free port on the Pacific, it would be strategically located to put naval pressure on Japan and a reunified Korea.

Already Moscow was moving its chess pieces forward. Probing the board for weakness.

Just as they'd taken advantage of China every time in history it had suffered.

She touched a knuckle to her lips, considering. Her task force had been built around *Savo Island*, two Japanese Aegis destroyers, *Chokai* and *Ashigara*, and one modern Korean unit, *Jeonnam*. She had four submarines, *Arkansas*, *Idaho*, *Guam*, and *John Warner* and *Utah*, replacing the lost *Guam*.

Antisubmarine defense . . . Her surface escorts were two missile frigates, *Goodrich* and *Montesano*. The unmanned Hunters moored alongside, USV-34, -20, -7, and -16, and Flight One Orcas

USS-4 and -13, would serve for early warning. As would her manned attack subs, which she would post farther north.

As for air defense . . . She had helicopters and onboard drones, but no carrier air on call. Four Aegis units should be able to fight off an air attack, though, and the Japanese Air Self-Defense Force should be standing by.

If, that is, Japan felt like confronting the Russians on behalf of the Chinese. Which might not seem in their national interest, considering their recent losses in the battles to recover the Ryukyus. Japan had so few young people, and robots couldn't do all the fighting.

No. She'd have to have carrier support. Something to ask for, urgently, right now, before getting under way.

She scratched under her arms, staring sightlessly down on the forecastle, where her undermanned First Division people were overhauling the lifelines. And what about her crew? They expected to go home. How would they take going to sea again? Possibly, going into battle, against a new enemy?

The 21MC lit again. Mills's voice again. *"Captain? We went to GQ down here on a sailing plan. Contacted* Chokai *and* Ashigara. Jeonnam, *we can't reach.* Goodrich *and* Montesano *will get under way from Sasebo.* Arkansas *and* Utah *are pierside in Pusan; they can be under way in four hours. Permission to get them to sea?"*

"Granted. What do you suggest as a rendezvous point?"

"Chief Van Gogh advises we head everybody to join up east of Tsushima. In the Korea Strait. That way if the Pacific Fleet comes down the Sea of Japan, we'll be in a blocking position."

She debated the pros and cons, but only briefly. Higher would send more specific orders. "Make it so. But set the rendezvous for farther north—around latitude forty. Give us more sea room. Present a less concentrated target."

The exec rogered and signed off.

She let herself out on the wing, and leaned on the splinter shield again. Below, on the decks of the Hunters, the indolent movements of the maintainers were already giving way to bustle and shouts. The itching flamed like maddening fire, at her armpits, neck, scalp. She closed her eyes, sagging into the steel. Suddenly wishing all she had to worry about was paperwork and inspections and training schedules. "Fuck," she muttered. "Fuck it to hell . . . they had to. They just had to do it."

Maybe it wasn't peace after all.

But she wasn't really sure she could stand doing war all over again.

4

USNS *Mercy,* T-AH-19
The South China Sea

IS chest is cast of solid pain. Each breath hurts as it's pulled
into his lungs, but *he's not taking those breaths.*

Horror. Horror . . .

Someone has jammed a sharp stick down his throat. His eyes
stream tears. Something hard slurps noisily down by his jaw, sucking drool from his scorched mouth.

Huge spidery shapes shift within the smoke, striding about.
They cut writhing mucus-yellow shadows from the bloody sun.
The gas-warning alarm in his mask chirrups, chirrups. A for-
mation of silvery disks whir over a hundred feet up. He searches
desperately for cover, but they hum on inland, ignoring his
squad. The big Indonesian, the guy with the Javelin launcher,
keeps asking a question he doesn't understand. Far above, con-
trails lacerate the sky like scars.

Confused. Everything so *pinche* confused . . .

The short, dark-haired Marine only very slowly becomes aware
he is not actually on the battlefield. That just now he seems to be
lying motionless in a soft bunk. Unless this too is just a dream,
within a dream. And that some machine is chuffing and clicking
beside his head.

His name . . . it's not . . . got it. It's Hector. Hector Ramos.

But where the fuck is he?

He's aboard ship, maybe? Still waiting to hit the beach? Hard to tell. But then, where's his weapon? He's a machine gunner. He remembers that perfectly clearly, though everything else is dim, dreamlike, muddled. The solid weight of the weapon. The king of the battlefield. *The king fucks the queen* . . . Who said that, who yelled it into his ear, on a hot day, in a hot wind choked with bitter dust . . . He can't remember. It slides away, vanishes, maybe a memory, maybe a dream, maybe a nightmare.

Groans come from around him. The thing, the machine, chuffs and clicks, on and on. When he pries crusted lids painfully open at last the light is a blue dim. He can't see much, and his head doesn't seem to want to turn.

But there really is something jammed deep in his throat. Something hard. A bone, sticking far down his *throat—*

He raises himself on one arm, clawing at it. Only *his arm doesn't move.* He fights with all his strength to lift a hand and jerk the foreign thing out. The bone. The stick.

But he *can't move.*

Sheer terror shakes him. He's been . . . *taken over* by some other being. A demon. An alien. He has to push it off, and get this choking, hard *thing* out of his chest. But he can't move. *He can't move.*

A light flashes near his head. Something hard is pinching his ear. He fights to breathe, to struggle, but he can't. The device chuffs and clicks. He can feel his chest rising and falling in sync with the labored noise. His lungs, inflating and deflating. But he has no control over his own breath. No control over anything. It's insane, it can't be real. The thing keeps puffing and clicking by his head, laboring, regular, maddening.

Oh Jesus oh God get this thing out of my throat.

Ayudarme, ayudarme.

Jesus God help me.

But Jesus doesn't come.

His brain spins dizzily down a twisting rathole of panic. Back to the beach. Back to the battlefield. Back.

He welcomes it now: the bloody sun, the mucus-yellow shadows, even the invigorating terror as the shapes shift in the murk ahead, around, behind them. At least here, he can move! He signals the squad forward, and trots toward the buildings in the distance.

Yet still, beside his head, something chuffs and wheezes, on and on.

A dark shape looms over Hector. It is the nightmare terror. His demon. He comes awake terrified all over again, struggling to move, but unable to. That's the worst thing. He can't fucking *move.*

The shadow speaks, this time in a woman's voice, "Sergeant Ramos? It's okay. You got to calm down, all right? Or we're gonna have to put you out again."

He puts a hand to his throat, gagging. Only his hand *won't.* His eyes water. The blue light. He jerks his eyeballs from side to side, trying to signal whoever this is. Something sharp is burning in his dick. *Ya vale madre*, he'd say, if he could say anything.

"Sergeant Ramos, I'm your nurse. Nurse Donovan. We had to put a tube down into your lungs, to let a machine help you breathe. Then we had to give you something so you wouldn't keep trying to pull it out. That's why you can't move. It's temporary. A drug-induced paralysis. But everything's going to be all right. We've got you. We're taking care of you. Do you understand? Blink for me if you understand. Please."

He fights to move his hands, to tear the foreign, sharp things out of his throat, out of his dick, out of his arm. But he can't. At last he focuses on the dark face over his. A black woman, in the blue dim. A strange alcoholy smell about her. Wearing some kind of uniform. For a second he wonders if it's La Planchada, the demon nurse, come for him. But at last he blinks obediently, squeezing his eyes shut. Opens them again.

And feels her hand squeezing his. "Good. Good! You're not going to be this way for too long, and you're going to be fine. You're not going back to Hainan. Okay? You have all your arms and legs. Your spine's not injured. This is just to help your lungs get better, from the gas they used on you. As soon as you can breathe on your own, we'll take these nasty tubes out and get you something good to eat. Oh, and—and the war's over, if you didn't already know."

He blinks ferociously and she pats his arm again. "Things are a little confused right now, but I'm pretty sure we won. So I'm going to turn this tap here, and in a couple of seconds you'll feel a lot more comfortable."

A warm tide rises, spreading all over his body, prickling and heating. A reassuring heat in his arms and legs. He's still terrified, but the tide rises slowly, like a warm soft woolly blanket drawn up over him when he's sleepy. A sleepy child. His mother squeezes his hand again.

"Mama," he whispers. Or tries to. But his lips only twitch around the rigid, mucus-smeared plastic.

HE wakes up again that night. Or thinks he's awake, though he's not.

He's back on Hainan. In the mask, the heavy suit. Sweating. Searching the targeting fog for the lurching things. They loom through the smoke, bodies sleek, metallic, spider-shaped, teardrop-shaped, with spiky antennas and bug-eyed oculars. Autonomous, like the Allied combat bots. Needle-thin, sporadically visible beams shoot out through the smoke, searching their surroundings.

He pushes forward, breath rasping in his ears. Rasping. Chuffing. Clicking. On and on. The squad follows him, but they keep bunching up. He has to turn and signal them furiously to spread the fuck out.

The school looms ahead. He grips his carbine, not wanting to see this. But he must. *He must.* He can't stop it or direct his steps away. He's helpless, here in the dream.

The grass between the bus and the school is carpeted. A patchwork quilt, all colors, unrolled on the dusty-gray grass.

Then he makes out the faces.

The children lie in ragged lines, as if they'd been in queues when the violet shells hit. Some still holding hands. They're all black-haired, like his nephews. They wear colorful plastic rain slickers. The boys in blue. The girls, all in pink.

When he walks in among them the bodies crunch and give way under his boots, crackling like fried pork rinds. He steps on a plastic pencil box cartooned with a pastel-colorful cat. All the kids have the exact same pencil boxes.

The Indo with him, the big Papuan who fired the Javelin into the bunker back by the beach, is whimpering under his mask. The cicadas of the gas-warning alarm go *chirrup, chirrup.*

Do you hate the Chinese? The twisted, rabid face of his old boot camp DI looms in the blowing clouds. DI Brady. *Do you hate the Chinese, Private Ramos?*

I hate the fucking Chinese, sir.

I will stick my bayonet into them and blow their guts over my boots.

HE wakes wanting to scream but still unable to and lies in stiff helpless terror in the dim blue light for many hours as the machine clicks on and off. He can't take this. He's going crazy. Now the others have come to gather around him, sitting on the bed. They gaze down at him, the way they looked up from the landing craft's wake on the way in to the beach. Oh, he knows they're dead. Fat useless Bleckford. Titcomb. Schultz. Vincent. Orietta and Truss. Troy Whipkey and Lieutenant Hern. Pudgy little Lieutenant Ffoulk. Sergeant Clay. Patterson, Karamete . . . they're yelling at him, mouths open. Or maybe chanting some kind of cadence.

He can almost make out the words, but he's afraid to hear them.

He knows what they want.

He sings all the songs he knows but without words. He says endless Hail Marys in his head but without belief. He tries to remember the rosary but can't. He keeps feeling someone there but when he opens his eyes again there's no one. Not his mom.

Not Mirielle. Not La Planchada. Not Jesus. Not any of his old squad. Where did they all go? Are they coming back? He almost misses them.

His eyes drift closed again.

He's back at Farmer Seth's. The Hanging Room. The Kill Room.

He's back on the Line, with the crew. José, Mahmou', Johu, Fernando, Sazi.

A long chain of stainless hooks sway from an I-beam, tinkling, like music. From them hang dozens of upside-down U's of heavy, polished stainless metal, each sized just right to trap a careless hand. The chain passes through a vertical slot in the concrete-block wall. Slot, wall, and floor are spattered with a brownish-black crust inches thick.

Hector stamps heavy steel-toes, testing his footing. The men fit goggles over their eyes. They rub Vaseline over their arms, then pull on thin gloves, or women's nylons.

"Ready?" the production foreman growls, his lone hand on the knife switch. He lost the other in an ice-grinding machine. Without waiting for an answer from the men ranged tensely along the line of glittering hooks, José jerks it down. The lights douse, then reignite a scarlet carmine. Hector sucks a deep breath, clenching his fists.

With a prolonged, grinding rattle, a clashing metallic clanging, the Line surges into motion. The chickens squawk and flutter as the crew pulls them out of their modules, fighting, pecking, spurring, but there's only one fate awaiting them. One after the other, dangling from the shining hooks, the Line carries them off, to vanish through the wall.

Then . . . he floats up . . . to

Something in his throat. Something hard, digging into his throat . . .

The blue dim, and him floating in it, tormented and alone . . .

Is this Hell already? This could well be Hell. He may really be totally fucked.

Not far from him, someone's moaning in the dark. Sobbing, but it sounds choked. Muffled.

It takes a long time before he realizes that helpless, weeping bastard is him.

ENDLESS eons later he's still lying awake as someone snaps the overhead lights on. So bright he can't see. People in white coats dart past. They glide in and out of his field of view. They seem to move extremely fast. Or maybe he's just thinking super slow. Sometimes when they do stop they discuss him in low mumbles. He can't make out more than an occasional word. Someone else in the room keeps groaning. The machine puffs and wheezes, and now it clicks too. Now he understands what's happening. And he's even more terrified. Why is it *clicking* now? It didn't click before. Did it? He can't remember. He *can't remember* . . . He's scared it will break or the power will be interrupted. If the plug gets loose he will die. And there won't be a damn thing he can do about it.

He'd rather land on a dozen mined beaches than lie helpless like this.

The woman from last night. Dark faced, round faced. She bends over him. "Sergeant? Sergeant Hector Ramos? I am your nurse. Do you remember? Blink once if you can hear me."

She has a funny accent, like the Pakistanis who run the convenience store down the road from the chicken factory. He squeezes his eyes shut. Feels tears trickle down his cheek, into his ears.

"I know it's scary, okay? But you're going to be all right. You're on a Navy hospital ship. The war is over, and we won. You're one of our heroes. But they used a new gas on Hainan. It hurts your nerves so you can't breathe on your own. Your family knows you're alive. The Marine Corps got that word to them.

"Now, this morning we're going to have to suction some bad stuff out of your lungs. It's not going to hurt, but the procedure might make you feel like you're choking. Blink those pretty brown eyes if you understand."

She lied. It hurts, all right. He chokes and dry vomits while they force yet another tube down his throat. The edge catches, ripping something deep inside his neck. So of course they have to suction some more. They mutter above his bed about blood and secretions. Then force more things into him. Tears leak down his cheeks. He can't help moaning. Why are you torturing me? Just let me die, he wants to yell. But of course he can't.

Even worse is the steady fucking patter one surgeon, or corpsman, or whatever he is, keeps up. A white guy with a sharp nose and a narrow face filled with hate. He murmurs a steady stream of "You're a three-landing marine, they say. The hero who raised that flag in Taipei? Well, I kind of expected a little more here. Expected a big shot like you to be able to take it. Not whine and cry like a little fucking pussy girl." Muttering close to Hector's ear, so the others can't hear.

Hector resolves in his heart to kill this fucking asshole as soon as he can get out of this bed. I will corner you in the fucking head and choke-hold you till it takes, motherfucker.

When they finally finish and back away he lies sweating, dizzy, wanting desperately to flee. Escape. Die. Anything but go through that again.

Across the ICU another man's staring back. A white kid. He's festooned with tubes, like an alien life form is sucking the life out of him. A computer screen draws jagged lines above his bed. He too is on a ventilator. His eyes are filled with terror. The blanket sags flat where legs ought to be. They stare at each other across the room. Hector musters all his strength. Contorting his lips around the tubes, he tries to send him a faint smile.

STILL later another woman comes in. A white woman, but with long dark hair. His nurse addresses her as "Dr. Andrews." She looks at him for a while and asks his nurse questions. Then starts talking to him. By now he's fading, exhausted, but she's saying something about how great he's doing. How they don't want to keep him on the ventilator. If they do, his muscles will weaken and he won't be able to breathe on his own, ever again.

"And we don't want that, do we?" She pauses, as if he could actually answer. "No, I didn't think so.

"So we're going to try weaning you off this afternoon. Discontinue the curare and see if you can breathe on your own. Could be a little uncomfortable, but it's the way out of here. You game for that, Sergeant?"

Blink. Blink. A long, long blink. Fucking *pinche* yes, lady, fucking more than ready.

She goes on talking—to the nurse, he guesses—about discontinuing this drug and the antagonist that and the dosage this. But he's not really listening.

Anything to end this.

Why didn't they just let him die?

Hector Ramos doesn't want to live.

But he has to. For a while. If only to get this fucking thing out of his throat.

Then he will find a way to kill them. He is a machine gunner, after all. He will find his gun again. Then he'll kill them. All of them. Every fucking white coat La Planchada devil in here. Everyone aboard this *pinche* fucking torture ship.

5

Xinjiang Province, Western China

THE smoke streamed steadily upward, only to be intercepted by the hut's roof. It slowly filtered along the ridgepole, to finally seep out through a reed-shielded hole. Shielded, in case an infrared eye peered down from the bright morning sky. In case a drone buzzed over, loitering above these crags and deep mountain valleys, missiles cocked, searching for a target.

Three stocky men sat cross-legged around a large brass serving tray steaming with heat. They scooped up clumps of soft, hand-pulled noodles with folded naan bread dipped in gravy. They picked out hot chunks of savory stir-fried camel meat, popped it into beard-fringed mouths, and followed it with hot sweet tea so strong it made their heads buzz. No chopsticks. The rebels disdained them as a foreign custom imposed by the hated Han. Women in black robes stood behind them, watching silently from the shadows. Outside, gravel crackled as a guard paced slowly back and forth before the little shepherd's hut, built of native rocks and roofed with native brush.

The Lingxiu sat in the center. His once dirty-blond beard, graying now, did not cover the furrowed scars that radiated out over a bronzed face from a potatolike nose. He wore the same threadbare shalwar kameez as the Uighurs, the same flat cap over braided hair. But wrapped around his shoulders was a ragged gray blanket, the sort that might have been issued to a prisoner of war. A black eyepatch covered the empty socket where his left orb had been torn out. His remaining eye was a cold, remorseless blue, like sunset seen through deep ice. His left leg was thrust out awkwardly. A titanium brace glittered, buckled tight over loose wool trousers. A Makarov pistol rested on the carpet inches from his right hand, and a Claymore remote-det mine lay in a carrying pack at his other side. From his belt hung a heavy, curved Uighur blade he'd taken off an enemy, after killing him in a knife fight.

Once upon a time the stocky mujahid with the eyepatch had been Master Chief Theodore Harlett Oberg, United States Navy. But no longer. Now he was Lingxiu Oberg al-Amriki, the Leader. Of the Resistance, of the Faithful. Deep in the mountains of western China, supported now and then with guns and gold by the CIA, he'd built a guerrilla force to distract and weaken the enemy from within. The Independent Turkistan Islamic Movement harked back to an earlier resistance the Han majority had ruthlessly stamped out. ITIM fought for the union of all the Turkic peoples from Azerbaijan, Kazakhstan, Kyrgyzstan, Turkmenistan, and Uzbekistan. And of course, above all, "Chinese" Turkistan.

Now the tallest of the three men, a spare lanky Uighur named Guldulla, sat back from the tray and beckoned impatiently. His long face was curtained by a heavy mustache, half white, half dark-haired. A girl slave hurried to fetch a damp cloth, then stepped back, gaze downcast. His pistol lay next to him as well, an older Russian automatic chased with intricate engraving.

He muttered, "You say we cannot stop fighting, Lingxiu? Even though the cursed Han have surrendered?"

Teddy shifted his butt and farted; the greasy camel meat had that effect on his digestion. "They haven't surrendered to *us*, Tokarev," he muttered, in the crude Chinese he'd picked up as a prisoner of war.

Camp 576 had been a death camp, working politicals and POWs to death mining radioactive rare earths. Five men had made it out, up a cliff, past a guard post, and through the apron of barbed wire, lights, and machine guns. But only two had threaded the mountains to safety. By now, after months with the rebels, he understood basic Uighur, but didn't speak it well enough to trust himself in complex negotiations.

He spread his hands. "Ever hear of Iraq? Saddam Hussein surrendered. After the Gulf War. Then used his helicopters to massacre his Shiite rebels."

The third man was heavier than the other two, and younger. A glossy black beard brushed his chest. A strange-looking apparatus lay next to him: rifle-like, yet not a rifle. A cable led from it to a solar panel deployed outside. A second cable led in, to a monitor panel, at whose readouts he occasionally glanced. He said little, concentrating on eating, but looked searchingly from face to face as the others debated.

"Jusuf, are you getting all this?" Teddy asked him. "You understand, this 'armistice' doesn't apply to us? It's only between the infidel powers. All it means is that now the Han can shift their forces in from the coasts, to reconcentrate against us."

Guldulla said tentatively, "The Hajji would have said—"

It was the Hajji's curved knife Teddy wore. The Hajji he'd had to kill. Teddy barked, "The Hajji's dead, okay? Old Imam Akhmad's dead too. We three have to formulate a strategy, here, Tok. A way forward. Otherwise, once a peace treaty's signed the Han are going to redeploy six Internal Security divisions and just overrun us out here."

"What is it that you suggest, Lingxiu?" Jusuf said quietly, picking through the remains of the meal. He glanced at the others, then flickered pudgy fingers at the women. They scurried quietly about, removing the serving tray, bringing more damp heated cloths, refreshing the tea. A heavyset one brought a dish of sweet date-and-nut cakes and set it before Teddy. The men ignored the slaves, though Jusuf filched the smallest cake from the tray as it went by. He nibbled it, sighing, closing his eyes.

Suddenly the console emitted a faint, repetitive beep. The younger muj squinted at it, then gestured angrily to one of the women. She rushed to the fire, dragging a thick carpet of blackened wool over it. Smoke puffed around the hem as the fire suffocated. The other rebels glanced at the technician questioningly. He studied the readouts for a few seconds, then shook his head and sighed. "It will pass us, in the next valley," he said in a soft, deferential voice. "To the north. This time. Inshallah."

"Inshallah," the others murmured too.

Teddy sucked a tooth glumly. He turned his head and spat a bit of gristle. "Well, keep an eye on it . . . You see, they're still hunting us."

"It is true, I understand, Lingxiu," Guldulla said. "And I agree, they will not stop. So what is our wisest path?"

Teddy inclined his head. The older man had rescued him, when the surviving escapees had stumbled into a rebel attack on a propaganda festival. They'd soldiered together for nearly two years now. He said, trying to sound reasonable, logical, detached, "I see two roads ahead. We can approach the new Han government, using our status as allies of the Americans. It is possible the CIA will speak on our behalf. Offering to end the rebellion."

"And what would our terms be?" Guldulla said. "Independence?"

Teddy shook his head. "We could *ask* for it. But the Han will never agree. They might compromise on some kind of separate status. Like Taiwan or Hong Kong, or Tibet, in this Chinese Federation the BBC radio speaks of.

"But to achieve that, we'd have to give up fighting. Surrender our weapons, and trust the Han not to break their agreement and come after us again five years down the road."

"We must not give up our guns," Jusuf said. "Without weapons, we will no longer be free."

Teddy nodded. "I don't disagree, my friend. But as I said, that is one path."

"And the other?" Guldulla asked.

Teddy shrugged. "Continue the battle, but reach out to our friends in Saudi, in Afghanistan, in Pakistan. Arm all the people, not just our fighters. And send martyrs to the cities, to Beijing,

Shenzhen, Tianjin, Guangzhou. Carry the terror to the Han where they live. Where they now feel safe."

Jusuf glanced quizzically up from under shaggy brows, and Teddy knew what he was thinking. This was the course the Hajji had pushed. The old fighter who named himself Qurban, the Sacrifice. He'd called for all-out jihad, with himself as their leader. Teddy had killed the al-Qaeda veteran hand to hand, knife to knife, in the doomed and failed attack on the missile sites that the Allies had called Operation Jedburgh. It had been al-Nashiri or himself, in those final desperate moments.

Teddy had lost an eye, but his opponent had lost his life. Pried out of his throat with the sharp edge of the same titanium brace he now wore, strapped to his torture-damaged leg.

He shook himself back to the present. Smoke filled the room, obscured the rock walls, milled in a dense obscuring cloud. He waved it away from his face, coughing, and said angrily, "It was the wrong strategy before. When we needed American ammunition, food, and equipment. We needed their shining gold, and they were generous with it. But maybe it is the right strategy now."

The younger muj looked doubtful, but said nothing. Guldulla said mildly, "Do you truly think things have changed so much? That your friend Vladimir will abandon us, now their war is done?"

Vladimir was the cover name for their CIA handler. Teddy gave them a sardonic smile. "Do you think America truly cares what happens to us? We were their tools. To attack the Han from behind while they fought them in front. Now that Beijing has surrendered to them, they'll have no further use for us.

"Learn from Vietnam. From Afghanistan, and Iraq, and Syria. The Shiites, and the Kurds. I have seen this before, with my own eyes. They are loyal friends so long as we are useful to them. After that, we will be sacrificed."

Jusuf leaned forward. "But if we fight? Align ourselves with al-Qaeda, or ISIS, the Caliphate—and fight?"

Teddy sat silent. Casting back to a moment two years before.

High on a mountain, starving, freezing, after weeks on foot wandering after the escape from camp . . . he'd been visited by something.

Or Someone.

He still had no explanation for what he'd experienced. Divine visitation? Dream? Revelation? Hallucination? But he still remembered the message.

There is no such thing as choice, the Voice that could not be questioned had told him.

No such thing as chance.

You have always done My Will.

You are My creature, and you cannot do other.

Trust Me, and I will never forsake you.

"Lingxiu?" Guldulla murmured tentatively, and Teddy Oberg came back shivering from that high, sere memory. Nothing else in his life had mattered since then. He'd been called, and he had to answer. He had his orders. From Higher.

Any SEAL could understand that.

He nodded, and compressed his lips. "It is well. All will be well, if it is the will of Allah."

"Allah's will," the others muttered, gazes downcast.

Teddy sipped tea and gestured for more. Once again, the heavyset woman slave stepped forward. He said, "If we choose total jihad, we can look for supplies from our friends in Pakistan and Saudi. Perhaps even from Iran. There will be money and arms from somewhere, I am certain.

"But if we take that road, we must become merciless. We must kill many innocents, and spread terror. Become devils in the eyes of the world. We must make our war so bloody and cruel and long, so expensive in money and men, the Han will be happy to let us depart from them.

"That is the hard road. It will cost many lives. And may take many years. But there is no path in between. We must take one or the other. And we have to decide soon. The CIA man will be here tomorrow. We need to choose by then."

He was glancing around at their faces when the warning console beeped again. They all stared at it. Jusuf turned a dial, frowning, watching the screen. "The other valley," he said at last. "Not ours."

"Wait a minute," Teddy said. "Which valley? The north valley again?"

"Not this time, Lingxiu. The south one this time."

He lifted his head, suddenly penetrated by an icicle of unease. A drone, one valley northward. Now another, this one to the south . . . "Alert your men," he snapped, and hoisted himself awkwardly to his feet.

OUTSIDE, the sky above the mountains was hard and glossy, a dark blue like fired porcelain. He shaded his eye and searched it, adjusting the Claymore slung over one shoulder, then the captured carbine slung over the other. Up the valley, then down, toward the desert that stretched away to the far south.

Then, far off, he saw it. No, them.

Tiny glints, high up, far off in the high blue. Not even specks yet. Just faint, disappearingly brief glints of reflected sunlight.

"Antiaircraft stations!" he shouted, in English. The men knew this command. Around him the rebels rose from between the rocks, evacuated open patches of ground, and spread out, manning weapons. Jusuf, behind him, jerked the charge cable out of the antidrone gun. Other rebels shouldered Stinger launchers and rocket-propelled grenades, or hastily set up machine guns atop sheltering rocks.

Teddy held out a hand. The heavyset woman he called Dandan, though that wasn't her real name, handed him a set of binoculars. They were CIA-furnished, gyrostabilized and with an infrared capability he didn't need in this hard bright sunlight. He aimed the glasses and pressed the stabilize button.

Z-10s. Gunships. Coming in fast, welded together in the tight wedge formation the Internal Security quick reaction teams used in these tight mountain passes.

The black sharkshadows flushed bad memories. Woody Island, with Echo Four caught in the open. The rotor wash blasting down brush and trees, the miniguns blazing like the fiery mouths of dragons. And again, in the passes to the west, when ITIM had attacked pipelines and power lines. Too many mujs had died under the guns of aircraft like this, or maybe even these same machines.

When he lowered his binoculars five degrees, there they were: the fatter, lumbering bumblebee-outlines of troop transports, flanked and escorted by smaller midge-shapes; escort drones.

Not just a strike. This was a major raid.

Which meant that somehow, the Han had known they'd be here.

He lowered his glasses and bawled orders. A young muj spoke rapidly into a cheap walkie-talkie, passing orders for the down-valley post to open fire, for other crews to take their assigned positions, for the young boys who carried ammunition to assemble at the caves. If he could draw the enemy's attention down the valley, persuade the transports to land where it was more open, the enemy would have to fight their way uphill to reach them, and spend longer in the kill zone.

But even as he shouted the Z-10s bored onward, roaring over him, before pulling up in tight chandelles that brought them heart-stoppingly close to the gray granite walls of the canyon. Despite himself, he bared his teeth in admiration. Flying like that took balls. These guys were pros.

But in the next seconds the gunships had come around and were bearing down on him. As if they knew exactly where he would be standing.

He limped-ran clumsily for a nest of five huge granite boulders, realizing the helos were aiming for the shepherd's hut behind him.

A spear of white fire jabbed down from the lead attack ship. The hut exploded into black smoke, fire, and thousands of rock fragments and metal shards. Something hit the back of his sheepskin coat as he dove, hard, sending him rolling into the shelter of the boulders.

Dandan, beside him, was pressing something into his hands. His carbine, which he'd apparently dropped when he was knocked down. His back felt numb, as if someone had just scourged him. But it didn't hurt yet. Maybe he'd gotten lucky and the heavy sheepskin had stopped the fragment. At least it hadn't set off the half kilo of explosive in the mine strapped to his back. He seated the mag with the heel of his hand, charged the carbine, and popped up to fire.

And found himself looking up into the barrels of the miniguns. Gazing, at a range of about two hundred yards, directly into the face of a pilot, one who stared back intent behind a slanted and no doubt bulletproof slab of glass above the already flaring muzzles of the pylon-mounted Gatlings.

Explosions ripped down the valley. Cannon shells, the bursts walking directly toward him as the three aircraft hurtled forward.

"No windage adjustment necessary," Teddy muttered. He aimed right at the pilot, adjusted slightly upward to allow for bullet drop, and fired out the full magazine, holding the chattering rifle tight, letting the recoil drive it straight back into his shoulder. The little bullets were high velocity, but too light to hammer through the windscreen. Still, if he could place a couple in front of the guy's nose, maybe crack his gunsight, it might discourage him from making such a low pass next time.

Teddy wanted him higher. Not so high he was out of the canyon, but not too low, either.

The turbines crescendoed into a terrific howl, magnified and confined by the encircling cliffs. Black blurs slashed overhead like flying sabers. Then they screamed off down the valley, canting and jinking. Flares arched out from their sides and fluttered outward in graceful burning waterfalls of white fire, drawing off the heat-homing Stingers that leaped from the rocky floor of the ravine to chase after them. Most of the hand-launched missiles followed the flares, detonating against the cliffs with hollow-sounding cracks and flashes.

But one ignored the distractions, homing relentlessly on the tail-end gunship. The helo pilot, picking up his pursuer, or hearing an alarm, pulled nearly straight up, trying to outclimb it.

The missile's fiery booster-trail bent in midair like a hot steel wire, went up the helo's tailpipe, and vanished in a balloon of tangerine-and-licorice flame out of which the forward end of the Z-10 emerged, still climbing. Momentum, plus the force of the explosion, drove it perhaps another hundred feet up before it faltered, nosed over, and pitched down and out of sight down into the valley to the east. It was succeeded by a huge burst of black smoke and a thunderous, crackling detonation like a major thunderstorm played in fast-forward.

Teddy eyed the transports next. They were touching down, lurching, heavy-bodied and awkward as they picked out landing sites. Sinking out of his sight line down the slope of the valley. But within seconds, black-clad security troops would be pouring out of them, heavily armed, aggressive as ground wasps. Their Level 4 ceramic body armor would stop dead the 7.62 projectiles from the AKs most of his insurgents were armed with. The enemy had helmet-to-helmet comms and were drilled for combat with irregulars. His snipers, up on the flanks with the scoped Remington M40s the CIA had sent in, would take a toll, slow them down. But they wouldn't stop them.

Not outnumbered five to one, the way he quick-figured the odds. Two to one, in a position like this, he could've stonewalled the attack. Held them, and maybe even counterattacked.

But not at five to one, against trained troops with this level of air support.

In other words, he didn't have a frickin' chance in hell today. A pitched battle would end with all his guys wiped out. Their only hope of survival lay in retreat.

As they'd had to so many times before . . . so many, he was getting pretty fucking tired of skedaddling. For a second that felt like a minute, crouching amid the boulders while Jusuf tracked a buzzing, jinking drone with his antidrone projector, Teddy debated taking a stand anyway. Dying in place. Pulling off an Alamo. Earning a place in history.

The drone flipped and destroyed itself against the face of the cliff. And Teddy muttered, "Forget it." Maybe the Big War was over. But if ITIM was wiped out, the Turkmens would never be free. All his guys would have died for nothing. And the Han would rule, forever.

A fighting withdrawal. The toughest option tactically any leader could face. If your troops lost their heads, or if you lost control, they'd all be wiped out.

Fortunately, he'd drilled *his* guys too.

He passed the command over the radios, and stood, arm-signaling it to those within sight. Two young boys scrambled past, ducking amid the rocks. They hugged green ammo boxes to their chests, headed for the front line.

Incoming spattered around him, blasting white scars into the rocks and filling the air with orange sparks and gritty dust. The noise was deafening. One of the boys buckled, dropping his box and crumpling to the gravel of the valley floor. The other looked back, hesitated; then picked up his companion's burden along with his own and scrambled on, crouching as more fire cracked and zinged off the rocks. Teddy ducked too, then edged around the boulders, to get the rear guard organized and returning fire.

Which they already were. His machine guns were chattering, in short bursts, the way he'd trained them, aiming fiery arcs down the valley. Pouring heavier slugs into the black-clad troops. The crack of grenades, the stutter of AKs, and the sharper barks of the high-velocity Chinese rifles rose from the front line. Smoke blew up the valley past him, the odor of burned powder and battle. Teddy snapped into the radio, "Peel!"

He couldn't see it, but noted the effect as his frontline guys reacted. Alternating left and right, each fighter retreated a few steps, then stepped out to the side. As the defense melted backward, keeping up the volume of fire, the offense saw what looked like more and more fighters joining the battle. And no troop, no matter how well supported, wanted to advance into strengthening opposition. Meanwhile the defense kept moving backward, and

from a steadily widening front with cleared fields of fire poured
it on. The heavier cracks of the M40s continued, deliberate and
steady. As the enemy line advanced, they'd expose their flanks,
then their backs, to the snipers, who were sworn to hold in place
and die for Allah.

Teddy permitted himself a tight grin. A nod to Jusuf, four paces
off. If his guys kept their heads, conserved ammo, and didn't get
overrun, they could pull back all the way up the valley like this.

He stood fast as the mujs scrambled past, looking white-eyed
to the rear. They caught his glare, his pointing arm, and turned to
fire once more as he slapped in another magazine and fired it out,
trying to pick his targets as black helmets bobbed amid the rocks.

But then what?

A renewed howl at the far end of the valley grew, swelled, became deafening even over the crackle of fire, the staccato clatter
of both sides' MGs. Black raptor silhouettes rose over the curve
of mountain, hurtling toward them at incredible speed. Rockets
streaked downward. They shattered boulders, throwing huge
stone fragments and human bodies end over end. Gatlings lit with
a tearing flame, raking the floor of the ravine and sending projectiles ricocheting crazily all around it like red-hot, lethal popcorn.
One hissed past Teddy's ear and cracked into the ground, blasting
a hole a yard across and pelting him with a lashing of gravel.

Once again, just as they had before, the aircraft chandelled up
after they passed over. He shaded his eyes after them. Were they
coming back down valley again? Yeah. They were.

He waited as the specks shrank, hovered, turned. Then they
began to grow again, headed back down the narrow, cliff-walled
valley. A little higher than they had the first time.

In fact, just about where he wanted them.

Teddy yelled to Jusuf, "Lariat!"

As the lead gunship swept overhead, in a blast of hot air, exhaust, noise, and kicked-up grit, fire lanced down from the high
cliffs on either side. Figures in baggy pants and shalwar kameez
popped up, balancing tubes atop shoulders.

Then the RPGs lanced out. More slowly than usual, it seemed. Aimed not directly at the helos, but ahead and above them.

Spindly black lines untwisted in the air, trailing the rocket-propelled grenades. They were thin, but far stronger than they looked. Braided Kevlar guy wire, looted from the Han cell towers his men had blown up.

The cables seemed to hover lazily, to drift through the air for a heart-stopping moment.

Then they dropped.

Directly into the spinning rotors of the lead aircraft.

The Z-10 snagged two of the falling lines in midair. They both came instantly taut, rigid, leading back to where they'd been bowlined off to projections of solid rock. The first line snapped at once, its cut-free grenade tumbling end over end to burst harmlessly in the air. But most of the line itself disappeared, wound instantly into the fiercely rotating rotor head and swash plate assembly like the string into a yo-yo.

The head assembly seemed to freeze for an instant. Then it jerked violently and exploded, shooting parts and detached blades flying off violently in all directions.

The other line held. Like a horse suddenly yanked back by the reins, the helicopter reared backward, nose pointing up and to the right. The two gunships following it pulled up radically, nearly colliding in midair, and still firing, though now their weapons aimed harmlessly into the sky.

The second cable quivered, elongating under the massive strain, but still didn't snap. The tail boom swept downward, and the tail rotor of the lead gunship brushed a jagged rock.

The tail rotor disintegrated. The aircraft twisted madly, like a hawk caught in a net. Still snagged in the line, the gunship's forward momentum brought the now swiftly disassembling tail boom around beneath it.

With stubs of its rotor blades still flailing loosely around the smashed hub, the machine flipped in midair. Rotating like a gymnast in a twisting back layout, it collapsed out of the sky directly onto the oncoming security troops in a massive bloom of black smoke and then bright saffron fire that carpeted the ground in flame, flying parts, and the electric arc flashes of onboard ammunition cooking off.

"Orqaga qayting. Chekinmoq," Teddy yelled into the little radio. Time to get the hell out. He fired out what was left of his magazine, aiming over the flames that now blanketed the whole lower end of the canyon, and limped as fast as he could back toward the cleft in the rock he'd pretagged as their fastest way out in a pinch. Always leave yourself an escape route . . . This one was barely wide enough for two men abreast, but that very constriction meant a rear guard could hold it while the rest of the rebels escaped. A second exit a half-klick up the valley debouched to the northward.

Scattering into two- or three-man groups, too many to pursue, the rebels would disperse into the mountain fastnesses, vanishing amid millions of square miles of tormented terrain. Then, later, reconstitute; as usual, they had a rendezvous point specified many miles to the west, not far from their old mountain base.

The smoke from the burning aircraft was heavy, choking, blowing up from the valley floor. The crackle of enemy fire had lessened. Good, maybe their attackers were having second thoughts.

Guldulla loomed suddenly out of the seething smoke. His face was so blackened with powder smut and dirt that even the white of his mustache was dyed black. He was panting hard. The barrel of his AK was smoking, the plastic handguard deformed and melting. "They are falling back, Lingxiu. Regrouping. But our lookouts to the south report more dragonflies on their way."

Their warning net covered every village north and west of the Taklamakan. Teenagers and old men with cheap handhelds, passing warnings and poems of battle from mouth to mouth throughout western China. Hajji Qurban had lit that fire before he died. Turned ITIM's struggle into a full-fledged jihad.

Now Teddy had to ride that unleashed tiger.

But first, he had to extract his guys from the fiery hell this once-remote valley had become. He stood by the cleft in the rock, waving men in. Urging, "Hurry the fuck up there. *Gankuài! Gankuài! Shoshilmoq!*" Dandan and the other slaves scurried past, heads lowered, burkas whipping against bare ankles and bare feet as they ran, carrying packs and cooking gear. Jusuf followed, with other young mujs carrying the Swiss drone-detection gear, the antidrone rifles, and the solar panels they charged from. Then came the rank and file, sweating riflemen and RPG gunners, some with charred and smoking hair and clothing. Those who'd been closest to the front line when the helicopter went down like a flaming Lucifer falling from Heaven.

Teddy didn't want to imagine what the guys directly under it looked like now.

The wounded staggered past, clutching shoulders, chests, bellies. They looked desperate to keep moving, no matter how badly they bled. As well they might . . . Shading his eyes, Teddy searched the battlefield. The pops of pistols came from among the boulders as the squad leaders, retreating last, finished off anyone too far gone to walk, plus any wounded Han within range.

He slung the carbine and drew his Makarov. Holding it out at arm's length, he limped forward, between the boulders.

The young ammo carrier who'd been shot down saw him coming. He couldn't be more than ten. He struggled to rise, holding his guts with both hands. His spindly arms were bare.

Teddy smiled down at him, and bent to pat his shoulder gently. *"Siz yaxshi jang qildingiz,"* he said. *"Bu shunday bo'lishi kerak."*

You have fought well. But this must be done.

The boy muttered something in return, but his words were inaudible in the din of shots and cries and screaming. He sank back on one elbow, nodded, and turned his face to the ground.

Teddy brought the pistol down to touch the black hair, the bowed head. He looked away, and pulled the trigger.

When he was satisfied they'd gotten everyone back who could still walk, that no rebel was left behind to torture and interrogate, he unslung the Claymore he'd carried all this time. Twisted the prongs into the gravel, and pointed it toward the enemy. Turned it on, and set the self-det to Auto IR. Then turned and limped as fast as he could into the shadowy opening in the rock, which was screened by an overhead ledge so that it was almost a cavern.

The dark closed in. He could touch both sides with outstretched arms. He hustled along, cursing as pain jabbed through the waning endorphins of battle. Agony shot up his bad leg.

Suddenly he paused. Standing motionless in the cleft as a thought paralyzed him. One he just hadn't had time to ponder during the engagement itself.

Who had known they would be here? Who had wanted, set up, arranged the meeting here with the CIA agent?

Had the CIA given their location to the Chinese?

Behind him the Claymore went off with a hollow crack that echoed down the cleft. It would hold their pursuers up, but not for long. Jusuf jostled him from behind, breathing heavily. "We must go on, Lingxiu," he said urgently. Recalled to the danger, Teddy limped forward again, hunched over, carbine at the ready. Just in case there were enemy posted at the exit, too.

Or was he being paranoid? Suspecting everything and everyone?

He didn't think so. Being paranoid didn't mean no one was out to get you.

Especially if you were the leader of a hunted, hated guerrilla band.

It would bear more thinking about.

The rocky slit narrowed until he could barely wriggle his way through. Then it widened, and light grew ahead. As did his apprehension. If their location had been compromised, this escape route might be blocked too. One of those transports could have landed here, debarked its black-clad troops, and lifted off. He could be walking into a trap.

He flicked his carbine's safety off, getting ready to dodge left, find cover, and return fire in one last, desperate shootout. Whatever happened, he'd go down fighting. With a weapon in his hand.

There is no such thing as choice.
No such thing as chance.
You have always done My will.

"I have always done Your will," he said aloud. And around him, ahead, behind him, screams and yells rose, deafening between the confined coffinlike rock walls. "God is great. God is great. *God is great!*"

II

CHAOS RISING

6

Beijing

PACING back and forth on the hotel terrace, nursing a cup of hot green tea, Blair hugged herself with one arm, shivering. The wind was chilly, as their hotel room had been all night long. Either summer was late, or the haze from the nuclear exchange was still diluting the sunlight. And the power was still off. All over the city, as far as she could tell.

Not that they'd seen much. Except for their hotel, and the Forbidden City, where the sessions were taking place. Today marked their fourth meeting with the provisional government, and Yangerhans had made it clear this would be the last. They'd all done enough posturing. Enough accusing. Enough advocating extreme positions and inadmissible concessions, none of which the other side seemed willing to consider.

Tomorrow, at the latest, they would wrap. The mission would convene to finalize and forward their recommendations to the Allied heads of state conference, scheduled two weeks from now. Transmit it, on the scrambling gear the DS people had brought with them. And then, finally, leave.

She shivered again and sighed, rubbing her arm. She was waiting out here for Shira Salyers. The petite State rep had been up late, looking over notes from the past negotiation sessions. Each

sit-down had been less courteous, less productive, as the differences between the Allied positions and those of the interim
government, apparently headed by Minister Chen, had only widened, ripping apart the always-delicate membrane of diplomatic
protocol.

State dinners were usually fairly sociable. But the one hosted
on their third evening in the city, in the Hall of Supreme Harmony, had been icy. Their hosts, standoffish. She'd faked it on
the toasts, not caring for the raw distilled baijiu the Chinese
bolted down glass after glass without flinching. Yangerhans and
Ammermann had tried to keep pace for a while, but given up at
last, red-faced and reeling. Only Bankey Talmadge had stayed
with them to the end, finishing by drinking General Pei under
the table. Boozily reeling away, the old senator had nearly fallen
down the steps. But he'd been steadied at the last moment by
one of the DPS personnel, a tall, darkly complected black agent
named Maple Chaldroniere.

The State rep came out onto the terrace at last, adjusting a
sweater over her shoulders. "Sheez, it's chilly out here, when you're
not in the sun . . . We have a problem, Blair."

"Another one, Shira? What now?"

"The Russians want in."

Blair frowned and sipped her rapidly cooling tea. "In? . . . Into
Manchuria? Well, we knew that. They have a long history there.
Not that it's right, but—"

"No. I mean, not just that. They want into this conference."

Blair's eyebrows lifted. "What? No way. They were in the
war all of, what, four days? And we're almost done here. Aren't
we?"

"Maybe so, but they've insisted. Their representative's arriving
this morning. Bankey says shutting them out wouldn't be a good
idea. The admiral agrees."

Ayala, the little translator, poked his head out. "Ladies. Time."

Blair finished her tea, and stared down for a moment at the

final settling flakes at the bottom of her china cup. Did they really foretell the future?

If only it were so easy.

THE videoteleconference was set up in the same bland room they'd met in after arriving. A quantum scrambled satellite link powered by a military solar generator was set up on the roof. The ever-present security people had swept the room again. Now two of them, with the tall DSS agent helping, were hanging the antieavsdropping curtain across the window. Each day of the negotiations had begun with a VTC, mainly because of the time difference with Washington. Beijing and Washington were twelve hours apart, meaning 8 A.M. in the former city was 8 P.M. in DC.

In some ways she thought it might have been better the other way around, reporting on the day just past to fresh morning eyes in DC. But she hadn't been asked for an input to that decision. It probably didn't matter. The advance party was down to seven principals now, not counting security people, translators, and aides. In rough order of rank, it was Talmadge, Yangerhans, Ammermann, Shira, herself, Tony Provanzano, and General Naar, though the old senator didn't typically show for the morning briefs, depending, instead, on a murmured summary from her as they were limo'd to the City.

When the screens came up, they were facing three people: the secretary of state, who looked more haggard and closer to eternity than Blair had ever seen him; the chairman, JCS, husky and beribboned General Ricardo Vincenzo, USAF; and dapper, silver-haired Edward Szerenci, the national security advisor.

Yangerhans opened the brief in clipped tones, recapitulating yesterday's negotiations, which had focused on coordinating Chinese and Allied humanitarian efforts, food supplies, and medicines. "They were grateful for the formula of the flu drug, LJL 4789. They requested additional electrical generation, food, water, and medical assistance in the port cities, as soon as we can provide it, plus teams to restore electrical generation and internet router systems. As you know, these were largely destroyed or compromised in the course of the war."

The SecState said heavily, as if short of breath, *"I'll so advise the president. But we're in rough shape here concerning the budget and the debt. I doubt there'll be much for foreign aid."*

"And little enthusiasm for providing it to a former enemy," Szerenci put in, looking more foxlike than ever. He waved. *"Hello, Blair. Do the Chinese still think you're my mistress?"*

She ground her molars. *Not* funny. Minister Chen had tossed that insult her way back in Dublin, at their first meeting. He'd called her "a pliable puppet, wife of the notorious war criminal Admiral Daniel V. Lenson, and most likely the mistress of the insane national security advisor, Dr. Edward Szerenci." She forced a liquid-nitrogen smile. "No, Ed. Nobody here's saying that anymore."

"Before we discuss helping former enemies, we have to rebuild our own forces," Vincenzo said. *"There are new threats emerging, and we're fighting rebels here at home. We've got to think about the homeland first. Restoring government. Restoring confidence."*

Yangerhans said patiently, "We'll have our recommendations ready for the heads of state well in advance of the convening date. Right now, I'll forward their aid requests via cable." The Department of State term for what the Navy called a "message." "Moving on . . . we'll be getting into some delicate issues today. Nuclear limitations. Conventional force limitations. Governmental structure."

Szerenci said, *"Our position should be total nuclear disarmament. Disband their Internal Security divisions. Stand down their surveillance of the population. No more than a five-division standing army, and limits on conventional missiles."*

Yangerhans let that hang. Finally he said mildly, "That may be a recipe for the fall of this government, sir. There are already active separatist movements in Tibet, Hong Kong, Xinjiang—"

The NSA smiled coldly. *"Let's be realistic, Jim. Tibet and Taiwan are already gone. They declared independence. The Russians are fomenting separatism in Manchuria. Hong Kong wants out too. They see this as their chance at independence.*

"But why should we fight that? Wouldn't disintegration be in our best interest? Let China fall apart! Let the warlords rule again! It's the last survivor of the old empires. The old imperial powers. It deserved to die long ago.

"If you can only keep a country together with oppression and surveillance, it isn't really a country. It's just one big prison."

He was going into lecture mode; to cut him short Blair cleared her throat. "That's . . . a defensible point of view, Ed. For the short term. But let's look farther down the road. If we divide China into smaller states, the humiliation will fester. These people have enormous pride. If we humiliate them, it could turn them against democracy. Mean another war, eventually. Like Hitler's crusade against Versailles. Or Putin's drive to rebuild the Soviet empire."

The SecState lifted a shaky hand. *"What would you recommend, Shira?"*

Beside Blair, the petite woman looked up from her tablet. "Mr. Secretary, I'd agree with Abraham Lincoln's advice. 'Let 'em up easy.' I'd concentrate on trying to gradually foster democratic institutions. The way MacArthur did in Japan. This provisional government, these former-regime Party bureaucrats, they're not going to be whom we're dealing with in a year. But this has been an authoritarian state for a long time. If the center loses control, we could have another Iraq, another Syria, on our hands. Only a hundred times bigger."

Blair started to speak, but Shira waved her to silence, taking a breath. "I think our primary mission for what time remains, sir, should be to clarify the shape of the government going forward. Work with the ROC and the Hong Kong democrats to outline a federal arrangement. A joint government, with an interim president. Sure, why not Chen, pending elections? Pull in the KMT and DPP from Taiwan for advice. Or to be the nuclei of new all-China parties."

"*Those few who survived General Pei's massacres,*" Szerenci said drily.

Vincenzo was looking doubtful. "*Do you really think democracy can work in China? Maybe some societies need authoritarian rule.*"

"*Another way of putting what I just said,*" Szerenci cut in. "*If they need a tyrant, they're not really a functional polity.*"

"The Taiwanese are arguing for a free China. We owe them that chance," Salyers said.

The secretary of state spoke again, and his age and illness were clear in the slow dragging way he pronounced long words. "*The real question, as I see it, is what is our foreign policy in this sit-u-a-tion. We need to rebuild. That goes without saying. But General Vincenzo is right too. Right now, with wartime losses, we have more commitments than we have resources. We've got vacuums to fill in Africa. In the Mideast. We have to arrive at some understanding with Iran, now that we have a temporary cease-fire with that power. And eastern Europe is under threat.*

"*When our accounts are insolvent, we don't prevent wars we could have prevented. And above all, right now, we need peace. So do the Chinese.*

"*So let's arrive at whatever un-der-standing we can get to now. So we can stand down out here. Any agreement is better than no agreement.*"

Someone was talking urgently to Szerenci, though off-camera; the voice was muffled. His smooth head was nodding. But when he pivoted back to the lens he looked grim. "*Some bad news. Zhang's resurfaced.*"

"Where?" Blair and Yangerhans both said, together.

"*Somewhere in Russia, with two of his former ministers. He's giving a press conference to the tame media there. Saying they still constitute the legal government of China.*"

"Oh, fuck," Ammermann said.

"So now there's a government in exile," Shira breathed. "You're right, Adam. This could complicate things."

Szerenci said, *"It doesn't change where we are, going forward. We have an armistice. He's out of the country. Out of power. But that's right. He'll still have active supporters.*

"Which may mean, now, we have to strengthen this ad hoc government. Go the distance with them, more than we would have liked to before."

He stopped. The room was quiet. Until the secretary of state said, *"Keep us advised."* His screen went blank. Then so did Szerenci's. And Vincenzo's, last of all.

THE hall was set up less for a brunch than for a sumptuous dinner. The Chinese masses might be starving, Blair reflected, but their masters were definitely well fed. Unless it was just a show, a Potemkin feast, to impress the Americans . . . The tables were filled with sliced roast pork, savory spiced dishes, mounds of rice. Western foods, too: a chef was slicing a huge prime rib. She loaded up with broccoli florets, red potatoes, and a whitefish fillet she suspected was . . . cobia?

The first table she approached was occupied by Chinese. They ceased talking as she approached, and looked away when she gestured a request to join them. A frigid silence supervened. No one met her gaze. She took the hint and moved on, to the one table that had only a single occupant. She was setting her plate down before she realized who it was.

The Russian. *He* was Moscow's representative? She'd met him once before, in a café in Zurich, where he'd introduced himself as Dick. He was tall, even seated, and his hair shone so blond it was nearly white. He looked to be about her age, or a little older. His blue suit bore the blue-white-and-red pin of the Federation on one lapel.

His real name, she knew now—of course she'd researched him, after Zurich—was Rostislav Pyzhianov. He'd occupied much the same position she did, but in the Russian ministry of defense.

These days, apparently, he was the special representative of the president of the Russian Federation on central Asian issues, and apparently, for China now as well.

They nodded warily over the place settings. "Am I still calling you 'Dick'?" she asked.

"Let's make it Rostek. Good to meet you again, Blair."

"I wish I could say the same. Is it true you have Zhang Zurong in custody?"

Pyzhianov smiled. "Not 'in custody.' He's visiting us. As a friend. Yes."

"Are you going to recognize his government?"

He shrugged. "We have for many years. Will you give us a reason to stop?"

"I see you're not sitting with our Allied delegation. Despite wanting to be treated like an ally."

"Russia's true interests may lie in other areas," he agreed gravely.

"Last time we met, your 'interest' was two trillion dollars."

Pyzhianov shrugged. "It's actually closer to three. But that's what is owed us. Our country made major investments in China during the war. Extended significant credits. If its repayment can't be guaranteed, then we must seek restitution in some other form."

"What 'form' might that be?"

But he waved the question off, and applied himself to a dripping slab of the roast pork. And not too much later, people began getting up, heading to the long polished table, surrounded by too-soft armchairs, where the last three sessions of wrangling, lengthy statements, protestations of innocence, and veiled threats had been exchanged.

Her hip hurt already, and the session hadn't even started. Maybe, she thought grimly, the diplomats really did earn all their little luxuries, one way or another . . .

ONCE again the formerly warring powers faced each other across the ancient lacquered surface, as if across a battlefield. Yeah, which this in fact was. Negotiation was wearying, sometimes boring, sometimes infuriating; but it was as real as any military engagement, and the results, good or bad, would be as long-lasting.

General Pei. Marshal Chagatai. Admiral Lin. And the guy who in some ways seemed the least in control: the premier, Chen. Over the course of the days, primed and instructed by Salyers, Blair had noted who was inclined to bluster, who refused to budge, who could be reasoned with, who seemed to lead and who to follow. As, no doubt, they'd been doing with the American delegation.

She couldn't help wondering where she ranked on that scale.

A technician, one of the men who'd scanned the room for bugs that morning, pushed a small device to the head of the table. One of Archipelago's instantaneous digital translators. Ayala sat to the side, looking displaced but hopeful. Maybe he thought the device would fail.

"Good morning. The first topic for discussion today," Yangerhans opened, "is the shape and magnitude of China's postwar armed forces. We'll treat residual nuclear forces first, based on the disclosures General Pei submitted to our staff on our arrival.

"I'll start by reminding everyone that these are preliminary discussions, to place options before the heads of state conference, now scheduled in Singapore in two weeks. Nothing will be set in stone here. Meanwhile, the armistice holds."

Immediately, Chen leaned forward to tap the table. "If we are to discuss China's nuclear capabilities, we must also consider those of the United States. If our armaments are to be reduced, it is only fair it be matched. A mutual reduction."

"Who exactly lost this fuckin' war?" Ammermann muttered, beside her. But not so loudly the Chinese couldn't pretend not to have heard.

"China is not the only possible opponent the United States faces," General Naar said. The Air Force officer had been silent for most of the diplomatic discussion but seemed ready to take point now. "We have worldwide responsibilities, from defending our allies in eastern Europe, to the Horn of Africa, to resuming anti-pirate and humanitarian activities throughout the Pacific. China no longer has a navy, or really an air force. And for at least the foreseeable future, you won't need one."

"Look at it as an advantage," Ammermann put in. "Y'all can concentrate on reconstruction. Which we are *not* going to fund."

Chen said, "Let us leave that for the moment, and address our requirements. China must remain a P5 state. A nuclear weapons state. This is not a point for negotiation. It may be possible to reduce the number of warheads—"

"We've already reduced the number of your warheads." Ammermann grinned. "Want to go for a second round on that?"

"Adam." Yangerhans's tone held a mild reproach. "Let's keep it civil. The premier has a point he wants to make. And we ought to hear it."

"But what about this," Naar put in. "China promised no first use. Since 1964. Not to be the first to use nuclear weapons at any time, or under any circumstances. That was your policy when the war started. Yet you struck first, at the *Roosevelt* battle group. An unprovoked attack. You say you need a residual capability. I have to ask—why should we trust you with one again?"

Chen blotted his forehead with a sparkling white handkerchief. "That was President Zhang's decision," he muttered. "That was not decided by us. That was not a Party decision."

"Zhang was the Party chairman," Blair pointed out. "How can you say that wasn't the Party's doing?"

The premier waggled his head like a cornered bull. He said stubbornly, "Asia is a field of highly complex security dynamics. We must be able to defend ourselves. Against India. Japan. Against—" He cut his gaze sideways, and Blair caught its direction—toward Pyzhianov. "Against other enemies, as well," he finished, rather lamely.

Admiral Lin lifted an eyebrow. "Unless the United States is willing to defend us? Extend the nuclear umbrella to China?"

Ammermann snorted, and Blair glanced at him. "Not a chance," he muttered. So that was the White House turning thumbs-down.

Yangerhans made a note on his pad, long horsey face imperturbable, as one of the aides passed out single sheets. English at the top of the page, a Chinese translation beneath. "General Naar has formulated a compromise. A suggestion, for discussion. You've disclosed a hundred and eighty remaining operational warheads. We propose you renounce any first-strike capability once more. Only this time, not just in words, but in force structure.

"That means dismantling and rendering unusable any remaining ICBMs, specifically any and all MIRVed missiles, whether siloed or road-transportable. Discontinue development and testing of any hypersonic or boost-glide weapons. And do not replace the ballistic missile submarines the US and Indian navies destroyed in the opening days of the war."

The faces opposite had gone rigid. After a few seconds, Chen said tightly, "What then do we retain?"

Yangerhans said, "China will remain a P5 + 1 power. You simply return to the same minimal-deterrence posture you maintained before Premier Zhang assumed the leadership.

"In outline: A central strategic force of no more than one hundred single-warhead IRBMs, limited in range to five thousand kilometers, for regional deterrence missions. Add to that fifty gravity bombs, and thirty warheads in reserve. This matches India's current posture and exceeds those of Pakistan and Japan."

Naar added, "Minister? Let me point out, this does not require you to dismantle any warheads you admitted to having. It assures you a credible, survivable, and deliverable second-strike capability against any regional threat. You may deploy any form or quantity of antimissile defense you wish. Such a limitation to be in effect for a term of twenty years."

The Chinese sat as immobile and expressionless as the terracotta warriors of Emperor Qin. Finally General Pei murmured, "This is not acceptable. Not for a great power like China."

Ammermann stirred in his chair. "Premier Chen. You present yourself as speaking for the provisional government. I think that's a fair offer. What do you think? Have we finally got a deal here?"

Chen slipped his eyeglasses off and fiddled with them. Rubbed the lenses with a scrap of tissue from his pocket. He started to speak, then glanced at Marshal Chagatai. He carefully fitted his glasses back on, and muttered, at last, "No. We do not agree."

"Obviously this requires further consideration." Yangerhans nodded, laying the sheet aside. "But I will warn you, there are elements in Washington who want China stripped of all nuclear capabilities whatsoever. Bear in mind, it would be far better if we could submit this to the heads of state as acceptable to China's provisional government. Much better for the stability, and continued existence, of that government, to be seen as party to a compromise, rather than having an agreement imposed on it by victors. I hope you see my point."

Again, none of the Chinese reacted.

Yangerhans sighed, and turned a page in his briefing book. "Then, we proceed to conventional forces. Your navy and air force have already been reduced to acceptable levels for regional self-defense. So the remaining question is that of land forces." He glanced at his watch. "But first, let's take a short break."

BLAIR visited the ladies' room, a tiny cubicle far down a shadowed, musty corridor. She doubted the empress dowager had ever used this room, but the toilets might have dated from around her era. The massive porcelain thrones, with cisterns high above eye level, were trademarked with the logos of long-vanished English companies.

She washed her hands, checked her mascara, and brushed her hair. Sighed, looking at herself in the mirror. No, the years were not kind to women, and unlike men, they were judged far more on their appearances, even now.

Well, at least, aside from her hip and ear, she still had all her

moving parts. She could still ride, though she hardly had time anymore. Maybe when she got back to Maryland, she'd take a weekend off.

But first they had to nail down a peace. Or what might pass
for one for a few years. She suspected no one back at that table
expected it to last forever. Even temporarily humbled, China was
too massive, too populous, her people too industrious, to fade into
obscurity.

But all the lives and treasure had to have bought the Allies
something.

THE conventional-force talks went no better. Their hosts seemed
to have lost interest in the discussions. They sat immobile, barely
reacting except for brief denials or terse rejections, as Yangerhans
sketched possible force structures.

Most of his proposals involved large reductions in the land
and internal security forces. "You've mobilized far more men and
women than you need for homeland defense," the mission leader
pointed out. "You'll need that labor for postwar reconstruction. If
you have to keep them on the payroll, transfer them to reserves,
at least. Let them return home, with the opportunity to begin a
peaceful and productive life. Start businesses. Look for other
careers, pursue education. It might be possible for us to under-
write some of those costs, since they don't directly strengthen
your armed forces."

Blair looked around for the senator—he'd be the one to introduce any aid packages on the Hill—but he still hadn't rejoined
them after the break. Should she worry? Bankey Talmadge was an
old man, and not in the best of health. What if he just hadn't woken
up? She crooked a finger at Chaldroniere, and after a whispered
exchange sent the DS agent to check on the senator.

When she tuned back to the discussion, Yangerhans was pro-
posing the disbanding of all internal forces and domestic surveillance operations of the Ministry of State Security. The infamous

Black Battalions had crushed dissent in Hong Kong, Taiwan, Tibet, and Xinjiang. Even before the war, they'd run a massive gulag system—the internment camps—rivaling that of the USSR at its most ruthless, and a system of digital surveillance and online "social credit" programs that made George Orwell's dystopia in *1984* look laid-back and genial. When he finished there was silence once more around the table.

At last Marshal Chagatai held up a palm. He spoke in Chinese, but the digital translator seemed to be mimicking his gravelly tones. "This is not acceptable. Stability forces are internal matters. Not subject to negotiation. We are facing serious uprisings in the far west and south. For the same reason, it is impossible to close the reeducation camps. We are of course repatriating all prisoners of war, as rapidly as the conditions of our transport system allow. In any case, what will remain are not concentration camps, as you seem to believe. They are only for de-extremization and reeducation. The residents are happy, well fed, and gaining advantageous new skills."

Blair exchanged a glance with Shira; the State rep, too, seemed to find it difficult to keep a straight face. Salyers said mildly, "Nevertheless, Marshal, they must be closed. It is possible your far west may become independent. That hinges on the decisions of the heads of state meeting."

The marshal huffed. "Impossible! Xinjiang is historically Chinese."

"Only since 1949."

Chagatai all but rolled his eyes. "You confuse the date of the People's Republic with the history of China. The Western Region has been Chinese since the days of the Han Dynasty. Over two thousand years. It is Chinese. *Thoroughly* Chinese."

"You forget the Uighur Khanate," Salyers said, but with a smile.

Chen smiled back at her, but much less pleasantly. "You know some of our history. But not all. The Tang withdrawal was only temporary. As the marshal says, it will remain Chinese."

"If it's so damn Chinese, why is it in armed revolt?" Blair asked him. Ammermann stifled a chuckle; Provanzano smiled silkily.

"The province is restive, that is true. But those who resist are terrorists. Bandits. Enemies of all law-abiding people." Chen eyed Provanzano balefully. "And as you know, they are being encouraged by your American intelligence. Sit there, Anthony, and tell me you have not supplied and armed them, from the beginning."

"Not at all true," Provanzano said evenly. "This is an indigenous uprising, caused solely by your oppression. They only want their liberty. If they had it, perhaps they would not be so determined to leave."

Blair reached for the water carafe. The atmosphere had definitely chilled today, in contrast to the collegial tone of the opening sessions. Obviously the Chinese were going to stonewall any attempt to disarm them, or weaken their iron grip on their minorities. Both would be stumbling blocks to any peace agreement.

And the Allies' ability to impose change was limited. China could not be physically occupied and forcibly disarmed, as Japan, Germany, and Iraq had been. But the victors couldn't leave a hardened, resentful Party in charge either. Or the war would have been fought for nothing.

They were sitting in silence when there was a commotion outside the doors. A shout from the guards, then countermanded orders. She twisted in her seat to look.

Talmadge lumbered in, bulling his way across the hall. Her heart sank. Just from his uneven, lurching gait, she judged he was half seas under. His noon scotch, followed, no doubt, by a few chasers. She looked away as the senator lunged into his overstuffed chair, nearly upsetting it. The Chinese looked away pointedly.

"Sorry, bit late," Talmadge mumbled. He skated a paper fluttering across the table toward Chen. "Here's what I got. See what y'all think."

The premier looked astonished, then offended, but after a moment picked it up. Gingerly, with the tips of his fingers, as if it were a shred of carrion. After a short study he looked up, frowning. "What is this, Senator?"

"An outline of your new government," Talmadge rumbled. "Based it on Sun Yat-Sen's 1912 constitution. You still honor Sun, right? Strong central government. Weak federal system. Five branches: legislative, executive, judicial, civil service, and inspector general. Headed by a president. Oh, and I wrote up a bill of rights. Just to backstop everything."

The paper trembled in Chen's hands. "*You* wrote this up? Senator?"

"No, *you* did. Minister." Talmadge lifted one haunch slightly, then settled back with a sigh. "It's the Chen constitution. Laid out with the advice of the senior sitting member of the United States Senate, though. You'll need to call a convention to ratify it. But it'll give you a framework to start out with."

Blair closed her eyes, breathless, unsure yet whether this was low comedy or the birth of a new China. The four men opposite gazed on stonefaced. Finally the premier murmured, gaze fixed on the paper again, "And where is the Party's role in this . . . Chen constitution?"

"The Communist Party leads the people in the transition to democracy. Over a five-year implementation period. After that, it competes with the others on a level field. Don't worry, everyone still has offices and retirements. Ever'body gets taken care of. Nobody left out in the cold." Talmadge reached for the water carafe, and barely managed to fill his glass without knocking it over. Muttering an aside to Blair, "I did tell you, Missy, constitutional law, Georgetown? Yeah, I thought so."

Heads together, the Chinese studied the document. Finally General Pei murmured, "And . . . prosecution? For war crimes? Senior officials must be protected. Guaranteed."

Talmadge waved fat fingers. "Well, to be frank, that's up to the heads of state. But committin' to democracy will make y'all look a hell of a lot better to 'em, that's for damn sure."

Admiral Lin murmured, "This will require time to study."

"Sure, sure," Talmadge said good-naturedly, flapping a hand. "Talk it all over. Won't happen overnight. But once you hold general elections, y'all can start a new tradition. No more Generalissimo Zhangs. Peaceful transfers of power."

"And the camps? The police?" Chagatai narrowed his eyes.

Talmadge wiggled his fingers again. "Believe you me, son, you transition to a rule of law, devolve some self-government to your provinces, you'll be surprised how fast these upsets can just simmer right down. But this here is somethin' I can take to the heads of state. Get you a treaty. A high level of positive engagement. Show the Foreign Relations Committee, and pry loose a few billion in transitional aid. Get trade and agriculture started again, get your country back on its feet." The old man shoved back from the table and looked to Yangerhans. "Jim, how about we let 'em stew on it awhile? It's a good offer. They'll be Fathers of their Country."

Chen waited for the translation of that, eyes nearly closed. He seemed to be thinking it over.

Finally he nodded, and stood. "No promises," he murmured. "But we will talk it over."

The others stood too, and forced thin smiles. It seemed the meeting, and perhaps the negotiations, were at an end.

YANGERHANS caught up with her as she and Salyers were descending the broad steps of the Hall of Supreme Harmony. "Blair. A word?"

She excused herself to Shira, and halted. What now? Had she been too aggressive with Chen? Too bad. They were shooting themselves in the foot if they stonewalled. The heads of state were in no mood for a soft peace. Not after the unprovoked aggressions against so many countries, the massacres in the occupied territories. Even the noncombatant nations had suffered, from famine and environmental disruption, the cross-border flood tides of hungry refugees, the worldwide spread of radioactivity from the exchange that had climaxed the war. She crossed her arms. "What can I help you with, Admiral?"

"Jim, please. This has nothing to do with the mission. Not directly, anyway. But I wanted to sound you out on something."

She glanced around. They were alone; the other members of the party were already far down the steps, heading for the limos that would take them back, accompanied by waiting sirens, to their chilly and still-unlighted hotel. Talmadge trailed them, limping, but the tall diplomatic security man was at his side, steadying his steps. "Uh . . . sure."

"You'd have to agree to keep this under wraps."

What the hell? She nodded reluctantly. "Okay. Agreed."

He dawdled like a small boy, looking down at his shoes. "Well . . . you know we have the election coming up. This fall. I'd, um, like you to join my exploratory team. Head it, if possible."

She bit her lip, not just surprised, but gobsmacked. "Uh . . . what did you plan to run for, Jim? Senate?"

"I thought we might start out aiming higher." He looked abashed; then grinned that sad, twisted smile. It looked out of place on his long, ugly face, but also she could see how it might be called Lincolnesque.

"Aiming higher . . . ?" she repeated.

"Since the president said he's not going to run again. Just to, you know, explore it."

"I see. And we're talking which party?"

He glanced at the sky. "Haven't decided yet. I'd run as a centrist."

"The middle of the road's where people get run over." Someone had told her that once.

"Perhaps. But I think the country's tired of being divided, at loggerheads. I could bring people together again. Or sure as hell try."

"As the architect of victory? Yeah, that'd be a selling point." God help her, she *was* thinking about the politics of it. America hadn't had a war hero for president since Eisenhower. Wait, maybe Kennedy. Perhaps the elder Bush. All for World War II service. But then, there hadn't really been a victorious war since then. Just more or less messy skirmishes that petered out, as often as not simply because the public had just had enough.

The wind was messing with her hair; she smoothed it back over her damaged ear. "Yeah, you could probably make a splash in the primary. But . . . Jim, look, I appreciate the compliment. But you realize, I'm already in government. And not terrifically popular with either party."

"Again, that places you in the center. A progressive, but one who helped win the war." He took her hand, but not in any untoward way. And he was married, anyway. Happily, as far as she knew. "I'm not looking for a huge persona. Just someone with organizational ability, clout with the funding sources, credibility. Maybe not head of the team. Necessarily. But high on the team. Essential." He waited a beat, then added, releasing her hand, "Anyway, I'd like you to at least consider it. We don't need to do anything more right now. But do tell me if you're definitely ruling it out, for personal reasons, or that you don't think I'm the right candidate, or whatever. I won't ask why. Just a simple no will be enough."

She smoothed her hair back again, stalling for time. Feeling that sense of the world shifting under her feet again. Of possibilities materializing, history happening. She'd felt it at the start of these negotiations. And again today, when Talmadge had seemed to make headway with the Chinese.

Oh, she knew why it felt so unreal. She'd just had to think about everything in terms of the fucking war for so fucking long she'd never had a chance to consider what might come next. But the postwar world was hurtling toward them all, faster than anyone could imagine.

He was still intently staring at her. Still waiting. She drew a breath. "Like you say, it's too soon. To give you a yes or no answer."

"Sure. I understand."

"But if you want some kind of response right now . . . for your own planning . . . I'm not instantly saying no."

Those unattractive features twisted into a delighted grin. Suddenly they weren't all that ugly anymore. But they were still sad, with the compassion of a man who'd seen war, and death, yet who still hoped the world could be made better, despite it all.

Yeah. She could see him in a campaign video, easily. With the right coach. Yeah. Absolutely.

"That's all I was asking for." He glanced toward the limos. "Guess they're holding a car for us."

"Oh yes," she said, pushing her hair back into place again. Feeling, for some obscure reason, a flush burning her cheeks. And together, they descended the ancient stone stairs.

7

35°17′02″ N, 130°34′55″ E: The Sea of Japan

THE sea was a black, heaving dark, and the wind was a blustery twenty-five to thirty knots. A summer night, but it didn't look like anyone's idea of summer out here.

High on *Savo Island*'s bridge, Captain Cheryl Staurulakis winced at a clatter of wind-driven spray on the windshield. She studied a glowing screen, wishing they had a moon at least. Commander Mills, her exec, was down in his bunk, snatching a well-deserved hour off. The underway watch was set, but compared to the ships she'd served on earlier in her career, there were all too few people up here.

Off in a corner of the pilothouse, the mumble of low voices: Lieutenant Max Mytsalo, relieving Noah Pardees as officer of the deck. Mytsalo had been an ensign when the war started. He still looked young, but the strain of wartime watches had engraved lines around his eyes and sagged those once-peach-fuzzed cheeks. The others, enlisted and officer alike, tottered about the bridge like robots supplied with insufficient voltage. Chief Van Gogh was nodding over the nav screen. There was no helmsman anymore, just a remote console the OOD maneuvered the ship from.

Lieutenant Commander Pardees was a lanky shadow, his tones almost lost in the hiss of circuits and the hum of fans and the renewed rattle of spray as the cruiser burrowed her bow into the trough of an obsidian sea. "Ma'am, um, properly relieved by Lieutenant Mytsalo."

She returned his salute in the dark, though neither could see the other. "Very well."

A younger tenor: "This is Lieutenant Mytsalo. I have the deck and the conn. Course is zero three zero, speed one five. *Savo* is the guide. All ships in formation sectors for night steaming. Ma'am."

"Very well," she said again, and nodded. "We've got half an hour to COMEX. Let's make sure we're ready."

Silence returned to the darkened bridge. She chewed a lip, matching the pips on the faintly glowing night-adapted screen to the formation she'd hastily set up.

Exercise Trident Junction hadn't been planned through the normal process, staffed and coordinated and deconflicted to support a mission-focused joint training program. Fleet had stapled it together overnight from old exercise op orders, with coordinates hastily rejiggered for a sea the US Navy had seldom cruised, let alone conducted fleet ops in. Except for Operation Chromite, the takedown of North Korea. That now-ravaged country lay to the northwest. To the south, behind her, lay Tsushima Island and Tsushima Strait, where the Russian fleet had come to grief back in 1905.

Yeah . . . Tsushima. She'd read about that battle, which bore a ghostly, unsettling resemblance to what might be taking shape now.

Early in the preceding century, Admiral Zinovy Rozhestvensky had steamed his coal-burning battleships eighteen thousand miles, nearly around the globe, to link up with tsarist forces blockaded in Port Arthur, and crush the Japanese. Instead, Admiral Togo Heihachiro had obliterated the Russians in an afternoon. Winning the war, and planting the seeds of the Russian Revolution and the eventual death of the Romanov dynasty and the tsar's whole family.

Now a new fleet was gathering, this time to the north, to retake that same chunk of China. Dalian had once been Port Arthur, a

Russian enclave. Once Moscow reoccupied it, Russia would sur-
round and dominate the mineral riches of Manchuria. Augmented
and reequipped with the profits the Russian Federation had reaped
from the runup in oil prices during America's war with China, the
fleet now headed toward her was far more powerful than either
Rozhestvensky or Togo could have imagined.

Which was no surprise to her, of course. But what concerned
her most was that it had recently been joined by *Peter the Great*.
Intel said that massive nuclear-powered battle cruiser had just
been updated with the Zircon-C hypersonic antiship missile.
Meanwhile, US forces had begun their drawdown after the end
of the war, headed back to Pearl and the West Coast for refit, or
mothball, or scrapping.

Which meant that, in many ways, the oncoming forces both
outnumbered and outranged those she could bring to bear. And
Higher had already said the Air Force strikes she'd requested on
the advancing ships would not take place, in order to avoid what
they called "premature escalation."

"Fuck," she muttered. A fierce itch triggered just under one
armpit. Mustering all her will not to claw at it, she scowled down
again at the screen.

To the north, the Sea of Japan narrowed nearly to nothing. A
four-mile-wide pinch point there separated it from the Sea of Okhotsk. No guarantee the Russians would thread that choke point,
though. More likely they'd skirt the northern tip of Sakhalin, the
same route she herself had taken to her anti-ICBM station a few
months before.

Entering the Sea of Japan via one of two international straits,
the *Peter the Great* group could join up with a Russian task force
already moored in Vladivostok. It was even possible, though Intel
judged it unlikely, that they might round the southernmost tip of
Japan, Kyushu, and enter the Sea of Japan from the south.

Resulting in a battle cruiser–centered task force nearly twice
the size and fighting capability of her own . . .

She pushed that thought away irritably as Pardees, still on the bridge, centered his tablet in front of her. "We're about to COMEX, Skipper. Here's the message, if you want to review Phase I."

"Any word from *Chokai*? *Ashigara*? Commodore Ota?" The Japanese Aegis destroyers would double the capability of her force. They'd operated with her during the war. She'd requested submarine and air support from the Japanese Maritime Self-Defense Force as well. But Pardees simply shook his head.

She sighed and accepted the tablet. Yeah, she'd have to review it. But the close-set paragraphs read like so much naval prose did, dense with acronyms and larded with clichés. After the usual boilerplate about "honing interoperability skills" and "demonstrating close operational relationships" it set up the overall exercise scenario. All in all, she reflected sourly, it was a terrific tasking. Whipped up overnight, the order outlined an ambiguous commander's intent, inserting full deniability for Higher, but pushing the risk down to her.

She sighed and buckled down to reading.

The order specified no dedicated opposing force—OPFOR, in joint terminology—for the events. Only a scripted enemy. The "Federation of Phosphora" was threatening a seaborne landing in eastern China. Blue naval and air units would constitute a blocking force in a constructive battlespace whose dimensions just happened to match the real Sea of Japan. They would intercept and warn the Phosphorian forces, but it was possible the scenario could degenerate into a limited conventional engagement. Phosphora's objective lay to the west, in the middle of the operating area.

"Fuck," she muttered again, kneading her brow. The opposing force's strength factors included a two-to-one advantage in surface forces, three-to-one in submarines, two-to-one in available aircraft, and three-to-one in missiles. Blue's strength factors included a slight technical superiority in antimissile defense and support from shore-based air to the east.

Phosphora also had the initiative: the freedom to choose the timing and method of their opposed transit of the strait. They were operating from comparatively short lines of supply, and had missile and aircraft replacements available within hours. Both forces were rated as equally acclimated to the operating area and at roughly equivalent levels of training.

"You read this?" she asked Pardees. "All of it?"

"Yes'm. Not too encouraging, on the face of it. The balance of forces."

"No shit," she muttered, wincing as a new lash of spray hit the glass two feet from her face like a fusillade. She grew heavy on her feet, then light, as *Savo* dipped and reeled in the near-utter darkness. "But if we have to engage . . . We need to see if the Marines can redeploy a couple of NEMESIS batteries from Taiwan. And if the Japanese will commit some from the Ryukyus. Get those land-based antiship missiles redeployed where they can help us out."

He nodded. "The Russians—sorry, the *Phosphorians*—are going to be handicapped too. They'll have to escort the amphibs for the landing. All we have to do is goalie. Keep them from landing in Dalian, and we succeed."

"Right, they have to come punch us," Cheryl agreed. Dalian lay to the west of the Korean Peninsula, past the strait she guarded now. "But whoever wrote this about levels of training being equal, that's bullshit. We've just come through a war. While they haven't fought a fleet action since, since—when?"

"1905?" Pardees ventured.

She grinned. "I was thinking the same thing, Noah."

The 21MC lit, someone calling from far below in the armored and sealed citadel. *"CO, Combat."*

Pardees leaned forward to depress the lever. "She's listening."

"Ma'am, chat message on the TF side. Chokai *and* Ashigara *do not anticipate joining."*

Cheryl took a quick breath; she and Pardees traded glances. "Uh, that's not good news. Reason given?"

"No reason, ma'am. Just a personal from their COs."

She acknowledged with a double click. Then sighed, blinking out into the seething chaos of night, and fog so thick it blotted out the stars. No, not good news at all. The Japanese would have brought more than two destroyers to the battle. Their modern submarines alone might well have tilted the balance in her favor, in these narrow, shallow seas.

"We might have to fight this one alone," Pardees muttered. "In which case . . ."

"Yeah." In a way, she couldn't blame Tokyo. The naval commanders, she was sure, would have joined her, given half a chance. But the Japanese government had played it cagey throughout the war. Hung back during its first months, until it looked like the US would really strike back at China. Then joined in full bore. They'd contributed mightily to the victory. But now, apparently, they weren't eager to make any new enemies.

Pardees cleared his throat. "Uh, Captain . . . this may be a little outside the box. But have we considered seeing if there are any Chinese capabilities left? That could collaborate, maybe join us in a show of force at least?"

She scratched her ribs absently as she pondered it. "Huh . . . It's not a bad idea, Noah, but I doubt they've got much left. We pretty much cleared everything out with the autonomous torpedoes, the air strikes, and so forth. And then the nuclear laydown. Even if there was, they wouldn't be interoperable with us in any meaningful way. But . . . I guess it's worth a try. Get a message off to, uh . . ."

She stalled out. To whom? There was no Beijing government anymore, as far as she knew. "Uh, maybe shoot it up to PACOM, okay? Ask if they can make the request via whatever channels they have, staff to staff. And expedite it."

He nodded, head down, making notes.

She said reluctantly, raising her voice to the inchoate shadows around her, "This is the CO. Let's shift the conn to CIC." And headed aft to take the elevator down.

COMBAT was icy cold and so nearly dark that even after being on the bridge, she had to wait a few seconds while her pupils dilated before she could make out the rows of consoles, the big vertical displays near the front. She paused at the coffee mess and poured herself a shot, black. Studied the displays again as she carried the cup to her seat at the command desk.

The screen showed Korea off to the west. Newly reunified, but by all accounts still in turmoil as accounts from the war got settled and the interim president, Jun Min Jung, tried to assert control over renegade generals in the North. To the east lay the angular, tortured coastline of Japan.

And behind her, the strait itself. Seventy-five miles across, with Tsushima Island stuck in the middle like a bone in the throat. A natural choke point, the kind anyone with the most basic strategic sense would choose for an ambush. Which Togo obviously had decided too.

The problem was, her own enemy had already pinpointed her location, and probably her dispositions as well. The Russians had improved their overhead observation all through the war, augmented with nanosatellites nearly as advanced as the Allied MICE network.

"They've got to pretty much know exactly where we are," she muttered to Chief Terranova.

The round childlike face of her lead sensor chief was unworried. "That's gotta be good, Skipper. Right? When they see us parked smack in their way." When Cheryl didn't answer, Terranova added, "We going to the helmets? I gotta know, ta run the displays."

She said reluctantly, "Uh, sure. I mean, yes."

"You don't much like that helmet, do you, Skipper? Wait'll you see the new upgrade. Uploaded it yesterday. You'll wanta live in there now."

Cheryl half smiled but didn't rise to the bait. She pulled the headgear down off the rack, adjusted her faded, threadbare olive-and-black shemagh for padding—it was about the only thing she had left from the old *Savo*, since most of her clothes and gear had gone down with the ship—and settled the heavy VR helmet down on her shoulders.

A moment of pinched dark, swimming with phosphenes. Then the world lit.

The screens swam before her eyes as she struggled to refocus. A stream of cool air caressed the back of her neck. The ship status readout glowed on. She could toggle through it to check every space, every system, and count the remaining weapons in her magazines.

She clicked past it to the battlespace display, and gasped. The Flight 8 software was so far past visual quality it seemed more vivid, more convincing, than reality itself.

She floated a hundred thousand feet up, looking down and across and around on 360 degrees of blue-green sea. Latitude and longitude lines crossed it, and the display instantly populated with altitude readouts when she blinked.

She blinked again, and the electromagnetic presentation appeared. Radar, radio, and microwave laser and data transmissions wavered, sheer slowly fluttering curtains of violet, cornflower, jade, indigo. Neutral, friendly, and hostile contacts were displayed as NATO symbols, though she could switch to video from drones, or even direct view when they were in line-of-sight range. The mirrors of *Savo*'s lasers doubled as powerful telescopes. When she glanced down, she looked through the hull, to a rugged, corrugated sea-bottom that wavered many fathoms down.

She cocked her head and her avatar rotated in the air. There was *Savo*, a blue JTDS symbol. She blinked and it transformed into real-time video. The cruiser was rolling, plowing through heavy, cream-topped seas the hard gray of wet steel. A wave rolled up her down-slanted bow, smashing apart as it hit a V-shaped shield, and *Savo* shuddered despite her massive size. White spray blew back over the laser mounts like gauzy veils as she slowly rolled upright again, plowing on.

Cheryl was viewing it through the lenses of a recon drone far above. And somewhere below, nestled within meters of steel and Kevlar armor, crouched a small, soft larva that was . . . herself?

And yet, not. Her old human self was no longer bound by its

old senses. She'd left it miles behind, sitting motionless in a foam-contoured chair, hands lying lightly on the armrests.

Only the maddening itch below her armpits, both of them now, reminded her she was still mortal.

A voice in her ears murmured. Though not a human one. AALIS, her ship, was fused and integrated now with Sea Eagle, the tactical AI that would direct the battle once it started. *"COMEX. COMEX,"* it pronounced in tranquil, sexless tones.

And the exercise began.

THE fleets of 1905 had converged in line ahead, battleships and cruisers steaming like articulated trains. Togo had won by "crossing the T," maneuvering to concentrate the whole weight of fire of his broadside-on line against one Russian ship at a time, as they charged toward him.

But since World War II, American task forces had transited and fought in concentric formations. The highest-value units—carriers and tankers—were nestled in the center. Cruisers and destroyers were stationed farther out, for antiaircraft defense. Beyond them, radar pickets reached out with electronic feelers to detect threats and localize targets. Aircraft had the job of searching even farther out, while beneath the waves submarines sanitized the line of advance, to guard against ambush.

That formation had had its advantages, when information was scarce and the outermost units served primarily as sensors, feeding information to a central decision maker. But now data could exist everywhere simultaneously. Each ship and plane was a node that shared information instantly with all other nodes. In other words, distributed operations.

Her formation now was anything but circular. And, really, nothing that would even have been recognizable as a formation to a commander from the twentieth century.

Cheryl hadn't come up with this disposition herself. DEVGRU-WEST served as the fleet's capability development hub. AALIS had communicated with Sea Eagle, the Navy's cloud-based AI there, which had in turn consulted with Battle Eagle, the overarching Allied strategic artificial intelligence.

After the mysterious demise of the Chinese AI, Jade Emperor, Battle Eagle had planned operations, fought back cyberattacks, and conducted its own crippling offensives in cyberspace. It had largely been responsible for winning the war, in the view of some pundits. Now, the op plan it had developed for Trident Junction included a tactical grid to connect the various nodes, plus backup data storage uplinked to satellites and downlinked to a surface-based comm chain. A way to connect the various ship and land-based AIs, to render tactical advice to the commander in real time.

The artificial intelligences had recommended a steaming formation unlike any she'd ever seen. Gliding effortlessly across the sky, her avatar looked down on a seemingly random mix of units large and small. Scattered across hundreds of square miles of sea, it hardly seemed organized at all. If anything, it was more like a random scattering, a crushable foam filled with far too much empty space.

Since the Japanese wouldn't be joining, her task force would consist of *Savo Island* and one single modern Korean unit, *Jeonnam*, currently en route from Pusan. She had four submarines, *Arkansas*, *Idaho*, *Utah*, and *John Warner*. Sea Eagle had placed three subs north of *Savo*, with *Utah* behind Cheryl, in the approach from the East China Sea. Which made sense, to guard against any attacks from behind. Her surface escorts consisted of two wartime-construction Improved Burke–class destroyers, *Dixie Kiefer* and *Christos Katsetos*, and three Wartime Flight 3 missile frigates. *Goodrich*, *Montesano*, and *Patrick Hart* had operated with her before; she knew and trusted their captains to fight smart and persevere until the end.

Far ahead, halfway up the Sea of Japan, the unmanned hunters scouted: USV-34, -20, -7, and -16. Most of the data streaming to her about the oncoming Russians were from them, and from the drones whose inputs they and the nanosatellites were forwarding. Her two Orca Flight 1 autonomous submarines, USS-4 and -13, were far out in front, covering Sakhalin and the Soya Strait. They were controlled from *Idaho.*

She toggled to the antisubmarine presentation. *Savo* herself was operating in fairly shallow waters, but to the northwest the depths dropped to over two thousand meters. Perfect operating depths for enemy submarines. AALIS highlighted five unidentified contacts strung along the coast, with three vibrating patches that denoted possible threats as well, though not yet localized enough for targeting purposes.

Five to eight possible subsea threats. Again, not a good force ratio.

She toggled to the air picture, but—aside from a few contacts over Japan and Korea, the latter probably humanitarian missions to serve rescue and reconstruction—the battlespace stretched empty. Thus far, at least. Her request to Higher for carrier air support hadn't been answered. But with three modern Aegis-equipped ships, she should be able to fight off a modest air attack.

A coordinated, well-timed barrage of hypersonic missiles, though . . . She was pretty confident her ABM defenses would take out a Zircon-C. The hypersonic traveled at Mach 9, and reports claimed it was shielded from radar with plasma stealth. But after discussing its parameters with Terranova, Cheryl felt *Savo* was up to the job. The chief felt she could tune above or below whatever electron plasma frequency the incoming warhead displayed.

But a ship's magazines carried only so many rounds, and those she'd expended at the end of the war hadn't been replaced. She still had lasers, but the forward mount tended to overheat and she wasn't sure she wanted to trust the ship's survival to the after one.

Bottom line: depending on how many missiles the oncoming fleet might fire in salvo, she could be overwhelmed. If the Japanese provided land-based support, that would help. But expending their remaining Patriot, THAAD, and Aegis Ashore missiles to save her would leave their homeland undefended, if Moscow decided on horizontal escalation.

She wondered when they would ever be satisfied with what they had. The Russians, that is. Hadn't everyone suffered enough?

Then she remembered.

The Russians hadn't suffered at all. Mainly, they'd just profited, cheering from the sidelines as the other superpowers clawed at each other's eyes and ripped each other's guts out.

Now, like some lurking scavenger shark, they were moving in, intent on tearing bloody chunks off the loser.

Okay, keep Higher informed at all times . . . She cut her eyes to bring up high side nanochat. Her fingers flexed, and some circuit she didn't see spelled out letters. Her message went out Flash priority, reporting her task force on station, and once more requesting air and tanker support. Requesting high-level intervention as well, to beg for Japanese missile support and any available forces from the remnants of China's navy and air force.

Requesting reinforcements, from anywhere they could be found.

It wasn't just to cover her ass. But if worse came to worst, no one would be able to say she hadn't sounded the alarm.

At last she hit Send, and sagged back in her chair. Her palms itched. She glanced down at her avatar's hands. They were smooth. Unsullied. The skin didn't itch, or erupt, or bleed. Her virtual hands looked perfect. Even the nails were neatly done, and squared off with French tips. "Nice," she muttered, envious.

Now all she had to do was wait.

The sea spread out below, calm, unfurrowed. Except . . . far below her, on the sea bottom, something was creeping into the field of view.

At first she couldn't tell what it was. Maybe just a disturbance, an anomaly, or a jutting rock marring the smooth sediments of the bottom. Gradually her brain assembled it into something recognizable, though. Lying on its side, half buried.

The crumpled, broken wreck of a ship sprawled far beneath, half digested by the muck of the abyss. She couldn't tell what kind, but it contained iron. The magnetic readouts told her that. Imperial Russian? One of Rozhestvensky's doomed battleships, from so many years before? Or a casualty of World War II, a Japanese maru blasted apart by American torpedoes?

She couldn't tell, and didn't really want to know.

She just didn't want *Savo Island*, or any of her other ships, to join it.

8

Headed East

DAN motored out Route 90, toward the sunrise. The first day out from Seattle passed in a blur of wind, noise, and speed. The highway stretched before him nearly empty. Now and then he'd veer into the passing lane to overtake a slower-moving truck, but not often. Traffic in the other direction, headed back toward Seattle, was heavier, but still sparse. Far fewer vehicles than he'd expected, even in the aftermath of a nuclear exchange. For hours on end he was alone on the highway, devouring four lanes of empty pavement with the only sound the dronesong of the engine, a vibration in his windscreen, and his worry.

The guy at the factory had said Nan was headed east, in a refrigerator truck filled with medications, being escorted by a motorcycle gang. But Dan saw no other bikes, much less a pack of them, though he kept his eyes peeled and slowed to peer carefully down each exit ramp he passed. His own machine felt heavy, awkward, and he wasn't sure why. Maybe it was built that way. It also had a wobble in the front end at around forty miles an hour, nearly sending him off the road once when he'd overcorrected.

So he didn't go forty.

Cryptic inscriptions started appearing on the road surface west of Spokane, spray-painted in big swoops of Day-Glo orange. Eventually, recalling the shipboard radiological training, he decoded it:

radiation dosages, probably in either millirems or millisieverts per hour, plus the date the survey had been taken. Eventually he deduced that whoever was spray-painting the markings was maybe three days ahead of him, also headed east.

The numbers climbed as he neared Spokane. As he motored through, the turnoffs and side streets lay eerily empty. Looking down from the overpasses as he went through, as far as he could make out the city was intact, but deserted. Evacuated early on, apparently, since he didn't see any smoke, fire, or other signs it had actually been hit.

Which was going to make it harder to do what he'd intended. Namely, ask along the way if anyone had seen Nan and her entourage-slash-captors.

A UPS truck stood parked at an off-ramp. No keys, but the gas cap was unlocked. He deployed his hose and filled the bike up with the pink-tinted high-eth wartime fuel substitute. He searched the nearby undergrowth until he found a couple of discarded two-liter soda bottles. He filled them, too, stowed them in a saddlebag, and pushed on.

But the orange numbers kept rising. When they hit 150 per hour he started to sweat. First of all, if it was in millirems, he was getting about ten times as high an exposure as it would be if it was millisieverts. The type of radiation mattered too—alpha radiation, neutrons, or gamma—but he was pretty sure fallout would be mostly alpha and thus a direct one-to-ten conversion factor. Accumulated over time . . . He pondered it uneasily for mile after mile. There was no *safe* dose. Once you hit about 100 rem, especially over a short period, you could expect active sickness: nausea, low white blood count, hair loss, weakness, immune system compromise, and so on. If those painted numbers got much higher, he'd be running a real risk just being out here on the highway.

But those were only the overt, immediate symptoms. Even at doses below the levels that made you noticeably ill, the risk of cancer later started to climb.

He shook his head, squinting into the wind, bent over the

handlebars as he blew along, goosing the Honda up to seventy, eager to get through the city. But then, the readings he was seeing were several days old. Surely some of the fallout had decayed since then.

Bottom line, though, there was probably a pretty damn good reason he was alone on the road. He was picking up dosage the longer he stayed out here. Letting himself in for some bad shit. If not immediately, later on.

Still, he pushed on. Didn't stop, except once to piss, and even then stamped the dust off his boots before he got back on. Keeping a close eye on the numbers. Which kept rising.

Until they peaked somewhere past Coeur d'Alene. Then began to drop as he turned south, crossed a bridge, and left the deserted suburbs behind for a long valley.

He breathed a little easier as the orange digits stabilized at 20. Not great, but he could stand it for a while.

The highway twisted between deserted-looking wooded hills green with summer foliage. Discreet signs informed him he was in a national forest. And that only he could prevent wildfires. The air was scented with pine and juniper and sun-warmed wildflowers, a hot dry summery smell, pleasant even when you were blowing through at sixty miles an hour. He stayed at that speed, with sixty-five on the downgrades. He had plenty of throttle left, but seventy had seemed scarily fast. He wasn't really used to the bike and had no idea how long ten-year-old tires would last. He didn't want to be going eighty if one blew. Especially since he was riding without a helmet.

Toward dusk the valleys deepened and the hills grew steeper. They were covered with dry-looking grass and low twisted trees and scrub. Along some stretches the builders had chiseled down through the rock that stood to left and right. Its drilled-out cross sections showed striated sediments in pale shades of red and gray and brown, pale jewellike tones hidden for millennia deep in the earth.

He grew worried again, and not only about his daughter. The

gauge had started out full, since the staff at the pharma plant had filled the tank. He'd refueled in Spokane, from the UPS truck. But as the day went on the needle seemed to fall faster and faster. Obviously, there wasn't as much energy in the pale pink ersatz gasoline.

He slowed to fifty to stretch whatever was left. The highway stayed empty, the valleys picturesque but still deserted. He didn't pass any towns, or signs for any kind of rest stop, plaza, or wayside. And steadily the hills grew more rugged, steeper, the rock cuts deeper, the valleys narrower and tiding with shadow. The air grew chillier too; he must be gaining elevation.

The low-fuel light glared orange. He pulled over and kicked the stand down. Swung his legs off, and stretched the kinks out of back and legs. Massaged his aching butt. Then poured the contents of both two-liter bottles glug-glugging into the tank.

The warning light dimmed slowly, as if reluctant. This amount probably wouldn't take him much farther. He pulled back onto the road, and a few minutes later spotted a side road that looked like it might lead to a forest service facility. Instead it dead-ended at a graveled turnaround. He had to skid to a halt, wheel the heavy bike around, and gun it back to the highway.

Another worry: the spray-painted notations on the highway were rising again, climbing once more as he pushed east.

Yeah, now he remembered. Some of StratCom's missile fields had been north of here. The numbers quickly reached 150 millirems per hour. Granted, that was last week's reading, but radiation didn't decay all that fast. Actually, it depended on what isotopes were in the fallout, but he had no clue to its composition.

If he was stranded out here for any length of time—say, from running out of gas and having to walk—he could easily absorb a really dangerous, even a fatal, dose. For the hundredth time he wished for some kind of dosimeter or counter. But aside from the staff at the evacuee camp, who'd worn badges, he hadn't seen anything like that since leaving the ship.

At long last, west of Butte, he spied a sign for a truck stop. He swung off at Ramsay. As he coasted in, though, a heavy stink of death, of sweetish rotten meat, met his nostrils. A miasma so massive and choking he could barely breathe.

The truck stop building was locked, so he rolled on through the town, a small, rectilinear burg of neatly kept homes. Modest houses with attached garages, a nice mid-American town, but oddly lacking any stores or factories or other visible sign of economic activity.

But no one was home. The short hairs rose on the back of his neck. He was remembering old films, old shows. Zombies and body snatchers, *Stranger Things* and *The Postman* and *The Walking Dead*. A weird combination of the frightening and the long-familiar. The absolute silence didn't help, nor did the thick, cloying stench. No dogs barked as he chugged down the main street, keeping it under forty, made a right, and rolled past the high school. He spotted a black-and-yellow shelter sign, and pulled into the principal's space. A sign taped to the inside of the front office window read LEFT FOR SISTER EVAC CITY ROCK SPRINGS WY and gave a phone number.

The door with the shelter sign was closed but unlocked. He groped his way down concrete steps to the basement, but had to halt there. No light, but the dank nose-twitching smells of mildew and long-dead mice were at least a change from the rotten-meat stink up in the sunlight.

Back in the saddle . . . rolling past a soccer field, its grass deserted, the nets hanging limply in the quiet sunlight. The only movement anywhere was that of the crows, who fluttered up from the pavement as he approached, and cackled noisily back down, cursing him out behind his back after he passed. They were eating what had at first looked like spilled grain on the road. But when he got closer he saw it was the carcass of some large animal, so flattened and smeared out he couldn't even tell what it had been. Not human. At least, he didn't think so.

He'd expected to leave the rotting scent behind as he got out onto the highway again, but instead it grew even heavier. He pushed on a mile or two, suppressing his gag reflex. The odor kept thickening, until it seemed to be physically slowing the bike, the air itself denser and more resistant to any passage.

Until he saw its source at last.

They lay in rows, as if felled that way. Penned in wire enclosures, overlooked by elevated walkways. Grotesquely swollen, red-brown and white hides puffed out like balloons, mouths gaping open. Black clouds of flies milled above them, the massed buzzing audible even over the mutter of his engine as he puttered past. He couldn't tell if they'd been shot, or gassed, or killed in some other way, but the cattle lay in windrows, hundreds of them, thousands, past a sign that proudly proclaimed MONTANA'S PREMIER CATTLE AUCTION HOUSE, *open Tuesday with sales on Friday for feeder calf and yearling steers and heifers in the fall, October through December.*

Okay, so it had to be the truck stop. He bumped across the divider, U-turned, and headed back.

The doors were shatterproof Lucite, but a heaved-with-a-grunt concrete block got him through a plate glass window overlooking the fuel pumps. The interior smelled dank, and the floor tiles were stained, as if something had leaked and dried and never been cleaned up. He used the toilet, though there was no water pressure to wash with, then browsed the sale aisle. Motor oil. Plastic jerricans that would fit in the saddlebags. Yeah, he needed to extend his range. Tire pump. Blue plastic tarp. Bungees. Patch kit. Maps. Flares. He didn't want to be a looter, but he needed this stuff, and no one seemed to be around.

He jimmied open the manager's desk with a screwdriver, found a loaded stainless Ruger .38, and tucked it into his belt. Montana seemed more deserted than threatening, but still he felt more secure with the revolver's weight dragging at his pants.

The food aisle . . . somebody had plundered it before evacuating, but he found canned Vienna sausages and onion Pringles. He munched them sitting at the table in the little café, washing it down with a warm Pepsi. Shades of *The Road* . . . He tried the telephone on the wall, hoping to call Blair, but the line was dead. And of course his cell registered no bars.

By now it was dark outside. He wished again for some way to measure the radiation he must be accumulating. The contamination here had been so severe the authorities had put down thousands of valuable cattle. But he couldn't think of any detection method.

The same protective measures you applied on shipboard, then. Keep to interior spaces. Close the doors. The building had been locked up, sealed against the fine radioactive dust to that extent, at least. A roll of duct tape and some cardboard patched the window he'd broken.

He discovered a discreet little bunkroom in back that long-haul truckers must have rented by the night, before the big freights had gone full driverless. The bunk beds were sagging, obviously hardused, but better than the concrete floor. He wedged towels under the door. Covered himself with a thick layer of on-sale sweatshirts. And lay there in the dark until it took him as well.

THE next day he rose at dawn, and shaved with bottled water. He deployed a hand pump from the store to fill his tank and two of the jerricans with gas from the buried fuel tanks. He crammed the Honda's top case with quarts of oil and Slim Jims and Lance ToastChee and Little Debbie fig bars. He left two of the tissue-thin hundreds on the counter to pay for his purchases, though it seemed a meaningless gesture.

The sun greeted him in long golden glints across the mountains, glowing off the dew-shining pavement as he hit sixty and then seventy. More confident now on the bike, pushing it harder.

Butte looked as deserted and abandoned as Spokane had been. The strikes on the missile fields to the north must have smeared a deadly plume across some of the most productive grazing lands in the country. No doubt the cattle in his wake weren't the only livestock to be put down. There'd be meatless days for a lot of Americans in the year to come. Maybe grainless days as well.

But in every nuclear-disaster movie he'd ever seen, hadn't food been scarce? The gaunt survivors reduced to an endless crawl across a desert, fighting over each scrap of sustenance, each mouthful of drinkable water?

Maybe science fiction had forecast the future all too accurately.

The spray-painted readings stayed steady for an hour, then started to rise again. Two hundred an hour. Two fifty. Not long after, an irregular structure poked up ahead. He rolled off the throttle, steered to center lane, and coasted in.

The roadblock was makeshift, two trailers parked across the lanes. Large hand-lettered signs read ROUTE 90 CLOSED. DETOUR. Crooked arrows pointed to the right. But that turnoff was blocked as well. A few yards up the hill behind it, an American flag hung fluttering from a MECO boom truck. A dark bundle swayed gently in the breeze below it.

As he rolled to a halt men spilled from a faded green mobile home parked on the berm. They were in civilian clothes, sheepskin coats and cowboy hats, and carried hunting rifles. Some had huge Western-style hoglegs in holsters strapped to their thighs. All wore flu masks and the red, white, and blue–blazoned armband of the Mobilized Militia.

A bearded older man with wild white hair stepped out last. He held up a palm and slashed a finger across his throat, pointing to the bike. Dan kicked the stand down and cut the ignition. The throaty roar of eighteen hundred cubic centimeters died, leaving an echoing silence and a high keening in his ears.

"Mornin', amigo," the old man said, ambling up. He scanned him up and down with a white phone-sized device, gaze lingering on his boots, while Dan waited. At last he snapped the counter off. "Warm, but not hot. ID, if you don't mind. Sorry to tell ya, 90's closed between here and Hardin. Heavy alpha contamination. Where we bound today?"

"I'm headed cross-country."

"I see that. Nice old bike. Headed where?"

"Basically, just east from the Seattle area. I'm due in Washington in a few days."

Two more men with shotguns came out of the mobile home and ranged themselves behind the trailer. They leaned against it, watching him, pulling their masks down, and lighting up what looked like hand-rolled smokes.

"Goin' in the wrong direction for Washington," the old man observed mildly, examining his ID.

"I mean Washington, DC."

"ID says Navy. That a Navy uniform you got on under there?"

He was still in khakis, though the windbreaker was from the truck stop. "That's right."

"Got orders? Registration for that there machine?"

"I'm traveling under message orders. Nothing on paper I can show you, if that's what you want. And the bike, I uh—bought it." For the first time, he wondered if he should have asked for some kind of receipt. But it hadn't seemed like anyone would be asking, in the aftermath of a nuclear laydown.

"Bought it. Says here you're a captain. Captain of what?"

A younger man joined them, in a tan barn coat and an Army battle dress cap, though he was in jeans and boots. Actually Dan was still an admiral, though only for the duration, but there didn't seem any point in explaining that. His ID, indeed, still carried him as an O-6. "Captain is a rank," he said patiently. "Equivalent to an army colonel. I'm headed for DC for my next assignment, and looking for my daughter on the way. Last anyone saw of her, she was leaving Seattle with a load of medicine, headed east on 90. In a truck. A lot of motorcyclists were riding with her. I'm not sure why. Seen anything like that?"

The old man tucked Dan's ID into his own side pocket and gestured to the mobile home. "No sir, can't say I have. We carrying today?"

"Got a .38 in the saddlebag. I'd like my ID back?"

"Actually, I 'spect you might could be a deserter," the old man said mildly.

"We hang deserters," said the younger one, unzipping his coat and suddenly fast-drawing a .45 from a leather holster. He pointed it and thumbed the hammer back. "Let's have the gun, mister. Carefully. Slow."

Suddenly the bundle hanging limply from the boom truck made sense. Close up, Dan could make out a boot hanging off one of its feet.

He raised his hands and nodded to the saddlebag. "The one on the right. You can take it out. But I'm not a deserter. I'm Captain Daniel Lenson, US Navy, on compassionate leave, looking for my daughter. I've been fighting in the Pacific for the last four years. You sure none of your men have seen her? She was in a refrigerator truck with about thirty Berzerkers. Kind of hard to miss, I would think."

"Oh, we don't miss much out here," said the old man equably. He nodded to the mobile home again. "Lot's changed since the war, Captain. I'm Colonel Rutter, Silverbow M&Ms. Come on, get down off that hog. Keep your hands where we can see 'em. We'll get you checked out, see if you're who you say you are."

"Better hope so," the younger man said.

"Take it slow, Derek," the old man told the younger one. "Not everybody's a antiwa or a looter. Captain here could be just who he allows to be."

Moving carefully, keeping his hands in sight, Dan dismounted and followed the old man. The "colonel." He lurched a bit, unused to walking after the hours of riding. The younger man, Derek, fell in behind. From time to time the muzzle of the .45 dug into Dan's back. "I hope you have that safety on," he said over his shoulder. But the guy didn't answer, just prodded him again, harder.

For the first time it occurred to him that though the old man sounded country friendly, he might really be in shit city here.

Inside a radio was tuned to the Patriot News. The announcer was blustering, bullying, pouring contempt on someone whose name Dan didn't recognize. Through a window, he glimpsed a so-lar array sparkling in the sun behind the trailer. A woman sat at a notebook computer. Smoke from one of the hand-rolleds curled up from a tray. "Can we run this boy, please, Angela," Rutter said, handing her Dan's ID. "Says he's on leave from the service."

Dan started over to the desk, curious what database they were accessing, but was steered away by Derek's pincer-grip on his shoulder and pushed down onto a plastic chair that looked like it had come out of a waiting room. The younger man stood over him, still pointing the .45.

"Y'like some coffee?" Rutter said, pouring himself a cup at a side table. "Guess we can spare a mug, for one of our fightin' men."

"If he really is one," Derek said, hovering like a concerned parent. Only he looked more threatening than concerned.

Dan said, "Sure, I could use a cup. Black is fine."

It was hot and strong and for a moment the little cramped trailer seemed almost hospitable. Until he looked out the window again, and saw more clearly what was swinging in the wind behind the array. Traitors. Deserters. *Looters*—with his top case jammed to the brim with what he'd taken from the truck stop . . .

"Fugitive from the Zone," the old man said, letting himself down into a worn armchair opposite Dan. "Guy out there, I mean. He showed up on the list, we judged him, took the appropriate action. Now. You said, your daughter."

Dan cleared his throat and looked away from the window. ". . . Yeah. She's a medical researcher. From Seattle. She rescued a pro-duction run of a new antiflu drug—"

"For the Chinese flu?" Rutter said. "That's hittin' pretty hard some places, I hear. About time they come up with something for that."

"—For the Chinese flu. Yeah. She's taking it east for distribu-tion, I think. The pharma manager said she was being escorted by a local motorcycle gang. Only apparently she never arrived wher-ever she was going. According to FEMA, and Archipelago, and whoever else ought to know. I'm trying to find her, or find out what happened to her."

The woman at the computer murmured something inaudible. Rutter twisted in his chair, then turned back to Dan. "Sounds like you're not where you're supposed to be, Captain. This says you're aboard a USS *Savo Island*, out of Norfolk, Virginia."

"Your database is way out of date. *Savo* left the East Coast before the war, and I left her about a year after the war started. I'm on leave now. I told you that."

The old man nodded understandingly. "But all we got is your word for it."

"Then contact the CNO's office. The chief of naval operations. They know me and where I am. That's who I'm reporting to in DC." A suspicion flared. "Do you really have connectivity? Or is that a freestanding database?"

He started to get up, but Derek moved menacingly to block him. "Don't worry about any of that, Captain," Rutter said. "We make our own minds up, out here."

One of the guys from outside pushed in through the door. He wasn't quite as gray as Rutter, but wasn't all that much younger. Actually, though he was more weathered, he looked to be about Dan's age. He leaned his shotgun in a corner and came over, taking off his hat. Regarding Dan with a bemused gaze from above his mask.

Dan nodded back, but the guy kept staring. Finally he said, "Lenson."

"Right. And you're—?"

"Simo Hardin." The man pulled down his mask. "From *Reynolds Ryan*. You were my division officer. First Division."

"Holy smoke. *Hardin*," Dan said, taking his hand as a rush of memory overwhelmed him.

His very first ship. The old destroyer, worn even beyond her many years, laboring in the terrifying seas north of the Arctic Circle. Intercepting a submarine that shouldn't have been there. And at last, torn apart and sinking, when her sick and fatigued captain had made one single wrong rudder order.

It might have seemed coincidental, running into a member of that old crew here. But it happened often enough that when you ran into old shipmates, guys you'd served with or under or had commanded, it wasn't a shock. He cleared his throat. "That's right. Hardin. You were from out West, weren't you?"

"From Wyoming, but I live here now. Got out as a first class, and took over my dad's construction business. Until the war, anyway." To Rutter, Hardin said, "We were on a tin can that went down after a carrier ran over her. Why're you holding him, Colonel? This guy's the real deal. A senior officer, now, I hear. Pretty much a hero."

"Also a looter, and maybe a deserter," Derek sneered.

"Not this guy," Hardin told him. "He doesn't have it in him. He was the fucking straightest arrow aboard. We all hated him, back then. But we respected him too. Whatever he tells you, you can count on. Saw his name in the news, over the years. He's been everywhere. Shit, this guy's got the Medal of Honor. You assholes should be kissing his feet."

"Thanks . . . Simo," Dan said, a little overwhelmed. Remembering the moments of terror as *Ryan* had been torn apart, flaming, destroyed by her own, because of her deadly cargo.

Remembering, too, what he'd always wanted to know from back then. Such as, who'd tried to kill him on an icy deck one black and freezing night. He'd always suspected Slick Lassard and his pot-smoking deck gang. And hadn't Hardin been one of them?

But maybe this wasn't a good time to bring that up. "Yeah, great to see you. And thanks for your service. In the Navy, and, uh, the Mobilized Militia."

The woman at the computer murmured something else. Rutter squinted, face darkening under the white beard. He sighed heavily. Got up, hoisted his pants over his gut, and glanced toward the door. "Guess we don't have enough to hold you on. Since Simo here vouches for you. I'll put a pass notification up on our chat. If you hit another roadblock that might help.

"See, we got our own network. When the government dies, citizens got to step up. Like it was in the old days. But I might have some bad news for you too."

Dan rose. "Bad news," he repeated.

Rutter looked away. "From some ways east of here. Angela here did a search for what you told her. They found a woman . . . midtwenties . . . a body, over near Chadron. Suspected murdered by a guy on a motorcycle. They're still looking for him."

Dan reached for support as the trailer reeled around him. "What are you saying? Do they have . . . did they identify her?"

Rutter steadied him with a hand. "Angela asked. No ID on her. Real sorry to tell you this."

"Well, maybe it isn't—can we get a—a picture?"

The woman turned in her chair. She was older, crag-jawed, but her eyes were kind. "This here system is hard-wire routed. We don't have the bandwidth for pictures. I'm real sorry."

"Where is it?" he forced through numb lips. "Chadron, you said. Is that in Montana? I'll go there. And see for myself."

"You'll want the sheriff's department. And no, it's in Nebraska. Good ways east of here."

"That's a hard day's travel," Hardin said. "More like two, on that bike."

"And he can't take Route 90," the woman said. "It's still too hot to cross. Full body dose, the levels they're reporting, he'd be toast. Gonna have to jog south. Maybe through Yellowstone. Then pick it up again on the other side, around Sheridan, or take 25."

"Get his bike filled up," Rutter told Hardin. "Give him some water. And Derek, give him his pistol back. He might need it, out on those roads these days. Captain, I'm real sorry about all this. I wish we had better news for you."

Dan might have answered, but he wasn't focused on what was going on. He felt poleaxed, like one of the dead steers back in the feedlot.

He stumbled back out to the bike. Tried to concentrate, to listen, as Hardin gave him directions. The woman came out, carrying a road map. They fueled his bike, tucked MREs into his saddlebags, patted his back. From overtly hostile, they'd suddenly become almost like family. Even Derek bumped fists and wished him good luck.

Dan accepted it all in a dazed stupor, as if he were watching a golem controlled from elsewhere. The golem accepted things. Muttered thanks. Remembered directions. But didn't seem to be all there. He climbed back on the Honda and hit the start button. But, the starter didn't work anymore. He kicked it several times and at last it caught. The militiamen dragged the roadblock aside to let him take the turnoff.

When he looked back, in the little vibrating handlebar mirror, they were all looking after him, growing smaller and smaller, until they too were gone.

9

The Tian Shan Mountains, Western China

THE donkey had bitten Vlad twice, once on the thigh and once on the hand, when he'd thoughtlessly strayed his fingers too close to its mouth. The Hunza with him kept apologizing, but in his heart seemed to be relishing it.

The animal's rider had high Slav cheekbones, but he wasn't Slav. Nor Russian, despite his cover name. "Vladimir" was in his early thirties. His dark stubble was rimed with white frost from the altitude. His nose was straight and thin as a box cutter. He wore a long, heavy black wool greatcoat that could have been issued by the army of the tsars, but with high-tech hiking boots and gloves that in these mountains were barely warm enough. He spoke four languages and carried an SKS carbine slung over his back. His earflapped fur hat made him look like a mountain hunter. At least from a distance.

He didn't look American. But he was. A Ranger before the war, now Andres Korzenowski was with the Special Operations Group, Special Activities Division. A paramilitary operations officer, specializing in raids, sabotage, ambushes, and the other brands of unconventional mischief the Allies had fomented behind enemy lines in Tibet, Iran, China, and Mongolia.

"There it is, their camp," the Hunza said.

Andres shaded pale blue, deeply hooded eyes rimmed with broken blood vessels. "I don't see it," he said in Russian.

"It is designed not to be seen."

"Of course." Digging out a bulky pair of binoculars from inside his coat, he set them to electromagnetic and scanned the deep, rugged mountainside before them. Nothing. He toggled to IR and scanned again. Still nothing. "It is well hidden indeed. If it is here."

"It is, sir. Somewhere. I do not know exactly the spot. Our guide will tell us."

The donkey was twisting its head again, trying to get at his foot with those huge yellow teeth. Korzenowski pulled his boot back and with one heel kicked the beast in the ribs.

"Do not abuse my animal, sir," the Hunza protested.

"I've paid you enough for it. The damn thing bites."

"One that did not bite would not have the spirit to keep on."

His escort had guided him over the mountains. Unfortunately they'd been delayed by a rockslide. Then, again and again, by drone warnings on the device he carried in his greatcoat pocket. Each time it sounded a discordant whine they had to take shelter, finding nooks amid the rocks and drawing the crackly plastic IR/EM blanket over themselves. They'd lost another whole day when Andres's animal had decided to chew through his tether and make tracks. Only hunger, in these high, deserted, treeless wastes, had finally brought it reluctantly back to them.

But the end result had been that they'd missed the original rendezvous, a shepherd's hut far to the east. The man he was meeting seemed reluctant to reschedule, though. It had taken several calls on the satellite phone before he'd reluctantly set a new meeting point.

And now they were here. But no one was around to meet them.

Suddenly the Hunza, several yards ahead, extended a hand. Gestured downward, as if patting the air. Andres reined in his mount, carefully keeping fingers and feet clear, and shaded his gaze ahead.

Where figures rose from nothingness, emerging like ghosts from graves from tumbled rock and gravel and patches of snow, to assemble themselves into ragged but fit-looking fighters. Men in shalwar kameez and sheepskin coats, pakul hats and black scarves wound around bearded faces. Their rifles were pointed at the new arrivals.

The Hunza lifted his hands to the sky. But Andres kicked his mount forward, passing him. The rifles' muzzles tracked him. Conscious of the 9mm tucked inside the greatcoat, but knowing neither it nor the SKS would help much facing a dozen AKs, he spread his hands pacifically. *"Selamlar. Ben beklediginiz Ameri-kaliyim,"* he said, forcing confidence into his tone. I am the American you are waiting for. Turkish, not Uighur, but both being Turkic languages, they should get the gist. *"Hanginiz benim rehberim?"* Which one of you is here to meet me?

A bulkily built mujahid with a heavy beard lifted a hand warily. He had what Andres recognized as a Battelle antidrone rifle slung across his back. "I am Jusuf," he said in Han Chinese.

"I do not speak the language of the Han oppressors. I am called Vladimir. We can speak Russian if you like."

They compromised on his Turkish, which made the other mujs furrow their brows and rub their mouths, but seemed to get the main points across. Jusuf narrowed his eyes at the Hunza. He gestured at him. "We must shoot this one. We are not taking him to our camp."

"He guided me here. Do not kill him, I beg. I trust him."

"We don't. So. He must stay here and wait for your return."

This didn't seem to be a good place to argue, and he didn't need the guy until it was time to go back. Shrugging, he explained this to the Hunza, who looked relieved. Andres counted out two gold pieces, Krugerrands, surreptitiously into his palm. "I know it is not in our agreement, and you will have to camp here. Perhaps this will help pay for feed." The guy ducked his head, gaze locked on the shining metal. There, that wasn't so hard.

Andres turned to the stocky Uighur. "You will take me to Chief Oberg?"

The other hesitated. He held out a hand; mimed a handgun with thumb and forefinger.

Andres handed over the carbine. Another mimed trigger-pulling, pointing this time at his chest. He slid the Glock out of the shoulder holster and handed it over too.

The muj reached to the small of his back, and Andres tensed. But what he brought out was not a gun, but a wadded black cloth. Jusuf shook it out into a hood and held it out.

"You got to be kidding," Andres said in English. Then, in Turkish. But the guy kept holding it out, insisting, and the men holding the rifles stirred, murmuring among themselves.

Unwillingly, he pulled the heavy cloth over his head. It stank of mutton grease. Raw, dyed black wool. He couldn't see a fucking thing. His breath came hot, and he fought claustrophobia and gritted his teeth to steady himself.

Jusuf said, "Now I will take you to the Lingxiu."

WHEN they pulled the hood off him at last, after a long stumbling walk during which he was led by the hand, they stood at the bottom of a deep defile.

Jusuf carefully scanned the sky before motioning him forward. The opening was narrow and he had to duck under the shelving rock.

It was a cave. The entrance, overhung by the rock, must have been invisible from a hundred feet away, and no doubt from any prying eyes roving that high clear sky. One of thousands in these ancient, raddled mountains, here at the very roof of Asia. They stretched west and became the Karakoram, the fabled Black Mountains; the jeweled Pamirs; then the Hindu Kush, even farther west, in Iran. And the Himalayas, loftiest and most remote of all, to the south.

He'd seen a lot of the area in the past three years, winter, spring, fall, and summer, on foot and on skis. Fomenting, supplying, and financing unrest and rebellion in the most distant and isolated areas left on earth.

Now he girded himself for what promised to be a difficult conversation, with a man already a legend nearly on the scale of T. E. Lawrence and Orde Wingate.

As he straightened warily, a vast cavern gaped below him, twisting down into the earth like a bowel. Water dripped somewhere, echoing in the dim. The steeply slanted floor was studded with rocks that seemed to have been roughly rearranged into a slippery staircase. As he descended, choosing where to step next with intent care, the light receded above him. To either side poles had been wedged into the descent. The air grew colder as he went down. At first he thought the poles might be burned-out torches, set to light the way, though they weren't burning now.

But then, letting himself downward, braking his controlled slide with difficulty and coming very close to wrenching an ankle, he made out what was perched at the top of the stick. He grunted in surprise, and nearly slipped and fell before he regained his footing.

The darkened, twisted clump jammed atop the stick was a human head.

He stared into desiccated sardonic eyeballs for a full second before jerking his gaze back to the treacherous, lichen-spotted, already-sliding scree under his feet. Water dripped from overhead, cold, limestone-dank.

More sticks dotted the zigzagging path down, each topped with its macabre decoration. Some still wore caps.

Breathing deeply, mastering his fear as the air grew ever colder, the gloom ever darker, he concentrated on placing each boot on a surface that would not tilt or slip away beneath him. But found all too few that looked like anything solid enough to trust.

THE man he'd come to see hoisted himself with evident effort from beside a low table as Andres neared. A stocky woman in black from head to toe helped him up. The titanium brace the Agency had sent in on an earlier visit lay to the side, on a priceless-looking antique Bukhara carpet. As did a satellite phone. A Chinese-issue rifle stood propped against the cave wall. Torches flared and smoked, providing a fitful, inadequate illumination. The stink of kerosene fought with the wet-limestone cave-smell, along with what seemed to be a musky perfume.

SEAL Master Chief Teddy Harlett Oberg had not aged well. His skin was darker, seamed by sun and altitude. His hair and beard were much longer than Andres remembered. And a black eyepatch covered one side of his upper face. Well, it had been almost a year since they'd last met. Before Operation Jedburgh, when the American advisor had led his rebels against the Chinese missile base in the mountains far to the east.

That hadn't ended well at all.

"Teddy, good to see you," Andres said.

"*Sizga salaam.* Come in, come in," Oberg said, a bit hesitantly, as if he hadn't spoken English in a long time. He was swathed in heavy-looking sheepskins with a tatty gray blanket over his shoulders, and unlike the others, he was bareheaded. He spoke rapidly to the woman, in what Andres assumed was Han Chinese, and waved her away. Then limped forward and gripped his hand. The big guy, Jusuf, stayed on his feet, taking up a stand behind Oberg, one hand on his hip.

"Teddy, shit, your eye. What happened?"

Oberg shrugged and slapped his shoulder. "Hey, I got a spare. So, they tell me your guide was Hunza. But you know the Pakistanis bought them off. Turned them against us."

"Now that China's crumbling, they like us better. Enough to take our gold anyway."

"An offer they couldn't refuse?"

"More or less."

"And you rode in on a donkey?"

"Donkey, my ass. That thing's half alligator. Bit me twice on the way up."

They chuckled together. Oberg waved him to a place on the carpet. "Am I still calling you Vladimir?"

"Why not call me Andy. Now that the war's over."

"Andy, sure. Good."

Oberg called an order back into the cave, and they settled in for tea. The way every negotiation started in this part of the world. Yeah, they were both Yankees, but it still greased things along to spend a little time getting reacquainted.

Especially considering what he was going to ask.

The stocky woman and another, thinner, perhaps younger one—he couldn't tell much through the black cloth—brought brass trays laden with sweet thick chai and the date pastries called baklava in these remote mountains, though it wasn't like the Greek variety. The older woman poured; the younger one hovered until Oberg selected a cake, apparently at random, and handed it to her. She lifted her black hijab to take a large bite, and Andres caught a glimpse of youthful, pouting lips.

Andres toasted his host gravely with the blazing hot brass cup. "To victory. At last."

"Victory," Oberg said, but somehow his version didn't have the same savor. Maybe with a twist of lemon.

They sipped and Andres helped himself to a cake. Then another; there hadn't been much to eat on the trail up. He noticed his host didn't indulge.

"We'll have lamb and rice later," Oberg said, watching him. "I can move dinner up if you're really hungry."

"Whenever you had it planned for. Sort of a celebration?"

"No, just the regular meal. But I wanted you to get some face time with the rest of my leadership."

"Guldulla. Nasrullah. And the Hajji."

Oberg's eyes flickered, though the fingers that held the tiny brass cup did not move. "Thought I mentioned that in the after-action report. Nasrullah turned traitor on us. Had to be shot. And Hajji Qurban bought it on the raid." For some reason his hand wandered to his belt, where he wore an ornately hilted dagger.

"Oh yeah, you did report that. Too bad, he was a fighter."

"He certainly was that." Oberg smiled grimly, as if remembering something he both regretted and found pleasant. "And you already met Jusuf here."

"Right." The bearded young guy who'd carried the antidrone rifle. Who now, catching his name, bowed his head slightly and smiled.

They sipped again. As a muj brought another torch the shadow of one of the grisly-headed sticks tracked across the cavern wall. Shadows on a cavern wall, Andres mused. Undergraduate philosophy. Something from Plato . . .

Oberg caught his glance. "Guess you saw my garden gnomes, on the way down."

"Yeah. They're . . . intimidating."

"I keep 'em in a chest, packed in salt, so we can move them along with the HQ element. That kind of thing helps when we bring in the tribal chiefs for a little talk. Especially if they recognize somebody they knew. Who cooperated with the Han. Or didn't contribute his quota of young men to fight. We take them along when we visit a village, too. Post them in the square, once we shut the government cameras down and shoot the teachers and other officials."

Andres cleared his throat, increasingly uneasy but trying not to show it. The dank smell, the cold, the flickering flame-light. The immobile, shadowed features of the man sitting opposite. It all made for an unsettling feeling. Something pale glowed behind him, against the blackened wall of the cavern. Not a source of light, but reflecting the light. He couldn't quite make out what it was. "Uh, yeah, well . . . we need to talk about that kind of thing, Teddy. Seriously."

"You want a status report? We have almost two thousand effectives now. Two thousand trained rifles, with good comms and a dependable intelligence network. Contacts in every village. Intel coming in from every Han office that employs a local."

Oberg grinned in his beard and leaned to refill Andres's teacup. "We're ready to take this rebellion big-time, Andy. Last week we got our first squad-level desertion from one of the Internal Security divisions. Complete with all organic weapons and a ZTQ."

This was a light tank optimized for mountain fighting. Andres nodded. "Impressive."

"Oh, it's just the start. Han rule's crumbling out here. They're evacuating their families. The people always feared them, sure. But now the word's out they're not invincible, the tide's running our way fast. All we need is for you to double the level of support, and we can grab this whole province right out of Beijing's hands."

Andres said carefully, "Before we get to that, there are a couple of issues that concern us, Teddy."

"Shoot. Oh, here's Tok. You remember Tokarev? Given name, Guldulla?"

The lanky Uighur with the two-tone mustache. "Hello. Uh, *selamlar*. Yeah, I remember him. Your exec." They exchanged a limp handshake.

"Actually we sort of share the leadership now. But yeah, effectively." Oberg spoke rapidly to the Uighur, who nodded, gaze reflective on Andres. The lanky man folded himself down, drew an ornately engraved automatic from his belt, and placed it beside him on the carpet. Cocked.

Oberg went on, "So, you were saying. Issues that concern the Agency?"

"Uh, yeah. We're getting reports of massacres of civilians. Decapitating collaborators, and leaving the bodies in town marketplaces." He grimaced, trying not to look again at the grisly trophies staked around them. But he waved at them. "Which I see is true."

"Terror works," Oberg observed. "Nobody wants his head on a pole."

Glancing past him, suddenly Andres made out what the source of light was. A curved, reflective surface that seemed to writhe in the twisting orange glow of the torches. He'd seen it before, at the old camp west of here, where Oberg and Imam Akhmad had first received him, long ago, when it had been little more than a lair of petty bandits. An ancient scimitar. Rusty then, but now repolished to a gleaming glow. An arc of old steel, its surface smoothed, lovingly reground, no longer pitted. Hand-whetted to a gleaming sharpness. He jerked his gaze from that shining-keen edge and murmured, "Uh, granted . . . but what about these massacres?"

"Fake news. I mean, there's probably been some collateral damage. Sure. When we remove the police, the street monitors, the local judges and mayors and so forth—and they're pretty much all Han—the people feel free to take revenge for what the Han took from them. Land. Homes. Jobs." Oberg shrugged. "You can't lay that on ITIM, amigo. It's just the price of freedom. And yeah, it also encourages any of 'em that remain to pack up and leave town. But that's what we want, right?"

Andres drew a slow breath, trying to disguise his unease. Sometimes there were negotiations the negotiators didn't come back from. It would be all too easy for Oberg to behead *him.* Doubtful he'd end up on one of the poles, but his skull's ultimate disposition, probably under one of these piles of scree, wouldn't matter to him. By then. "Well, there's been some discussion back at Langley. About postwar plans, and how you fit into them."

The lanky Uighur had been following the exchange back and forth, though Andres was pretty sure he didn't have the English to extract much content. Now he said, in broken Russian, "Will you continue supplying ammunition?"

"Let me deal with him, Tok," Oberg said, patting the guy's hand, then letting his own rest on his fellow rebel's. He said to Andres, "Proceed," but his scarred features showed the beginnings of a scowl. "I really hope you're not thinking about selling us out, Andy. Like the Vietnamese or the Iraqis. The Afghan government, after we left it for the Taliban again. The fucking Kurds, holding the bag in Syria."

Andres said carefully, "Let me make one thing perfectly clear. No one's proposed abandoning ITIM in the field. But remember our original verbal contract, when the Agency agreed to fund and supply you . . . Do you remember that, Teddy? That we direct your operations?"

The other didn't respond, so after a beat he went on. "The end of the war means both our overall strategy and our tactics on the ground have to adjust. At the moment, all we have is an armistice. The peace talks are going on now, in Beijing. One of the demands from the other side is stopping our support for the separatist elements in Hong Kong, Tibet, and out here.

"So we have to prepare. Get our ducks in a row. You said to me once, 'the world changes.' Well, it's changing under us now. We have to shift our focus. From defeating the enemy at all costs, to building some kind of postwar order."

Oberg nodded, and for a moment Andres thought the guy was going to see reason. But then he said, "I think I'm getting it. So you can use us as a bargaining chip. Or as a threat. 'Make peace, or we detach Xinjiang.' Or, 'Play nice, and we'll give you these nasty bandits for you to disappear.'"

Andres shifted on the carpet, suddenly aware of sweat trickling beneath his armpits despite the wine-cellar chill. He pulled the greatcoat a little tighter. "That's a cynical way to look at it. And untrue. Rest assured, we're not hanging any of our allies out to dry. Including irregulars. But we have to look at those end states that are achievable, and that might contribute to a stable postwar Asia."

"Does that include independence for Tibet? For Taiwan? For Turkistan?"

"That'll be the subject of the negotiations," Andres said, only half lying. His instructions had been quite clear: Make no hard promises. But he *could* utter half-truths, in order to wrap up this mission.

And Theodore Oberg was very definitely a loose end. ITIM had tied down six Internal Security divisions and over a hundred combat and transport helicopters by the end of the war. A huge contribution to the war effort, and probably one reason the invasions of Taiwan and South China had succeeded.

But the administration, and the Allied heads of state steering committee, were still undecided on what form the Beijing government would take following the treaty. Multiparty, certainly, with both the KMT and DPP from Taiwan and the DP and NPP from Hong Kong guaranteed the opportunity to participate. But whether a unitary state or a federation was still up in the air, as was whether Taiwan would go its own way or rejoin the mainland at last. Tibet, too, would probably have the opportunity to decide to stay or go, most likely in a plebiscite.

But this guy didn't need to know the big picture. Andres said carefully, "Whatever the politicos think at the moment, Master Chief—"

"Lingxiu," Oberg corrected him.

"—Lingxiu, of course. Whatever they think right now, ITIM may well be asked to participate in the final settlement. We'd want a rep in Beijing for that. Maybe Guldulla here? For obvious reasons—"

"Right, it can't be me." The Lingxiu nodded heavily, and at last permitted himself a date cake. He spoke at length to the stocky woman again, who bowed deeply and left.

Guldulla spoke then, but in Uighur. Andres could catch only a word here and there. Oberg noticed his frown and translated. "Tok says we will not remain part of the People's Empire. The ITIM wants full independence. Not to be part of a federation, still taking orders from the Han. If Tibet is to be free, Taiwan to be free, Xinjiang must be free as well. We can't compromise on some kind of halfway house. Or trust that ten years down the line, the Han won't be back. They are like . . . they are like something on goats, I think he's saying. Fleas? Worms?"

Andres said, "There are still a lot of Han in Xinjiang, Lingxiu."

"Fewer every week," Oberg said, grinning, and the wavering torch-flame threw a grisly shadow once more. "Give us a free hand, and they'll all leave. Go back where they came from. East of the Taklamakan, east of the Altun Shan. If you want to weaken China for good, detach Tibet and Xinjiang, with their mineral resources. We'll promise you airbases and a defense treaty. This is the heart of Asia. From here, you can dominate the continent."

The agent eased a breath out and sat back, reconsidering. The

guy thought big, all right. In one way, it was a glittering opportunity. But America wasn't interested in central Asia anymore. If it
ever really had been. Weakened, bankrupt, facing famine, with the
lid barely held down on the South and Midwest. With a crippled
nationwide electrical grid, grainfields poisoned with radioactivity,
rival militias clashing in Missouri and gangs the only functioning
government in LA, Washington was in no mood to seek an expensive hegemony half a world away. An end to the war, at nearly any
cost, was the most likely reading.

But he only said aloud, "It's a grand vision, but I don't know if
the Agency could commit to that, Lingxiu. It's way above both our
pay grades anyway."

"Will you take it up the line? Run it past whoever you report to.
See if it flies. I think it might."

"It doubt it will, even if I take it up the chain," he said, seeing an
opportunity. "But if *you* could . . ."

The other stiffened in the dim. "If *I* could?"

Andres shifted on the carpet again. Sweat trickled, and he
hoped the strain wasn't showing on his face. "Teddy, let me put
this to you straight." He nodded to the lanky mujahid, who had
been following the conversation, face unreadable. Then to the
younger one, who was scowling, glaring down at the low table.
"We want to send Guldulla to Beijing. But we need you to come
home and report. Brief us on the local politics. Give us expert
insight. How realistic an independent Xinjiang . . . or if you want
to call it Turkistan . . . could be. Argue that grand vision. Help us
craft the peace."

He leaned forward and tapped the other's knee. "And the deal
we mentioned last time I was here? Back pay. Combat bonus. Get
your leg fixed, the right way. Get that eye looked at. A senior position with the Agency, if you want it. Desk officer for central Asia.
Did you read that letter I gave you, the one from your old girlfriend? What was her name—Salena? You can have your life back.
A good life. A better one than here."

The two Uighurs looked to Oberg. Andres wasn't sure how much of the exchange they were following. Probably enough to know what he wanted.

"I already told her, the guy she knew is dead," Oberg said heavily. He snapped his fingers at the women. The younger one hurried forward, picked the tray up, and carried it off, bare feet slapping moist rock. The older one stayed, motionless against the cave wall, like a caryatid carved of coal. "A lot has changed here, Andy. Even since you first came out. You want to extract me?"

"To help us out. And to help ITIM out."

He spoke rapidly to the others, who listened with visages of granite. They answered in monosyllables. Oberg turned back to him. "Guldulla will go to Beijing. But I will not return to the United States. Not until Turkistan is independent. And maybe not even then."

Andres shifted uneasily, restraining the urge to fidget. The darkness seemed to close in. The heavy kerosene stink, the basement-smell of the cave. The aftertaste of strong boiled tea. He eyed the cocked pistol. Tokarev's automatic, an arm's reach away across the carpet. But when he looked up the muj was smiling sardonically at him. He picked up the handgun and set it down on his other side, away from Andres.

"I have a question for you, Andy," Oberg said gently, pincering something from his beard and examining it. Then flipping it away into the dark. "Does the Agency pass our location to the Han?"

"What? No. Never." As far as he knew anyway. He tried to make his outrage convincing. "Why would you think that?"

"Because someone knew about our meeting point last time. And sent a quick-reaction force after us."

Andres met that pale blue eye. "That's kind of paranoid, Teddy. Lingxiu. Or whatever you've decided to call yourself these days. We don't burn our assets."

"You sure about that?"

"Look, whatever you've done here, and you've done more than we asked, way more than anyone could have imagined, you're still in the Navy. A SEAL obeys orders. This is an order. We're pulling you out."

"The asset you knew is dead." The other smiled grimly, and struggled to his feet. Without the brace his foot twisted awkwardly when he put weight on it. It had to hurt like hell, but nothing showed on the seamed, wind-roughened face. The pale blue eye was cold. Remote. As if seeing something that wasn't there. "Do you believe in God, Andy?"

"In *God*? As in, in God we trust? Not really. Why?"

"In Allah?"

"Definitely not in Allah." He grinned, unsure if the other was joking, but got no wink or smile in return. Instead all three men stared at him, and each one's expression was exactly the same. Each bearded visage, the same. Setting aside differences in age and conformation of the underlying bone, he seemed to be looking at three iterations of the same face. Intent. Determined. Fanatical.

"He gave me a mission." Oberg grinned, a terrible grimace to see, but still, a grin. "Sounds nutty-fuck, right? Yeah. I fought it for a long time. Told myself it was some kind of hallucination. A high-altitude psychosis. Or just being so fucking hungry for so fucking long, up there in the Altun Shan, after we escaped from Camp 576."

"You can't mean that," Andres said. He dusted crumbs from his coat. This was getting beyond him. He'd come to get the guy back in the fold. Extract him, like an infected tooth. Not . . . whatever this was turning into. Some kind of theological chess match. A shadowy, ominous, demented debate deep in the darkness, in the heart of the earth.

"But it was real. You can't look away from something that feels that . . . absolute. Y'see, that whole free will thing, that's something we just got wrong. There's no free will. There's no such thing as chance, either."

Andres felt disoriented, as if he were losing his equilibrium. And for some unclear reason, suddenly angry. "You're saying, it's all predetermined. Set in stone. Right from the get-go?"

Oberg spread his hands. His voice took on an incantatory

monotone, like this was something he'd chanted again and again, like a mantra, or maybe rehearsed again and again in his head, since he had no one out here to speak English with. "It's already happened, partner. It's like, cast in glass from the beginning of the fucking universe. We're all one creation. All one piece. Everything that's happening, already has. Everything we see. Everything we do. Us, and everybody else. We do His will. Because that's all we can do. His will."

Andres shifted on the carpet, looking into the guy's face. Yep. Just . . . plain . . . nuts. "So let me get this straight. These killings, cutting off heads, all these murders—they're God's will? Allah's will? Not yours, because you're so fucking far off the reservation you don't even have a map back?"

Whoa. Too blunt, Andres. The truth, but he'd put it way too frankly.

His hand itched for his Glock. But it wasn't there.

Oberg hesitated, as if in thought; then nodded. And without having been spoken, his agreement hung there in the dank air. Until finally he added, "I know how it must sound, but that's how it fucking is. So I won't be extracting. Just to get that straight."

"You still need . . . medical help. Your leg. Your eye. We can make it a short visit, to get that taken care of. Then you can come right back, and—"

"I'm not going back with you," the leader of the rebels said. "And I don't need 'help.' Take my offer to Langley. Get them to think about it. This place shouldn't be part of China. We owe it to these people, the ones who fought for us. Tell your bosses what we can win here. Mineral resources. Rare earths. Forward bases. Strategic depth. The heart of Asia. It's all on the table. All they have to do is say yes."

He held out a hand. After a moment, Andres took it. The others stood too, smiled, and extended their hands as well. He tried to disguise his relief. Apparently he was going to be allowed to leave, instead of getting salted away.

But he still couldn't be absolutely sure.

He sat through the dinner, putting on as hearty a face as he could manage, though the lamb and rice congealed in his stomach. Afterward, Guldulla showed him to the guest room: a side cavern. A stone-faced guard squatted on a rock just outside its entrance, wrapped in a sheepskin and leaning his AK against the cave wall.

HE lay sleepless for a while, apprehensive in the dark. Gripping a sharp stone—the only weapon available—in one hand. But he was exhausted. Every limb and joint ached from days on the donkey. The heavy meal didn't help. Eventually his head sagged.

He came awake sometime in the deep night, at the whisper of bare feet over rock.

A breath in the dark, and the scent of perfume. Cloth rustled, and someone plucked the blanket up.

He groped for the rock. Found it, gripped it, ready to swing and hammer. To defend himself against the assassin.

Instead she slid in close beside him, and covered them both with the blanket. She lay there silently for several minutes. Then her hands searched until they found him, under the blanket.

He resisted for a time, then gave in.

THE next morning he munched naan bread spread with a piquant fig jam around a shielded fire. But Oberg never showed. None of the other leaders seemed to be around either. His unease returned. It didn't help when the hood came out again. They covered his head, and rough hands shoved him up the slippery not-quite-a-staircase toward what he hoped was the exit. He thought about asking for his guns back, the carbine and the Glock, but decided not to push it. He could always get others.

It would be all too easy for him just to disappear.

Hours later, hours in the stumbling dark of the blindfold, he stood motionless in the wind. High in the open air, unable to see, but he sensed emptiness around him. He stood shivering in the cold for a long time before feeling sure he was alone. Finally he reached up and touched the hem of the hood lightly. No one objected. Panting, he jerked it off his head.

Rock. He was circled by walls of tormented rock, and roofed by a brazen sky.

Not far away, a donkey brayed, the sound distorted by echoes but recognizable. He scrambled to a rise, and saw with dawning relief where he was. Just above the valley where he'd left the Hunza guide and the bite-happy donkey. He was overjoyed, now, to see them both.

He breathed out, accepting that he'd survived. Relieved. Though not eager to take back the news that he'd failed. But at least he still had a head on his shoulders. At least he could still make his report. And tell them the bad news.

Teddy Oberg was a spent asset.

10

Camp Pendleton, California

HECTOR sits on the sidelines, watching the smooth white sphere arc back and forth. The players are evenly matched, and the steady, rhythmic clicks as the ball shuttles this way and that are reassuring. Hypnotic. He can close his eyes and almost, for a while, forget.

The Corps calls it the Wounded Warrior Regiment. It's like a hospital, but not exactly. The division sent him here after the hospital ship got him off the ventilator and, eventually, okayed him for air travel.

The Wounded Warriors live in hundreds of mobile homes lined up in ranks behind the headquarters building at Pendleton. The trailers were trucked in and set up fast and cheap to house the thousands of casualties streaming back from the Pacific. There's not much going on to keep everyone occupied, though. Some local folks, mainly vets, widows, and older people, retirees Hector figures, have organized outings for the recovering troops. Softball games, trips to San Diego, picnics on the beach. Donated money to send them sports equipment, like the Ping-Pong table here in the rec room.

He went on one of the outings a week ago, to San Onofre. The same town he and his School of Infantry squad went to on liberty, years ago, before shipping out. Back then the gate had been blocked with orange Jersey barriers, HESCO bastions, and concertina. JLTVs with mounted .50s had overlooked it, while armed sentries paced the flanks, frowning down at the new Marines as they ambled out on their first liberty.

Now those barriers were gone, dismantled. Instead, two lone guards snapped to attention, saluting the veterans as they walked and limped and crutched and wheeled past toward the waiting buses.

When they reached the beach, the guys who could walk were assigned to bungalows. The ones who couldn't had special tents, right down on the shore. The people running the rec area had set up for a campfire that night, and after a cookout with hot dogs and chips and pizza and macaroni salad and even a thirty-two-ounce can of Bagby each, a guitarist had led a sing-along.

But he left shortly after it started, and walked down the beach alone. Looking up at the stars as they wheeled down to die in the sea. Listening to the surf. A siren song that was chilling, unpleasant, because it took him back to Itbayat, where his company had been pinned down and almost wiped out.

He'd watched the moon glittering on the waves.

Glittering, above their faces . . .

He didn't want to. But he couldn't help it.

He looked down, into the water. And there they were.

Some were waving to him. Others had their mouths open wide. The ones who hadn't made it. They seemed to be shouting, but he couldn't hear their words. Anyway, he knew what they wanted.

They missed him.

They wanted him with them.

He stood watching them for a long time, there in the wind from the sea, and at last waded out. In his boots. In his MARPATs. Out into the surf.

He hesitated as the cold reached his crotch. Drew a breath, shuddering.

Now they sounded closer. A distant but definitely more distinct murmuring. Though he still couldn't quite make out the words. Maybe a little closer . . .

He took another few steps into the rolling surf. Now the sea was at his chest.

The moon glittered on the waves, sparkling like diamonds, cold as rimefrost.

He took another step, and suddenly the bottom caved away beneath his boots. He sucked a breath just before his head went under. Flailed, beating at the water, and clawed himself back up to the air.

He broke the surface gasping, unable to stay down, yet struggling to keep his nose above the water. Suspended. Between. The sea icy cold. Numbing. He'd never been a good swimmer. Failed the test in boot camp. Except back then, at the start of the war, it'd been impossible to fail. You just got kicked back to the Booger Squad, to do it all over again. Until finally they gave up and shipped you out anyway.

Fifty yards out, sculling desperately to keep his head above water against the steadily increasing pull of wet boots and soaked cloth, he stared out to sea, out over toward the far Pacific, remembering.

A voice lifted behind him. Higher, clearer than the rest. For a moment he thought it was Lieutenant Ffoulk, then remembered: she was dead, shot by a sniper while they were hauling down the flag in Taipei. Her head haloed instantly with a pink mist.

An icy crest rolled over him, submerged him, and he came up even less buoyant, gasping, sputtering. The voice called again, more urgently. A woman's. So maybe it *was* Ffoulk. Or Orietta.

Maybe now, so close to rejoining the ranks of his dead, he could finally hear them clearly . . .

He cocked his head, splashing, coughing, choking on new mouthfuls of salty sea in the gathering darkness. No, it wasn't

Ffoulk. Somebody was yelling at him. From back on the shore. "Hey you! Out there in the water!"

He sculled around, mind still roiling, to a sight that instantly cleared it. He stopped fighting then, staring instead, and instantly started to slip under.

The woman was shedding her clothes as she ran, tossing away her uniform blouse. Kicking away her boots. Then bending, stripping off trousers. Until, all but naked, pale-radiant in the moonlight, she arched like a dolphin over a breaker and plunged into the surf. Her head emerged a moment later, as she shook out long dark hair, then jabbed at the sea in a savage crawl.

Toward him. He floated there, flummoxed, gaping at her until the ocean flooded his mouth and choked him again and he snapped it closed, sputtering. She ducked under a roller and emerged again. Her back glowed in the moonlight. The sea seemed to glow around her as she thrashed through it. It seethed with a greenish-yellow silent luminosity, a phosphorescent torpedo-wake as she plunged forward, turning her face upward at every alternate stroke to draw breath.

When she reached him, she yelled something uninterpretable, and grabbed his shoulder.

Before he could react she punched him hard in the gut, doubling him and emptying his lungs. She spun him as he choked and sputtered, circling his neck with a muscular forearm. Then she began towing him back toward shore with powerful, downward-thrusting chops of her free arm.

He fought her, dragged willy-nilly along on his back, but his flailing fists encountered only the unresisting sea. After a few more futile thrashes and useless jerks he sagged, winded. Gave up and lay back, letting her tow him along with those powerful one-armed strokes, tireless as a tugboat.

At last his dragging heels brushed a foothold. A sandbar, a few yards out from the beach. She relaxed her grip and let him find his footing. The sand caved softly, yielding under his heels. The surf battered them, nearly knocking him down.

She steadied him with a hand on his arm, regarding him in the blanched light of the full moon. "Y'okay?" she gasped.

"Uh . . . yeah. You . . . anyway. Thanks."

"Looked like you were. In trouble. Out there," she panted out, still winded. "Sorry I . . . had to punch you. If I hadn't, you'd've grabbed me. Drowned us both." She let go and bent too, hands on knees, sucking in air. They leaned together now, bracing each other as another comber hit them, like a couple of drenched linemen.

When it passed on he blinked salt sting from his eyes and saw her clearly for the first time. In the moonlight, the wet bra and white panties were transparent. He gazed at goose-pimpled arms, little erect nipples, hard muscular arms, a dark delta at the crotch. Sturdy thighs and stockinged feet. Dark hair straggling down over above a face oval, yet almost masculine, with a taut jaw and black eyebrows that nearly met in the center. He shivered in the cold, gaze riveted to dark eyes.

She held him at arm's length, regarding him too with a cool yet still worried expression. "Carlina Farnaccio."

"Hector Ramos. Second of the Third."

"A marine."

"Yeah . . . you?"

"Navy. Corpsman. I gave you your Chink Flu meds when you got here, remember? At least I think that was you."

"I don't remember . . . wasn't in such great shape."

"No, a lot of you really aren't." Grabbing his wrist, she led him toward the shore. Tossing back, "What the fuck're you doing out there anyway? This isn't the swimming beach. Aren't you afraid of sharks?"

"I just . . . felt like it."

"Out here, all alone. You weren't having intrusive thoughts?" Leading him up toward the dunes, she suddenly reverted to some kind of clinical mode. "You weren't trying to—?"

"Huh? Oh. No, fuck no. I was just cooling off."

"Well, looks like it worked. You're shivering pretty bad," she said. As they reached the trail of her clothes, she bent to pick them up. "Jeez . . . I'm gonna be wearing sandpaper the rest of the night." But instead of pulling them on, she felt his forehead, like a mother checking on a fevered child. "Wow. You're really hypothermic . . . Here, let's lay down. Out of the wind."

She smoothed her clothes down on the sand, like a patchwork blanket, between the waving grasses. He relaxed obediently. She knelt, then slithered forward, covering him with her nearly naked body. "I better warm you up. Body heat, you know?"

Her weight felt reassuring. Firm, yet giving. Accommodating its shape to his. Her skin felt clammy at first, as cold as his, warmthless and unliving as the sand beneath them.

But gradually it warmed. Her cheek lay close against his. Her arms enfolded him. He closed his eyes against a sudden prickle of tears that welled from some depth he couldn't plumb. He panted, trying to muffle his sobs.

"Better?" she whispered, breath warm on his ear.

"Yeah . . . yeah." He closed his eyes, then opened them again to the moon. Feeling the warmth slowly return to his skin. And trickle downward . . .

She wriggled slightly, then lifted herself and glanced down the length of their entwined bodies. "Hey . . . what's this shit? Are you fucking *kidding* me?"

He grimaced. "I'm sorry—it's just—"

"It's been a while, hasn't it?" She grinned. Felt down between their pressed-together bodies, and to his astonishment and near horror lightly traced the outline of his erect penis under the wet fabric with thumb and forefinger.

He shuddered, closing his eyes involuntarily. She sighed, and raised herself a little on both arms, peering over the top of the dune. Then placed her lips next to his ear and whispered, so softly he almost couldn't hear it over the rustle of the wind in the sea grass, over the high endless song the machine guns had left in his head, "If you want, you can take off your pants and fuck me. Hector. Get some of that shitty war out of your system. But *only* if you want."

AND now he's sitting in the MWR hut, watching two clueless corporals each with only one hand left battering a fucking little plastic ball back and forth as seriously as if it meant an Olympic medal. The posters on the walls are about something called Warrior Games. Hector can't care less. He has no interest in power lifting, or rowing, or shooting clay pigeons, or any of that shit. Actually, if you gave him a shotgun, he'd probably start shooting the people around him. Like he'd feverishly sworn to do, back on the hospital ship.

He closes his eyes and shudders. Remembering the helplessness, the terror. Having that *thing* down his throat. Paralyzed, unable to move or fight, trapped like the quarry of some predatory alien, enwebbed and hung to season before being devoured at leisure.

The trouble is, there really isn't anything that interests him. At all. Except maybe for Carlina. And he's not sure yet what that means, other than that they get it on at every opportunity.

He doesn't have any other friends here. There are some other dudes from the Second, but he didn't know them downrange and feels no connection. He does know his RCC. His care coordinator's a bouncy always-smiling white girl, Sergeant Brinnell. She made a joke about being hard when they first met, but he didn't get it. He has to go to therapy every weekday afternoon, in the Head Shed trailer, where he and ten other guys and girls sit around and try to talk about their days. Which are always the same, of course. And their nights, which suck and are sometimes pretty tormented.

The white Ping-Pong ball clicks, takes a sudden wild spin off the table, and flies directly at his face. He flinches away, dropping, hitting the floor with both hands and rolling. But no one laughs. No one in the whole hut laughs, though they all glance over to see what made him hit the deck.

There's that, at least. They're all in the same boat here.

USS *Totally Fucked.*

THAT afternoon at session a fat civilian in a too-long blue Patriot tie gives a speech. He talks about the continuum of care and its three phases: recovery, rehabilitation, and reintegration. He's from the VA. Not a Marine. Hector tunes out after the first three seconds. He's heard it all before, but then, he's been here longer than some of the new guys.

Under the drone of the lecture he drifts back to that first night with Carlina. Her teasing smile in the rimefrost moonlight as the sea grass waved above them. The ripping, succulent pain of release. Then, her lying next to him in the dark, gently manipulating an organ he'd nearly forgotten he possessed.

Until it rose again, and she rolled over once more atop him, this time stretching and working until she too achieved a short, choked cry that mingled with the shrieks of the seabirds and the booming crash of the surf.

Surreptitiously, under the shield of the Recovery binder he has to bring to each session, he strokes himself under the rough digitally patterned fabric.

THAT night he wins a remote availability. You sign up for it in advance, and there's some kind of lottery, since connections are still tough to get. He lines up outside the video booth, a half-enclosed setup between the trailers. No one likes it because there's no privacy, so you can't do a sex call, but it's better than nothing.

Anyway, he isn't interested in a sex call. Carlina has taken the edge off that. They've met twice more, once at her hootch when her bunkie was out, the other time out in the dunes behind the camp. Spreading a blanket, and talking, then getting it on. In a savage, almost tigerish way he's never encountered before. Certainly not in the awkward gropings in his old Kia, behind the high school football field. She takes him from above, savagely, as if commandeering his dick for wartime use. And something repressed and angry in him responds, and they copulate savagely under the stars again and again until they roll apart exhausted as if they'd just staggered out of the surf together once more.

He shakes this intrusive thought off as his mom appears on the screen. She looks exhausted, in a rumpled green smock like hospital scrubs, but smiles broadly at the sight of him. *"Héctor. Como estas hijo, estas mejor? Te veo pronto en casa?"*

For the first time in his life it feels weird speaking Spanish. After so long away . . . "Hello, Mom. How's everybody there?"

"Your sister esta muy bien . . . Your hermano called from Mexico, he has a new bebe . . . I am a grandmother! So proud. You will see pictures, when you come home. When will you be here, in the casa?"

"I don't know. Don't know what they're planning to do with us."

"What will you do when you come home, mi hijo? Work at Farmer Seth's? They have to give back your old job when soldiers come home, they say so on Patriot Network."

The processing plant. Most of the workers were immigrants; Americans wouldn't work the way the lines demanded. All the lines: deboning, whole bird, grading, cut up. These ran at different speeds, but no one could ever stop or rest. Five minutes off every hour. Half an hour for lunch.

He squeezes his eyes shut, remembering the Hanging Room. The rattling clang of the stainless hooks. The blood. The shit. The fluttering, squawking, terrified birds. The snarl of machinery, the whir of exhaust fans, the mutter of forklifts bustling cartons of disassembled meat off to the freezers. Above, looking down from their offices, the Bosses. And the clattering endless whine of the Line echoing, stainless, rubberized, greased with fat and blood.

But the chicken's cheap in the scarlet packages, with cheerful, friendly Farmer Seth, lanky and white-bearded in trademark yellow bib overalls, grinning out from the plastic wrapping.

He jerks his eyes open, sweating. No. No way is he going back there.

"Héctor? Son?"

"Uh, *no lo creo*. There's got to be someplace better to work."

"Yo tampoco lo creo." Doubt in her voice. *"Not a-round here. It's not so bad, though, is it? They don't pay much but the work is steady. La gente siempre va a comer pollo. And if you get hurt they give you another job. Like your friend with the one arm, what is his name—"*

"José's not my friend," Hector grits out. "He's the production foreman. And he only got that job after he lost his arm in the ice machine because he said he'd sue the company."

He hears the exasperation in his voice and tries to rein it in. Confronting her concerned, worn, tired face on the screen . . . She only wanted what was best for him. But a job, citizenship, to no longer have the fucking Loyalty League harassing them, that would be heaven on earth for her. "What are you doing now, Ma?"

"Oh, I am taking care of old Mrs. Custis. I stay there at night. Make her supper. Take her to el retrete. Keep the place clean. You know how it is."

"I wish you didn't have to work so hard, Ma. Wish you didn't have to at all."

"Oh, it is not too bad. It keeps me busy." A pause, during which someone outside the partition yells he's going over his five minutes. Hector shouts back, "Fuck off, knuckle fucker!"

His mother frowns. *"What was that, mi hijo?"*

"Nothing, nothing, some ass—some guys here crowding me. I can't stay on too much longer."

"You want to know about Mirielle, I guess. I have not seen her. I think she and her mama may be out of town. She's a good girl, Mirielle. You could do worse."

Someone bangs on the outside of the booth. "You're eating my time too, asshole. Hang the fuck up! Other guys wanna talk!"

Hector yells back, but he's got to wrap this up. His mother asks worriedly what's going on there, why they are shouting. Is he safe?

He doesn't want to think about Mirielle. He'd carried the rosary she gave him. For a while. But after the shambles and death on Taiwan, then Hainan, she'd dropped astern like garbage in a ship's wake. Become a hazy distant memory, no longer even a dream. "Uh, Ma, no way. Okay? I got too many problems now to foist them off on her. She'd be better off without me. You can tell her that, okay? Look, that yelling, that's just the other guys wanting their turn on the vid. I'm doing okay, Ma. A lot of people here're a lot worse off than I am."

"Tell me you will come home safe, Héctor." Her voice was pleading. Fuck, she was shaking out a tissue, which meant she was going to cry.

"I got to go, Ma. Love you!"

"Vaya con Dios, Héctor, mi amado hijo. Call me again soon."

THAT night he meets Carlina again. This time, out behind the trailers. There's a baseball diamond hardly any of the patients use, though the amputees sometimes come out here to practice walking the bases on their new legs. Which look nearly real, Hector has to admit.

His own injuries are less evident. If only they could replace his brain with some computer box strapped around his neck, like the ones that control the artificial legs . . .

She's waiting for him in the dugout. Somebody's equipped this as a snake pit, with a narrow bunk mattress, cheap bead curtains, a box fan, and a battered red-and-green Yeti cooler. It's apparently obscure enough, or maybe notorious enough, that the roving patrols don't come here. Hector wonders how she knows about it.

Other than her hootch or the dunes there isn't any other place to get together on site. He wonders why. Is not getting laid supposed to help them recover? Certainly being with Carlina has dragged him a little bit out of his head. If only to make him get boners during session.

They strip down and within seconds fell on each other like starving jungle cats. He keeps trying to roll on top but she won't let him. "You wanna do this, we do it my way," she states. There's no arguing with this, so he rolls off and positions himself on his back on the stained, mold-stinky mattress.

The smell reminds him suddenly of the one time he got it off during the war, other than the hand job from Orietta at boot camp, and popping his nut into a MWR napkin. Like most everybody else in the platoon, which sometimes left the ground outside their foxholes littered with gray-green tissues.

The Indo senior enlisted had taken him to a massage and spa place in Bongkaran, where he paired off with a pouty and actually pretty hot little whore who said she was into Hispanic guys. She'd giggled when he asked if she was a ladyboy, and pulled down her pants to show him she wasn't. He'd been careful to wear a banana burka, though. Which he isn't doing now, but Carlina's never said anything about protection.

Then he forgets everything as she leans over him and tucks it in. To that warm welcoming place where he can forget all the things he doesn't want to know, doesn't want to remember. The reproachful dead faces he doesn't want to see but can't look away from. The numb horror he doesn't want to carry inside his head, like a fucking bullet the fucking surgeons can't get to, so they just leave it there. To fester and work itself closer to his heart, gradually, to kill him, sometime, no one can tell when.

Her thrusting hips take him out of himself but he falls back. Coming close. She increases the pace, up and down, sliding, smiling down at him as his face tightens, as his whole body strains upward.

He fires, grabbing her shoulders, the grunting agonized cry

bursting out of him in the dugout beneath the earth. Buried, like so many good fucking Marines.

He just hopes that whatever's going to be at the end of this purgatory, he gets there soon.

THEY lie exhausted on the flaccid mattress, looking up together once more at the stars twinkling above the outfield fence. Bright and clear tonight, as if they're at sea. Past that glow the marigold night lights of the camp. He's stroking her hair. She's talking about cutting it short, but he doesn't want her to. He doesn't like short hair on girls. And so far, at least, she hasn't. Maybe just for him? He doesn't think so, but can't help wondering.

She murmurs, "You feelin' better now?"

"Yeah. A lot."

"No more walking out into the surf, and not coming back?"

"Told you, I wasn't thinking about that," he lies.

"Like fuck you weren't. I looked at your record, Ramos. You were some fucked up. *Are* some fucked up."

"My breathing's a lot better."

"I'm not talking about your lungs. You were down for compromised immune system, eye damage, complex PTSD, alcohol addiction, moral trauma, and dissociation. As soon as they removed the restraints, you tried to choke one of the doctors on the hospital ship. Your shrink recommended a suicide watch. He wants you red-flagged on a watch list when they release you." She rolls over and frowns. "You do *know* all this, right?"

He takes a deep breath. Shrugs. "All I know is, I can't stop thinking about stuff. And I don't care about what happens now, or getting home, or anything. DGAF, you know?"

She cradles his face in both hands and sighs. "You went through some dread shit, Hec. Nobody can say you haven't, a three-island Marine. And you still came back. In one piece. More or less."

He takes another breath, and to his astonishment tears start to burn again. What the fuck, over? Every time he makes it with this bitch, he cries. What kind of pussy is he turning into? But now, instead of toughing it out or laughing it off he mutters, surprising himself, "I don't feel like I should have. Come back, I mean."

She chuckles bitterly. "When your buds didn't. Yeah. I hear that all the time. Hector, it's just that, you won the lottery. You got lucky! Sure, go ahead and miss them. But there's nothing you can do about it. Or that you *have* to do about it. Just try to remember them, and get on with life as best you can."

Pretty much what the fat civilian in the too-long tie said too. But somehow, coming from her, here, now, it seems to mean more. Maybe because he's starting to wonder if maybe he loves her.

It's a scary thought. Not quite as puckery as riding an ACV in to the beach while the Slants are shelling the shit out of you, but still, scary in its own way.

And maybe she knows this just from him not saying much, because she says, still looking away, "You know, pretty soon now you're going to get mustered out."

"You think?"

"I know. They don't want to keep you guys here any longer than they have to. They'll unload you on the VA, give you a pat on the back, and that'll be it."

He sighs, not wanting to think about it. Wanting to hold on to this instead. This night. Their night. Whatever it means.

But she won't stop talking. "So what are you going to do?"

"Me? I was thinking about . . . staying around here. In San Diego. Until your tour's up."

"Until my tour is up." Her tone is flat, neutral. "What's that mean? I hope, not what I think."

"I mean . . . I like you. I thought you liked me."

She rolls off him and sits up. Reaches for her bra, huffing, looking away. "That's beside the point. You're getting out. Going home. Wherever that is.

"But me, I'm staying in. I'm a regular, Hec. A fucking lifer, unnerstand? I'm gonna make master chief and retire on twenty. Maybe do enlisted-to-medical. At least get my degree." Her shadow seems to be farther away somehow, even though she's still sitting on the same mattress with him. "I like you, sure. But this is nothing special, for either of us. I'm not going home with you, or making this forever after. Just to get that clear."

He lies waiting, he's not sure for what; maybe giving her a chance to change her mind. "So this is just a hookup?" He can't keep the hurt tone out of his voice.

"You needed it. And, yeah, I liked it. But you ain't the only patient I liked this year."

"Oh, I get it. You fucked me as . . . part of my therapy."

She barks a laugh, buttoning her blouse, then stands to work her trou up over her hips. "Sure! Just part of the treatment. CT scan, blood work, psych counseling, and get it off with Carlina. That's pretty fucking insulting, you know that? Or it would be, if it didn't work better than the meds."

He sits up and grabs her wrist. "I didn't mean that. Don't go away mad. It . . . I got to say, it does kind of . . . work. It kind of got me . . . interested again."

"It got you *horny* again." The tension seems to ease off; they're both laughing now. Though his sounds forced, even to him.

"You really think I'll get out of here pretty soon?" he asks.

"I shouldn't tell you this. Don't tell anybody. But they'll discharge you next week. You know, not enough beds, not enough staff. They can only keep the troops so badly wounded they can't go back to their families. Facial wounds. Nutcases. Quads. You're Olympic material compared to some of these guys. As you well know."

"As I well know," he repeats. He'd wandered into one of those wards last week. And never wanted to see stuff like that again. "Maybe you're right."

"Oh, I'm right, all right." She straightens from zipping her boots. "You'll have a great life, Hec. Go home. Find some local cutie. Squirt out a few brown-eyed puppies. Forget the war. Forget me. Pretend everything's cool. And someday you'll realize, it really is. Believe me."

A scuffing, followed by a faint clatter of tiny glass spheres. He lies half naked, spent, the wind cold on his exposed groin, arm over his eyes. When she doesn't say anything more he mutters, "You still there? Carlina?"

When he opens his eyes, the dugout's empty. She's gone, but the stars still glitter through the swaying beads of the curtain, reflected and refracted from bead to sparkling bead, so they seem to be twinkling all the more brightly.

III

SPENT ASSETS

11

Chadron, Nebraska

I T took Dan a while to find the sheriff. He rolled down the streets on the bike, pulling over now and then to ask directions from pedestrians. This town seemed crowded after the long emptinesses he'd traversed. The sidewalks bustling, jaywalkers keeping him on edge, the way a place ought to be, the way towns all across America once had been. Several of the folks he stopped to ask just shrugged, saying they weren't from here, they were evacuees from Denver, and had no idea where the sheriff's office might be.

It had taken two days to get here from Montana. He'd doglegged south around the no-go areas, following Hardin's directions and the fallout map the militiawoman had printed out for him. Then angled east again, and crossed Yellowstone.

The park had been closed, but he'd nursed the bike around Jersey barriers and motored around the wide placid blue lake on a narrow two-laner. His engine echoed from the mountainsides. It was probably scenic, but somehow he couldn't see it as anything but distance to be conquered. A single ranger vehicle turning out from the lodge had trailed him for a time, but he'd sped up and it finally gave up the chase. If it had even been a chase . . . He'd slept in the open that night, snatching a few hours with the bike pulled into a copse of fir along a creek. Its channel held only a trickle, but he washed his face in it and drank some, then gnawed at his processed food, though it was tasteless. He didn't care whether the water was potable or not, contaminated or not. It just didn't seem to matter.

He couldn't stop reproaching himself. What might he have done, could he have done, *should* he have done, to keep Nan safe? How had he let her take a job so far from home, on the far side of the country? Jack Byrne, an advisor on Yangerhans's staff and an old friend, had warned him to get her out of Seattle. "She's sitting right on the bull's-eye," Byrne had said.

But he hadn't done a thing. Just *assumed* she'd be safe. Or, no. To be exact: hadn't thought much about it. Just told himself she was adult, she wouldn't obey. Would feel it her duty to stay, and keep trying to produce the drug that would save lives and bear her name. Or at least her initial.

But he should have tried. Even if he didn't think she'd leave, he should have *tried*. Sentiment aside, it was, at the very least, his biological duty.

Yeah. He should have worried more about her. Back when worrying could have done some good.

He lay staring into the dark. He could blame his ex-wife. He could blame the war. He could blame Nan.

But the only one he really had any right to be angry at was himself.

THE next morning he'd hit the road again at dawn and powered on through the day. The highway ran along mountainsides, then through valleys. Past lakes, then through much deeper ravines barriered by lead-colored mountains. Some serious peaks rose above and beyond them to the north. He guessed he was in the Rockies. At Wapiti he found an open gas station, and was asked for a ration card for the first time. He didn't have one, of course, and the guy made an issue of it, threatened to report him, but at last accepted the .38 in trade for a fill-up.

There, for the first time, he got a hit when he asked about the truck. Yeah, the station owner said, he'd seen it. A refrigerator truck, with five motorcyclists riding escort. They'd pointed rifles and demanded gas and food. Dan had agreed, that was beyond acceptable behavior. Had one of them killed his daughter? He drank a cup of boiled-down coffee, used the dirty toilet-paper-less head, and got back on the road again.

East of Wapiti the countryside seemed little by little to return to something resembling normality. More cars dotted the road, though still far fewer than in peacetime, or at least in what peacetime had been like before the war. He was stopped twice more, but each time was let go once he presented his M&M pass. He was getting the feeling that the federal government's writ, never popular out here, had been supplanted by the sheriffs and the Mobilized Militias since the Exchange.

The hours passed in a blur. Valleys and plains were painted a deep verdant green with new crops, though no one was working in those fields and he saw little agricultural machinery. He motored through more endless valleys, the engine cocooning him in a soothing omlike hum that emptied his brain.

When he wasn't thinking he wasn't remembering. Was no longer dreading what he was going to find at the end of this ride. Instead, it was as if he were riding from life into a deathlike realm he'd never expected to visit. A gray underworld through whose mists he wandered like a wraith.

He'd always thought, hoped, expected, his daughter would outlive him. That he'd never have to confront this worst doom that could befall a parent.

But apparently now he would.

A mountain pass, winding roads, great trees towering to either side. Waterfalls. An honest to God state road crew, repairing a washout. They waved and cheered as he roared past, and he lifted a hand in acknowledgment, a little puzzled by their enthusiasm, before the numbness returned.

The land flattened. It became planed-smooth grasslands that

stretched to the horizon like a calm, occasionally wind-ruffled green sea. Hour after hour of flatness, the asphalt blurring beneath him as he pushed the bike to eighty, to ninety, to near a hundred. Then eased off, realizing he was courting something he didn't want to name. Another gas station, in Gillette, let him fuel without a ration card, only asking an exorbitant sum per gallon. He handed the bills over reluctantly. He was running out of cash, and even the mention of a credit card earned him a look that suggested he was crazy.

At long last, late in the afternoon, a sign welcomed him to Chadron. *If You Lived Here, You'd Be Home Now.* Wide fields stretched away on either side. Farms and the occasional metal-roofed, pristinely kept barn perched on low hills. The rest of the land reached away almost to infinity, sealike, disorienting. Then the open view across the land gradually gave way to the usual beach wrack of small-town outskirts. A church, a brick-pillared cemetery, a nursing home; then trailer parks, convenience stores, car lots, a Wal-Mart, and the bland faux-glitzy normality of a shopping mall. A Taco John's was even doing business, with a blinking OPEN sign, cars parked out front, locals chatting by the door. So here they had electrical power . . . He was terrifically hungry, but pressed on, dreading what lay ahead but also strangely eager to get it over with, confirmed, accepting the blow and the blame even though he had no idea what it would be like on the other side.

Telling himself a lot of other people, dads, moms, families, had known this moment, in this war. He wasn't alone.

But that didn't seem to help.

Eventually he found the sheriff's office, pointed the last couple of blocks by a friendly older woman in a painter's apron, who was retouching a faded sign in front of the public library. He coasted into a diagonal parking slot in front of the three-story building that held not just a sheriff's department, but the district judge and the county offices. It all looked so normal and everyday that his heart lifted just a tiny bit. Before he remembered why he was here.

The sheriff was named Kit Larsen. A deputy stood by as he was ushered into her office. She acted reserved until he told her why he was here, half in uniform, hatless and windblown and stubbled and probably smelling of gasoline and dirt.

"Ah. You're her father," she said in a flat midwestern accent, **pointing to a chair. "Sit down, sir. Please."**

He slid it over and sank into it, the old springs protesting audibly. "Maybe. Maybe. That's what I'm here to find out."

"We never discovered any ID on her, and we don't have the connectivity back yet to do fingerprints." She started to open a file cabinet, then seemed to change her mind. "The face . . . I mean, she wasn't in good shape. Whoever left her out there beat her up pretty bad."

Dan swallowed. He forced himself to ask, "Do you have any suspects? I heard it was a motorcycle gang—"

"Not a *gang*. Just a stranger on a Harley. Or at least the bartender down at EJ's said he'd seen her with him. Some time before she was found at the creek.

"See, there are a lot of new people in town these days. 'Vackers,' we call them. People look past them, most of the time. Since we know they might not be here for long." She frowned. "See, we're between two big fallout plumes here. We're all just hoping the contamination doesn't move south or east. There are supposed to be monitoring teams out, but we're not getting their reports. A lot of folks think it's worse than what they're telling us." She sighed. "And that this cease-fire might not hold."

"I think it will," Dan said. "Just my opinion, but both sides are pretty damn sick of this war."

"Yeah, us too." She sighed again, placed her hands on the desk, and rose. "We don't have a county morgue. Body's being held at Hertich's. Local funeral home. So, let's take you over there."

THE patrol car smelled like he expected a small-town police cruiser to. Unwashed bodies, greasy fast food, and the ghosts of vomit past. When they pulled up a few blocks distant, a corpulent man in a black suit, white shirt, and blue tie was waiting at the curb. The mortician shook Larsen's hand and introduced himself, though Dan didn't register his name. He was abstracted. Not really here.

He was asking a power he hoped was there for help. For strength. Not for a given result, not for it not to be her. He wouldn't ask for that. Because then he'd just be wishing horror and grief onto another father, another family, instead of his own. He couldn't pray for that.

Only for the strength to bear whatever came.

The mortician ushered them through several curtained and carpeted parlors, down a flight of steps, into an air-conditioned, fluorescent-lit basement.

Here the air smelled like cinnamon and acetone. The director cleared his throat. Unsmiling, deliberate, with the air of a robing priest, he pulled on a crackling green plastic embalming gown and green nitrile gloves. Talc drifted in the still air. Clearing his throat again—a tic?—he rolled a dressing table out of the way and unlatched the door to a gleaming stainless three-body mortuary cooler.

A single shrouded bundle lay on the top rack. The tray extended with a squeal of bearings. The pale blue sheet atop the body was dotted with brownish fluid. "She was unclaimed," the director said. "So I didn't put much time into prettying her up." He looked shyly at the sheriff, then at Dan, as if expecting to be chided.

"Go ahead, Rog," Sheriff Larsen said.

The director cleared his throat again, grasped the upper hem of the sheet with thumbs and forefingers, and drew it back with a respectful yet somehow still showmanlike flourish.

Dan felt iced, emotionless, as if walled off by many meters of frozen asbestos from some devouring flame. He forced unwilling legs to dolly him forward.

The face was obliterated, hammered by blunt force into black bruises, so distorted the bones beneath must have been smashed out of shape. The head lay cocked to one side, as if in mute question. Why? Or maybe, Who? No, this victim must have known her assailant. The damage was so up close, so personal a violation.

But confronted with this swollen, distorted wreckage of a face, Dan couldn't tell if it was familiar or not.

"We figure about five nine, maybe one thirty, one forty. A little taller than average for a woman, but not that much. Mid- to late twenties. Hard to tell race. She's pretty banged up," the director said, half admiringly, as if he were describing a used but durable car he was selling. "If you asked me, I'd say she was dragged. There's a lot of abrasion damage."

The sheriff said, "Then maybe beaten, so she wouldn't be recognized?"

"Could be," the director said. "But that could've happened in a car crash, or a motorcycle accident, too. I see a lot of young adults come in here like that. Those are always sad. Donorcycles, they call the bikes, down at the hospital."

The icy sheath was melting. He felt queasy now, ready to bolt for a toilet. He'd seen the dead before. Many times. But none had been his own daughter. "Can I see her hair?" he muttered, only realizing he'd said it aloud after the words were out.

The director nodded. Those green nitrile gloves lifted the head and fanned out the hair. Dark brown, like hers. But . . . it was short. He blinked, fighting voices in his brain lifted in argument. Nan hadn't worn her hair this short. But . . . she could have cut it. Even, probably *had* cut it, working in a lab environment.

Her mother's hair had been jet black. His own, lighter, almost blond. She'd been nearly blond once, when she was small, but it had darkened as she grew up.

Without being asked, the director flirted the sheet downward. Uncovering a torso and chest, also bruised. The skin was mottled red and brown, lacerated and stripped down to raw meat.

Dan closed his eyes, and put out a hand to brace himself against a utility cabinet.

"Did your daughter have any identifying markings?" Larsen asked, beside him, in a not unsympathetic tone.

"A, uh . . . a tattoo. A tennis racket. With some kind of design around it. Leaves, or flowers. She got it when she was at college, thinking about going pro."

The director murmured, "Where was it, sir?"

"Right wrist. No, left, I think . . . Actually I'm not sure right now." He ground his teeth, fighting down the nausea. He had to stick with this. Had to know. One way or the other.

The director pulled the left hand from under the sheet and turned it over. The skin was mottled, but there was no sign of a tattoo of any kind.

"The right one?" the sheriff, Kit, said.

The director tucked the left hand back under the sheet, re-folded the sheet, and took out the right hand. His deliberate, mea-sured movements were enraging. Dan squeezed his eyes shut, then forced them open again.

On the right hand, the skin was gone from above the elbow down nearly to the fingertips, scooped or scraped off, leaving raw red muscle and white tendons.

"That's what we call road rash," the director said. "It's instinct. You tend to push your arms out when you go down. Try to break the fall. So maybe, whatever happened to her, it started with a wipeout."

Dan rubbed his face. He tried to remember what his daughter's body looked like, but all his mind gave him was pictures of her as a child. Bony, long legs, long arms. Her slightly awkward, stiff-legged run. This body was the right size. Five nine was about right, and the weight was ballpark. The skin appeared slightly sallow, at least in the uninjured areas, more or less like he remembered hers looking like when she'd been indoors studying and hadn't gotten much sun. Which she probably hadn't, working at Archipelago.

But he couldn't tell, and he wavered, standing there, between wondering if he was just denying what was in front of him, or if this truly might not be her. The undertaker and the sheriff stood watching. Waiting for some decision.

But he just couldn't look at the poor broken thing in front of him anymore. As if some force field, or magnetic repulsion, wrenched his gaze away. He had to think about breathing just to get air down to his lungs, and the room kept trying to spin. At last he said, inspecting the green-and-white tile floor, "You can cover her up now."

"So, is that your daughter, sir?" the sheriff asked, taking his arm.

"I . . . I'm sorry, but I just can't tell. What about clothes? What was she found in? That might help."

"Found her pretty much just like this," the sheriff said. "Covered in leaves, out where the highway crosses the White River, north of the airport. Stripped naked, lying under the trees. Jogger who spotted one hand called it in."

"Can you do something else to ID her? Fingerprints, blood type . . . DNA?"

They looked at each other. The director cleared his throat. He shook his head and whispered something to the sheriff that Dan didn't catch.

Finally Larsen said, "It's not exactly like CSI or the movies, Captain. Not out here, these days. We could maybe do DNA, but it would take a while. The sample would have to go to Lincoln. Like I said, it would take a while. Weeks. Maybe months, I don't know how much backlog they have, with all the . . . you know, the remains, from the Exchange."

"I'd be happy to pay, if that would help." Dan wished he felt icy again. Now he felt hot, sweaty, and his legs were beginning to quiver. "Look, I don't know what to say. I really can't tell for sure. It's probably her. But I can't be certain, so I don't want to . . ." He caught his breath; could see from their sympathetic yet baffled expressions he wasn't making sense. "Look, I'm going to have to get out of here."

"Sure. Sure." The sheriff took his arm again and they climbed back up the steps, back through the floral-scented parlors, outside into the fresh air.

When they reached the patrol car his knees buckled under him. He felt dizzy, sick, ill. He dropped to a crouch on the curb, covering his face with both hands.

The others patted his back, murmuring in consoling tones. Hands slid under his armpits, to lift him, but he twisted away, fought to stand on his own. Finally he made it, but barely, swaying.

He leaned against the patrol car, fighting just to breathe past the sucking black hole in his chest. Wishing now that numbness would return. That feeling he wasn't really involved. Was not seeing what was right in front of him.

But this nausea, and this endless and bottomless horror, felt like they were here to stay.

12

The Sea of Japan

SAVO ISLAND had been at Condition Three, wartime cruising, for over a day now. Cheryl had spent most of it slumped bonelessly in her chair in the Citadel. Occasionally dozing, until jerked awake by some interruption, or reports, or a particularly insistent itch. Finally Mills had persuaded her to retire to her cabin for a few hours. But she'd spent most of those staring up at the overhead, arms tense, waiting for the general quarters alarm or a call on her Hydra.

God. She hated waiting. The worst part of war, or the run-up to it.

She still wasn't sure exactly which one this was.

Maybe the whole idea of peace had been, in that great Navy acronym, OBE—overtaken by events. Maybe the world would just keep fighting from now on. Just changing the names of the enemies. God, but that was a horrible thought.

If this really was a new war, or a resumption of the old one, though, the oncoming fleet would already have been suffering a withering gauntlet of fires. From unmanned penetrator aircraft, long-range missiles, attack submarines, and Space Force hypersonics. From land-based Marine and Army batteries too.

But Fleet and PACOM had made clear that would not happen in this case. Not until the approaching Russians demonstrated hostile intent.

The United States wasn't going to start this war. And it wasn't going to happen by accident, either.

On the other hand, her mission was to block that fleet's passage. To abort their landing in Dalian, and takeover of the former Russian grant there.

If they kept coming, how could she do that without initiating hostilities?

An insoluble dilemma. An impossible mission.

But she had to figure out how to accomplish it.

Somewhere in there, though, she must have managed a few minutes' troubled shut-eye, for when she next forced her lids apart the clock had moved on. She rolled out, splashed her face and scrubbed her armpits, smeared on ointment, pulled on a fresh set of coveralls, and went down to the messdecks. They were serving breakfast, and she bolted buckwheat pancakes and a ham slice, sitting with several young enlisted women.

Then, back to Combat.

Now she sat at the command chair again, feeling levitated from the three cups of coffee she'd chugged and gravitated from the heavy flapjacks and ham. Maybe they counterbalanced each other, but she felt leaden. Even though she'd lost fifteen pounds over the course of the war. She'd gained a couple back since the armistice. But now, she guessed, I'll be losing again. Fuck.

If only that were her biggest problem . . .

Chief Terranova turned to her. "Captain? Seein' a change in their formation."

Reluctantly, she donned the heavy VR helmet once more.

And was floating in midair, gazing down on a scribed and virtual sea. Which by now seemed more genuine than the ocean outside. A sight she hadn't seen for days.

Tilting her head slightly, she sped forward above its monochrome blue. Until contacts loomed up over the ever-receding horizon. Warships, like her own. Only *not* her own. And beneath the waves, other contacts swam like sharks, their locations less well defined, the edges of their probable locations fuzzier, but there. And all headed her way, as surely as locomotives on a track.

Russians.

The Northern Task Force had filtered in via the Soya and Tartary Straits, with the Japanese reporting numerous submarine passages of the Tsugaru Strait, between Hokkaido and Honshu. Their tightly interlocked steaming formation showed that they expected attack, or were guarding against it. She hovered, counting ships, occasionally zooming in for a closer look when drone or nanosatellite video was available.

The new arrivals were in a conventional sector screen, with *Peter the Great* and associated logistics ships and one Priboy-class Wasp-equivalent assault carrier at the center. Intel expected the assault carrier to be equipped with the new fifth-generation fleet defense fighters, which would be augmented with land-based MiG-31s out of Vladivostok to provide air cover.

Her heart sank. Together with those submarines—the Russian Pacific Fleet numbered over twenty modern boats, most nuclear-powered or advanced air-independent conventional— the oncoming force disposed of far more striking power than she could call on.

If it came to a battle, she'd lose, and it wouldn't take long. Her ships would be overwhelmed by hundreds of missiles striking in a coordinated mass attack. Any survivors would be finished off by torpedoes and missiles at close range, once the subs penetrated a degraded ASW barrier.

Unless she made sure of her ground, and fought for every inch of it.

Or . . . unless she made it perfectly clear to her opponent that she was both prepared to fight and capable of inflicting heavy damage.

In which case, Moscow might decide it really didn't want Dalian enough to risk a full-on war with the United States.

She sighed again, and boosted the suddenly heavy-as-lead

helmet off her shoulders. Now, all at once, she felt shrunken. Impotent. Dazed, with the realization she was only a tiny worm in a thousand-acre field, instead of the master of the universe. Could see only the nutshell-interior of this black-ceilinged compartment, instead of infinite space.

"I don't like these odds, Skipper." Noah Pardees slid into the seat beside her. The ops officer stretched flexibly as a cat, but he too looked worried. "We should have spanked these guys as soon as they started through the straits."

"We're not at war yet, Noah. And we can't strike first."

"Who says? Otherwise, we just wait to get whacked? What the hell's PACOM thinking?"

She glanced at the geoplot, lit on the large-screen display in front of them. "Their declared destination is Vladivostok. Until they turn south from there, we're not even sure they're headed for China."

Pardees rubbed his chin, looking stressed. "Oh, sure," he said bitterly. "But by then it'll be too late. They'll have their targeting dataforces fused. Hit us with hypersonics, cruises . . . we could have two hundred missiles inbound at once. We'll be friggin' toast, Skipper."

She dragged a hand through lank sweaty hair. "You're not telling me anything I don't know. If we had the Japanese with us, the numbers'd look better. But I agree, this isn't a good force ratio. If anything, we might just be a tripwire."

The ops officer grimaced. "Tripwires get trampled."

She bobbled her head, unable to disagree, but wary of coming across as defeatist. If anyone aboard had to project stone confidence, it was the CO. Not only that, she had to convey it to her other units.

She regarded the geoplot for a bit longer, then began keyboarding.

At the front of CIC, one of the large-screen displays reversed. Lifting her fingers from the keys, propping her chin on a fist, she studied it.

This was what things looked like from the point of view of the oncoming fleet. Of Admiral Vitaly Aznavuryan, commanding what intel was now calling the Combined North Pacific Task Force, or CNPTF.

It might be worthwhile knowing more about this guy. Back to the keyboard . . . to call up the classified personnel summary on him.

It was sparse. A Nahkimov scholar as a teenager during Soviet times. Graduate of the Kuznetsov Naval Academy, the Moscow Higher Command School. Commanded two submarines—a submariner, then, before becoming the senior assistant to the commander, Pacific Fleet. A picture of him, obviously an official photo, in the grotesquely high-crowned combination cap the Russians had inherited from the old Soviet Bloc. It told her little, other than that he had five o'clock shadow on those pudgy cheeks.

The only personal information was based on an attaché's chat with him. It noted that he was from Smolensk, married, with two grown children, boy and girl. He spent his free time fly-fishing and bicycling in the country, when he could. Aznavuryan also enjoyed American movies and seemed to like discussing them. She wondered about his name, which didn't sound Russian, but there was nothing in the bio about that.

She left his picture looking back at her from her command desk screen, sighed, and contemplated the bulkhead displays again. Trying to figure out how this guy would proceed.

Okay, she thought. Let's assume he joins up with the forces already in port in Vladivostok. At that point, they'd be pretty much centered in the widest bowl of the Sea of Japan. Then he heads south.

But as he makes southing, the coastlines of Japan and Korea will funnel his line of advance more and more narrowly.

Until Tsushima Strait.

Back in 1905, Admiral Togo Heihachiro had engaged Rozhestvensky's fleet after it entered the strait from the southward. Here, the situation would be reversed. She, Cheryl Staurulakis, would be blocking this new threat's advance from the north.

She got up and valved coffee into a CIMSEC-logoed mug at the mess table in Sonar, then came back and settled in again.

Her stomach felt like it wasn't doing so well with the pancakes. Or maybe it was just nerves. She sighed, pondering her options. Which seemed to be pretty fucking limited, given that she'd been ordered not to strike first.

How had Togo handled it? A few seconds on SIPRNET answered that. A simple blocking maneuver, then directing his line ahead so as to cross his oncoming opponent's T. Obviously, not a tactic she could adopt, given modern weaponry. And since Japan and Russia had already been at war back then, it didn't matter who had opened fire first, although apparently it'd been Togo.

She cocked her head suddenly. Uh-*huh*. But was there, maybe, a smarter way to position her forces? One that, maybe, the AI hadn't considered?

To the oncoming admiral, after all, her own formation must look like a random scatter. It conveyed no intent to hold. More like a hopeless gaggle, uncoordinated and maybe even uncommanded.

It might well be the optimal setup for distributed, networked operations. But it was hardly the stuff to strike fear into an enemy.

On the other hand . . . if more forces were on the way to her, she had to make sure the loop was closed. That any new ships or subs on the way knew exactly where to station themselves, and that Blue air, if it was called in for a strike, couldn't confuse her ships with Aznavuryan's.

She called up a tactical publication. Then another, toggling through the pages rapidly.

Finally she logged to high-side nanochat. Her own call sign was Tangler; Fleet was Replay.

TANGLER: Tangler actual here. Request Replay actual.

REPLAY: Actual not available. Got a question?

TANGLER: Requested air support and liaison with pos-
    sible former enemy force support. Need update and
    anticipated time on station please.

REPLAY: Issues being worked as per previous comms.
    Diplomatic efforts also under way. No update available.

She hesitated, fingers over the keyboard. Hmm. How to phrase this . . . Finally she typed,

```
TANGLER: UNODIR intend commence tactical repositioning.
```

She waited, bent over, surreptitiously scratching at her madly itching shins, under the coverall cuffs and above the socks. Pardees shot her a quizzical glance and she snatched the hand up quickly.

```
REPLAY: Roger, out.
```

"Ohh—*kay*," she whispered.

The anonymous staff officer who'd just answered in the admiral's name hadn't had a problem with a repositioning of her forces. Or more likely, didn't understand that the formation had been dictated by Sea Eagle. Carefully calculated by the AI to interlock sensor networks, weapons capabilities, fields of fire, and the other variables that would determine victory or defeat once battle was joined.

Once battle was joined.

But since she led the inferior force . . . wouldn't it be better not to fight at all?

Regardless, her own lily-white butt was now covered, at least as far as her orders were concerned. She leaned back in the form-fitting chair, digging her fists into her kidneys to ease her back. Now to concoct something more intimidating.

She told Pardees, "Noah, how about asking the XO if he can spare me an hour or two."

SOME five hours later she sat in the same chair, in the same compartment, buzzed from far too much coffee and a hastily bolted turkey-and-cheese sandwich in place of whatever meal this was supposed to be. A fresh patch of itching had broken out right in the middle of her back, exactly where she couldn't reach it. And there was no way she was going to ask a junior officer or enlisted to scratch her back . . . There was no dawn or dusk, no noon or midnight, in the digital no-time of Combat. Only the uneasy anthracite seas in the images from the deck cameras told her it was night now.

The fleet dispositions on the central display were quite different now. On both sides. Evolving, in ways that would no doubt be studied in the future. At the War College, if her idea worked. At her court-martial, if it didn't. She and Mills and Pardees had worked this out together, gamed it a bit, with the limited resources available onboard.

But she was in tactical command. If it all went south, this would be on her.

Aznavuryan's force had been joined by four additional destroyers and possibly two more submarines out of Vladivostok. This brought his fleet total to more than double that of her own. But like an atom absorbing extra electrons, he'd simply reduced the size of his concentric sectors, densifying his screen.

If "densifying" was a word . . . Anyhow, back in the VR helmet, she hovered above her own dispositions. The coast of Korea lay to the left, as it narrowed toward the strait, with Pusan the closest city. She'd managed to contact an ROKN ship moored there, which was beaming its fire control radar out to sea, presenting a threat that should keep the approaching Russians well offshore. Japan lay to her right hand, and she'd requested a shore battery of antiship missiles to carry out a drill that night, adding to the threatening emissions and, again, tending to nudge any approaching force to the midline of the strait.

Just behind her lay the slug shape of Tsushima Island itself, dividing the passage into western and eastern lanes. But as Aznavuryan closed from the north, whichever channel he decided to take, he was limited to a forty-mile-wide approach lane. Which the threats from both sides would tend to make him stick to.

Her own disposition was different as well.

Instead of a loosely knitted, nearly random scatter, her units were on their way to new stations. Once in position, they'd be lined up along the approaches the oncoming fleet would have to negotiate to pass.

She'd left the forty nautical miles in the center wide open. An invitation. Or, maybe more accurately, a set of open jaws.

To either side, she'd arranged her teeth. Frigates, destroyers, and *Savo Island*. They formed a gauntlet, with recon drones, attack UAVs, and manned fighters flying CAPs above them. She'd pulled her submarines, too, in toward her surface units. The Russians probably had less insight into their locations, lacking the inputs from the Allied land-based sonar networks that Cheryl could access. But just to be sure, she'd pulled them out of the center of the channel as well.

There would be no such thing as surprise this time. Sonar aside, the Russians had just as good targeting information, from their radars and satellites and long-range drones, as she did. The battlespace was known. The chess pieces were out in the open.

Chief Terranova stood beside her, arms crossed, her too-young-looking face engraved with the first frown lines Cheryl had ever seen on her as she scrutinized the lineup. "You're givin' away a lot of tactical advantage, here," she observed. "Skipper."

"Only if it comes to a battle, Chief." She didn't *have* to explain herself, but doing so was part of training the next generation. "The AI positioned us optimally for a meeting engagement. I've repositioned us for a different reason. A more . . . psychological impact. How about you? Look at our dispositions, pretend you're the enemy commander. What do you see?"

"Well, I gotta say, it looks to me like a fuckin' trap," the Terror said. She rubbed her arms, still looking doubtful. "Ma'am."

"And you don't stick your nose in a trap. Do you?"

"I don't know, ma'am," she said. "I guess if they order the guy to, he will."

She nodded grimly. Yeah. If Aznavuryan had orders to bull through regardless of casualties, he could stand off and plaster her with missiles, then roll up their lines from the north, on both sides of the lanes. The Tsushima Strait would smoke once again with the wrecks of burning ships. But not Russian ones, this time. American.

She stared at the displays, wishing she could hand this job to someone else. But there didn't seem to be anyone else around. And she still wasn't hearing anything constructive from Higher.

She shivered and rubbed her crossed arms, the same way Terranova had.

Waiting. Always the toughest part of war.

What a fool she'd been, to think for even a moment that it was over.

SOMEONE was shaking her. She popped upright in the command chair, gasping, nearly choking.

"Captain? Fleet's on the horn for you." Matt Mills, looking pale, holding out the red phone. His grimace and upward-cast eyes conveyed the message: *And they don't sound happy.*

"This is Tangler actual," Cheryl said, trying to push herself upright in the chair. Why was her hand so greasy? Oh yeah. The fucking ointment.

"This is Replay actual. What in the hell is going on up there, Captain?"

No one could sound quite as irate as a pissed-off admiral. "Uh, sir, current status. Russian Northern Fleet is proceeding toward Tsushima Strait. Speed two zero knots. Formation course—"

"I know that. I have that on the screen! But your formation doesn't match the order from PACOM."

"Sir, I have tactical command. And I requested permission to reorient. At approximately . . . five hours ago, on nanochat. Your staff watch officer—"

"My SWO is not me. Those stations were generated to maximize your combat power. You don't have tactical command in

order to make off-the-cuff decisions! Not with my task group. Why are you weakening it?"

"Sir, based on my reading of the—"

"I hope you haven't really fucked up, Captain. I sincerely hope you haven't really fucked everyone out there."

She swallowed. "Sir, we can return to the generated formation. Are those your formal orders?"

"Not according to the SOA I'm seeing. CNPTF is going to be in weapons range in about two hours." The distant voice shaded from anger toward sadness. *"Now I have to decide if we initiate hostilities. Because I don't see any other way you can prevail. Do you understand now? You're forcing me to start another war. When we just got finished with the last one."*

She swallowed again. "Sir, I don't think . . . I don't think we should give up on this just yet. I'm just not sure combat efficiency is the only thing we should—"

The voice on the other end turned steely. *"You've committed us, Staurulakis. Now we're going to have to live with what happens. The reason we didn't send you more forces is so we don't lose more than we can afford. And from what I've seen, that was the right decision. Your career just ended, Captain. You can count on that. Fleet, out."*

She resocketed the phone, trying to catch her breath. Her career? She was an O-6. She'd never expected to go even this high. Getting through the war had been her only real goal. Getting through it, and being with Eddie again.

Which was never going to happen now. He lay somewhere under the East China Sea, tangled in the wreckage of his fighter, his bones probably picked clean . . .

"Skippa?" Terranova's Jersey-accented whisper. "Y'okay?"

She shook herself back to CIC. Where watchstanders at consoles were stealing glances at her. Evaluating her reaction . . . She straightened in her chair. "Nothing major," she said coolly. "Let's finish this . . . Get *Arkansas*, *Idaho*, and *John Warner* to ping active." The three submarines now lay to the north of the oncoming Russians; behind them. *Utah* was still playing backstop south of the strait. "I want both our Orcas going active too."

"To ping?" Mills said, looking doubtful. "That gives away their position. You really want to do that, Captain?"

She nodded firmly. To ratchet up the pressure. "Yes. Do it now, XO."

After a slight hesitation, as if to allow her a chance to rethink, he began keyboarding.

She stared at the displays, fighting fear. Then remembered. In the Sea of Okhotsk, she'd actually talked to the Russian commander. Colonel-General Sharkov then. Sharkov had warned her not to intercept the Chinese missiles over Russian soil. But she had. Without really any blowback.

Unless this oncoming fleet was part of the retribution for that move . . .

She stared up at the screen, gnawing her lip.

Fucking . . . waiting.

TWO hours later she slumped in the chair. Not asleep; she was too agonized, too jittery, too fucking tense even to close her eyes. Not for the first time, she wondered how her previous CO had managed to keep his cool. Lenson had taken them into some tight corners. Places it didn't look like the old *Savo* would ever get out of. But he'd never looked like he felt a moment's fear or an instant's uncertainty.

Or perhaps he had, and just not shown it? She smiled wryly, wondering where he was now. Last she'd heard, he'd been pulled back Stateside for some kind of trial. Then she dismissed worrying about him. He could take care of himself.

The five-thousand-some men and women in her task group . . . she had to worry about them now.

She twisted violently, trying to scratch her back against the chair, but the soft padding was no help. The fucking rash itched like some malevolent Martian virus, eating her from the skin in.

Mills glanced at her. "We doing okay, Skipper?" he muttered.

"It's just this . . . *fucking* . . . itch."

"Yeah, I can see it bothers you." He hesitated, making sure no one had eyes on them. Then reached over.

She relaxed back into the scoring of his fingernails. It was close to orgasmic as relief flooded over her. But as soon as he took his hand away it started again. *"Fuck,"* she muttered.

Her nanochat pinged. *"Incoming from Fleet,"* AALIS said in her earbuds.

REPLAY: Replay to Tangler actual.

TANGLER: Tangler actual here.

REPLAY: Orders follow. Withdraw all units surface and
    subsurface plus reconnaissance assets to southward via
    Tsushima Strait. Proceed to Shanghai Harbor for
    humanitarian relief duty, passing to south of Jeju
    Island. Prepare helicopter assets for transfer ashore.
    Prepare to tie into shore systems for electrical
    power generation. Detach USS Montesano to escort
    relief shipping from Nagasaki. Furnish course points
    ASAP. Confirm.

She stared, disbelieving, at the words. Higher was *backing down.* "Oh, this is not good," she muttered.

Beside her, Mills stiffened. She thought at first he was reacting to the message. Then, cutting her eyes toward him, she caught that he was staring up at the large-screen display.

On it, a single contact, already far in advance of the oncoming formation, had suddenly detached itself. It hurtled forward, directly at the center of the strait. She lifted her head, frowning, as he toggled to zoom in on the contact.

"Track 0145 inbound," Terranova called. "Identify as Ohkotnik."

Cheryl forgot about the withdrawal order. Okhotniks were

heavy, persistent fixed-wing drones. They were stealth optimized, but *Savo*'s finely tuned radar had picked them up. The same UAVs had shadowed her in the Sea of Okhotsk. The Russians had used them then mainly for reconnaissance, but they could carry weapons as well.

At her coordination console, Terranova clicked busily. The rightmost display came up with video from one of the massive reflecting telescopes *Savo*'s lasers doubled as. Two objects were slung beneath the inbound contact's wings, but she couldn't make out what they were.

"AALIS pattern identifies as Sukhoi S-80 Okhotnik-B, probably carrying dual Zircons," one of the watchstanders called. "Mach 8 antiship missile. Radar and passive IR guidance. Seaskim capability. Heavy conventional penetrating warhead."

The noise level in CIC bumped up. She ignored it, focusing on the blinking yellow tracer which indicated the drone's line of advance. If it stayed on the same course, Its closest point of approach would be less than five miles east of *Savo*, and much closer to *Dixie Kiefer*.

"That's an overt threat, per the rules of engagement," Mills said.

"I concur," she said. "Desig track 0145 hostile, stand by to take with laser." She flicked up the cover over the red switch in front of her.

Another line scrolled up on her command desk computer.

REPLAY: Confirm receipt. From highest levels: US is not
    committed to defending Chinese territorial integrity.
    Not at cost of new war.

"From highest levels." So the order to retreat was from the national command authority, SecDef or the president. Not from PACOM or the Joint Chiefs.

Not that it made any difference to her. Not now.

"Locked on," said Terranova. "Designating to forward laser."

Cheryl hesitated for the merest fraction of a second. *Not committed. Withdraw.*

Those were her orders.

But they were under overt attack. If she allowed the drone to close, and if those objects it carried were really hypersonic missiles, there would be too little time to respond.

And Americans would die. On this ship, or another one under her command.

No matter what happened next, she had the right of self-defense.

She muttered, "Laser released," and hit the Weapons Release switch.

The console operator must have been tracking the Okhotnik already, because the video didn't blink or waver even as the white-hot spot ignited on the incoming drone's wing root. At the same moment, the overhead lights in Combat dimmed as the laser soaked up power from the generators and capacitor banks.

The spot dwelled there for nearly a second, juddering only very slightly.

A dainty, twisting wisp of whitish vapor, or smoke, began to trail the drone.

She tensed in her chair, gripping the armrests.

One of the drone's burdens had dropped free. Intentionally released, or burned off, she couldn't tell.

In the video, the elongated object, drop tank, missile, or electronics pod, rode below the parent drone for an instant or two, bobbling slightly in the airflow, before dropping farther. Gaining separation.

She stared up at the display. Don't, she thought desperately. *Don't*—

With a sudden flash, a flame appeared at the rear of the object. The missile accelerated out of the frame almost instantly, gaining velocity with the enormous impulse of a huge solid-fuel booster.

Above it, the drone's wing buckled and crumpled. The aircraft lurched sideways. The burning spot followed it, remorseless, but flicking off the airframe now to dwell directly on the nose of the second missile. It was still on its pylon under the undamaged wing as the drone began oscillating, losing control, starting a spin.

"Forward laser overheat warning. Need to unmask rainguns, need to unmask aft," the weapons controller said urgently over the circuit.

"Hard left rudder," Cheryl snapped, understanding instantly. "Steady two niner zero."

The Okhotnik disappeared in a soundless blast, a flash of white light succeeded instantly by black smoke out of which pieces tumbled. Then the video winked black, at the same instant the controller said, *"Forward laser, overheat indication, automatic shutdown. Commencing LNX dump for chilldown."*

"Aft mount, take the missile," Cheryl said into her throat mike. "Take the fucking missile! Now!" Her other defensive weapons, RAM and evolved Sparrow, were too slow to stop a Zircon. It would rip through her defenses like a cleaver through cream cheese. Even the railgun would be useless unless it connected with the first shot. The ramjet-propelled weapon was just too fast.

Only photons were speedier. But her forward laser was offline now, until a liquid nitrogen dump could cool it down. And both lasers tended to overheat and shut down far too often. The system worked, but it wasn't robust.

She'd just have to push the after one until it broke too, and hope that would be good enough.

Chief Terranova toggled the display to remote video from one of their own recon drones. It wasn't as sharp as before, but Cheryl could make out the Okhotnik still corkscrewing down toward the sea far below. Pieces kept falling off it and fluttering away, and it bled a stain of brown smoke as if the sky were rusting. She couldn't see the incoming Zircon at all. The video slanted left, searching for it, but caught only a single canted freeze-frame glimpse of a blanched smoke-trail, low over the wavetops. Headed her way.

A low ping diverted her attention from the video.

REPLAY: Confirm receipt.

Without conscious input, outside her knowledge until she saw it on the screen, her fingers and some subroutine in her brain typed,

TANGLER: Under attack engaged archer zircon incoming.

The laser controller: *"After mount locked on. Dwelling . . . target destroyed. Warhead detonation. Range, eight thousand yards."*

"Fuck," Mills breathed, beside her. His voice shook. "That was just too goddamned close."

She stifled a hiccup, and clicked to the weapons control circuit. "This is the CO. Barrel temperature, aft laser? Status, forward laser?"

"Lima Two, temp high but operational."

"Lima One, still down. Chilling."

Video came back up, this time from a flight deck camera. A monstrous bloom on the jagged wave-horizon. Frighteningly near. Fragment-splashes boiled the blue-gray sea beneath it. Beam on to those seas, *Savo* was picking up the roll, big as she was.

The compartment tilted around her. Cheryl eased a breath out, suddenly feeling sick to her stomach, hiccuping again. Wondering now if she should have been running this from within her VR helmet. She'd have better access, better overall picture . . . but right now she just didn't have the ten to twelve seconds it would take to plug in, settle it on her shoulders, and orient herself. "Status, foward laser," she snapped into her throat mike again. "Keep me updated, I don't—*hic*—want to have to keep asking!"

"Still emergency cooling, Captain."

"Cool it fast, we need it back." She took a deep slow breath. Sometimes that stopped the hiccups.

Mills said, "Did they *intend* to fire that missile?"

She blinked at him. Said, without letting go of her held breath, "What do you mean?"

"We hit it with the laser. Started burning it. Then it dropped the missile, and the booster ignited. I'm saying, maybe nobody actually sent it a fire signal. As such."

She frowned. "XO? You agreed, overt threat. Before it ever fired."

"Yeah. I did. But I just—"

Ping.

REPLAY: Overhead assets report explosions roughly your
    position. Status.

"Screw that, I don't have time to update them," she growled. "Let's slow to . . . no, that'll make this roll worse. And degrade our tracking. We need to stay beam to." She didn't need to add, to protect the ships behind them, who didn't have lasers.

"Two more drones leaving main formation," the surface warfare coordinator said in her earbuds.

"This isn't good," Mills said.

Too many voices were trying to talk at once, fouling the command circuit. She pushed a button, and pressed the lever on the ancient 21MC box in front of her. "Comm, CO. Do we have a deconfliction frequency with the Russians?"

A second's delay, then a surprised voice. "Captain? Uh, no. No, we don't. But . . . we have international distress up. HF common single sideband. They should be monitoring that."

"Get them on the horn and patch me in. Ask for their task force actual. Ask for"—she hesitated, not knowing what the Russians actually called their task force—"ask for the admiral. For Vitaly Aznavuryan. Say, the American commander asks for Vitaly Aznavuryan."

She twisted in her chair to face the ops officer. "Noah, you were comm-oh. Who do we have who speaks Russian?"

"Petty Officer Golubuvs speaks Russian."

"Right, the electrician. Get him to—no. Get him up here, please."

On the displays, the lead units of the Russian force were tracking on converging courses. As if they planned to approach her funnel in a more compact body. Well, that made sense. Interlocking their fields of fire. Concentrating their forces in one solid punch-through, like the liquid metal jet fired by a shaped-charge warhead. A jet that would penetrate many feet of hardened steel.

Like the warheads the Zircons aboard those rapidly approaching Okhotniks carried.

Terranova called, "Aircraft launching from Priboy."

The Wasp-equivalent assault carrier. Each STOVL fighter could carry from two to four antiship missiles. And those still-only-vaguely-localized submarines on her left flank would carry dozens more.

"He's launching an attack," Mills said. "They'll use those UAVs to kick open the door, then push the strike train through the breach."

"Might just be defensive CAP." She frowned. Carrier air patrols, to protect the formation in case of enemy attack.

"If it's a strike, each of those planes has two to four antiship missiles. Maybe not all Zircons, but threats. And we still don't have firm datums on those subs, on our left flank."

She studied the displays, mind racing as fast as she'd ever thought. No sleepiness now. Even the hiccups had stopped.

Well, the fucking *waiting* was over anyway. Hours doing nothing. Now death was streaking at them. Regardless of its formation, her force was going to take hits. They would already be at general quarters, but she put the order out on TG chat.

Enemy strike imminent. Condition One air, surface, ASW.
    Acknowledge.

Ping.

HUSKY: Interrogative.

Husky was IndoPac, Honolulu. Bypassing Fleet to ask her, essentially, what the fuck was going down. "God *damn* it," she muttered, suddenly so enraged her hands shook. Could they not *see* what was happening? Could they not let her deal with it, without interrupting every sixty seconds? She seized the keyboard.

> TANGLER: Under attack. Preparing to receive missile
> and a/c strike. Request air support. Request missile
> support. ASAP.

Beside her Mills was talking urgently into the IC phone at the same time he was typing. Cheryl snapped to the Weps Control circuit. "I'm not hearing a status on that forward laser."

"Forward laser still in overheat shutdown."

"Crap . . . Stand by on railguns. Slow to ten knots." They'd roll like a pregnant pig, but she had to make electrical power available. Reroute it from propulsion to recharge the massive capacitor banks. The lasers sucked electrical power by the megawatt. The railguns propelled terminally guided slugs, but they too would deplete her banks, and their rate of fire wasn't that great. Ten rounds a minute, less if the lasers were drawing power at the same time. "Stand by on RAM and decoys. Nulka to automatic. XO, did we get a roger from every formation unit? EW, you on the line?"

Mills: "All units rogered up."

The electronic warfare petty officer: "Standing by, Captain."

A husky, smooth-faced, butter-haired petty officer edged around into her field of vision. "You called for me, Captain?"

"Pavel. Yeah. Hold on a minute, may need you to translate." She hit the 21MC again. "Comm, CO: is my circuit to Aznavuryan up yet?"

"We have a staffer on the line, Skipper. Asked him to patch in the admiral. Not sure if he will. Or can."

She gnawed her lower lip, trying not to look concerned, but sweating under the coveralls. If her opponent didn't want to talk, that meant her whole strategy had been so much hopeful bullshit. And they were all toast. Not to put too fine a point on it.

Yeah, they'd be avenged. The US was still mobilized for war, and overall the Pacific Fleet and air forces already in theater dwarfed anything the Russians could bring to bear.

But that wouldn't mean much to scorched, swollen corpses bobbing in the Sea of Japan.

The 21MC clicked on. *"Putting you on terminal 2, CO. Staffer says the admiral will be there in a minute. Remember, this is open frequency."*

"Got it. Put it on speaker. We may need to translate." She pushed the button to activate the handset and tucked it under her chin. Above their heads, a hidden speaker crackled and hissed. A live circuit. Distant, muffled voices.

Finally a single one, louder, hoarse. A smoker's rasp. *"This is Admiral Aznavuryan."*

"Uh, this is Commodore Staurulakis." Not an official rank, but commonly used for a squadron or task group commander. "Welcome to the Sea of Japan, Admiral."

More muffled voices. Then, *"Commodore. You have shot down unarmed reconnaissance drone. This is act of war."*

"Your armed drone was approaching with hostile intent. A violation of the Code for Unplanned Encounters at Sea." She hesitated, unsure just how to play this. Maybe, conciliatory at first? "However, if it will help, I apologize."

"Apology not enough." Angry-sounding Russian followed, which Golubuvs translated as "You will provide my force safe passage through strait."

Okay, being nice wasn't going to work. She exchanged glances with Mills, and regripped the handset, which was growing slick with hydrocortisone ointment and sweat. "My orders do not permit that, Admiral."

"I am transiting the strait. If you fire again, I will destroy you."

She took a deep breath, making sure that when she responded her voice was as firm as she could make it. With even a hint of glee. "Do you really want to? I have eight submarines behind me, if you manage to make it through. Three carriers on their way to back me up. America's already mobilized, Admiral. Locked and loaded for another war, if you want one. So . . . *make my day.* I hope you feel lucky, punk."

Golubuvs gaped. At her console, Terranova snorted, a sound that came out as if she were choking. Mills looked shocked. Disbelieving.

But Cheryl felt pretty sure anyone who liked American movies would get the reference. And apparently her Russian counterpart did, because for a full eight seconds there was just hissing silence on the line.

"I accept apology," the hoarse voice said at last. *"But we must pass. I have orders too."*

"I suggest you see if they can be changed, then." She grinned at Mills, but the exec didn't look amused. At all. She scribbled on a Post-it and pushed it to him. *To all units. Initiate lock-on with all available fire control radars.*

Another few seconds of empty air. Sweat trickled under her arms. The compartment reeled around her, and she checked the clinometer. A ten-degree roll. The lasers could cope with that. She scribbled again. *Stand by to take incoming drones.*

"Maybe we won't have to," Mills muttered, laying a hand over hers. Then, as if remembering himself, quickly removed it. *Sorry,* he mouthed. And nodded toward the displays.

She lifted her gaze, to see the two Okhotniks that had been approaching shifting gradually to split left and right. Skating across the front of her own formation.

Aznavuryan, on the circuit. Sounding angry. *"I am requesting orders."*

She adjusted her grip on the gray plastic handset. It nearly shot out of her hand, it was so greasy. She grabbed for it, but kept her tone icy cool. "I understand, Admiral. I will stand by for your decision." To Mills, letting up on the Transmit button, she added, "You're on nanochat to Fleet, right? Ask where that fucking air is. Don't we have fighters back in Okinawa yet?" She'd stalled the Russian advance, but they could resume it in mere minutes. She needed backup, *now.* Reinforcements. Something that would show up on her adversary's radar.

The surface warfare coordinator spoke in her earbud. *"Captain,*

*lead ships on the oncoming formation's screens have slowed.
Steering various courses . . . appear to be zigzagging within
their sectors."*

"Very well."

Four contacts suddenly popped on the display. To the west,
over Pusan, South Korea. Their readouts spun as they gained altitude. She hooked them and queried. EEFI information appeared
beside the readouts.

"ROK Air Force," Mills said. "T-50s, out of Gimhae."

"That's got to be about all they have left." Cheryl wondered why
they even had those. "Didn't they lose most of their planes when
the North occupied them?"

The air warfare coordinator again. *"A few escaped to Japan."*

Cheryl hissed in through her front teeth as the readouts spun
upward. The new air contacts contracted into a diamond formation, so tight that from sweep to sweep the radar occasionally registered them as a single blip. They accelerated, still maintaining
that incredible closeness. She muttered, "What the . . ."

The FAWC said, *"T-50s . . . jet trainers . . . I'm thinking this
might be their national aerobatics team."*

"Aerobatics?" She rubbed her face, incredulous. A stunt team?

More contacts winked on, this time populating above western
Kyushu. *"F-15Js,"* the AWC said. *"Counting two, three, four . . .
six."*

Maybe Fleet and PACOM hadn't been as unconcerned as she'd
thought. She steadied her voice. "We might have a chance, folks.
I don't know about the aerobatics team, but Aznavuryan might
not know that's what they are. And if the Japanese back us up, or
even look like they might be about to, this could be a different ball
game."

THE next twenty minutes stretched out interminably. She rested
her forehead on the tips of her fingers, elbows planted on the desk.
Closing her eyes, and counting slow breaths. In. Out. Sensing the

intermittent trembling of her muscles. The sigh of air in and out of her nasal passages. Fortunately the hiccups stayed gone. Scared out of her, no doubt.

Suddenly she yearned to live through this. To bring them *all* through. Everyone aboard, and the rest of the task force. No one needed to die for Dalian. Moscow was just scavenging for whatever they could snatch, as long as nobody else was watching. Gambling human lives for a little more land.

Well, the world was watching now.

The T-50s closed the range rapidly, maintaining the same diamond, so tightly packed they consistently registered as a single return, even to *Savo*'s highly discriminating radars.

The F-15Js proceeded west at a more leisurely pace. They settled into racetracks near the outer edge of Japan's Self-Defense Identification Zone, just south of Tsushima Island.

The Korean jets crossed the strait, still holding that tight formation, as if they were entertaining a crowd at an air show. They executed a slow 180 and hurtled back, passing south of Cheryl's rearmost elements. She made sure Air Control deconflicted them. This wasn't the time for any blue-on-blue casualties.

The Russians, Okhotniks and strike fighters, crossed and recrossed her front, just out of Standard range, though her Alliances could have reached them. Each time they altered course she tensed, staring up at the displays. Would they come out of their turns headed for the task group? But no; they stayed distant. A threatening display, but not yet quite an attack.

Her command desk screen blinked.

REPLAY: USAF scrambling Taiwan for your support.
   F-35s + Valkyrie UAVs + tanker support.
TANGLER: Good news. ETA?
REPLAY: Launch approx 8 minutes ETA to follow.

"Outstanding," she murmured to Mills. "They haven't forgotten us."

"They were probably just stood down, after the armistice," the

XO said. "Took them some time to get back on line. But, yeah. Some fighters out front, that'll make 'em think twice. Maybe not even bother to try."

She was allowing herself a tentative smile when Terranova called from her console, "Skipper! You need to see this. Putting it on the left LSD."

The picture came up, expanded so far to the north that the strait and the tip of the Korean Peninsula were not even visible. She looked down on Okhotsk and Kamchatka. Above them, air contacts were blinking into existence. Rising from distant airfields. Eight. Ten. Twelve. More.

"Bombers," Mills said, and his tone was flat. Dull. Dead, almost. She snarled, "I don't need you to tell me that, XO!"

"Sorry, Captain—"

"No, *I'm* sorry." She took another deep breath. In the last minutes of their lives, she didn't need to be biting pieces off her own people.

They weren't the ones at fault. The diplomats and higher-ups had failed, again, and it was the sailors at sea who would pay. "We'll take whoever crosses the ROE line first. Then expend our Alliances on the bombers as they come into range. Fight as long as we can, try to cover the rest of the force's retreat. That's all we can do."

Her exec's handsome features hardened. "Hold and die?"

"I'm afraid so, Matt."

Her desk pinged again.

REPLAY: *Russian Federation Defense Ministry announces major strategic maneuver exercise "Vostok." Combined arms groups including elements Eastern Fleet will engage in simulated air strikes and air defense. Goal of exercise: improving command and control of joint military operations across multiple services in the eastern theater of operations. Coordinating operations between Pacific air forces and the Pacific Fleet. Exercise will take place in the northern areas of the Sea of Japan, Sea of Okhotsk, and northern Pacific.*

She stared at the words, trying to reorganize them into sense. Beside her Mills was shaking his head. "What the heck—"

REPLAY: CJCS informs IndoPacom that negotiations for mutual
    withdrawal of US and Russian forces from Sea of Japan are
    concluded. Tangler will withdraw south of Tsushima Island
    and resume play Exercise Trident Junction in area bounded
    by sepcor until further orders. Acknowledge.

Fingers trembling, she typed,

TANGLER: Acknowledged. Wilco. Tangler out.

"We're *both* pulling back?" Mills sounded shaky too.

"Both retreating, saving face," she said. "Pretending we were both just carrying out exercises."

She closed her eyes and scratched under her arms, for once totally without inhibition. Yeah, it was good news. *Great* news. But she'd been so whiplashed over the last few minutes, with panic, fear, relief, rage, resignation, relief again, that her body felt like it didn't know how to respond, or what to feel.

On the display, the lines of advance of the oncoming units were altering. Clicking around clockwise. The opposing units were turning away together. The UAVs, too, were heading for the barn. Turning back, for their launch platforms.

She sagged in her chair, and even though her skin felt like a full-body rash was breaking out, and she was wet through with sweat, and stank from nearly a day stuck in the chair, she closed her eyes and heaved a silent thanks.

Then remembered: it wasn't just she who needed to be reassured. She hoisted herself out of the chair's too-soft embrace, steadied her knees, and stood. Turned to face the rows of consoles, the expectant, frightened faces, and mustered a smile.

She spread her arms, palms up. "It's over," she told them all.

"Both sides are backing down. We're headed south. Probably to Shanghai for humanitarian ops. Keep an eye on things. But it looks, thank God, like we're out of the woods."

Her desk pinged again, and she cringed, gut cramping, and whipped her head back to the displays. But the Russians were still in their turns. Still heading north. So what now? She bent quickly to the screen. No, she thought. Don't let the wheels come off this now. I can't go through it all again.

HUSKY: Personal confidential for Tangler actual.

Confidential? Everything on high-side nanochat was TS compartmented. What could be personal and confidential? She typed shakily, dreading the worst. Her mom? Maybe her dad? But they wouldn't notify her this way about a death in the family.

Filled with dread, she keyed in a terse response.

TANGLER: Actual here.
HUSKY: Muster list of personnel to be repatriated in POW
    exchange received from Beijing includes one Edward L.
    Staurulakis LCDR USN previously listed as missing in
    action, presumed KIA. Further status unclear. More
    to follow after formal exchange takes place but
    thought you would like to know soonest. Compassionate
    leave available if desired. Congratulations, Justin
    Yangerhans, Admiral USN.

Mills was patting her back. Telling the others, since he'd apparently read it over her shoulder. In seconds, Terranova was excitedly relaying the surprise development to the other enlisted.

Someone started clapping. Then they all jumped from their seats, applauding, cheering, shouting. Congratulating her.

She smiled uncertainly, blinking back tears and trying to hold it together. Nodding and smiling wordlessly. Shaking the outstretched hands as she walked among the stations.

The applause wasn't just for her husband, or for her. It was for themselves. That they would live through this war, and go home. See those they loved again.

The clapping went on and on, as if no one wanted ever to stop. She reached the far end of the compartment and turned to face them, to applaud *them*. Her crew, and all the crews. The new *Savo*. The old *Savo*. The ships and planes that had gone down, the men and women who'd burned and drowned in a war that never should have happened.

But who'd done their duty, to the end.

She clapped until her palms stung, tears hot on her cheeks, but not caring anymore. Not wanting to stop either, not wanting to stop ever, grinning now. Unable to fully join in their glee, but unwilling to dampen it either. They deserved it. They'd all come through, and won.

As to what came next . . . well, she'd think about that tomorrow.

13

McLean, Virginia

THE concrete and glass building was set amid a forest. It sparkled in the sunlight like a spaceship just arrived. The roads of a city enwebbed it, but a green space shielded it from view, cradling it like cerebrospinal fluid does a brain.

"Vladimir" sat in a windowless room on the third floor of the west wing, waiting to defend his report. He'd shed the greatcoat and fur hat for slacks and a blazer and an open-collared shirt. His cheeks were still blistered with frostbite, though. He still wore dark glasses, too. His eyes watered, exquisitely sensitive from exposure to the glare of the sun at high altitudes.

A young man and two women had just joined him at the table. A digital projector hummed overhead, projecting a map of the western Pamirs onto the wall.

The door opened and another, taller man in slacks, sport coat, and hand-tooled Black Jack western boots sauntered in. Anthony Provanzano was the assistant deputy director for operations. "Hey, all," he said. "Kaylie. Josh. Beverly. This must be Korzenowski, right? In from the cold. Good to meet you, Andy." He wrung his hand, the two-handed grip beloved of politicians. Then took the seat at the head of the table.

Provanzano kicked off. "Our tasking today is to clarify the situation in Xinjiang, try to predict where events are going, and what that means for long-term US interests for the postwar settlements with China, Iran, and Pakistan. All of which, what's happening in western China is going to impact. The output will be included in the presidential daily brief and furnished to the negotiators in Singapore.

"The usual reminders. Close hold personal notes, no recordings other than the official one, and focus on reporting, not policy. Our State and DoD reps will make their recommendations up the chain based on what they learn today. Plus of course their own sources of information.

"For the record. Present today are a rep from State, Josh, one from DoD, Kaylie. The desk officer for western China—Beverly—and Andy Korzenowski, just in from Xinjiang with the latest and greatest from the field. At considerable risk, I understand, since the fighting's still going on up there." He sat back. "Andy, give us the situation on the ground."

Andres started with the Hunza, the tribe that inhabited the high uplands of Pakistan, Afghanistan, and China. They'd sided with the Allies early in the war, then switched support to Iran. "On my last trip in, I spoke to four of the highland tribal chiefs. All four understood China's been defeated, and what that means—that the Allies will turn to Iran and Pakistan next. They're pliable. Willing to realign, given the right assurances.

"If they do, our supply lines up into western China will become much more secure. With better logistics, it might be possible to provide additional support to the ITIM forces in Xinjiang than we've managed so far."

"Provided we wanted to do that," Josh, the young State rep, put in. The others nodded too.

Except for Andres, who inclined his head gravely. "Yes sir; provided we wanted to do that."

He finished reporting on the Hunza and their disenchantment with the Iranians. Then pulled up another slide, zooming in on western China.

"Moving eastward, my next stop was the Tian Shan. I met with agent SKFROG. For those unfamiliar with his history, SKFROG is a senior US Navy SEAL operator. The Chinese captured him in the South China Sea early in the war. They subjected him to enhanced interrogation before sending him to a POW camp where he and other Allied prisoners were being held under starvation conditions. Eventually he escaped. Five men left the camp; only two made it out to safety.

"During his trek to the west, SKFROG encountered and was eventually taken in by a small group of ethnic Uighur bandits located deep in the Tian Shan. He contacted us, asking to remain with them, embed, and take on an advisory role. He proposed that the group be built into a resistance movement, to divert enemy forces into fighting a guerrilla war in the west. His proposal was passed to us through military service channels.

"The director cleared us to pursue this action. It was presented as part of the revised LC-INFRA Joint Operation Plan to the OSD/JS/Agency working group for transmittal to the Office of the Secretary of Defense. Approved by Defense and State, it formed part of the heads of state Joint Comprehensive Strategic Plan of Action. The concept was further refined and developed by the appropriate Agency, DoD, and CENTCOM authorities. It became part of the LC-INFRA strategy of diverting enemy forces by supporting revolts in Tibet, southern China, the Baluchi movement in Iran, and elsewhere."

He took a breath. Best to keep it short, but these people needed the deep background to make the right decisions. "Accordingly, we've supported this resistance, renamed the Movement for an Independent Turkistan, or ITIM, for the last two years. We supplied gold, medical supplies, weapons, ammunition, and second-tier communications and antidrone equipment. Our best read is that these efforts pinned down or otherwise kept from the front as many as six Chinese Internal Security divisions and over a hundred combat and transport helicopters, with associated logistic and support elements, including heavy artillery and drone reconnaissance and cyber support. Together with related LC-INFRA efforts in south China and Tibet, they succeeded in diverting major enemy attention and resources from the central war effort, and contributed to the success of the invasions of Taiwan and South China."

The State rep raised a hand. "Do we have any estimate of costs?"

Andres hesitated. "Are you referring to casualties, or—"

Josh smiled. "I'm assuming any loss of life was confined to local forces. My question was budgetary. That could impact whether to continue the program going forward, right?"

Provanzano, the deputy director, said, "I'll take that, Andy. Let me get those figures to you a little later, Josh. We'd have to pull the numbers together. But all in all, I doubt ITIM's cost us more than forty million, total."

Kaylie, the Defense representative, had a question too. "Sounds like a lot of bang for the buck. But I've heard some disquieting reports about massacres, reprisals, pretty savage stuff going on in that part of the world."

Provanzano lifted his eyebrows. "Jeez, where did you hear that kind of thing, Kaylie? I wasn't aware of anything like that. You say it's been in the news?"

"No. Anything like that, the censors would take care of, I assume. It's just . . . rumblings. Hearsay. But things that could embarrass us if they surfaced after the war. Or worse, during the armistice negotiations."

Their eyes turned to Andres, who hesitated, at a loss how to answer. Trying not to think about skulls on sticks. A dank cave, and the stories he too had heard, traveling the mountains. Tales that exceeded both in barbarity and scale anything that had filtered to the outside world. He sighed and thrust his hands into his pockets. "Well, as in most unconventional wars, there've been civilian losses. Chinese reprisals for ITIM actions included gassing villages, shelling population centers, mass incarceration, and targeted assassinations." He tried to think of some graceful way to put it, but there really wasn't one. "Both sides have probably been guilty of some unpleasant acts. And yes, those include actions we wouldn't want to be associated with. Even at a remove."

The DoD rep pressed. "But we have deniability?"

Provanzano waved a hand, taking the floor back. "Built in from the start. We supplied non-US weapons. European antidrone technology. Commercial comms. And all subventions were provided in Krugerrands, which was all anybody in that part of the world wanted anyway. There are no fingerprints on this operation." He grinned. "Unless someone in this room leaks it. All right?" He looked back at Korzenowski. "Andy, you can finish up. We have four other items on the agenda. Including cuts to the budget, which we are gonna have to be ready for if this peace process succeeds and we start winding down in earnest."

Andres cleared his throat. "Um, sure. My collection requirements when meeting with SKFROG and the senior leadership of ITIM included determining the number of effectives and whether the movement was broadly enough based to serve as a viable interim government for Xinjiang. Also, to determine if our asset could be extracted in case it was decided to slate the program for termination."

Provanzano sighed audibly. "Can we move this along, Andy? To your conclusions. Like I said—"

"Yes, sir. Fast-forward to my conclusions." He took a deep breath, aware of the focused gazes, aware that his next words could be seen as a betrayal. Could doom hundreds if not thousands of innocent people. "I believe ITIM is evolving from a sectarian rebellion into a more radical version of Islamic terrorism. Akin to the ISIS, Daesh, and Boko Haram groupings we were fighting in several countries in the prewar setting."

The four other attendeees avoided looking at him. Some studied the table's surface. A couple looked up at the ceiling. None met his eye, or ventured a comment. At last Provanzano said, "Beverly, you're Andy's desk officer. What's your take?"

"I think he's pretty well nailed it," she said firmly. "I don't need to remind anyone about our history supporting the Taliban against the USSR in Afghanistan, and what that morphed into. ITIM's methods are ruthless. They've targeted teachers, government officials, healthcare personnel, mayors, anyone cooperating with the central government. Yes, that's classic guerrilla strategy. But in some ways, they're coming close to genocide against ethnic Chinese.

"Early in the war, they operated effectively against strategic targets for us. But the most recent operation, Jedburgh, against missile sites in the mountains, was a failure. Going forward, our evaluation is that they will increasingly operate independently and not in a manner calculated to further the peace."

Kaylie frowned. "So your recommendation is to terminate our support?"

"*We* don't recommend squat," Provanzano said firmly. "Remember? We provide information. It's up to you guys what you do with it. So don't saddle us with providing some kind of advocacy for any given course of action."

Josh said, "What about our asset? This SKFROG. Can we pull him out safely before we terminate support? Because otherwise, he's likely to get whacked, right?"

Andres tried to game it out in his head. Actually, he'd thought about this for a long time, about the end game if the program was shelved. "Um, I'm not sure he would be. He seems to be respected by the rebels. Integrated with their top leadership, which has turned over several times during the rebellion. In fact, he's converted to Islam."

"Indeed." Provanzano squinted and leaned back in his chair. "He wasn't a Muslim originally?"

"No sir."

"A real conversion? Or a false flag?"

"Genuine, as far as I can tell. He even told me he'd had a personal talk with Allah once."

This seemed to give everyone pause. Finally Josh pressed, "But we can extract him? Um, he's actually DoD, right? You said a Navy SEAL."

Andres nodded, but then shook his head. "Yes, but I believe he's left that behind some time ago, sir. I discussed his future with him. Offered him promotion, back pay, surgery—he has a crippled leg, from the torture sessions after he was captured. Then, either retirement, a return to the Spec Ops community, or possibly a position in Special Activities."

Beverly, the desk officer, scribbled a note. "And what did he say?"

Andres said reluctantly, "He says, the guy we knew is dead."

The State rep: "He have a family? Would they be any help?"

"He's single. Parents dead. A former girlfriend in San Diego. No siblings or kids."

Provanzano mused, "So we really have very little hold on him."

"We actually have *no* hold on SKFROG," the desk officer clarified.

Andres said, "If I could insert a personal opinion? I respect this guy. He's given up a lot to make this rebellion work. I believe he's just . . . lost his way. Possibly suffered from some form of mental illness or psychological trauma. I'd argue for inserting a team and returning him involuntarily."

"For what purpose?" his desk officer said. "Just to retire him?"

Andres turned to her. "Well, maybe not, Beverly. He needs medical attention. After that, reeducation and treatment. He could be a valuable asset again, if he could be returned to service. An advisor on the internal politics in Xinjiang, if nothing else."

"Wait a minute. You said 'mental illness.'" The deputy tapped a pen on the table. "Explain that. Like this chat with Allah you mentioned. He's unbalanced? Insane? A loose cannon?"

Andres turned to face Provanzano. "Uh, not exactly, sir. He still seems to be a competent commander. But he's shared with me that he had some kind of . . . experience, up in the mountains. It's convinced him he has a, um, mission. One that justifies, I guess, pretty much anything."

"An experience," the DoD rep murmured. "A mission. You mean, aside from his tasking from you guys? Like, a mission from God?"

Chuckles rippled around the table. Andres didn't see much encouragement in their grins. The DoD rep rolled her eyes.

"So, a kidnapping," the State rep said. "In the Himalayas? From a group of armed guerrillas. Is that really practical?"

"Anything can be done if you throw enough money at it," Provanzano told him.

"And enough lives," Kaylie said. "So, we insert a special ops team and snatch him from these jihadis. We could lose a helicopter. Could lose the whole fucking team. And for what, exactly?"

"We could send SEALs," Provanzano suggested. "In the end, he's still a DoD asset."

"No way. He's your problem now. If you want him back, you go get him," Kaylie said. She and Provanzano glared at each other.

"We have an obligation." Andres tried to keep his voice level. "This guy's spent the war in prison camps, then in the mountains with the rebels. If his health's impaired, it's been in the line of duty. Kaylie, Tony's right. He's a military member, remember, only seconded to us. Not an Agency asset, strictly speaking."

"If you mean he's our problem, we can wash our hands of him," the DoD rep said. "His service record can show he went MIA on his raid. Or we can carry him as deceased in captivity."

The State rep said, "The Chinese might dispute that."

Kaylie shrugged. "And admit to his escape? I think not. Anyway, do you really think they kept records on their death camps? Did they ever give the Red Cross a POW accounting on him?"

"Not that we know of." The desk officer sighed.

"So as far as any records go, he went MIA years ago. He's a ghost." The Defense rep folded her arms. "Fuck him."

Andres looked from face to face. An interagency dispute? Really? He said again, more forcefully, "*Somebody* has an obligation here. If DoD's planning to disavow him—"

"He hasn't been under our orders for years," Kaylie said, rolling her eyes again. "No, you ran him, he's your mess. You clean it up."

Andres clenched his fists under the table. "You may want to write him off, but the Agency shouldn't. In my book, he deserves a star on our wall."

"Those stars are reserved for deaths in the line of duty," Provanzano observed.

"Well, maybe not that then. But the guy came through for us, at great personal risk. We gave him an award, remember? The Intelligence Medal. We owe him more than 'fuck him.' Extraction, treatment, care, rehabilitation. At the very least."

The senior CIA man pushed back from the table. "I get your standing up for him, Andy. Does you credit. But you said he refused repatriation. Correct?"

Andres nodded unwillingly. He could see where this was going.

"So it would be an involuntary extraction. Essentially, a kidnapping, as Josh pointed out. Let's look at the downsides. A, we lose people pulling him out. B, his existence goes public, and we get linked to enabling a mad dog, supporting genocide and terrorism.

"I just don't see the advantage to bringing him back, Andy. He's a spent asset. And a risky one to keep around, even if we could get him back. What if he goes back here? Decides to start his own little franchise of the jihad right here at home?"

Andres stood without words. He looked down at his hands, then around at the faces around the table. "We owe him," he said again.

"He knew the risks," the DoD rep said.

"The downside's too steep, I agree," said the State rep.

"Beverly? It's your department." Provanzano turned to Andres's desk officer.

She too shook her head, and made another note.

The deputy massaged his chin for a few seconds as the others watched him. Finally he said, "Some tough choices have been made in this room. Probably, some well beyond what we'd think of as moral, in our personal lives. But I'm gonna quote Machiavelli here.

"'The way men live is so far removed from the way they ought to live, that anyone who abandons what is for what should be pursues his downfall, rather than his preservation.'"

He looked around the table. "He said the prince had to set aside his personal feelings and act for the good of the state. Bearing only that in mind, and not what people deserved, or what anyone thought of as justice.

"Granted, it's four hundred years later now, but what's changed? We, here in this room, are in the position of the prince. We're not free to act the way we would prefer to in private life.

"We've looked at the downsides. Considered the upsides. I'm confident we've examined this case to the extent we need to, or can at present. The next step, if there is a next step, is going to depend on what the policymakers decide."

He nodded to Beverly. "Okay, let's go to the decision tree."

She passed out a single piece of paper to each participant, and waited as everyone studied it.

The deputy resumed, "If the heads of state approve independence for this part of the world, as part of the final treaty, we have to ask: Can ITIM transform into a viable political party, willing to participate in a democratic process? If they seem willing to, we can help. Subject to budget and manning constraints, of course. One stage in that process is to gauge whether the instigators of violence can be publicly rehabilitated into more acceptable figures, both to the international community and local opinion leaders. Then, whether they have enough popular support to become a viable political movement.

"Beverly, can we look for an assessment from you on that point?"

"Yes sir," the desk officer said, making a note.

Provanzano went on, "If, on the other hand, the final treaty retains Xinjiang as part of China, ITIM will have to undergo a harsher process. Shut it down, and remove the leadership, possibly coordinating action with whoever emerges as the final authority in Beijing."

Andres said, "And give our agent a last chance to return?"

Provanzano smiled thinly and nodded toward the door.

"Thanks, Andy. Good report. We'll take it from here. And let you know what we send up the line."

At the door he glanced back over his shoulder. At the gleaming table, the scraps of paper on it, the bent heads around it. He wanted to go back and argue the point. Pound the table. Insist.

But would it do any good? Unlikely. Had he fought hard enough? He thought he had. But it was out of his hands.

As he walked back down the corridor, toward the little cubicle office he got to use only two or three days a year, he kept telling himself this.

But he couldn't make himself believe it.

14

Singapore

THE lights in the eighty-fifth-floor conference room dimmed and brightened automatically as clouds slid across the face of the sun. If she glanced over from her notebook she found herself looking down at a vertiginous drop of hundreds of feet. So far that her head swam and she had to close her eyes and fight for composure.

Far below, across a wide expanse of manicured garden threaded with footpaths, shone the Singapore Strait. Dozens of ships lay moored out there, along with massive shining white structures many blocks long: floating apartment complexes, built to accommodate the swelling population of the land-poor island. To her right stretched piers and breakwaters, unloading cranes, and varicolored mountain ranges of shipping containers. International trade through the South China Sea, shut down during hostilities, had reopened since the armistice. Today a steel queue of containerships, tankers, and liquid natural gas carriers marched away over the hazy curve of the planet eastward and then out of sight.

She sighed, and turned back to her screen.

She'd left the Sands only once since getting here, for a brief foray to a mall and tea garden. Just to say she had . . .

She and Shira had walked there via an elevated way lined with trees and vaulted above a highway thronged with nearly silent electric cars, vans, and trucks. Vertical wind turbines spun between the lanes, recovering energy from the passing vehicles. Singapore seemed to be taking its obligations under the new climate treaty seriously. The city, futuristic and wealthy, was densely populated but carefully planned. Compared to it, postwar Washington seemed shabby and worn. Deteriorating, with its potholed, flooding roads, abandoned plywood-covered storefronts, whole neighborhoods even the Loyalty League didn't dare go into at night.

Now, back in the office, Shira Salyers sat across from her, head down, intent on her own computer. Behind her, pinned up on the wall, was a large, minutely detailed, brilliantly colored geographic and political map of China. At other tables, or collaborating on the same documents in real time from other rooms, sat Australian, Japanese, Russian, Vietnamese, Indonesian, and Indian staff members. They were searching the minutes of the day before, embodying voted-on agreements and amendments into the final report.

She glanced out the window again, unable to resist. Then gritted her teeth, steering her mind back from the image of hurtling hundreds of feet down to the pavement. You just have too much imagination, Blair, she told herself.

The hotel was three huge towers of pale curved concrete. Across their tops cantilevered a pool and topiary garden as large as the deck of an aircraft carrier. She hadn't been up there yet, though, and had absolutely no desire to go.

But aside from that hour at the mall, she'd been locked indoors since she got here, either sitting in the tight circle of wallflowers and aides around the semicircular tables of the bigger conference rooms down on the second and third floors, or toiling deep into the night to reconcile the clashing positions and embody the compromises in black-and-white text for the ages.

But the work was drawing to an end. The final session of the heads of state conference would take place today, with the treaty-signing ceremony tonight. And as usual in most negotiations, the final terms were being fought tooth and nail down to the closing bell.

Leading the Allied Powers was the United States, represented by the deputy SecState, Ransome Teague, since the secretary was too ill to travel. Adam Ammermann was "assisting" him, which really meant keeping him toeing the line—this administration being deeply suspicious of bureaucrats, even if they were their own appointees. The president of Australia was here, as were the foreign ministers of Japan, India, and Indonesia. Only Russia was represented by a military man, Marshal Yevgeny Sharkov. Britain and the EU had attended as nonvoting observers.

And each ally had come fully primed to fight for its own country's utmost advantage.

The Chinese, putatively the defeated power, were right in there with brass knuckles ready as well: the disadvantage of not insisting on unconditional surrender . . . Chen Jialuo represented the provisional government, as he'd done at the meetings with the advance mission in the Forbidden City. He denied any responsibility for the war itself, blaming everything on Zhang, while insisting on China's continued status as a superpower. He'd schemed, coaxed, and threatened the smaller allies, especially those who'd have to live cheek by jowl with his still-powerful country whatever the postwar government looked like. Chen was trying hard to break the united front and weaken the terms of the final settlement.

Fortunately, he didn't have a vote. But his arguments and proposals had to be heard, evaluated, debated, and rebutted. The smaller countries had to be reassured that their allies would stand behind them in case of renewed aggression. It all took endless palavering and horse-trading behind the scenes.

Over the past days, four resolutions had been introduced, hotly debated, amended, and voted on again and again.

Blair sat back, sighing, and like some weird pull of gravity the drop attracted her gaze once more. She turned her head away, and reviewed each point, one by one.

The first resolution specified territorial adjustments and residual military forces. Point One included formal independence for Tibet, for "Miandan," the Chinese puppet state in northern Myanmar, and ceding of the islands in the South China Sea that Zhang Zurong's regime had fortified. They were going to Vietnam, Indonesia, and Brunei. The Allies would retain permanent military bases in Itbayat and Pratas Reef, with a ten-year lease in Hainan.

Point Two dealt with a second tranche of adjustments. Taiwan and Hong Kong were to decide their own futures by plebiscite, choosing between full independence or participation in a democratic, federal Chinese state. Xinjiang had been on this list too, until State had struck it off. Without explanation; but Blair had a pretty good idea why. The Islamist rebels there were gaining ground. The administration feared it would become another radical fundamentalist state. With a choice between that and leaving it to China to police . . . that decision had been made.

During the Point Two negotiations the Russians had put in a claim, insisting that Manchuria be added to the list of newly independent states and that Dalian, formerly Port Arthur, become a Russian leasehold once more. After considerable argument, Sharkov had agreed to a compromise. Manchuria would also go on the plebiscite list, to vote for either China or independence. In turn, Russia would abandon her claim to Dalian.

It sounded to her like a recipe for another gray war, like the ones Moscow was already fomenting in Eastern Europe and Finland. Low-grade infections, to sap the health of fragile states. Still, that was how the Allies had finally voted.

Point Three dealt with the postwar military and government. China's conventional armed forces would be reduced to ten divisions, her nuclear deterrent to one hundred warheads, and research into artificial intelligence and quantum technologies would be subject to international supervision for a period of ten years. As to its government, Minister Chen had arrived armed with a modified version of Bankey Talmadge's sketch constitution, with a return to the 1912 flag and a new name, the Federation of Chinese States.

Talmadge wasn't mentioned, but Sun Yat-Sen was. China's twenty-some provinces would be federated under a central government in Beijing. It would have five branches, headed by a president elected for no more than two four-year terms.

The Allies had debated it at length, with Russia pushing for acceptance and finally moving the question. Unfortunately, the bill of rights Talmadge had drawn up had vanished along the way, and Chen had added language continuing a leading role for the Communist Party. So the other allies had voted against, and the motion was defeated.

At that, Ammermann had spoken up. As a junior White House staffer, he'd been involved in the writing of the Iraqi constitution following Saddam's fall. He'd outlined a process where a committee appointed from Chinese elements drafted a constitution during a transitional period. The first assembly elected under that constitution, whatever it was called, would review it, amend it as necessary, then submit it to the population for ratification. There would be no mention of parties at all.

Everyone except the Chinese seemed to like this, and it passed on a voice vote while they sat with arms crossed and angry scowls.

"Excuse me, Blair?"

Recalled from her mental review, she opened her eyes to an anxious young face. Harold Lichtman worked for the US trade representative. She pushed her chair back, caught another glimpse of the fall to the pavement below, and was suddenly tense again.

Okay, yeah, now she got it: why she felt so threatened. Having been trapped in the North Tower on 9/11 meant she would never thereafter feel comfortable more than ten stories off the ground. She couldn't help glancing up, searching the sky, but it was empty of approaching airliners.

"Ms. Titus?" He cleared his throat nervously.

She flinched, jerked back from the memories of story after story collapsing above her, like the heavy footsteps of an enraged giant striding closer. "Sorry, I was . . . never mind. What do you need, Harry?"

"Well, you know what we're pushing for, right? Dismantle war-time barriers. Open Chinese markets to American businesses, and build in hard protections for copyrights, patents, intellectual property. That was one of the causes of the war, right? Unfair trade."

"Okay, sure." She tried to keep impatience from her voice. "I understand. So what's the problem? I'm Defense, you know that, right?"

"Um, right. But you did a study once about floating the yuan?"

"Oh." She blinked. "Why, yes . . . for the Congressional Research Service. But that was ages ago. Way before the war."

"I came across it looking up references . . . See, now we have to make some decisions on whether to insist on a stable new yuan, or couple it to the US dollar, or let it float, or—or, well, what?" He swallowed. "I'm sorry—didn't mean to interrupt. I know you're busy . . ."

She frowned. Did she really come across as that scary? The kid looked totally intimidated. She gestured to the chair opposite. "Grab a seat, Harry, and I'll try to help. Well, you know that their currency regime's been state-controlled. Their central planners tried to keep up with the market, the money supply, interest rates. They screwed up as often as they got it right, but it gave them weapons we don't have in the Fed, for example. For one thing, they can devalue on demand."

He blinked. "Which means . . ."

"They can commit to, say, a huge loan, then devalue, and suddenly it's twenty-five percent less in hard money."

Lichtman said, "That would also make their products cheaper. Right?"

"Not only their products." She suddenly saw where this was going. "Um, is this linked to the state enterprise liquidation scheme? Where they have to go to the highest bidder, even if it's a foreign company?"

"It could work to our advantage," Lichtman said, gaze sliding away.

"Meaning, fire-sale Chinese industry to multinationals at pennies on the dollar? Hmm. I'm not comfortable with that, Harry. I know, victors and spoils. But if anyone really owns those companies, it's the Chinese people."

He leaned forward. Said earnestly, "But it's not like that, really. We did it wrong in Russia. Sold off to domestic entities, and they ended up being owned by the old KGB and the Mafia. This will be the free market at work, Ms. Titus. Spurring development through the private sector. Integrating China with the international community. And they *did* lose. After all."

She exhaled, searching her brain for historical parallels, but couldn't think of any. Even after the fall of Germany, Krupp had stayed German. Boeing hadn't taken over Mitsubishi. The Bush administration hadn't appropriated Iraq's oil.

But really, bottom line, this question was outside her wheelhouse. "Um, sorry, but I can't really give you any useful advice, Harry. Postwar currency stabilization's a balancing act. You want to peg the exchange rate at a realistic level. Reassure business, so they can convert to peacetime production, restore the living standard, rebuild some kind of social safety net. All of it, all at once . . . um, do you know Mr. Ammermann? He was in Iraq. At least he'll be able to tell you what *not* to do."

The staffer nodded, not looking very enlightened, and left.

She sighed, and pressed the heels of her palms to tired eyes. Then returned to her screen, and the contemplation of the final point of the peace treaty.

Which could turn out to be the most dangerous.

Point Four dealt with responsibility for war crimes. Sixteen persons were specified under the Allied indictment. The International Court of Justice at The Hague would carry out the trials, assuring an independent and disinterested process.

At this point, Minister Chen had popped to his feet like a jack-in-the-box, spluttering, near apoplectic. "This," he protested, "is victor's justice." He ticked it all off on his fingers: Allied forces had committed crimes as well. They'd damaged nuclear generating stations, endangering large areas with the release of radioactive materials. Bombed coastal cities, inflicting thousands of civilian casualties. Fomented rebellion by religious extremists. American scientists had unleashed diseases. Medical personnel had withheld knowledge of essential drugs.

If the ICJ was to sit in judgment on Chinese generals, admirals, and statesmen, it had to include those Allied personnel who had brought on the conflict, who'd violated the laws and usages of war and of humanity. He'd held forth for minute after minute, face reddening to violet, until Blair had feared for his heart. But at last he'd stammered to a halt.

And been ignored. Chen had stood astonished, mouth still open, as the Japanese foreign minister spoke next, ignoring his protests. He'd stared around, bewildered. Then finally slumped back into his chair, shaking his head and cursing. Behind him the other members of the delegation—some, like Admiral Lin and General Pei, themselves named in the indictments—had put their heads together in an urgent confab.

And Blair had turned to Salyers, beside her, to exchange horrified looks. Chen had just been publicly humiliated. And all of China, of course, with him.

The Nazis had built a movement on just such a humbling at Versailles.

A new stir at the door jerked her from her thoughts. Another staffer, who called, "DepSec wants you, ma'am."

Blair and Shira looked at each other, confused. "Me? Or Shira?" Salyers was State; she, Blair, was still Defense. Though of late, her days seemed to be numbered. Denver Barley of the *Post* was speculating Blair Titus would be the next wartime join to be ejected from the administration. Which, now that hostilities were over and an election in sight, had no need to pretend to make nice with the opposition party.

"Ms. Titus, please. He's up by the pool."

SHE stepped out of the elevator to a truly dizzying view. Nothing but sky above. The calm blue surface of the pool in front of her, and a few teens splashing each other at the deep end. A palm-thatched tiki bar was doing a desultory business. The warm air was scented with chlorine. She dragged her gaze away from the edge of the pool that was just clear glass, separating water from air with a mere inch of transparent plastic . . . No. Uh-uh. She wasn't going anywhere near that.

A wave from a deck chair; Ransome Teague smiled as she hesitated a few feet away. "Blair? Come on in. Water's fine. Bring your suit?"

He was joking, of course. He was wearing gray suit trousers and a white shirt, crisp starched sleeves rolled up. He hooked another pool chair with a foot and pulled it over. "Thanks for supporting us during this conference. And all during the war, of course."

"I did it for the country," she said, trying to muster a half smile in return while trying to ignore the abyss that lay to every side. "Who wouldn't?" But she had to guard her words. Teague was administration through and through. A political appointee. Which meant that very soon now, they'd probably be on opposite sides of an election. So . . . polite, but wary. "How can I help you, sir? We just about have the final wordsmithing done on Point Four."

"Good. Excellent. I just wanted to let you know, the loan was approved." He waved her toward the chair again. "Since you have juice on the Hill. Might be good to let them know in advance what we're planning there."

She nodded, keeping her knees together as she eased down into the much-too-low deck chair. The two-trillion-dollar loan would be underwritten by the IMF and Qatar. Ostensibly it was meant for the rebuilding of the Chinese economy. But a confidential codicil specified it could also be used for "settlement of outstanding debt."

This was a euphemism. What it really meant, though it would take considerable research for an outsider to understand, was that the bulk of the loan would actually be going to Russia, in payment for arms and energy deliveries during the war. This quid pro quo had been the price of Moscow's abandoning claims to Dalian, and setting the military plans to retake that city on hold.

At least until the cash was paid over. She forced obligingness into her tone. "I'll do that, sir. Informally?"

"Sure, just a heads-up to grease the wheels. Now." He inclined his head toward a man in dishdasha and ghutra, the long Arab robe and headdress, sitting off to the side. She'd not noticed him, so quiet and motionless had he been. Dark glasses shielded his eyes from the sun, and from her inspection. "I think you know this gentleman," Teague added.

Blair nodded; yes, she did. But didn't extend her hand. "Dr. al-Mughrabi."

Dr. Abir al-Mughrabi inclined his head, and murmured a greeting in return. He was a former Appeals Division judge, International Criminal Court. They'd met in Dublin, during a conference on human rights violations and war crimes. Al-Mughrabi was from Morocco, though Shira said his family was Lebanese. He'd been involved in prosecutions for civil war and genocide in Lebanon, Rwanda, and Syria, and also overseen investigations into alleged Coalition war crimes in Afghanistan.

She smiled, trying not to appear as hostile as she felt. "Doctor, so good to see you again. I'd expected you earlier in the week, to be frank."

Al-Mughrabi said carefully, "I had expected to be here as well." His English was precisely enunciated, but French-accented. "Unfortunately I was detained on another matter. But now I would like to see if we can find common ground."

She nodded, and Teague gestured to a mustached server at the tiki bar. He brought a pitcher of iced coffee, cups, saucers, sugar, cream. The jurist accepted his with a murmured *"Shukran."* He touched his beard, stealing a glimpse at her, but not meeting her gaze. At least as far as she could judge through the sunglasses. Two deeply tanned teens in bikinis strolled past, chatting in Chinese. A scent of coconut oil on the breeze . . . Finally he muttered, "I fear we do not yet have an agreement about these trials. I understand yesterday there was a question raised about that in the plenary session."

"Point Four will treat that in detail," Teague said. "It was settled at Djakarta. The Australians and Indians insisted that the ICJ hold the trials, rather than an Allied court."

"We are aware of that, and have made preparations. We're still discussing the venue, though it will probably be in either Germany or Holland. But I wanted to raise the issue of our indictments of Allied accused."

Blair touched her forehead with the back of her hand. The cool water was looking better every minute. She kept her arms held close, hoping she wasn't sweating through her suit jacket. Or at least that it wasn't showing.

Teague shook his head. "No, sir. I don't think the Allies will submit to the ICJ. The United States withdrew from compulsory jurisdiction in 1986 over Nicaragua."

"Unfortunately, neither does China signal an agreement to comply." Al-Mughrabi sipped his coffee, as if to give all three time to reflect. Finally he added, "But there have been instances whereby major powers managed to cooperate nonetheless. The world these days demands a balanced and transparent process. You may be able, as an occupying power, to force the defeated to appear. But if only Chinese are held to this standard, the proceedings will seem one-sided. Prejudiced. Even vengeful."

"We can live with that." Teague half-winked at Blair.

Al-Mughrabi seemed not to notice. "I am not thinking of you, but of the Chinese. If these present negotiations are to result in peace, the Party and military have to reintegrate willingly into a democratic polity. If they resist, the result could be continued turbulence. And for you, continued expense."

A burst of excited screaming echoed from the far end of the pool. Blair glanced over. The teens were chicken-fighting. The girls, perched on the boys' shoulders, were splashing gouts of water at each other. Both men shifted in their chairs, giving them better angles on the action. "Exactly," said al-Mughrabi. "A balanced, open judicial process will help the new government begin with some credibility. Placing personnel from both sides on trial will assure that balance."

Teague tapped his fingertips together. "This might be something we need to kick up to the secretary himself. Whom, precisely, are we talking about here?"

"Actually, very few individuals on the Allied side." The Arab smiled delicately, and turned back to her. "I do regret, however, to say this: one in particular may be of interest to you, Ms. Titus."

"To me?" She straightened as the old hip injury jabbed her. Curse this low chair . . . "What do you mean?"

"The German government has asked us to indict your husband. For abandoning a civilian ship and crew to the fortunes of war, when he was obligated to render assistance."

Suddenly, but far too late, she saw the trap. Laid for her not by al-Mughrabi, but by Teague. No doubt, he'd been advised by Ammermann and her other enemies within the administration.

Dan had written her about his being forced to leave the torpedoed tanker. His cruiser had been too valuable to risk so close to a submarine's known location. Now, if she objected to his indictment, she'd be opposing administration policy. But not for any praiseworthy motive. On the contrary; it would be nepotism, a wife protecting her husband.

But if she agreed with the White House that Americans should *not* show up for trial, she'd not only be throwing Dan under the bus, she'd be contradicting her own party's policy on international justice.

And by the gleam in his eye, she saw that Teague saw that she saw. While the jurist glanced from one to the other, looking puzzled.

She mustered herself. "If that's true, I can't believe any court would find him guilty. He had no choice. It was operational necessity, under combat conditions."

The server, a tray under his arm, cleared his throat politely. "Will madame, or the gentlemen, care for more coffee? Something to eat, perhaps?"

Al-Mughrabi dismissed him in Arabic. When the man was gone, he smiled again and spread his hands. "No doubt you are right. But the operative question here is not guilt, but the act of submitting to judgment."

"That'll be up to other authorities than me," she told him, inclining her head toward the deputy. "To the secretary, probably. I'm sure he'll make the right decision."

Teague said casually, "Have you talked to Harry Lichtman, by the way?"

"Lichtman . . . oh, yes. He asked me about, um, stabilizing the yuan?"

"And also about denationalization, I think."

She nearly grinned now, seeing where this was going. If she went along with selling off Chinese industry to the multinationals, Dan wouldn't go to trial.

And once again Teague smiled, in recognition of her recognition.

She had to admire it, as a tactic. The most rigorous ethics counsel could hardly point to a definite subornation. But they'd closed the jaws on her. She could really see only one way out. "Well, I'll have to take that under advisement. And as far as whether any given individual shows up for trial, I'm sure what *I* think will have very little impact."

Teague cleared his throat and leaned back, as if content for the moment. At the far end of the pool in the sky, the adolescents screamed in high, keening notes, like seagulls squabbling over some discarded fish head. "Then we'll just kick it upstairs, all right? And Doctor, we'll have an answer for you soon, I'm sure."

BY late afternoon she was limping. Her hip throbbed. Really, she was going to have to look into replacement surgery. Once this was over, once they were home.

But this was a historic event. So she bit her lip, smoothed the pain lines from her face, and forced her spine straight again.

The garden lay a few hundred yards from the hotel. But not

just any garden. Huge artificial "supertrees," concrete-and-steel mushroom-shapes hundreds of feet high and sheathed with plantings and solar panels, rose above the natural palms, shading the gardens and walks below. A pedestrian skyway webbed the supertrees, and network lenses glittered down. Viewing stands had been set up on a manicured greensward. It wasn't the teak deck of USS *Missouri*, but she had to admit, it was a very impressive setting. A long table on a dais covered with an ornate, gold-encrusted tapestry formed the centerpiece.

She, Salyers, Ammermann, and the other staffers and junior officials were ushered to a position a few yards behind the table, cordoned off by velvet ropes. Singaporean cops cradling automatic rifles eyed everyone as the principals filed in, each finding his or her seat as their country's anthem played. Foreign ministers and senior generals. The president of Australia. DPS and Singaporean security stood at each entrance to the garden in dark suits and smart glasses, scanning the noisy crowd seated below the dais, mainly press and local dignitaries. She spotted a tall, very black man in a dark suit, scanning the throng as he murmured into a lapel microphone. The DPS agent who'd accompanied the mission to Beijing, Chaldroniere.

To her surprise, Teague walked up the ramp to the dais. The secretary of state must not have been able to make it, even for the ceremony. Which was strange . . .

She shifted on her feet, wishing she could just sit down. Salyers leaned in. "You okay, Blair?"

"Just my fucking hip. I'll live."

"And . . . there he is. I wondered if he'd show up personally." Her petite co-worker nodded to where Chen, in a dark blue suit and red tie, was striding in, comet-trailed by his ministers and generals. Looking grim, he headed for the table. Then did a double take as an Indonesian usher in a military uniform touched his elbow, steering him to a smaller, desk-sized one, off to the side. Chen wavered. Then, seeing there was no room for him at the head table, reluctantly took his seat there.

The ceremony began as dusk fell. The giant trees began to light up in coruscating, lambent tones of lavender, peach, turquoise, and violet. Brighter lights, spots, came on from the skyway. The effect was fairylike, ethereal, like a glowing universe suspended above their heads.

In turn, each of the Allied representatives stood to deliver remarks. The Japanese, Indonesian, Vietnamese, and Russians spoke in their native tongues. Teague spoke in English, but briefly. It seemed to be left to the president of Australia to give the keynote. She covered the run-up to the war, its history, and explained the treaty being signed, in exhaustive detail.

It wasn't the specificity but the length that was getting to Blair. She staggered at a sudden wave of vertigo and clutched Salyers's arm. Whispered, "Um . . . I'm not feeling so hot."

"Blair? You haven't looked good all day."

"The long hours. Too much fucking work."

"If you need to, step back. There's a planter behind us you can perch on . . . You know, there's one man I wish was here too."

"Who's that?"

"Dewei Chagatai. The Butcher of Hong Kong. They didn't bring him, I guess. And I know why."

Blair glanced back. Yeah, a planter, with a wide lip that would make a great perch. But if she sat there, she'd miss the climactic moment, screened from it by the standees. "I'm going to try to gut it out. But if I go down, break my fall, okay?"

A smile and a squeeze of the arm were her answer.

The Australian came to the end of her peroration and bent to the microphone. "We will now proceed to the signing."

Four uniformed troops brought out a folio-sized folder on a separate table. They placed it square in the center of the amphitheater.

The Australian said, speaking slowly, "Signing for the Russian Federation."

Marshal Sharkov stood from the table, strode to it, and bent stiffly in his bemedaled tunic to inscribe his name.

"The People's Republic of Vietnam."

They were being called up in reverse order of when the country in question had joined the Allies. One by one the signers stood, walked to the document, and inscribed their names and titles. Some used several pens to sign, pocketing the extras.

The deputy secretary of state stood when "the United States" was called. Blair frowned. *Teague* was going to sign? While Justin Yangerhans, the Allied commander who'd actually won the war, was roped off with the observers? Oh, yes, it was obvious why. She glanced over, caught Yangerhans's eye, and got a poker-faced wink back.

Teague straightened from signing and looked proudly around, flourishing a gold Montblanc, beaming for the cameras.

The presiding officer bent to the mic again. "The representatives of the People's Republic of China."

Chen sat immobile, hands pressed down flat on his desk. He'd flushed again; his face was beet red. Once more, Blair feared for his heart. Or a stroke. If the guy had any aneurysms lurking, now was when they would probably blow.

But the seconds ticked past. He didn't sag in his chair, or grab at his chest.

But neither did he rise, or look like he was going to.

The younger man, Xie Yunlong, bent to whisper urgently in his ear. Still Chen sat immobile, hands splayed out in front of him, lips clamped in a pale line.

Then, at last, he rose. Slowly, with reluctance in each studied movement. Chen circled his desk and paced the length of the high table, studying each face. The Allied representatives stared back expressionlessly as more lights came on high above, illuminating them all like actors on a stage.

At the signing table, the generals and Admiral Lin joined Chen. The senior minister bent to sign, flicking the pen angrily across the paper, then threw it into the bushes with a violent heave.

General Pei stepped up. He signed and also flipped the pen away, sneering.

Admiral Lin signed quietly, setting the pen aside on the table.

They returned to their places in silence. And the president of Australia bent to the mic once more.

"These proceedings," she said, "are closed."

At a command the Singaporean troops wheeled. They marched around the table and took positions behind the Chinese delegation. The military men looked uncomfortable. An officer stepped forward to confide something to them. As Chen stood alone, the soldiers led the others away.

Suddenly, as if that had been the climax, the mood broke. The floodlights died, leaving only the blue-violet tracings of the super-trees to illuminate the faces that milled and chattered below. Blair eased a breath out and staggered toward one of the just-vacated chairs.

Her hip flamed. She felt like throwing up.

The war was over. Chen and his generals had signed. But they'd done so angrily, and been humiliated to boot.

Had they all just sown the seeds for a second Pacific war?

15

The Eastern Shore, Maryland

WORKING on the old Kia is frustrating as hell. This is the third day he's been at it, and he isn't even getting a spark.

Bent under the open hood, Hector Ramos mops sweat off a dripping forehead with a bare forearm. He can feel he's leaving gritty grease on his face but doesn't care.

The heat's terrific. He's gotten up Corps early, at zero five, but already it's over a hundred and four, the radio says. And airless, not even a breath of a breeze off the bay. His mom's brown mongrel dog, Ham, lies panting in the shade of the azaleas, eyes glazed, pink tongue hanging out. Behind the garage a dry, parched field of dead yellow cornstalks stretches to distant trees, baking in the relentless heat. Their withered leaves hang motionless. Heat eddies over the road and the cornfields as if the atmosphere itself is melting. In the other direction, next door, is Mrs. Figueroa's yard. She used to keep a brown mare, but there's no horse there now, just an empty, rotting shed where the animal used to shelter when it rained.

If only it would rain now.

The Eastern Shore. He's grown up here, but it doesn't seem as wild and natural and endless as it did when he was a kid. Everything's smaller. Shabbier. Poorer. The once-white shell drives are covered with dead grass. The decrepit old wooden houses, some of them mere shacks, that his people live in here, sag toward the earth, as if being sucked inevitably back into it.

"Me cago en la leche," Hector mutters, kicking the front tire with a combat boot. The old car was a piece of shit before he joined the Corps, and three years under a leaky garage hasn't improved it.

Then he looks down, puzzled. *"Cago,"* he mutters again.

The tire he just kicked has crumpled apart into curved shards and gray powder. It's dry-rotted, a useless, crumbling shell of desiccated rubber.

He'll have to bicycle down the road again.

After his release from the Wounded Warrior regiment, then his discharge, the Corps issued him a train ticket home and a wad of hundreds, since a lot of the country still doesn't have credit connectivity.

The train stopped twice for ID checks. Troops in black uniforms threaded the aisles, facial-ID'ing everybody and matching them against red-flag lists on their phones. They looked his discharge papers over and photographed them too. "Combat vet, three wound badges," they said, impressed. "We could use a guy like you, patriot. What was your specialty?" And when he told them 0331, machine gunner, they called a sergeant over to give him the hard sell about something called the Special Action Forces. Hector told them he was fucked up in the head, on heavy P meds. But the sergeant just shrugged. "That don't matter, we got other Devil Dogs just as bad."

And Hector remembered then, again, why he'd gotten out.

He just doesn't want to see any more of his people die.

He left the train in Philly and hitchhiked south. In uniform, it wasn't hard to get rides, though there weren't many cars back on the road. The big driverless rigs, three and four trailers long, tore past, swerving only slightly away if their lidar picked him up standing on the berm. Sometimes, though, they didn't, and the blast of their passage knocked him back a few steps.

The people who gave him rides never asked where he'd been. As if they either knew, or didn't really care. Or maybe they were afraid of him. He was just as happy not to have to talk. Just to sit there silently watching the country go by, then rolling out to stand in the heat again when he'd gone as far as they could take him.

He's been home for a few days now, not doing much of anything yet. Getting up early, though he doesn't seem to be logging much actual sleep. Sitting on the back porch, a warm beer in one hand, staring at the trees and vaping the cheap nicotine they sell at Dollar Tree. Popping the pills morning and night, though he doesn't think they're doing much good. Or maybe the dreams would be even worse if he weren't taking them.

His Marine greens hang in the closet upstairs. His old clothes feel strange: too light, too loose. But they're much cooler in the growing heat than a uniform would be. It seems a hell of a lot hotter here now than when he was a kid. Or maybe he's just not used to it anymore.

His mother's glad to see him back, but she's warned him not to go out at night. She's scared of the Loyalty League, mean local whites who beat up resisters and burned their homes during the war. He's already stopped by Mirielle's house, but there's no one there. One of her old girlfriends who works at the NAPA store says Miri's visiting a cousin down in Virginia. She doesn't answer her phone, either.

So now he's trying to get the car started, to regain some mobility. Be able to go somewhere. Salisbury, maybe. Or Dover, to the casino that just reopened.

Or else he'll just fucking go nuts, all alone here in the house all day long.

"*Cabrón*," he mutters. He kicks the tire again, knocking another piece of tread loose to hang and sway. And finally wheels his old coaster bicycle out once more, onto the baking, buckled asphalt of the one-laner that leads to town. The brown dog follows him for ten yards, tongue lolling out, then gives up and trudges very slowly, lifting one paw at a time, back to the house.

M&W has a tire his size, but Hector's appalled at how much they want for it. He thought his back pay was generous, but it's obvious his whole idea of what money's worth is way off now. He offers $350, but the guy shakes his head. "No way, amigo. That'd be less than I paid for it. Four hundred, take it or leave it." He turns away: "Plenty others need tread, my man. Good rubber's like gold these days."

In the end Hector has to peel off four of the flimsy, limp new hundred-dollar bills, hardly more substantial than toilet paper.

THE fucking wheel bolts are rusted solid. By the time he gets the nuts chiseled off, in the hellish heat, he's ready to pour gasoline over the fucking car and nuke it. But finally he gets the tire fixed. He fiddles under the hood and coaxes a spark at last.

Finally the motor turns over. He lets it run for fifteen minutes to charge the battery and get the oil moving around. Should change it, but the worn-out four-cylinder burns oil so fast it makes more sense just to top it off every other day. He kicks the concrete blocks out of the way and slides in.

Inside, the front seat is still damp and feels somehow squishy. The interior stinks chokingly of mold, which has blackened the liner. Webs glitter in the sun, flecked with dead flies and the equally dead spiders who wove them. He inspects under the seats, hoping there aren't any live ones crawling around. Spiders creep him out. Ever since Hainan . . .

He brushes the webs and old wrappers and dust out with a broom and saws out a piece of scrap plywood to cover the hole in the floorboards. Gets in again and guns the engine. Ta pocketa, but it runs. The car squeals as he rolls it forward and then back, listening to the transmission.

He twists in the seat to make sure he isn't running over the dog, then backs out of the garage. The driver's side door still sags, so he can't lock it, and the brakes yield slowly, like foam pillows. But aside from a furtive rustle under the backseat and a musty smell of mouse pee, he's back on the road. He drives a block, then remembers: *discharge papers.* He two-points around on the one-laner, goes back, and gets them.

He drives past Mirielle's house again, but still no one's around. No cars. Thistles are growing tall in the driveway. Maybe they've moved away? He debates stopping, knocking again, but finally drives on.

He rolls slowly through town. A lot of stores are closed, but there are two new thrift shops and a storefront church. He takes the bypass north to the highway. And pretty soon, as if magnetized, though he doesn't remember setting out to drive here, he's back in front of Farmer Seth's.

The plant's going strong, with feathery plumes of steam rising straight up off the cooling towers. Fifty or sixty geese stand about on the grass. They look fat and stupid. The smell's the same: a dense, eye-stinging stench of burned feathers, chickenshit, and ammonia. He applies the brake gingerly and coasts to a halt by the now rust-specked sign. DEFENSE ESSENTIAL PLANT. AUTHORIZED PERSONNEL ONLY. DEFENSA ESENCIAL INSTALACIÓN. SOLO PERSONAL AUTORIZADO.

Jessup isn't in the guard shack. Instead, a woman he doesn't know peers down. "What c'n I do for you, 'migo?" she says, looking his car over with a cocked eyebrow. Taking in probably too his black T-shirt, the camo uniform pants, his dark issue glasses, the tattoos on his exposed forearms. She doesn't look impressed.

"I'm Hec Ramos. Used to work here."

A metallic crashing, underlain by the hum of electric motors.

Stainless hooks march steadily along, dangling from an I-beam. From them hang upside-down U's of heavy, polished metal. The concrete floor is spattered with a brownish-black crust inches thick.

The birds fight desperately as they're yanked out of their modules. The workers wear thin gloves or women's nylons to protect their hands from beak and spurs. They flip bird after bird upside down and hook the claws into the loops.

And with a musical jingle, an electric hum, the Line carries them on, out of sight, through the slot in the wall.

"Hey. I ast you. So what you want, yeah?"

Hector blinks. "I'm back from the . . . from the war. Thought I'd see if there's anybody around I used to run with."

"Well, this ain't old-home week," she says. "Only current employees, current ID. Unless you want to see about working here again. That'd be the office, though. Out front."

"Yeah, I know." Hector nods. "I just wanted to go in for a minute. See if José's here, Fernando, Sazi—"

"I don't recognize none of those names, sir. You best go to the office." She sets her lip and reaches for something behind the lower sill of the window, out of his sight. He tenses, suddenly at full alert; is she going for a gun? Shit, and he's fucking unarmed here. He searches the floor for a wrench, a screwdriver, some kind of tool at least, but there's nothing. He needs something to carry. At least a pistol. Where can he pick up a gun? Maybe then he'd sleep better.

But when she straightens all she has in her hands is a colorful puzzle book. He fights to relax, but his grip on the wheel feels like it could bend the thin metal and plastic.

Past the gate he can just see the loading ramp. A truck's backed up to it ready to off-load. Plastic cages, crammed with perfectly still white-feathered birds. Behind it, leaning in the shade of the overhang, a heavy fortyish woman in a blood- and shit-spattered canvas apron is sucking on a cigarette with quick nervous gestures. The smoke rises, drifts, thins, mingles with the steam. Vanishes.

She takes another puff, looking off into the trees. Slumping, as if her very bones are melting. Then throws the butt away, pulls her mask back up, and turns back into the building.

"Go on, get out of here," the guard says. And carefully, mastering his overwhelming desire to get out and beat her fucking head against her cage, Hector puts the car in reverse and backs away.

SIX hours in the VA center don't make him happier. He's been here before, but after a long wait they sent him home to bring back his discharge papers. Which is why he made sure to bring them this time. But apparently Veterans Administration Affairs and the Marines don't talk to each other. They don't have his medical records yet. He sits with growing impatience all through the morning, then to noon, as the staffers at the counters banter with one another and eat their lunches. He can't leave, or he'll lose his place. The flimsy paper ticket grows damp with sweat in his hand. The number fades, blears, until he has to blow on it to dry it out, lest he lose out entirely.

The center's in Salisbury. He's nursed the Kia here in a cloud of blue smoke, wondering as he goes how he's going to afford his next tank of gas. Fuel is fucking astronomical, and most of the stations he used to go to are closed. Now he sits hunched over, avoiding the eyes of the others. Other vets. Some of them, probably, from the same battles and campaigns he's survived. But he doesn't feel like talking.

One, a black kid, wanders past, then halts. Looking at Hector's buzz cut, at the camo pants, the furrowed scar on his scalp, the brass burns on his neck, the long blackened scars on his forearms. "Hey, amigo! Bwe-nos di-as. You Army?"

"Marine," Hector says unwillingly.

"Oh yeah? In any fighting?"

Hector glances away. "Some."

"Oh yeah. Oh yeah. I never got overseas. Riot duty, LA, the Big Island. Got this in a rollover." He pulls up a pant leg above ragged Nikes to show a faded patch of skin. "A real bad scrape. Still hurts sometimes."

Hector gives him the hard look. "It would behoove you to go sit the fuck down and shut the fuck up, jackass."

Two women sitting across from him halt their conversation and avert their eyes.

The room quiets. The kid, who looks to be about nineteen, wavers, opens his mouth as if to bluster, but finally decides not to push it. He stalks away.

Hector folds his arms and stares straight ahead. Fucking pogue.

What a waste of time. Shoot him between the fucking eyes and do the world a service.

He takes out the phone he bought at Dollar Tree. Plays with it some, but there's still no wifi here and it doesn't seem to connect to anything very well, or only occasionally.

"Now serving: four hundred and sixty-three," the PA system rasps. He looks at his tab again. 458. For a moment he wanders, confused. Has he missed being called? Gone UA in his head? He looks around, counting the people, loses track, counts again.

Then gets up and approaches the counters, stepping in front of a woman so old she couldn't be a vet, or maybe just not from this war. "Hey," he says, trying to keep his voice down but not doing a great job of it. "I been here since eight and you're calling numbers after mine. But you never called mine."

"If you left, sir, you'll have to take another number. Over by the door."

"I din't leave. I been fucking sitting right here."

"No need to curse at me, sir. If you do so again I'll have to ask you to come back another day." A short tubby black woman, she wields a glare like a drill sergeant. Like Sergeant Brady, back at boot camp. No. Like little Lieutenant Ffoulk's. So withering, and that's such a bad memory, recalling what happened to Ffoulk, that he shuts up and starts back to his seat.

But he recovers and wheels back. No way is he going to take another number. Like some fucking baa-baa sheep. He draws a breath, anger welling. The fat cop at the door glances over. He straightens, and lays a hand on his gun.

But the old woman he pushed aside steps back and gestures him ahead. "You can take this boy ahead o' me," she says to the clerk. "Look like he done been through a lot. You go ahead, son. I'll just wait an' go after you."

The clerk acquiesces, but he can tell she doesn't like it. She reviews his information on her screen, scans his DD 214 and discharge and his civilian driver's license, though he thinks surely they have to have him in the system by now. Finally she points him to a back room. "The counselor will see you soon," she says. Then, to the old woman, "Now tell me what you need, honey."

More plastic chairs in a dingy hallway. A half hour later the door opens and a weary voice calls, "Next, please."

The counselor's white, super fat, bald. Wearing a suit that even to Hector's untrained eye looks like it doesn't fit. Half-moon glasses are pushed down on a fleshy nose. A window unit whines cold air. "Okay, hello, Sergeant Ramos. Have a seat. First, thank you for your service. Looks like you went through a lot over there." His accent sounds like he's from up north, maybe Philly.

"Thanks," he mutters.

"Let's see what we can do for you . . . What are your plans? I see your civilian occupation was factory worker."

"I worked on the kill line at Seth's."

"I see. Well. Law says your employer has to offer you your old job back. At the now-prevailing rate of pay. If you still want it. But let's look at your service record first." A keyboard tap; a prolonged pause. "Okay. What's an MRAP license?"

"Mine resistant vehicle driver."

"Uh-huh. Any other qualifications? I'm not too clear on some of these."

"I was a 31. Uh, MOS 0331. Machine gunner. Also I hold rifleman and assault. That's an 0311."

The guy pushes his lips out, like a fat duck. Like that wasn't what he was hoping to hear. "Any computer skills? Maintenance skills? Welding?"

Hector drops his eyes and mutters, "No, just the . . . I was just infantry."

"Well, Farmer Seth's has openings advertised."

Hector says, keeping himself calm, "I didn't plan on goin' back there."

"Okay, I can understand that. It's hard work."

Is this asshole insulting him? "I don't have no problem with hard work, *sir*."

The counselor waves his hands without looking Hector's way.

"Sure, I didn't mean anything by that. Just that . . . you're older now. Seen the world. So what's the plan? Give me something here, and we'll see what we can do for you."

"I never been great with numbers," Hector says. "So I never thought about college. But lately I been thinking, maybe I could work with people. Returning troops. People with depression, maybe. Or like that . . . there anything like that I could do without college?"

"All right, let's pursue that. You're talking about something like a two-year counseling degree. Or maybe even just a certificate of completion. I've seen vets go into crisis intervention, drug programs, youthful offenders. Does that sound like the sort of—?"

"Yeah, something like that might be good." He's actually starting to get excited. Maybe helping other people would help himself. Get out of his own fucking head. Since it's not very nice in there.

"Well, let's check out what's available." The counselor taps his screen, moves things around. Then frowns. "Uh-oh . . . when exactly did you become a citizen, Hector?"

"When? Uh . . . at boot camp. They gave citizenship to everyone who enlisted."

A sharp glance over the glasses. "Right, when the war started, right?"

"Yes sir."

"Well, problem is . . ." More scrolling, then some keyboard tapping. "I'm sorry. Says here, the Patriot GI bill doesn't apply to service members who became citizens after they entered military service. Only to those who were already Americans when they signed up."

The guy reads some more, frowns, shakes his head. Then rolls his chair back from the desk and shrugs. Searches in his desk for a business card, and scribbles a number on the back. "I'd go for the old job back, if I were you. Here's the hiring number over at Seth's. They give you any shit, come back to me and we'll set them straight."

"I don't think that's gonna work," Hector says, and something in his tone seems to warn the guy, because he suddenly looks down and goes quiet, no longer smiling.

But Hector gets a grip and leaves out of there before anything bad happens.

BACK in the car, he takes a P pill, hesitates, then dry-bolts another. Sits there shaking.

It don't matter.

It don't matter at all, he tells himself.

But he can't shake the feeling of threat, the dread, the rage. No GI benefits, after all the shit he's been through? All he fucking gave? Something's not right. The white guy, the counselor. Was he smiling? Was he laughing? Was he holding out, fucking with him? Maybe he better ask somebody else. Make sure. But he isn't going to take this lying down.

He drives past Mirielle's house again. But the empty driveway, the vacant windows, all say no one's home.

IV

THE JUDGMENT
OF THE FATES

16

Washington, DC

THE Gold Wing sputtered and nearly died, making Dan wonder if the old bike was going to last the final few miles in to the city. It wouldn't top fifty now, even at full throttle, and trailed a wake of black smoke in the early dawn. Well, he could probably walk in the rest of the way to the Pentagon. Fortunately there was hardly any traffic. He remembered this section of four-lane, heading into the Beltway, as jammed solid with traffic as early as six in the morning. But today his engine coughed on through what was otherwise near silence.

He'd been on the road for five days after viewing the body at Chadron. After that, Mobilized Militia roadblocks and warning signs had shunted him in a sweeping dogleg through southern Nebraska. Then south again to avoid Omaha, which the M&Ms said had "gone dark," whatever that meant. Somewhere in there, at a police station in some anonymous small town, he'd managed to get through on a phone. To his ex-wife, to see if she had any news. That had been an unpleasant call, but the upshot was that she'd heard nothing either. He'd left flyers on "refugee bulletin boards," as people were calling the telephone poles along the roads where vackers left despairing messages for the missing. He'd left the number of his and Blair's home phone at each roadblock he stopped at. But he'd heard nothing since Wyoming.

He didn't want to accept that the battered, flayed corpse he'd viewed there had truly been his daughter's. Yet her trail seemed to have ended there. Gone cold.

So he just tried not to think about any of it as he pressed on.

Through Missouri, Illinois, Indiana, Ohio, West Virginia. The hills gradually climbed again, his headlight sweeping in great curves through the dark as he pushed up into the Alleghenies. Fuel was a worry, and he didn't have a ration card. Sometimes his military ID worked. Often he had to beg, and once had stooped so low as to siphon a gallon out of a tractor left in a field. The ersatz high-alcohol "war fuel" made the Honda sputter and hesitate. And at each roadblock, he'd been faced with the same narrowed eyes, the same questions and demands for documents. Was he a deserter? A spy? An antiwa? The pass from the M&Ms had helped. But after a while he'd started taking side cuts, back roads, country roads. Avoiding the cities, even when it cost him time.

Because more than once he'd seen other corpses dangling, and freshly dug graves behind those roadblocks.

Day after day he'd settled into the trip. Hour after hour, to the roaring music of the twin cylinders. Bedding down long after dark, in motels, where they were still open. Or else crawling into a worn, mildewed sleeping bag he'd found in a wrecked, abandoned camper east of Beatrice, Nebraska. Bolting down beans heated over a campfire.

And the hills and plains had brought a measure of peace. As if occupying the eyes with passing scenery, the ears with the buffeting of wind and the drone of the engine, absorbed the brain to the exclusion of memory.

But only a measure.

She was gone. Vanished, like millions of others. Fed into the maw of this insane war, which seemed more futile the longer he contemplated it. What had either side won in the end?

He shook his head, motoring grimly east under a gray and frowning sky.

THIS morning he'd followed his headlights down out of the mountains for the last leg toward DC. From Washington to Washington. A checkpoint slowed him east of Front Royal, but the National Guard had waved him past a battery of pylon-mounted cameras without even an ID check. So maybe things were loosening up at last. From there he'd powered east under that same pewter sky, watching it gradually gray toward dawn.

Until the Dunn Loring Metro station, where 66 crossed over the Beltway. Humvees and Oshkoshes loomed ahead, and the sloping camouflage-painted hull of an armored personnel carrier. Above it a small dish antenna rotated, with a larger panel behind it pointed up at the low morning-lit clouds. Yellow signs warned SLOW. PREPARE FOR INSPECTION.

This checkpoint looked more permanent. Almost like the entrance to a military base overseas. He let the cycle coast, the engine blipping and farting as it braked, and maneuvered among looming barriers, tons of rocks netted into huge square gabions with galvanized steel mesh. Other signs separated "civilian" traffic and "official" into lanes. He hesitated, nearing the decision point, and countersteered at the last second into the "official" lane.

Troops, not M&Ms. Armed, unsmiling, but they seemed to be regular forces. And he didn't see any gallows or body bags, thank God. He lifted a glove to the sentry and coasted to a halt. A sign read DO NOT PROCEED PAST YELLOW LINE UNLESS INSTRUCTED TO. DEADLY FORCE AUTHORIZED. NO PROCEDA LA LÍNEA AMARILLA PASADA A MENOS QUE SE INDICA. FUERZA MORTAL AUTORIZADA.

"Cut your engine, sir," the sentry said, emerging from his booth and flicking a flattened hand across his throat. He was in full gear, flak jacket, helmet, and carbine, but Dan didn't recognize the black one-piece uniform, even up close. "Open your saddlebags and any storage compartments. Then step away from your vehicle. ID and travel pass, please."

He handed over what he had. The guard flipped through them, expression indecipherable, and finally pointed him to the side. "Clear the lane. Park there. Check in at the blue booth to your right." He didn't meet Dan's eyes.

In the containerized office a sergeant, also in black uniform but with Army-style rank rockers, studied his documents again as Dan explained once more. Home from the Pacific. On leave. Headed for DC. He leaned in, examining her silver cap insignia. It seemed to represent the head of the Statue of Liberty, surrounded by a laurel wreath.

The sergeant flicked a fingernail at the note from the M&Ms. "What's this, patriot?"

He blinked. Patriot? "A pass. From the Wyoming militia."

"Are you a member of the Wyoming militia?"

"Am I? No. They gave me a pass to help me through their road-blocks."

"Why were they letting you through their roadblocks, sir?" The "sir" was there, but the way she said it didn't make it an honorific. And maybe "sir" in place of "patriot" wasn't a good sign either.

"Why . . . well, because I was on leave, headed here. Like I said."

"You're a captain, sir? In the Navy?"

"Correct. As my ID says." His wartime rank hadn't made it onto his DD Form 2. And anyway he was probably reverted to O-6 by now; Niles had made it clear his promotion was for the duration only. He was still wearing khakis, with his jacket and dress shoes rolled up in the saddlebags. Probably ruined from rain and engine heat by now . . . "What are you guys, if I may ask? Army? Guard? I'm not familiar with your uniform."

"No sir. Homeland Battalions."

This was new. "So what's the problem, Sergeant?"

She didn't meet his eyes. In fact, hadn't since he'd walked in. "The problem, sir, is that the militia in this pass is on the list as a suspect organization. Part of the Covenanters. The Midwest separatist movement."

He blinked. "Well, all I have from them is that piece of paper. I didn't know they were . . . mutineers, or whatever. Rebels?"

"The Rebels are to the south, sir. RECOs. Reconstituted Confederacy."

"I see. Well, sorry I'm behind the times, but my leave's expiring. I need to report in to my next command."

"I don't see any orders here, sir." She shuffled the pile. "Do you have them with you?"

"They were telephone orders. From the CNO."

"What is that, sir?" Still not meeting his eyes, clicking busily on a small tactical computer.

"The chief of naval operations. Admiral Barry Niles. I'm TAD to his office. After helping win the fucking war."

He regretted that last crack; insulting her for her service at home wasn't going to help. He apologized and explained again, trying not to sound impatient. But the sergeant was turned away, studying her screen. "Just one moment, sir," she muttered.

At last she looked up. "We've been tracking you on FR, sir. Facial recognition. Since Front Royal. So we know who you are. You're not on any red flag or watch list. At least the ones we have access to here. Homeland Security. Patriot Network. But you're not on the District access list either. You don't have a pass as a civilian resident. And you don't have written orders assigning you to a command here."

He took a breath. "You can look me up online, then. My service. My decorations."

"Antiwa groups are very active online, sir. They attack our databases every day. We can't trust anything on the internet."

"So, let me guess . . . How do I get on this access list? To the District?"

"Your home command has to enter you."

"Which they won't do until I report in. Right?"

An impassive shrug was all he got back.

They regarded each other across the counter. An impasse. Finally he coughed into a fist. "Can I speak to your senior officer?"

"I'm OIC at this post, sir."

"Then here's what I'm gonna do. I'm going to get back on that bike and head east on 66. Toward the fucking Pentagon. Where my orders say to check in! If you feel like shooting me in the back, well, I've been shot at before. You can write me up for running the roadblock. If you feel you have to."

For answer he got pursed lips and averted eyes. Then a reluctant "Forward together, patriot. But you'll have to present an inoculation card."

He didn't have one of those either, and had to submit to a nasal spray that apparently was for the Chinese flu.

Back on the bike, gunning it, wheeling out into the exit lane. Locking eyes with the black-clad guard. Who was looking across toward the office. Where the sergeant stood, arms folded, in the doorway, scowling.

He wanted to hunch low over the bike's handlebars, to present a smaller target, but forced himself to remain upright. Still, he didn't feel safe until he was a mile down the road.

THE way grew more familiar with each passing mile. Cherrydale. Highland. Then the Potomac to his left, screened with woods. Roosevelt Island. More traffic now. Black sedans and SUVs, headed probably for the same destination as he. But very few civilian cars. The city seemed still asleep, even—he turned his wrist, glanced at the oil-smeared face of his Seiko—at 0600.

The National Cemetery to his left. Somewhere up there was the memorial to the Roosevelt Battle Group. Ten thousand sailors and marines and airmen, immolated in the opening hours of a war that had lasted nearly four years.

And one that was, apparently, still ripping America apart, to judge by what the sergeant had said back at what had looked very much like the entrance to a closed city in hostile territory.

Then, ahead, the gray granite walls of the fortress from which that war had been fought. The engine hesitated, cut out, started again, jerking him so hard he nearly lost the bike as he turned for the lot.

He sucked a deep breath. It felt good to be back in the military world. But then, why did he also feel nervous? What could they do to him, after all? Send him home? Make sure he couldn't be sent to fight again?

Well, he'd done enough. If it was shitcan Dan time, he was ready. That old Navy saying: Every career ends with a failure to select.

He coasted up to the river entrance, steered into one of the motorcycle spaces, and shut down. Swung stiffened, nearly crippled legs off, staring up at the entrance.

Whatever they served him up, he was pretty sure he could take it.

IN the event, he had to get another dose of vaccine, a shot this time, since the version Homeland had given him hadn't been approved by DoD. Then he had to cool his heels for two hours before he got to see the CNO's flag secretary.

She was new, and didn't seem to have any idea who he was. And of course since he was in a rumpled, oil-stained uniform, and probably stank of exhaust and sweat and too many days sleeping rough, he had to explain. Looking skeptical, she'd gone in to notify her boss.

And come out smiling. "He'll be with you shortly, Admiral. I'm so sorry. I should have recognized your name. Task Force 91, right? Operation Rupture Plus?"

"That's me."

"I wish I could have been there. But some of us had to hold the fort here in DC."

"I understand completely." Dan forced a smile and got up, but staggered as a wave of dizziness rushed over him. From the dual vaccinations, probably.

"Are you all right, sir? Should I call—"

"Yeah. I'm fine. Just been . . . I'm fine." He braced a finger against the bulkhead until the vertigo passed, then followed her into Niles's office.

His old mentor, then enemy, then reluctant rabbi again, had lost a shocking amount of weight. Barry "Nick" Niles's service dress blouse sagged loosely on a once-massive frame. His shirt collar gaped around his neck. His color seemed less that of a healthy African American than the hue and texture of gray wax. And he'd apparently gone to the shaved-head look. But his first words, from behind his desk, were robust. "Where the hell have you been, Lenson?" he boomed, just like the old Niles.

Dan came to an awkward attention. "I had leave, Admiral."

"That doesn't mean you drop off the face of the planet. Where were you?" Niles squinted. Sniffed the air. "Do you smell gasoline?"

"I bought a motorcycle. My daughter was kidnapped. So I . . . I was trying to pick up her trail across country."

The CNO nodded. "And did you?"

Dan swallowed, fighting a tickle in his throat and a sudden desire to weep. The dizziness peaked, then receded again, like a tide. He blinked rapidly, looking toward the shatterproof windows. "No. No, sir. I lost track of her in Wyoming. No telling where they went after that, or . . . what they did with her. There's a body in Nebraska that . . . is . . . that *may* be her. I couldn't make a positive identification."

The CNO nodded heavily. Grunted. Muttered, after a moment, "Sorry to hear. I know it doesn't help to hear it, but a lot of other people are missing relatives, friends, kids . . . two of my nephews, working oil out west, not a word since the laydown."

"Things are confused out there, sir. They could just be in one of the camps."

Niles waved his hope away and picked up a piece of paper. Seemed to remember Dan was standing, and pointed to a chair. No offer of an Atomic Fireball, as in the old days. The bowl was empty. Maybe they'd stopped making them during the war.

He sagged gratefully into the armchair. Cleared his throat, and tried to focus as Niles set the paper aside.

"You been home? Seen Blair yet?"

"No sir. Came straight here."

"Uh-huh . . . uh-huh. Well, good work out there with Rupture, Dan. If I haven't made that clear. If you hadn't stopped the clock to build up your ammo and fuel reserves, then kept shoving when the going got rough, we'd have gotten kicked back into the China Sea."

"Yes sir. Resistance was a lot heavier than I expected."

"Than anyone expected. Including our intel and our AI. That took a lot of moxie, to keep driving ahead when you were looking at casualty reports of twenty, thirty percent." Niles tented his fingers. "Of course, if that'd been the wrong decision, we would have hung you by the balls."

Dan figured that for a rhetorical statement, so simply nodded. And waited for the other boot to drop.

Niles searched through what was apparently Dan's personnel file, though it seemed odd that it was printed out. He rumbled to himself, as if musing, then said a bit louder, "Your stars may be permanent."

"Oh. Is that right, sir?" It didn't seem that important, but he tried to look gratified.

"At least you're on the postwar list for Senate confirmation. Nothing's guaranteed these days." He sighed, sat back, glanced out the window. "We're having to fight for every flag billet. There's a lot of pushback about anything to do with the Pacific. We need to pull two carriers back for core replacement and overhaul. That's going to be a major fight in the next budget. There are already calls to scrap them, rather than refuel."

"Then, thank you, sir. For the nomination, at least."

Niles shrugged and rolled his eyes, and Dan added, "I saw something new on the way in here. Something called a Homeland Battalion."

"Uh-huh. In black uniforms?"

"Yes sir."

"Uh-huh." Niles tilted a massive head. "Homeland Security's amalgamating loyal Guard units and militias into Blackies. Also known as Special Action Forces. And they want general-officer billets for them. They're not DoD formations, they're DHS, but they count against our general and flag authorized strengths."

"That doesn't sound exactly . . . fair, Admiral."

Niles's eyelids flickered. "There's worse coming over the horizon. Posse Comitatus may be suspended. To fight the unrest in the cities, and out west. And the closer we get to the elections . . . the slogan's 'Forward as one,' but the reality may be that we're headed for one-party rule."

Niles looked away. "Some of us are determined not to let that happen. At least, not if we can prevent it."

Dan weighed that last sentence. Then, despite himself, glanced around the office.

The admiral caught his reaction, and waved a large hand. "You can speak freely. This room's a SCIF. Noise suppressors on the walls, and we sweep it every morning. One island we keep as sane as we can. The Joint Chiefs, I mean. Just don't face the windows if you're discussing anything you don't want overheard."

"Yes sir." He wanted to know more, but decided he'd better digest what had just been intimated first. Because Niles's words could be construed, in the wrong hands, into something close to treason.

Niles reached for the empty candy container, but halted his hand halfway. He rumbled, "I'm going to be stepping down pretty soon, Dan. We won, if you can call losing ten million lives a win. And I'm tired."

"Ten million," Dan repeated blankly, horrified. This was the first he'd heard of any round figure. Most of the deaths must have taken place within the areas he'd routed around in his trek east. Plus fallout effects, carried by the wind. Radiation, looting, revolt, disease . . . so the dying wasn't over yet. He straightened his shoulders. "You're punching out, sir? Retiring?"

Niles rubbed a palm over his bare scalp. His smile resembled a sardonic jack o' lantern's. "I have pancreatic cancer, Dan. They're treating it, but as you can see, it's a losing battle. I'd rather not die walled up in this fucking office. Scenic as the view is."

"No sir. Of course not. I don't—I'm very sorry to hear that."

A tap at the door, and the aide stuck her head in. "Five minutes, Admiral."

Niles sighed. He stood from behind the desk. Dan, rising too, saw anew how shrunken his old senior's body was beneath the now nearly tentlike blues. Niles shrugged again. "That's the cookie . . . Anyway, you'll want to know what's next for you. It's still up in the air. Jun Min Jung called. He wants you as ambassador to reunited Korea. I told him that was a nonstarter. No way the administration would go for it, and you weren't a fucking diplomat anyway."

Dan nodded, not chagrined. Dealing with Jung could be stressful, and he wasn't eager to leave home again. "Yes sir. So what were you thinking?"

The CNO waved the question away. "Let's talk about that next time you come in. For now, go home. Take a shower. See Blair. Get some sleep. We all need a rest. Still got that boat of yours? Go sail it. Come back in when you feel up to it. Three, four days or so. Tell Marla to give you a District pass and a ration card."

Niles looked at the papers again, a contemplative, lingering glance. Then shoved the chair back and came around the desk. He didn't move like a lumbering bear anymore. His steps seemed tentative, cautious. His grip, though, was still strong as he pincered Dan's shoulder. "We go back a long ways, Lenson. All the way to Crystal City and the JCMPO. I've been hard on you at times, I guess."

Dan forced a smile. "No more than I deserved, sir."

"But I fought for you too, when you needed it. The way I hear you do for your own people."

"Your example, Admiral."

"An officer who knows when to take a risk, even dares to disobey, for the good of the service—that's a rare thing. We were headed for a zero-risk Navy for a long time, before this war. I tried to fight that, whenever I could." Niles held out his hand. "I guess after all these years you'd better make it Nick. In private, at least."

Dan's eyes stung. At the Academy, spooning—a senior's giving

a junior permission to use a first name—was a time-honored tradition. One never given lightly. He cleared his throat and took the
proffered hand. "Yes sir. I mean, Nick."

"Sir?" said the aide, from the door. "Before you leave. Legal
wants a word."

"Legal? Hell. Well, make it short," Niles said, turning away, letting go Dan's hand, clearly annoyed.

A tall woman in blues introduced herself. She carried a red
striped folder. "I heard Admiral Lenson was in the building."

"Get to it," Niles growled.

She turned to Dan. "The notification by the ICJ. Admiral, has
anyone discussed this with you?"

The International Court of Justice. "Uh, my wife mentioned it."

"Blair Titus," Niles clarified. "Undersecretary of defense."

The legal officer nodded. "Yes sir. I thought as long as he was
here, we could go over the administration's stand. That no US citizen will be judged."

Dan said, "But doesn't that mean the Chinese won't attend
either?"

Niles shook his head. "They're trying to take that position. But
they signed the treaty. Giving up war criminals was one of the
stipulations."

"That's actually a political question, Admiral." The attorney
clasped her hands primly in front of her, elbows out. "It goes to
war guilt, if we still want to align ourselves with that concept. But
if we do, the ICJ may indict Americans as well. As they may with
Mr. Lenson, here."

Niles said irritably, "Forget it. He's not responding."

"What happens if I don't?" Dan said, accepting that he probably
wasn't going to, but also curious as to what would happen if he
didn't.

"You wouldn't be able to travel, probably," the advisor said.
"At least to Europe, the UK, the other standing members of the
court. If you did, you'd be subject to arrest, extradition, and
trial."

Niles patted his arm. "Don't lose any sleep over this, Dan. This'll all get settled way above our pay grades."

He nodded to the aide, who stepped aside to let them both pass.

DAN stopped by Blair's office, but her people said she was overseas, in Singapore. "Oh, yeah," he muttered. "The peace conference." He stopped in at the cafeteria and put a lunch on his new ration card.

Next stop: home, in Arlington. And just about time; the bike was down to a top speed of forty, and its smoke trail was like a burning bomber's.

He shut the engine down and rolled the last few feet down the driveway.

The house looked . . . deserted. Desiccated pine needles carpeted the roof, with patches of green moss. One of the gutters had come loose and hung down like a torn hem. The shingles needed attention. The lawn had grown two feet high, and Virginia creeper and the red hairy cables of poison ivy twisted through the undergrowth and up the trunks of the pines, clinging and strangling. He'd have to take a machete to them.

Around back, he found the spare key under a brick in the patio. Let himself in to first quiet, then alarmed mewing. He scooped Blair's cat up and cradled it, ruffling its fur. "Hey, Jimbo." Remembering suddenly how he'd cradled his daughter the same way, so many years ago.

The house smelled musty. No wonder; the windows were taped over, as if for a hurricane, and duct-taped shut, no doubt as a preparation against fallout, though it hadn't reached this far east. He fed the cat, then let himself down the narrow steps to the basement. Here, in his study, it smelled even worse, as if the books were moldering. He went back up and checked the air-conditioning. But a crimson sticker sealed the breaker in the off position: *Save Energy for Victory.*

So he went around untaping and opening the windows and

sliding down the screens. Not much of a breeze, but it might cool
the house a bit. He checked the refrigerator: empty. The pantry
was bare too, except for a few staples: olive oil, beans, rice, canned
stuff, bottles of wine. Blair must have been getting her meals at
work.

He stood at the window, watching squirrels squabble and play
in the pines. Feeling suddenly . . . aimless. Apprehensive.

Fuck that! He should feel relieved, right? The war was over.
And the US had "won."

Yet he'd lost too much to feel relieved, or happy, or even curious
about what came next. An indictment? He couldn't muster concern for that, either. Like the legal beagle had suggested, maybe
the whole concept of "war guilt" was a thing of the past. Quaint,
like honor, or virtue, or truth, or the idea noncombatants weren't
legitimate targets.

He just felt . . . empty. Peculiar, out of place, as if this were
some uncanny, alternate world he'd never expected to inhabit.
And guilty, too, as if by surviving he'd betrayed those who had not.

The wine, in the pantry. He could uncork it. Forget all this. Blot
it out, if only for a few hours.

No. He'd been sober for too many years. The craving faded. It
wouldn't help. When he woke up tomorrow, his daughter would
still be dead.

He'd have to learn to live with that. Somehow. Like millions
of others, all across the US. Across China. Pakistan. India. Indonesia. Iran. Vietnam. In all the countries this war had wrecked,
trampled, and poisoned. Remember that, he told himself. You're
not the only one. He looked at the coffeemaker, but decided Niles
was right. He needed a shower, a good long sleep more.

Upstairs, to a rumpled bed. The comforter was pulled up hap-
hazardly, as if his wife had left in a hurry. Stooping to the pillow,
he could smell her. Her lotions and emollients stood lined up in the
bathroom. He peed, got a quick shower, then lay down. Blinked at
the ceiling.

He didn't bother to set the alarm.

17

Nagano, Japan

THE monkeys were much bigger than Cheryl had expected. About the size of large dogs. At the moment, five of them were lounging in the pool.

Leaning on the rail separating her from the steaming springs, she stared down. Their bright red faces were rimmed by long grayish fur. They reclined in the murky water, or paddled slowly across it to clamber awkwardly out onto the rocks, their wet fur slicked down, looking like drowned cats. There they desultorily groomed one another, picking things from each other's heads. Or squabbled in squeaky, aggrieved tones, like seniors in the golf course locker room. It was easy to picture them as lazed-out retirees. All they needed was cocktail glasses and bingo cards.

"Think they're naturally that way?" she asked Eddie, beside her. "Those red faces?"

Her husband stood hugging himself, his shockingly thin frame concealed within the heavy padded parka she'd bought him in Tokyo. The weather wasn't really that cold. She herself felt fine in thermal leggings and hiking boots and a Navy windbreaker.

The pictures on Booking.com had all showed the *onsens*—natural hot-spring pools—in the wintertime, with snow down to the edges of the springs and lying deep on the rocky hills beyond. Now those hills were bare. The whole region was volcanic. Wisps of steam bled from the rocky ground here and there, rising to eddy and swirl in the wind along the short trail they'd walked down from the hotel. The stink of sulfur mingled with the rank stench of the monkeys. They had no compunction about letting go in the pool, to judge by the floating turds.

Finally he said, as if forcing some response, "Maybe they're just flushed from the heat."

"Or embarrassed about being naked. In front of an audience."

That got a faint smile. "I doubt being naked would embarrass a monkey."

She grinned. "Well, obviously shitting in the bathtub doesn't."

"But actually you don't know. Do you?"

She looked away, feeling in the wrong, or as if she was overlooking something important. Something beyond missing her ship, which of course she did every minute she was away. It felt weird, not having that responsibility. But *Savo* was safe now. Inport Wakkanai again, with Matt Mills keeping an eye on things. And the war, thank God, was over.

She cleared her throat. "No, I guess I don't." Wanting to add something like, In fact, I can't tell how *anybody* is feeling. Unless he tells me.

But she didn't. Shit, the poor guy had just come back from a living death. A Chinese POW camp. Carried as missing, presumed dead, since his strike fighter had gone down in the Taiwan Strait during Operation Recoil.

Three years had been a long time for her, too. She'd mourned him. Then finally moved on, with a union rep from the shipyard.

She shivered, remembering Teju. His cocoa skin had felt smooth as a cat's back. Except for his hands, a worker's hands, stronger and rougher than Eddie's had ever been . . . She should feel guilty about that. Shouldn't she?

But whether she should or not, she didn't. After all, she'd believed her husband was dead.

But now Eddie "Chip" Staurulakis was back. Gaunt, hesitant,

pale. Pain had drawn his face tight by the end of the easy twenty-minute walk here from the hotel. He leaned on the paint-scarred railing beside her now as if exhausted. This husk was nothing like the brash, arrogant fighter jock she'd married, oh so long ago.

"Look at that little one," he said, too cheerfully, as if trying to mimic being entertained. He lifted his hands, flexed the wrists, and winced. Then crammed them back into the parka pockets. "He's kinda cute."

"Yeah. Kinda." She shivered. The little one *was* slightly more appealing than the others, if creepy, too. A cross between a puppy and a human baby. It was eating something it had found in the pool. She hoped it was food. A bin of what looked like peanuts or soybeans was set up a few yards down the slope. More turds littered the rocky ground around it. Yeah, these monkeys were famous. But she had absolutely no desire to get any closer to them. "Do you like the ryokan? I mean, is it all right?"

They were staying at a traditional hotel, a terrifyingly upscale place ostensibly favored by the imperial family. Their sunken tub looked out over the fog-shrouded northern mountains. The daily price was daunting, but they both had back pay on the books. She'd reserved a room with Western-style beds. But Chip hadn't been able to sleep. He said the mattresses were too soft. Before they'd left for the springs this morning, she'd asked the desk to shift them to one with futons.

He didn't answer for a few seconds. Then his shoulders lifted and fell. "I'm cool with it."

"Did you get baths in the camp?" But the moment she asked this she thought, Fuck, Cheryl. What a stupid, *stupid* question. Why remind him? You're supposed to be getting his mind off that. Helping him come back.

But he only shrugged again and squinted up at the dreary sky. A moment later she heard it too: the distant hissing roar of a jet. Invisible above the clouds, but he'd picked it up right away.

"Twin engine," he said. "Probably commercial."

A feral shriek jerked their heads around. At the far end of the spring, two monkeys had turned on a third, smaller one. They were screaming, their shockingly long yellow fangs bared in snarls. The small one scrambled up out of the spring and crouched shivering on the rocks, hugging herself. The larger ones glared. Then turned away, returning to their heat-soaked trance. They ignored her, beyond an occasional intimidating glance.

"They're pretty fucking territorial," her husband observed. He sighed, face tense, as if he'd just recalled some unpleasant event. "Like us."

She wanted to ask what he was remembering. To know what he'd experienced. To share some of his pain, if it would help. But the counselor had said, "Give him time. It was hell in those camps. No food. Beatings. Worse, if you resisted. His story isn't going to come out overnight. Some of it," she'd added, "he'll probably keep to himself for the rest of his life."

She took his arm now and leaned her head on his shoulder. Yeah, her husband was back. She'd yearned for this. Dreamed. Then lost all hope, and just grieved. And finally, come to terms with the loss.

Now, years later, here he was again. But this was not the same man. Not at all. He'd slept badly. Twitching, jerking, and muttering all night long, so she'd only fallen asleep well toward dawn. In the morning, he'd gaped at their breakfast trays, as if fish, rice, pickled veggies, and pumpkin soup were an emperor's feast.

And of course, he hadn't touched her, other than a peck on the cheek that wouldn't have offended a maiden aunt. Not at all like the horny jock she'd married, ready to launch hot on a moment's notice. Once, she couldn't even change her bra in front of him without a grab. Which she'd not always fended off . . .

"I just wonder what it was all about," he muttered now, rubbing his lower jaw. The Navy said he needed serious dental work—he had gum disease, needed root canals and tooth replacements—but had let him postpone it for a few days, so they could get reacquainted.

"What . . . what *what* was all about, Eddie? The camp, you mean?" she murmured, looking up. Hoping for maybe a hug, or a quick kiss, but he wasn't even looking at her. The monkeys seemed to interest him more.

Shit, what had the Chinese done? He'd been a randy goat. Now he was acting like some kind of detached, celibate guru, floating above earthly desires. He hadn't even touched breakfast, except for two bites of rice, a pickled carrot, and a few sips of hot green tea.

"No . . . the whole fucking war. What it was about." He nodded at the monkeys. "Was it just that . . . like that?"

She blinked. "I'm not following, Eddie. Like what?"

"Like, they wanted us out of the pool? And we didn't want to go?"

She blinked again, thinking for a moment he was joking. But he wasn't smiling. After a moment she said, trying to banter back, "Or we owned the water, and they wanted in."

Where was *this* coming from? The guy she'd known had never thought deeply about anything. Well, about football. Golf. And flying. But maybe being in a prison camp gave you time to think.

"Sorry, I guess I'm tired," he said. "That was kind of a rough path."

Actually it had been easy, a smooth gentle slope. But she nodded. "Yeah, it was a bit of a climb. Want to go back?"

"No, this is all right. Let's grab that bench over there."

A Japanese couple, gray-haired, a head shorter than the two Americans, smiled and half bowed as they passed. Cheryl smiled and bobbed her head back. They settled on a concrete bench overlooking the pool area.

"So," he said, not meeting her gaze. "You turned out to be the real hero in this war."

She took his hand, which lay lifeless and rather cold in hers. "I think we both did okay, Eddie."

"You got the DSC. I get the POW medal."

They were comparing decorations? "Yeah, but . . . you're getting the Heart too, right?"

"I don't know. They might not give medals for cracking your

head open when you punch out." He huffed a sigh, still not looking at her. "What is it with you, Cher?"

"With *me*? What is what?" She smiled, squeezing his hand, but not getting anything back. "I don't understand. Explain it to me."

"Something's different. You're like, not the same. You were always nervous. Anxious. That was kind of what I liked about you. Plus that you were incredibly hot, of course." A slight grin; a *very faint* glimmer of the old Chip, as if seen darkly beneath many layers of aging plastic.

"You're attracted to anxious girls?"

"You know what I mean. Like, I had too much self-confidence. Well, you gotta have some of that when you're going down the chute in Case Three seas, low fuel and no divert. But it was like . . . I guess I thought we could share. I'd help you out there, and you'd help me in the brains department. Help me figure life out. I don't know. I was only twenty-five."

She turned the gold ring around on her finger. He didn't have his anymore. Said they'd stolen it and his watch on the fishing boat that had pulled him out of the East China Sea. He'd ditched his pistol as soon as he hit the water, and his radio hadn't worked, damaged in the bailout. The fishermen had beat on him some after they pulled him aboard, then turned him over to the military cops. Who'd relieved him of the rest of his survival gear.

Beyond that, he hadn't said much about his captivity. Only that they hadn't gotten much to eat, and that after a group of prisoners had escaped from another camp, they'd spent the nights locked into steel trash containers, huddled together for warmth.

Well, maybe he was starting to share now. She'd just have to be patient and wait.

But she had something to share too. And she wasn't looking forward to saying it. But it had to be done. Here, now, today. Time wasn't going to improve the news. And she'd truly thought he was KIA, after all.

More screaming erupted from the pool. The monkeys were throwing feces at each other. Really, they'd looked cute and funny in the pictures, but she was getting the unvarnished experience now. Still, the mountains were lovely, and she and Eddie would have their own hot bath, without floating poo, back in the room. Or a communal soak at the humans-only *onsen* up the hill, stewing alongside naked Japanese. Probably mainly older couples, like the pair who'd bowed to them.

She said in a low voice, "And I'm not like that anymore. Is that what you're saying?"

For an answer he fumbled in his parka and took out a pack of the cigarettes he'd bought at the exchange, despite her askance look, while she'd been shopping for hiking boots. She'd started to ask, When did you start, but didn't.

Once again, she choked back questions. Just tried to go with the flow, and let him set the pace.

He lit up with a disposable lighter and puffed morosely, watching the animals. More were arriving now, trekking down from the hill, where they apparently lived. More tourists were arriving too, toiling up a rugged path from the direction of the train station. They looked Asian. She and Eddie were the only Europeans at the hotel, too. If white Americans could still be considered Europeans.

She took a deep breath and crossed her arms. Boy, she didn't want to do this. But the longer she let it go, the worse it would be. "I'm really glad you're here," she opened. "I mean it, Eddie. I thought for so long that you were . . . well, gone. Never coming back. The Navy told me that. Missing, presumed dead. Nobody knew you survived. And the Red Cross never got an accounting from the camps until the armistice. So I just—I just had to accept that."

He smoked morosely, but nodded. Still watching the pond, where the small monkey, trying to creep in again, was being ejected once more, with screeches and bites and flailing arms. "Yeah," he muttered. "Must've been rough."

What the hell did that mean? She tried to ignore it, to not take offense; had to just plow on. "What I mean is, I mourned you, Eddie. I went through all those grief-stage things. But we were at war, and I was a CO. I had my people to look out for. I was devastated at losing you. But I came to terms with it. That I'd have to live without you."

He flicked ash off the cigarette, staring at the ground. "Okay, sure. But it sounds like you're working up to some kind of apology, I think. So . . . why?"

She took another deep breath. "Anyway . . . I want to be honest with you. I got involved with a guy, in Hawaii."

He didn't react at first. Just kept staring at the fighting monkeys. She picked at the skin between her fingers, which seemed to be itching again. Maybe it was the dryness here. Oh, shit, she thought. I should have waited on this. Waited until he felt better. Was she just trying to make *herself* feel better? She cleared her throat. "Um, did you hear me? Chip?"

"Oh yeah. Loud and clear. Who was it, one of your officers? That tall asshole. Mills, is that his name?"

"Who, *Matt*? No. God, not him! Nobody aboard ship. Not anyone you know. A civilian."

He nodded, acknowledging, but still not really reacting. She rushed on. "Like I said, I didn't know you were alive. And it didn't last. Just one weekend, really. I wanted you to know. To get it out in the open, so we can talk about it."

One weekend she'd never forget, an idyllic time she'd always cherish in that secret corner of her brain no one else could access. At least not without the kind of imaging equipment Archipelago Systems and the CIA were rumored to be developing to interrogate spies. Maybe with that they could actually hear the swish of waves on a Hawaiian beach, feel the sand in the crack of your butt after a round of incredible sex . . .

But Eddie just sat there on the bench, watching the monkeys and nursing his smoke. She scratched her head, fretting. Was he even *registering* her confession? She wanted to shake him. Hurt, being wounded, even rage would be better than this . . . passivity. This appalling apathy. It just wasn't him. He just wasn't whom she'd married: mercurial, funny, rambunctious. Sometimes a caveman, yeah, but always *there*. So finally she did shake him, gently, by the sleeve. "I need some kind of reaction, Eddie. Say you hate me, or whatever. What are you feeling?"

"I don't feel much of anything these days," he murmured, and sighed. "To be real honest, I don't feel much about you, either way. So you had like, an affair, while you thought I was dead. Well . . . fine. So did I."

She cocked her head, puzzled. "You had a . . . I don't understand. I thought you were in that camp the whole time."

"I was."

"There were women there too?"

"It wasn't with a woman."

Her nod was a mindless reflex. She hovered between shock and numbness. "I'm not—I didn't—I never knew you—had impulses. I mean, that way."

"I didn't. Still don't, I guess. Or maybe I do. That's part of what I've got to figure out." He sighed again, more deeply this time, and stubbed the cigarette out on the bench's concrete arm. Flicked it to the ground. She bent and retrieved it, slipped it into a pocket. He jammed his fists into his parka again. "Along with a lot of other things," he added. "Like, whether to stay in. Whether I'll ever get back to flight status. Probably not, given what they found on my physical."

"Is that right? I didn't know . . . You didn't say what the results were."

He shook another cigarette out, but didn't light it. Just stared at it. "And, I guess, whether we stay together."

She tried to keep her tone neutral. Unemotional. "Oh. I see."

"And until I get some of that uh, figured out, yeah, it might seem like I'm kind of, not all here. Or whatever."

She let the silence elongate. His words weren't exactly a commitment, either way. But at least he was talking. She eased a breath out and patted his shoulder.

They watched the monkeys for a while longer. Until he said, "What are *your* plans, Cher? Postwar, I mean?"

"Uh, it's kind of up in the air . . . Captain was just a wartime rank. I'm still a commander, officially. *Savo*'s in port, safe. She's new, but a lot of the older ships will be decommissioned. I'd have six months left on my command tour if I hadn't put her in commission in wartime. But now, who knows. I'm long overdue for a shore tour . . . but a lot of my peers are getting out. Hoping for civilian jobs."

"Which may or may not be there," he muttered. He fished in his pockets again, probably for the lighter, and she almost said, You're smoking too much, but didn't. "I might need to stay in, at least for a while," he added. "Given the medical crap I need to take care of. And the dental. They'll probably give me a desk someplace. Limited duty. We'll see. You?"

"I'll stay with the ship until they reassign me. I should call the detailer. There's a lot going on right now in the surface community. Not just ships. Manpower issues, funding . . . end strength, promotion planning, billet base, bonus structures—" She stopped herself, realizing she was beginning to chatter. Weird, she felt nearly as scared now as she had in the Tsushima Strait.

"Probably be a lot of early separations," he said. "Might be good for you promotion-wise. But flying? For me, I think, it's the end of the line."

"Uh, maybe. Like I said, a lot of changes are coming down the pike." She hesitated. "Is there—you used to say, someday you wanted to play golf professionally. Any thoughts about—?"

"Professionally?" He flexed his wrists again, the same habitual way he had since returning. "After they stamped on these, and broke them . . . No, I don't think so. Might be able to coach. Yeah, I could probably coach something. Maybe college ball, college golf. Or teach flying somewhere. In light planes."

She thought about saying that might not be much of a challenge for him, but regarding his downturned face, the slump in his back, she might be wrong.

But then, he'd only been back a few days. She had to give him time. He'd always loved golf. Had talked about it endlessly, to the point of boring her. She'd played a little, mainly when invited along on wardroom outings, but nowhere near his level. But the idea of coaching, or teaching something, that was new.

"Or maybe politics," he said.

She flinched. *"Politics?"*

"Just thinking about it. So all that"—he waved his hands, indicating something bigger than these mountains, but farther away— "all *this*, doesn't happen again. That's the most important thing now, I think."

He lit the fresh cigarette automatically, without looking down, as if not noticing what he was doing. They sat on the bench, watching as another clump of tourists arrived, chattering excitedly as the pond came into view.

So were they together? She still didn't know. But at least she'd told him. Gotten that off her chest, off her conscience. Not that she had any reason to feel guilty. But still.

"Getting cold out here." He shifted on the seat, turning a slightly remote gaze her way. "Thanks for the parka, but maybe I should've worn a sweater under it. How about you?"

"Yeah. Maybe. I guess."

"So, time to go?"

He flexed his wrists again, winced again, and stood. Stretched, his hands to the small of his back. "Let's try that big heated bathtub. That's gonna feel good." He almost sounded eager. The most animated he'd been since his return. About a hot bath. Still, it was something.

She looked back one last time at the pool as they left. Remembering again what he'd said, and the incongruous wrongness of it. Reducing the horrific years just past to monkeys fighting over an increasingly fouled pool.

No. That wasn't why she'd fought. Why she'd risked defeat, and death, time after time. Why people, her people, had died, aboard the old *Savo*, aboard *Jeonnam*, *Guam*, all the other lost ships, all the wounded and burned in her task force. Why he had lost three years of his life, and ruined his health. It wasn't like that. Couldn't be like that. God, if he really believed that . . . but surely he couldn't. No sane person could.

"I'm really looking forward to a dip in that hot tub," Chip said again, beside her.

She turned back to him, dismissing her vision, and forced a smile. "Yeah. Me too."

And after a moment, tentatively, he took her hand. His fingers felt icy. His grip was weak. But he'd reached out, and touched her, finally.

Yeah. Nothing in life was guaranteed. Nothing had been agreed between them. But . . . maybe it had been clarified, at least a little.

They'd have to just let it all settle out. And then, see what came next.

A few steps on, she linked her arm through his.

18

Republic of the Covenant, Missouri

THE line was just as long today. Out around the block before the doors even opened. Not that they really ever closed; the clinic, set up in the basement of the building, was open around the clock.

The bone-thin, spindly-legged, haggard woman in dirty scrubs dragged herself toward the back. Each lifted foot was a slog. A kerchief over her head hid the patches of bare scalp where her hair had fallen out.

Nan had noticed the first effects—nausea, diarrhea, and loss of appetite—shortly after the shoot-out at the roadblock. At some point in their trip east, she and her escort of bikers had crossed a patch of fallout, or a shift in the wind had brought it down on them. Or maybe it was just from that initial blast of neutrons as she'd huddled in the stairway at Archipelago, arms locked over her skull, as the scarlet flash tore through her brain like a guillotine blade.

Anyway, the *when* of her exposure probably didn't really matter. Most people here, just south of the main strikes on the missile fields, had been toasted to some degree.

She'd been here for weeks, but it seemed like months.

Her escort, a Seattle gang who called themselves the Berzerkers, had gone violent during a face-off with the militia. Barreling down the highway, convoying her truck in her escape from the stricken city, they'd disobeyed a shouted command to halt. Probably Ish, their leader, had expected to bulldoze through the roadblock, and signaled his men to open fire from the saddle fifty yards away. But the yokels hadn't fled, and they'd been better armed than the bikers. The gang had been caught in a withering crossfire on the open highway, without cover other than their toppled Harleys and Indians.

When the shooting ended the bikes were burning, and Ish, Rollvag, and the other gang members lay dead or wounded. The Covenanters didn't seem interested in taking prisoners; a shotgun blast to the head finished off any lingering sufferers.

When the fight was over, they'd dragged her out of the truck too. She'd screamed at them as they dragged her toward the heap of twitching corpses. But at last she'd convinced her new captors that she was a medic, not a combatant. That the crates in the refrigerator truck were essential to stemming the Central Flower virus spreading through the Midwest.

"The Chinese flu, you mean?" one of them had said at last, and held out a hand to push away the muzzle of a shotgun.

But they hadn't let her go. Just shunted her upward in their own command structure until she and the crates of still-chilled LJL 4789 had ended up here, in this rural community hospital, which had been hastily converted into a frontline aid station.

Since then, she'd been stuck here, helping Dr. Merian Glazer and his forcibly drafted hospital staff fight the outbreak. No one knew exactly how or why the Flower had gained a foothold here, and the Centers for Disease Control was no more welcome behind the Covenanter lines than any other federal agency. But, fortunately, the insurgents at least realized the disease had to be contained. Especially since radiation effects had weakened the people in the northern half of the area where they held sway, making them susceptible to any opportunistic infection.

Now, as she let herself into the operating room, Glazer was bent over the operating table. A sweet reek of ether and alcohol filled the air. The generator hammered in the basement; the lights flickered. A muffled *boom* vibrated the air. Not far away: a missile from an HS drone, artillery? They knew very little down here about how that battle was going. Only that the enemy wore black uniforms and seemed to have unlimited ammunition.

But the locals knew the terrain, and guerrilla fighters with scoped rifles and hunting camouflage were apparently taking a deadly toll.

"Lenson." The head nurse jerked her head toward a cabinet. "We saved you some breakfast. Feeling any hungrier today?"

Nan hugged herself, shivering, wishing she did. Food was scarce. But the very thought of eating was nauseating. "It's sourdough, fresh baked, from that flour they captured. Rayfield sent it over special," the nurse urged, her eyes still on the open chest cavity on the table.

Marshal Dallas Rayfield was the Covenanter leader. The provisional president, he called himself. Nan sighed. "I'll try." She opened the cabinet, but closed it again as the yeasty reek hit her nostrils.

The head nurse patted her back. "Are you really going out today? You look terrible."

"She has to," Glazer said over one shoulder, suturing by feel as the lights flickered off, then on again. "There's nobody else, and the flu's still spreading."

"I'm just saying—"

"Yeah, I'm going," Nan said flatly. "Release me another five hundred doses, please, Doctor."

Glazer cocked his head. "You sign. Use my name. I'm wrist deep."

She faked his signature, in huge loopy letters, and took the chit downstairs.

OUTSIDE, she tucked the packet into the saddlebag of a bullet-scarred Harley—yes, one of the Berzerkers' machines—and threw a leg over. Hit the start button, and was rewarded by a hearty bellow.

Fuel was scarce, but a chit from Rayfield allowed her one gallon a day of home-brewed alcohol, eked out with raw gas from the single fracking-fed refinery in Covenanter territory. And a bike had another advantage, or so she hoped: the black drones that crossed the sky might be unwilling to expend an expensive missile on two-wheelers. At least they'd held off so far. But the black flyers kept coming over, so often that the rebel children included their threatening geometry in their scrawled drawings. A cross, with propellers. A black quincunx, hovering, omnipresent, ominous, ruling the blue now alongside the sun and moon in the crayoned pictures.

Her cooler contained five hundred doses of L packed in ice. She'd mapped out a distribution schedule and tried to hit three towns a day. Other than her supply, the rebels had no vaccines, though Patriot Radio said they were available in government-controlled areas. Whether that was true, she had no idea. Anyway, she needed to keep a continuous patrol going, skirting the steadily expanding radius of infection, treating those in the early stages and urging their quarantine until the danger was past. Fortunately the antiviral she'd rescued from the wrecked factory hadn't lost its potency. When she could administer it in time, the initial fever held for about forty-eight hours, then dropped. Further symptoms, the deadly ones, didn't seem to develop.

A heavyset, fiftyish white woman threw a thick blue-jeaned leg over another bike and started her engine too. Floral Puckett rode shotgun with Nan on her rounds. Literally. Puckett carried a twelve-gauge sleeved in the scabbard of her own motorcycle. Whether to protect her, or to prevent her escape, wasn't quite clear.

The highway stretched empty to the horizon. They were headed for a small town to the south, near the border. Nan kept a wary eye on the cloudy sky. Government drones would strike rebel convoys, occasionally individual vehicles, but so far they'd not bothered the two riders.

The main fighting was raging farther east. Optimistic bulletins over local radio said the rebels were winning. Nan had her doubts, but kept them to herself. The Covenant Council dealt mercilessly with naysayers and suspected government sympathizers. She didn't know a lot about the fighting, or about the Covenant, or about the Council. Mostly the Covenanters talked about freedom from government itself, which of course made it difficult to persuade them it was vital to take public health measures. What she received, fuel and food and security escort, was grudgingly given. But every kid she saved was a kid saved, after all.

She was telling herself that again when Puckett hit the horn. When she glanced back, the other rider jabbed a gloved finger at the sky.

Just below the clouds, a black shape slanted down. For a moment Nan thought: *drone*. Every muscle tensed and she nearly swerved off the road. But then she saw it wasn't a drone after all.

It was even more dangerous.

The huge swollen-bellied aircraft, painted dead black, was a dark angel descending. Its steady swoop was accompanied by the faint, obviously muffled whine of idling jet engines.

She searched for a turnoff, a concealing copse, a viaduct, even. But the highway that stretched ahead was empty, flat, coverless. She glanced at Puckett, who'd faced forward again. Pretending, probably, to ignore the cameras that were even now zooming in on them. The craft was close enough now that Nan could make out the guns pointed from turrets beneath its belly.

Whoever was behind that camera guided those weapons. Or maybe there wasn't a person there at all. No human heart with mercy or forbearance, but instead a program: a cold mechanical intelligence, sorting them against threat profiles with the speed of digital thought; evaluating; categorizing; deciding. Two riders. *Hostile, friendly, nonthreat, ignore . . .*

Kill.

Sweat broke under Nan's jacket despite the cooling wind of her passage. She relaxed her death grip on the throttle to slow, then reconsidered and sped up again, to sixty. A steady mile a minute. When she glanced back again Puckett was a few yards behind. No; her partner was dropping back, edging slowly away. Maybe a good idea. Spreading out, so it would require two bursts of whatever those turrets carried to take them out. Nan sped up even more and the highway between them widened.

She stole another glance up. The black aircraft was pacing them. The gunship was much larger than she'd thought at first. So huge it seemed to float, nearly motionless, from her perspective, though all three vehicles were rushing along the highway. An angel of death with lifted sword. Coldly eyeing them. Trying to decide.

Fire, or refrain?

Destroy, or let them go?

She tried to master her breathing. Then reached back, into the saddlebags. Felt around, as the bike wobbled. Her fingertips brushed a square shape, yielding, but with harder objects within. Nearly twisting her shoulder out of its socket, she hauled the box free. Held it out, at arm's length, so that it dangled by its strap, twisting in the blast of the wind.

Her medical kit. With the red cross on a white background.

When she glanced back Puckett's face had gone pale. She was mouthing words, but nothing Nan could make out over the howl of engines, the now-oh-so-clearly audible whine of the black plane's jets.

She glanced up again, and caught a gunflash. No . . . light sparkling off a lens. Which was apparently focused on her.

For several seemingly eternal seconds they rode locked together, observer and observed. Her arm tired and she had to lower the med pack. She hesitated, then tucked it behind her, to brace her back with. Her bangs whipped her forehead in the wind as she wondered with each heartbeat if it would be her last.

The black plane canted slightly, and banked off to one side. The turreted lens tracked away from them. With a surge of power, a renewed thunder of engines, it rose again.

Climbed.

Shrank.

Vanished, once more, into the low clouds.

Nan slumped in her seat. She eased her breath out, and returned her attention to the road. She pressed shaky thighs into the soft cushioned saddle, and tried to relax shoulders that felt like tightened wires. Suddenly she was nauseated all over again, though whether from fear or from the radiation exposure, who could tell. She craned over the side, turning her head away from the blasting wind, and tried at least to keep what she vomited off her pants.

THEY were headed for a town down south, near the Tennessee border. Reports of any kind were scarce, but someone had called in a new outbreak of what sounded like Flower. She had basic first aid stuff and reusable syringes in the med kit. Puckett, who'd been an EMT before the war, was up to speed when it came to treating and stabilizing most traumas, though she didn't seem confident about infectious disease.

When they pulled in, the main street of Lime Bluff looked deserted. A few nineteenth-century and early-twentieth-century brick storefronts lined it, a block or two of shops, most with rain-warped particleboard nailed over the windows. Zooming around her to take the lead, Puckett steered them onto a side street, to a brick-and-aluminum one-story clinic building. AID STATION had been clumsily painted over a still-visible PLANNED PARENTHOOD sign. Two men in green-and-beige turkey-hunting camouflage, the Covenant patch prominent on their billed caps, stood guard outside. Puckett yelled, "Meds are here," and after a moment's hesitation the guards waved them to a loading zone.

Puckett handed Nan a face mask, then tied her own on. Snapped on green nitrile gloves. Nan gloved herself just as carefully. They had to recycle items one usually disposed of, soaking needles and scalpels in a weak bleach solution, but the supply of gloves, masks, and bleach was growing short.

Inside, one back room had been taped off with plastic into a rough isolation unit. Nan nodded approvingly. The single nurse back there wore blue scrubs and a face shield. Nan gave him the first injection, though he said, "I don't feel sick yet." The patients seemed mostly to be teenagers. "We had two older folks, but they died," the nurse, Logan, added, rubbing his arm as he led them down a narrow aisle between what looked like folding camping cots. "This is Twila. She was the first one they brought in."

The girl was restrained in the bunk with gay red-and-white poly rope. Nan bent over her for a quick exam. Twila stank of diarrhea. She was gasping for breath, cheeks purpling, with white blotches. Bloodshot eyes fixed on the nurse, then rolled away in panic as the teen struggled to suck in air. "One-hundred-and-three-degrees fever, pulse 93, blood pressure 170 over 120," Logan said. "She's in hypertensive crisis, I think. I treated her with intravenous saline for hydration. Gave her Cipro, too."

"Antibiotics aren't going to help. Save those for injuries, wounds, and secondary pneumonia," she told him. Across the bed, Puckett was unwrapping a disposable airway. They had no respirators, of course.

Nan bent to the girl. "Twila, can you hear me? Blink twice if you can."

The teenager stiffened, gasped for breath, then seemed to relax. She blinked with both eyes. Once. Twice.

"Good, she doesn't seem confused," Nan noted. "Just scared. Any seizures?"

"No, Doctor."

Nan didn't correct his honorific. She broke the ampule and filled the needle. Puckett lifted a sleeve, patted for a vein, and swabbed the site with alcohol. Nan double-checked the needle for air, then slid it in. She drew the girl's sleeve back down and patted her shoulder. "You'll start to feel better pretty soon, Twila. Give it a couple of hours. Rest, and let the medicine work." Please God let it be still potent . . . but she'd kept it refrigerated; the antiviral should still be good.

Working swiftly, but with a reassuring word to each patient, they went from cot to cot. One of the men lay limp and unresponsive. She debated saving the dose for someone not as far gone, but finally injected him, too.

When she looked up from the last patient an older fellow with a close-cropped white Vandyke was watching from the door. He nodded when he caught her glance, and turned away.

Puckett came up. "About ready to head back, Floral?" Nan asked.

"I don't think we're going back," the heavyset woman said. "At least not tonight."

Nan frowned. "Sorry . . . what?"

Puckett lowered her voice. "There's somethin' going on. A 'push,' they're calling it. The major here wants us with his unit."

Nan frowned. "Wait, I'm confused. We're due back. Rayfield *shoots* people for disobeying orders. I had enough trouble persuading him to let us fight the flu instead of waiting for it to come to us."

Puckett murmured, "Sure. But we may not have a choice."

The men who'd been guarding the door sauntered in. They grabbed the male nurse—Logan—Nan, and Puckett, and hustled them out. They thrust them toward a makeshift convoy of battered vans and pickups spray-painted in various conceptions of camouflage. Men and women sat in the beds, weapons propped on their knees. A battered Dodge Ram had a machine gun bolted atop the cab. A hastily welded tripod of unpainted steel pointed it at the sky.

"What's going on?" she demanded, but was only boosted ungently into a van behind the machine-gun truck, along with Puckett and the nurse. The rear seats had been removed, so they sat on the floor. More Covenanters hurried out of the clinic, carrying cardboard boxes of bandages and boxes of sanitary napkins and throwing them into the van.

"Hey." The woman driving craned back in her seat, looking down at them. A strawberry blonde in aviator-style sunglasses, freckles nearly invisible under smears of green and black camo paint. In cammies, with the Covenanter cap at a jaunty angle and a white armband stenciled with the Red Cross. She thrust back a hard, not very clean palm. "Tracy."

"Floral."

"Um . . . Nan." She thought about asking again where they were going, but decided not to seem too curious. These people shot spies, too.

"Logan," the nurse mumbled.

"Cool, good to meet cha. Which of you's the doctor?"

"She is." Puckett pointed to Nan.

Who shook her head. "No, I'm not a medical doctor. Just a bio-chemist. I worked on developing advanced drugs. Look, we're here to fight the flu, not—"

"Yeah? A biochemist? Cool." Tracy pulled armbands from in-side her fatigue blouse and forced them into the reluctant hands of all three passengers. Nan's had suspicious-looking brown spatters on it. "Congratulations, you're gonna be part of the big push south. Eastern front's linking up with the RECOs. The Re-Confederates. We manage this linkup, we cut the country in half. But there's a Blackie force headed this way too. We're beefing up the flank, in case they try to cut us off. You're part of my team now, so put those on. We're not covered by Geneva, but it might could get you better treatment if you're captured."

Nan gave up and pinned it on. Maybe the insignia had helped earlier, with the gunship. Who knew.

The convoy groaned and clattered into motion, gradually, like an uncoiling rattler. Raw exhaust from homemade fuel made her cough. Tracy pushed Nan's scarf back and squinted at her nearly naked pate. "What happened? Dose of rad?"

"I was in Seattle when they nuked it."

"And you made it out? Jesus God. Hey, you guys hungry? They issued us some sausage. Might's well eat it now."

Nan didn't like the undertone of that last comment, but ac-cepted a thick cut of intestine stuffed with ground meat. It was bland and unspiced, but after so long without protein she tore chunks off, wolfing the pork so greedily one bite stalled halfway and she nearly choked. Puckett pounded her back helpfully and she gulped again, then again, forcing it down her esophagus. The nausea still lingered, but miraculously her stomach didn't reject the food. Was her appetite finally returning? That would be a good sign.

The convoy rolled between cornfields, then woods. The team on the machine-gun truck ahead of them swung the long barrel back and forth while a lookout searched the sky with binoculars.

"So how'd you get into this?" Nan asked Tracy.

"Into the militia, you mean?" She grinned like a happy kid. "Oh, I was in long before the war. My dad started me off when I was thirteen. He's a tractor mechanic. I went to musters with him. Got some medical training, and then came the war . . . I was gonna join the Army, but then I realized we weren't just fighting the Chinese. We were like superheroes, fighting the whole idea of tyrannical government. I mean, they tried to take our guns away. Nobody I know turned anything in. Then they started seizing crops, paying shit money for them—confiscating our livestock, drafting our kids. We just said, enough."

Nan had heard the rest working at the hospital: return to the original Constitution, Second Amendment sanctuary, America for Americans, Jefferson and insurrection theory. She couldn't disagree with some of it. But in the face of a war against a foreign enemy . . . and now that war was over . . . she shook her head and ground her teeth into something hard and bitter in the last bite of sausage. She lowered a window and spat the wad of gristle and bone over the side.

The lead vehicles turned off the pavement onto a dirt track paralleling rusty rails. The van lurched and banged over ruts. Dust rolled up, smearing a yellowish paste across the windshield. Tracy hit the wipers and squinted ahead. Horns blared. Brush scraped the side of the truck like fingernails.

After half an hour on the dirt track they came out at an open field. It sloped gently down toward a flat sheet of lake, bounded on the far side by a straight concrete line. A reservoir. A dam. Tracy slowed, letting a gap open between her and the technical. She peered up at the sky. Then floored the accelerator, vaulting the van rocking and jolting across the open field before plunging into the tree cover again at the far side, where the dirt track resumed.

It was late afternoon when the convoy finally turned onto an asphalted road, went another mile, then turned right into woods again. A man on foot gestured them to pull off and park.

Tracy squinted ahead. "Good. They put us beside a stream." She ratcheted the hand brake, cut the engine, and turned to them. "Looks like we're here, folks. Grab the supplies. There's a tent in that soft case. Let's get it set up. Go fifty yards out from the campsite along the stream and build us a fire. But keep it small, with a bucket of water beside it. They're gonna have drones out, looking for us."

BY the time the aid station was ready for business it was almost dusk. The woods were tangled with vines, dark and deep. Huge flies and mosquitoes buzzed, crawled, and bit. The so-called stream was barely a trickle. Nan shuddered when Tracy casually dipped up a tin cupful and drank it down. "Running water, it's good to go," she said when she caught Nan's horrified glance.

"No it isn't. There's all kinds of fecals and pathogens in surface water. Vibrios, salmonella, shigella—"

"Been drinking it since I was little. A stomachache now and then? So what." The battle medic flirted the dregs out of her cup and yelled, "Not *here*, fuckhead! This is an aid station. At least two hundred yards away."

Nan didn't see who the woman was yelling at, until a heap of moss stirred. A human figure stood, shrouded in netting festooned with twigs and leaves. It moved silently off, blending back into the forest.

She walked downstream, looking for some privacy to pee in. The sky showed between the trees ahead. The wind was rising, shaking loose leaves and bits of mistletoe down from the treetops.

The temperature was falling. Something bad was on its way. She shivered, hugging herself. Then halted.

A line of men and women were lying or sitting cross-legged, fiddling with reflective tarps, just within the tree line. Some had already spaded fighting holes; others were just starting to dig, grunting and cursing as they battled roots and rocks. Most were older men, but there were women, too, and teenagers. An older officer in baggy utilities walked from position to position, squatting for earnest discussions in low voices. The bearded guy she'd seen back at the hospital. The "major." Hunting rifles and shotguns lay beside the rebels, with hearing protectors and boxes of what looked like hand-loaded ammo. Some wore bulky vests stitched with squares of bathroom tile. They wore a wild assortment of helmets: old Army lids, motorcycle helmets, those who wore headgear at all; many didn't.

She edged forward a little more and peered out. An open field dropped away in front of them. A small farmstead lay a half mile distant. The fields were weedy and overgrown. The roof of one of the sheds had fallen in. A victim of the trade wars that had preceded the actual hostilities, she guessed. The sun was setting over her right shoulder. So they were facing south, or southeast. Waiting. For what, she didn't know.

When she got back another tent was going up not far from theirs. Tracy stood watching, fists propped on hips, scowling. Her nipples showed through her beater tee. As Nan came up she turned her head and spat. "Fucking headquarters pogeys," she muttered. "They gotta set up right here where we are. Which means we're gonna get targeted too."

Nan frowned. "Do you really think we'll get—what—bombed?"

The medic shrugged. "Guess we'll find out."

A distant rumble turned both their heads; "Thunder," Tracy concluded at last.

Nan wondered if there was any sausage left. She hesitated, but finally asked. Tracy lifted her eyebrows. "Jeez! That was a day's ration you scarfed down. Now you want more?"

"I haven't had much of an appetite lately. The radiation—"

"Well, good that it's back, I guess. There's some dried apples in my pack if your tum-tum's burning a hole." She waved a hand vaguely toward the tent. "Then, better get some sleep. You never know when you won't be able to."

SHE was headed back to the tent when a distant roaring penetrated her consciousness. It echoed among the trees, a rumbling so deep she couldn't tell which direction it was coming from. Not thunder. Not this time, although a distant flash of lightning flickered among the clouds now and then.

Excited voices rose at the command tent. A man came out with a small hand-launched aircraft. He powered it up and pitched it overhand. The drone climbed between the treetops and headed off. Another man squatted, studying a tablet that she guessed controlled it. Others, officers she guessed, gathered around.

She staggered back, blown nearly off her feet by the explosion. The missile, if that was what it was, had streaked downward too fast even to register on her retinas until the blast. When the smoke and airborne pine needles cleared, and clods of dirt stopped falling, Tracy charged out of the medics' tent. The crater was still smoking, with a bitter, acrid stench. Nan staggered after her, dazed, ears ringing.

Only two of the five or six men who'd been gathered there were left alive, and both were missing legs or arms. Tracy tried to render first aid, but they bled out in minutes.

The growling grew. It echoed off the trees. Tracy shepherded the others out of the aid tent and thrust med packs into their hands. She drew a gun on Logan when he didn't move fast enough. Urged on by the muzzle of her revolver, they trotted through the darkening woods, which were ominous with a cold, searching wind. Toward the scattered flat cracks of gunshots.

When they reached the front line some of the rebels were firing desultorily, but Nan couldn't see what they were aiming at.

Just down toward the old farm, apparently. Faint lights flickered from that direction, separated by wide margins of darkness. Even fainter blue lights hovered a few hundred feet up, weaving complexly, as if intelligent fireflies were coordinating a spectral dance. Then, all at once, they winked out.

The growling grew closer. A few people got up from their foxholes and trenches and faded back into the woods. They were followed by catcalls and curses from those who stayed. The major shook out a banner, a coiled rattler on a field of red and white, and staked it in front of their positions. "Stand fast!" he yelled. "They'll shoot rubber bullets, and we'll shoot real ones. Not one step back!"

The yells and cheers were blotted out by ponderous, incredibly loud words from the dark: a crackling loudspeaker, from down by the farm. *"PATRIOTS! WE ARE PATRIOTS TOO. WE DON'T WANT TO FIGHT OUR FELLOW AMERICANS. LEAVE YOUR WEAPONS ON THE GROUND. COME FORWARD WITH YOUR HANDS UP, AND WE WILL PROVIDE FOOD AND MEDICAL CARE."*

A scowling woman with a huge black automatic rifle walked the back of the line, shouting, "They're lying! They shoot prisoners. Whoever leaves his hole, I shoot. Whoever leaves his hole, I fucking waste." Some of the insurgents glanced around nervously, fingering their weapons; the older men calmly checked their sights and rearranged their ready ammunition. No one got up, and no one went forward to surrender. But no one else retreated, either.

The minute that passed felt very long.

On some unseen signal, the engines down by the farm gunned again, a renewed growl that swiftly deepened.

Lightning flashed in the gray-lined thunderheads. By the flash, silhouetted against the clouds, Nan caught small objects flitting toward them through the sky. She counted the beats: two thousand, three thousand—

A flash of heat seared her face, like a broiler grate suddenly pressed to her cheeks and forehead. At the same moment a high-pitched, incredibly sharp sound assaulted her ears. Pain stabbed her eyes. She ducked, unable to keep standing, rolling behind a tree and clapping hands over ears.

"Microwaves!" Tracy yelled. Along the line, sticks twanged into the air, snapping the reflective tarps into shape.

Someone yelled, "Fire at will!" and the riflemen opened up all along the line, though Nan still couldn't see what they were aiming at. She huddled behind the tree, wanting to flee, to escape the heat and incredible drilling whine boring deep into her brain in spite of her firmly clamped hands. But the scowling woman was pointing her rifle directly at her. Nan screamed and held out a shaking hand; the woman shook her head in warning and moved on. Something buzzed through the air and smacked into a tree with a shockingly loud *clap*.

The pain ray moved on, though the piercing whine kept on. When she looked out again one of the older men was angling a tube. With a hollow *thunk*, actinic light ignited above the field.

The brilliance illuminated four hulking shadows rolling slowly up from the farm. They approached at a walking pace, deliberately, as if unsure of what they faced, or maybe too unafraid of it to hurry. Between the larger shadows human figures, or something like humans, but with smaller heads, paced along with strangely mechanical rigidity, spaced out so that the entire line was some two hundred yards across.

"Fucking tanks," Tracy breathed, beside her in the dark. "We're fucked. We only got one AT gun. From in front of an American Legion post, and hand-loaded the rounds. And what are those things in between them?"

Nan ducked as something new droned overhead. It didn't sound like the bullets, but was a lower, slower, even more ominous buzzing. As if some winged predator hunted just above the treetops. She sank to a crouch, clutching her med pack to her chest. Wishing she had something to defend herself with. Even Tracy had a pistol.

Then thought: What good would it do?

From off to her right, a terrific crack and boom, a gush of

fire. She glanced up to see sparks fly from the lead tank. The violently painful siren-noise cut off instantly. The tank slewed slightly, but steadied again. Lightning flashed, closer now, and a drop of rain plinked onto her cheek, shockingly cold after the heat of the day.

A second flare burst. In its light she saw the riflemen working the bolts on their guns, aiming, firing. Distant clangs showed they were finding their marks, but the tanks and the walking things continued their advance. Tracy was down on one knee, revolver propped on a tree branch, cocking and aiming with careful deliberation.

"THIS IS YOUR FINAL WARNING," the loudspeaker intoned. *"LEAVE YOUR WEAPONS AND RETREAT FROM YOUR POSITIONS. WE WILL TREAT ANY WHO REMAIN AS INSURGENTS AND TRAITORS."*

The firing slackened. Then, to renewed yelling from the officers and sergeants, resumed, building to a steady roar. Lightning flickered. In its glare one of the black stalking silhouettes faltered, staggered, and toppled heavily to the ground. The defenders cheered. Shrill rebel yells and insulting catcalls rolled along the line. At the same moment, a gust of icy rain descended, rattling the leaves and surrounding the fighters with a mist that glowed in the flarelight.

Suddenly, with a deafening growl, the tanks accelerated. They bounded forward, rocking slightly, long barrels of their guns remaining steady. The leftmost one rotated its turret and with a bluish flash fired. A beam of solid light projected to Nan's left and was succeeded instantly with a deafening explosion, followed by terrified screams.

The tank itself neither slowed nor stopped. All four advanced rapidly now, rocking over the furrowed field. Through the gusts of cold wind and bursts of scattered icy rain the heavy machines rolled up into the woods. They knocked down trees with shattering cracks, rolling over the hastily dug pits and their occupants and crushing everything under spinning steel. Broken rifles and parts of bodies spewed from under the treads. As one, the machines pivoted—two left, two right—and bulldozed along the firing line, rolling over screaming men and women. Fiery tracers floated off into the woods, searching for fleeing shapes, pinning them, flinging them down like broken puppets. Above the trees something buzzed, and again, sharp reports snapped. Snipers fell from the trees like stunned squirrels, trailing camouflage netting, breaking branches on their way down.

Nan huddled behind the tree, watching a tank chew a flattened path away from her. Then heard a growl behind her, and turned.

The other tank loomed out of the rain, charging toward her. Men and women screamed as it rolled over them, then pivoted, grinding its tracks down into the shallow fighting holes. Trees toppled. Tarps whipped viciously, tangled and then ripped apart beneath the steel tread plates. The tank rolled over the rattlesnake flag and the old man stubbornly clinging to its pole, waving it in front of the oncoming machine until a machine-gun burst cut him down. A teen-aged girl ran in from the side, carrying two bottles, each capped with a flaming rag. She hefted one to toss, and the rag fell out. The fluid spilled out and ignited on her arm. Still she ran burning and screaming toward the tank, and smashed the other bottle against its armor before she too disappeared under the treads.

Nan shook off paralyzing horror and bolted, sprinting for the deep woods. Crashes and buzzing echoed from above. The heat ray returned, scorching her back. She panted as she fled, stumbling through underbrush and wait-a-minute vines that snagged her clothes and raked her exposed skin and finally tripped her flat. Bullets stitched a ragged seam just past her.

"*SURRENDER AND YOU WILL BE SPARED,*" the enormous voice intoned.

When she rolled to her back a dark form stood over her. Huge, but with a small, misshapen head. When lightning flickered she saw it wasn't human. It pointed a rifle at her. It said, "*Where is your wea-pon?*"

"I don't have one. I'm medical. Medic. First aid."

"*Where is your wea-pon?*"

"I don't have one, I said. Don't you understand? What are you? I'm a medic. Red Cross! A doctor!"

"You self-identify as noncombatant personnel?"

"I do. I do! Yes!"

"No wea-pon detected. Stand up and turn around. Hands behind your back."

She stood, knees shaking. Something wet sprayed her lower back. When she tried to bring her hands around again they were stuck to her clothing, to each other; she couldn't move them.

"Turn front," the audio commanded. She closed her eyes as another spray coated her chest and face. When she opened them, her chest and upper body glowed ghostly green in the night woods. *"Walk toward the sirens. Do not attempt escape,"* the robot commanded, then wheeled and stalked off, rifle jerkily pointing from bush to bush as it crashed through them.

She staggered back through the woods, which were on fire now here and there, the flames flickering low to the ground, struggling to survive against the pelting rain. Past bodies and chunks of bodies, exposed gristle and tendon and bone, splayed corpses burst like bags of blood where treads had run over them, the shot, the burned, the maimed. Floral Puckett lay facedown, still gripping her shotgun. Nan bent, but with hands bound behind her she couldn't help, couldn't even check for a pulse. She didn't see Tracy or Logan anywhere. She left Puckett behind and staggered out of the trees, out into the furrowed, smoking field. Past more tanks, immobile and hulking, ominous in the rain and lit only by lightning.

To join a line of bedraggled women and teens and old men waiting in front of a tent. Some were sobbing. Others stared blankly ahead, obviously in shock.

Here LED lanterns dangled garish light. Three officers sat at a folding table of white plastic under a dripping tent fly. Two male, one female. They wore black uniforms with silver insignia. Black-uniformed troops in tactical gear stood behind them, rifles at the ready. The line moved slowly, people shuffling forward reluctantly.

After a few words, some were led off to the right. Others, to the left, where shots cracked from the darkness.

Finally it was her turn. She faced the judges, but one of the troopers turned her roughly around, grabbed her pinioned hand, and shone a violet light on it.

"Do you speak English?" one of the seated officers said, the youngest one, on the right.

"Of course I speak English," she blurted, and instantly regretted her tone.

The leftmost officer, the woman, said, "You are a detainee of the Special Action Forces, Department of Homeland Security. What is your name?"

"Nan Lenson, Archipelago. I was taken prisoner by these—"

"Ms. Archipelago. Do you have any identification?"

"No, it was taken from me. And my last name's Lenson. I *worked* for Archipelago before I was taken—"

"State your allegiance."

"United States of America. My father's a Navy admiral."

The man in the middle, with graying hair, looked up for the first time. "How did you end up with these people?"

"I told you, I was taken prisoner. They wanted me as a medic. I worked for Archipelago until the nuclear attack. I escaped from Seattle with medications and was distributing them. Trying to fight the Chinese flu. Which is becoming epidemic north of here."

The younger man said, "Yet we find you down here, fighting in the rebel ranks."

"No, not fighting. They drafted me as a medic. As I said. See the armband? Red Cross. And we have wounded in the woods. A lot of wounded. Are you going to—"

"Green slime means captured without weapons," the woman said, cutting her short. "And GSR shows she wasn't firing."

"Remanded for further processing," the older man said, and the others nodded. The woman pointed her to the right.

Slogging through inches of greasy mud toward waiting cattle trucks, Nan struggled with whatever was pinioning her arms, and finally tore them loose. Maybe rain dissolved it. The goo dripped from her sleeves in rubbery strings. At least her hands were free. But the black-uniformed troops lining her path did not look away. Seeing no chance to run, she climbed at last up into the truck.

The rain blasted down harder now, cold and violent, suddenly unrestrained, a freezing deluge pelting the prisoners as they huddled in the bed, which still smelled of cattle and shit and blood, and now fear and ozone. And she huddled there, shivering, hugging herself, looking back toward the woods. Which stood dark, deserted, and now, except for the occasional muffled *pop* of a distant shot, completely silent.

19

The Pentagon, Washington, DC

LIGHTS flashed in her brain. Her hip flamed. Blair winced, then sighed and sat back, rubbing her eyes.

Her office was in the E ring, but it wasn't one of the most prestigious. Those faced outward, with views of the river, Arlington Cemetery, the 9/11 Memorial. Hers faced in, yielding a bleak, restricted vista of nondescript concrete walls and the blank-eyed windows of the next ring in. And above that, a gray sky that threatened more rain.

"You need a break, Blair," her aide said. But at the same time slid another folder in front of her.

She sighed and flipped it open. Plans for the postwar garrisons of Itbayat, Pratas, and Hainan. The strips and repair facilities would be maintained as Allied bases. Never again, or at least for the foreseeable future, would the South China Sea be a Chinese lake.

Until the next pulse outward, the next beat in the systole and diastole of the millennium-long flux of empire and power. The Chinese understood that time frame, and worked with the long view in mind. The United States never had. A perennial victim of historical amnesia, it never looked to history to understand the way forward. So it charged ahead blindly, pursuing each whim or crusade of the moment. Only much later to realize, and regret . . .

She clenched her teeth and shook her head angrily. Enough cynicism, Blair! She forced herself to read at least the executive summary. Sighed, and signed off. Handed it back. "What else?"

"Decommissioning ceremonies, medals, the rest of the morning, ma'am. After lunch, your remarks in the auditorium. The IT awards. Then the appointment with SecDef you wanted me to set up."

"Thanks. I appreciate it." She rubbed her eyes again, feeling terrifically exhausted. But then remembered, and smiled beneath her masking hands.

Dan had showed up at the house a few days before. Exhausted, gaunt, smelling of gasoline and the road. And miserable about Nan, naturally. He'd crossed a continent searching, only to discover her body in a small-town mortuary. His daughter was dead, plowed under in the brutal, confused aftermath of the greatest catastrophe to ever test the nation.

And Blair could do so little for him . . . so little. She'd never had a child, but she could imagine the pain.

The aftermath . . . the enemy nuclear strike had torn the heart out of four states, and smeared radiation, terror, famine, and revolt across half the rest. Over ten million Americans were missing and presumed dead, and no one could yet put any number on the wounded and the sick. The Central Flower flu was spreading, despite CDC doing all it could. The food situation looked especially grim. The harvest had been scanty, and millions of tons of corn, soybeans, and food grains were unfit for consumption, even though the administration had tripled the permissible level of contamination. Imports from Europe and South America would help, and foreign countries were contributing humanitarian aid; she'd seen offers from Belgium, Austria, Italy, the United Kingdom, Spain, Portugal, Turkey, Poland, and Slovakia. But the wartime rationing system would have to continue, maybe for years to come.

Which could be disastrous. A weakened, hungry population would be ripe for both pandemic and revolt.

"Uh . . . ma'am?" The aide cleared his throat.

She glanced up and forced a smile. "Thanks, that'll be all. And in case I've forgotten to say so, I appreciate your being with me through this war. Through everything."

The grin on the young man's face was worth millions.

SHE worked through the morning, feeling a brief return of her old energy. Broke for a tray lunch, salad and baked haddock from the executive dining facility. Then went to the auditorium. The ceremony featured her as the keynote, and for a change, she'd written her own speech.

A sea of faces, so very few of whom she actually knew. Oh well. She smiled, and began the opening remarks. She kept them simple, thanking both individuals and teams in the IT community for their contributions to the war effort and final victory. Most particularly, in cyberdefense and in the development of the vast artificial intelligence that had battled Jade Emperor.

She glanced down at her tablet. "Your friends, your husbands and wives, may not know this. May not be able to appreciate it . . . But you have fought a long, hard shadow war beneath the war they read about. A battle that perhaps will be declassified fifty years from now, the way Ultra was revealed only decades later.

"But you know the sacrifices you made, and your contribution to our victory. It was every bit as real and as meaningful as those of any soldier, sailor, airman, or marine in the front lines."

Maybe a little over the top. But hell, they deserved it. She glanced up to read the vibe from the audience. A mix of celebratory and . . . apprehensive? Of course. So she veered away from her prepared remarks to try to address that. Speaking slowly, and as reassuringly as she could. "There will be downturns in funding now that peace is here. Some of us will depart for civilian life once more. That's inevitable. But those who remain will have a continuing role in federal innovation and transformation. Not just within DoD, but in the other branches of the federal and state infrastructures as well.

"We have a major job ahead. We must rebuild the bomb-damaged and contaminated areas of the country, fight disease and hunger, and regain the trust and confidence of disaffected regions to the west and south as they reintegrate into the national fabric. You here will be called on again for the missions of peace, just as you were for those of war. And I have no doubt you will prevail in those as well.

"So with that, I say thank you, and farewell."

She stepped down to tepid applause, and surreptitiously blotted her brow. The hip was really stabbing her today. Another collection of clichés and platitudes, leavened with enough praise to keep their noses to the grindstone. At least she'd been able to reward a few of her best people with medals and promotions. They thronged her now, gushing thanks, jostling one another to shake her hand. So many that, for a few minutes, she couldn't break away. Maybe her little talk hadn't been as disappointing as she'd feared.

Until the aide pushed through, showing her the time on his phone. "Ma'am, we're just about due for the SecDef. Uh—can y'all excuse us, please? The undersecretary has an important appointment. Excuse us, *please*."

THIS was the biggest office in the Pentagon, and it was luxuriously quiet. Blue-carpeted, spacious, with a mahogany table large enough to serve a state dinner on, to the right of a massive walnut desk. A portrait of George Marshall hung over a bank of monitors. They were all turned off. The autumn-scarlet forest lining the Potomac was visible through the windows. Beyond it rose the impossibly slim, shining spire of the Washington Monument.

Behind that polished desk sat a shrunken, trembling man in a wheelchair. Leif Strohm half rose as she was shown in, then slowly sank back, gripping the armrests with gnarled fingers.

As she approached, she tried to hide her shock. His cheeks were sunken into shadowed hollows. His bare scalp was visible through straggling wisps of white hair, much sparser than the last time they'd met. Rumors had it the SecDef had only a few weeks left, but he looked ready to die at any moment.

He weakly waved her to a chair. "Blair," he muttered, frowning, as if he was trying to recall something difficult. Then he brightened. "Just a heads-up. We're planning a little ceremony for you later this week. Well deserved, I might add. Can your husband be there? Your daughter?"

Okay, so this might not be as easy as she'd expected. "Sir, I appreciate the thought. Very much. But that may not come off when you hear what I have to say."

"Oh? How so?" He sat back, tented tremoring hands, and waited as she gathered herself.

She drew the envelope from her jacket and slid it across the expanse of polished wood. "Sir, I've come to submit my resignation."

"Resignation?" He frowned, looking uncertain, even frightened, as if he didn't know the word. "I'm . . . not sure I understand. I was counting on you to stay on. To help us march forward as one. I thought you'd . . ."

"Several people have mentioned that to me, sir. A single, united party, dedicated to the regeneration of the country. They made a convincing case. But I think it's . . . well, time for me to move on. There's such a thing as outliving one's usefulness, and with the signing of the peace treaty—"

Strohm waved blue-veined, age-spotted hands as if shooing off bothersome gnats. "We still need smart people here to solve problems, Blair. This country's in bad shape. Yes, the war's over, but now DoD has to help out with internal pacification. And the Russians—they're up to something bad. Especially in the Arctic. I guess, since it's melting, warming—"

She frowned. "The Arctic? What's going on up there?"

"We're not sure. No one is. Some kind of deepwater ocean base? Anyway, we still need you. *I* need you. What do I have to offer to get you to reconsider? I had you in mind for the deputy spot someday soon. Until then, we may be able to—"

She smiled patiently as he groped about for whatever prize or price he thought would keep her aboard. A pity, really. The old man was one of the few members of this administration she'd actually respected. To save him time and embarrassment, she inserted gently, "That's very generous of you, sir. But I can't think of anything that would change my mind. So, really, you don't need to try."

He waved his hands again, irritably this time. "No? So regrettable. Sad, really. At least I hope we can count on your continued support for the administration. These will be difficult times . . . many challenges . . . have to stick together . . ."

She debated for a moment how to respond. And finally decided to come as close to the truth as she dared. To be honest with a dying man who'd always treated her decently. "Leif, I haven't really supported a lot of the president's initiatives. Of course, I've tried to run my office to the best of my abilities. For victory. But to be frank, I've never felt like part of the team. Nor have I really tried that hard to be, I guess. To be perfectly fair. But, forward as one? That's just not going to happen with me as part of it."

She left the old fellow slumped over his desk, staring after her with empty eyes. And as she closed the door behind her, feeling—though she really thought she had no reason to—intensely guilty.

HER conversation with the national security advisor, by phone, was considerably briefer and much sharper. Edward Szerenci asked about Dan first, and she reassured him; her husband was in reasonable shape, physically, at least. But then she told him about her decision to leave.

His tone turned angry. *"You already submitted your letter? No. No! I'm shocked, Blair. I insisted on bringing you in, against advice. Kept you on, when Swethi wanted you fired. Now you want to jump ship, just when we've come through the fire? I'm disappointed, Blair. Very. I hope it wasn't something between us that made you decide this."*

She held the phone away from her ear and took a calming breath.

It was true, or at least partly so. Szerenci had put her on important committees. The Hostilities Termination Working Group.
The DoD/State Joint Working Group, which she'd chaired. He'd
visited her at the hospital after her plane had crashed. Once,
very early in the war, she'd accused him of being partially responsible for its outbreak. But knowing him better, she'd realized she
was wrong, that he was less the warmonger—though certainly he
sounded like one now and then—than someone trying to be as
objective as a human being could be, when millions of lives hung
in the balance.

She'd thought about it a lot over the years. And come to a con-
clusion. No one person had brought that war on. Not even Zhang
Zurong, though he bore the largest tranche of responsibility. It had
been inevitable, a clash of a rising power with a status quo one, of
West with East, of authoritarianism with democracy. Unavoidable,
probably, as an earthquake, when tectonic plates ground together.

And as messy and violent as things were now, she didn't even
want to imagine what a world with Zhang and his fellow authori-
tarians triumphant would have been like.

She murmured, "That's all true, Ed. No, it was nothing you said
or did. And for what it's worth, I'm grateful."

A cynical chuckle. *"Gratitude? Doesn't exist inside the Beltway. You have no idea how many times I've stood up for you."*

That was a bit much. "Maybe not. But I never had the feeling we
were exactly on the same side. Rather, that you kept me around as
some combination of devil's advocate and punching bag."

His voice turned earnest, or at least as earnest as the "Prince
of Darkness" ever got. *"Not true, Blair. Not true at all. Rid yourself of that illusion! Your ideas were on point. Your objections
were always based on the facts. But some were, frankly, non-
starters with NCA."* She heard a distracted breath; a muttered
aside to someone else, off-phone. *"Anyway, I hope you'll keep
our little disagreements private. Or at least hold them for your
memoirs."*

She didn't answer, and after a pause he went on. *"So where're you headed? Industry? Consulting? You were with CSIS before, right?"*

Time for a half-truth, a false trail. "Leidos. They held a vice presidency open for me."

"Uh-huh. Well, stay in touch. Maybe we can work together in the future."

And that too was vintage Szerenci. In the sealed world of DC, what went around always came around, and today's enemy could be tomorrow's ally.

Still, the sharp click and dull hum as he hung up signaled the end of a chapter in her life.

SHE stopped by the human resources directorate that afternoon to file her official notice—the letter handed to Strohm had been largely ceremonial. Then called the library and history division about her papers. Since they covered a wartime period, they'd be of historical interest. She disposed of several other items of business, made good-bye calls to colleagues she respected and those she owed favors to, and emailed the heads of committees she sat on, notifying them of her resignation. Then she called in her deputy. Sat him down, gave him the news, and reassured him that he could manage as the acting undersecretary until the West Wing could appoint someone new.

By four she was exhausted again. The brief spurt of energy that had flared around noon was gone, and the fatigue of anxious years gnawed at her very bones. Time to go home to the boys, Dan and Jimbo Cat. Kick her shoes off, mix a shandy, put her feet up, and relax. Maybe a shower, then see how Dan felt. But she felt so wrung out; maybe it wouldn't be the best idea to encourage him.

The blast of humidity as she descended the steps of the entrance staggered her. Wasn't this supposed to be fall? Yet waves of heat rose from the granite, from the asphalt, eddied over the starkly angled 9/11 commemorative benches and drought-stricken plantings near where Flight 77 had hit. As she did each time she passed, she tapped out a mental salute in that direction. She herself had nearly died that same day, though in New York. And had nearly been killed again, in this war, Los Alamos.

Maybe she'd been spared for a reason. Or maybe that was just how everyone felt after a near miss. Still, she thought she had more to give the country.

But not as part of this administration. Not anymore.

Her driver was waiting, with the black SUV. She settled into the back, then leaned forward and tapped his shoulder. "John, just to let you know, I submitted my resignation today. It's supposed to be two weeks' notice, but I probably won't be coming back in tomorrow. You'll get reassigned shortly. It's been great having you drive me. I'll leave a glowing evaluation, believe me."

She was rewarded with a back-turned face, a wide grin. "Been great driving you, too, Miz Titus. We'll all be real sorry not to see you around the Palace."

"Thanks." She smiled and pulled up the number on her phone. Feeling a sense of completion, and of new beginnings. A sense of a new leaf being turned over.

"This is Blair Titus," she said. And after a moment, "Yes . . . yes. I just called to say, please thank him for the offer. I've just resigned. I'm free now. And I will be very happy to accept."

20

Xinjiang, Western China

THE pony was so shaggy the Lingxiu figured he didn't need to grab the saddle horn to hoist himself. Instead he grabbed the mane, and nodded to Jusuf.

When the big muj boosted him powerfully with linked hands, he closed his eyes, nearly crying out as an agonizing spear ripped up his crippled leg. The foot was warping to the side, pulled by some contracting ligament, and the muscles cramped in agony as they twisted tighter and tighter. The empty socket of his vanished eye throbbed too. He lived with pain every hour of the day. The poppy-seed tea Dandan brewed for him helped, though it tasted like bitter mud, but it made you sleepy, languid, and he had to stay focused. Stay on task. Get things organized.

Especially today.

He kicked the pony in the flank and it flinched and started down the ravine. The cave was safer than outdoors under the open sky, but you couldn't run a rebellion from a cave. Much less a full-on jihad.

Which this was now, since he'd given the Agency its walking papers.

The pony jogged out from the shadow and the cool of the mountain into a ponderous dry heat. Tokarev walked behind him, carrying an AK at port arms. The Uighur co-leader had taken Teddy's

decision with his usual stony expression. Saying only, "I pray that
we have taken the right path, Lingxiu. We could lose many men
attempting this."

"If Allah is with us, who can stand against us?" Teddy had
asked. Rhetorically, sure, but he believed it too. Anyway, they'd
come too far to stop now. To stand down, and let the Han keep
ruling the proud, self-reliant people he'd come to think of as his
own.

They deserved better. They deserved no less than independence.

Today, maybe, he might be able to win it for them.

NINE hundred miles to the west, Andres Korzenowski's boots
sank deep into soft gray sand as he stepped out of the helicopter. The blades rotating above him blew grit and dust away in dun
cyclones, obscuring the view. Which in any case was only of drab
yellow sand and even drabber clay hardpan, dotted here and there
with dead-looking scrub brush and the occasional rambling tumbleweed.

Turkmenistan. The installation was windswept and sere, surrounded by miles of dry, generally flat desert. Razor wire and a
bulldozed berm enclosed everything, with towers at the corners
mounting perimeter search radars. A long-range hypersonic battery was dug in on one side. A squat farm of yellow-green conex
containers, glinting black solar panels, and barracks tents
walled the other.

He could have observed today's action from a computer screen
in Germany. But he'd wanted to be as close as possible. Not actually on the scene, though. The deputy director had turned down
his request for a last talk with the asset. A last approach, a final
attempt to reason with him.

"Sounds like you've said everything you could, trying to wrap
this up more gracefully," Tony Provanzano had said, patting
Andres's shoulder avuncularly. "Some boar hogs we just can't

perfume, no matter how hard we try. You gave SKFROG every chance. And you definitely are not going back in country. You're burned too on this, so we're gonna have to find something else for you to do. Maybe Latin America, we can use some fresh ideas there. Okay?"

So he hadn't gone back in. Just come as close as he could.

Which was here, in this windswept desert, with the occasional tumbleweed bouncing across it on a mindless pilgrimage, pursued by the sigh of the wind, the harsh hiss of sand abrading everything that had form. Eroding it all, like Time itself.

He wished he'd asked the guy more about his vision. Made him explain. Describe it. Oberg had sounded so certain. He probably *was* mad, like Langley seemed to think. Unsound. But maybe he'd just seen deeper, glimpsed something only saints and mystics usually had access to.

He shook his head. No. Like the old Gary Larson *Far Side* psychiatrist-office cartoon, the SEAL chief was Just Plain Nuts. That was the simplest explanation. And likeliest to be true.

The conex was so crammed with equipment he had to slide sideways to get in. He shook hands with three unsmiling women in Army desert-pattern battle dress. One white, one black, and one Asian. The OIC introduced herself as Major Zein. She was the Asian-looking one, or maybe Filipina, with deeply lined features, short black hair, and a fierce squint. As if she were frowning into the sandstorm building outside.

The wind gusted, shaking the thin steel walls. A pair of scissors hung from a string, clacking against an equipment rack as the container vibrated. The women didn't react. Zein led him toward the consoles that lined the back wall. It was a little roomier back here, at least for three. With him added, though, it was tight.

"What are we looking at?" he asked.

Zein planted herself in front of the screen, and he leaned over her shoulder. Below, slowly, unscrolled a tormented land. Deep valleys furrowed it. Pits swallowed shadow. Here and there patches of snow glowed on corrugated mountains. A glacier twisted down, a moraine of rubble at its head showing where it had retreated over the past few years. She said, "This is from the MQ-3E Black Eagle high-altitude, long-endurance unmanned aircraft system. More capable than the old Predator. Sharper sensors. Solar powered, for longer range and indefinite linger. Your tasking pulled us off a mission for the Army. We were watching nuclear weapons sites in northern Iran."

Andres nodded, fighting a twist of nausea. Zein pointed to a copilot's chair set just behind hers. The two sergeants were in the other seats, to her right and left. "Understand you're here to identify our target. Any questions?"

"Uh, yeah. We know this group has Swiss-sourced drone detection. How are we going to get past that?"

"It won't pick us up." She swept a hand over a bank of readouts, and Andres recognized a spectrum analyzer. "We're IR masked, quiet electric motors, and we don't use GPS or radar. Inertial navigation, backed up by lookdown terrain analysis."

"But it's transmitting video. They won't pick that up?"

"No. It's a scrambled uplink, microburst, direct to nanosatellites overhead. We also use delta frame video. All that gets transmitted is the changes from the previous image, which cuts maybe ninety-five percent of the bandwidth you'd need for raw video. You could monitor from fifty feet below it and you still wouldn't pick up a thing."

She reflected for a moment, then added, "There's a *very* slight chance they could detect our radio commands, which go down via the same sat channel. But they'd have to have some pretty sophisticated analysts to figure out what that signal was."

He nodded, and Zein settled headphones over her ears and handed him a pair. "You'll hear the video going out, and a series of tone clues that keep us informed as to motor cooling, battery status and drawdown rate, and so on. When it's time to deploy weapons, you'll hear tones from that too as the missile initializes. Then a separate tracking tone, which tells us it's live. When that cuts off, the mission's complete."

He fitted the headphones, which were still warm from whoever had just taken them off. The scrambled video, or at least he guessed that was what it was, sounded like a high-pitched warble.

"This is a personality strike, correct?" Zein said. "Against a person specifically designated on the kill list? I have to have that on the record." She held out a clipboard and pen.

"He's not in the disposition matrix," Andres said. "This is special handling, as per a finding of imminent threat. No permanent record, and all video to be erased." He extracted a folded paper from inside his jacket and handed it over.

She glanced over the order, then handed it back. As if she didn't want to keep her fingers on it any longer than necessary. "Not a problem. We'll just carry it as a recon, and the weapon as expended for practice. But I'll still need a signature. If the time comes. That's just how the Army does things, sir."

Andres nodded. "Okay. Sure." He wasn't going to sign anything, of course. But he could tell her that later, after it was done.

FOUR hours later, after Guldulla had split off to lead the assault force, the Lingxiu slid down off the pony. Sweating in the oppressive, growing heat, aching in every bone, he pulled his drag pack off its rump. He patted the animal and threw the reins to one of the boys who trailed after the rebels, sometimes picking up fallen weapons to fight alongside them. Staying low, in a combat crouch, he limped uphill.

Just before the crest, he dropped to his belly and low-crawled forward, binoculars clutched to his chest, drag-bag strap in his other hand. The way he'd once carried a sniper rifle, in Ashaara, years before. On a mission to kill a man who'd thought he was directed by God . . . and now, ha ha, you had to grin at the irony . . . Jusuf crawled close behind, carrying the antidrone gear, a rifle, and a pack with water and food and grenades.

Concealed between two large flattish stones, Oberg looked down from the crest at a magnificent panorama. The valley ran southeast down from the mountains. A river glittered like wind-blown tinsel where rapids shattered it into bright shining scraps of silver. A road ran alongside it, though no vehicles moved there. No, not with the many IEDs his rebels had sown the length and breadth of this land . . . Far ahead the terrain flattened, inter-rupted only by low hills. To this side of them, barely visible from up here, a strangely regular reticulation of gray interlaced a flat-tening green.

His fists tightened on the binoculars. That green was soyabean paddies. The gray, the insectile hives of the Han. Their interlock-ing concrete compounds marched across the land like a great wall dividing the Uighur from the interlopers. A thinner line ran from east to west: a highway. And beyond the low hills rose the polluted haze of a city, set down on the land like the nest of an invasive species.

Like creeping bamboo, the Han would spread and spread, unless they were burned out, their roots torn up, the soil seeded with salt. Until it was made plain they were no longer welcome in this land they falsely claimed as theirs.

Jusuf flourished a radio. "Convoy on its way, Lingxiu."

"*Bu yakshi*. Give me a heads-up when it passes Kilometer 304."

They settled in for a stay. Jusuf pulled a flask of mare's milk and a wad of dates and bread out of the pack. Teddy shared it with the big muj, chewing thoughtfully, staring up at the passing clouds. Re-membering other hides, other stalkings. He'd always sought some-thing, without ever knowing what it was. Once he'd thought he'd found it in the Teams. Then, trying to put a film together in LA.

Now, for the first time, he truly knew peace.

Peace was when the outcome was out of your hands. When you didn't have to make choices, or worry if you made the right choice.

When really no "choosing" existed. Since everything had al-ready been decided. From time immemorial. For the best, and all he had to do was . . . go with the flow. Let it happen. Trust Allah.

You have always done My will.

He said a brief dua that the old imam had taught him. "Lord, all praise be to You, to Your might and your greatness, amin."

You didn't need to do much, to resign yourself. Simply accept. Submit. That was all.

The sun glittered on the rapids far below, and a bird twittered below them somewhere on the hill. The world was filled with stunning beauty. The mountains behind him, incredibly sere and distant in their granite sky-reaching. The plains below, warm and rich and fecund where they drank of the pure melted waters from the high snows.

Uighurs had lived here for a thousand years. Then the Han had come. Not content to live alongside the original inhabitants, they'd clamped down a heavy yoke. Closed mosques, shuttered madrassas, prohibited firearms and beards and knives and traditional dress. And when their subjects still persevered in the old ways, herded them into concentration camps for "reeducation." Monitored them with facial recognition. Rated their "social scores" online, to reward those who conformed, and punish those who persisted in being what they'd always been. What they and their ancestors had been born to be. *Free.*

Killing a few hundred people . . . it was little enough. He had to smile, thinking of the objections the CIA agent had raised.

Jusuf rolled over to place his bearded lips next to Teddy's ear. He murmured, in Uighur, "Tokarev is with the leader."

Teddy nodded. "Pass a standby while we wait."

Settling into the glasses again, he panned left, and saw them. But only the turrets. They were parked hull down behind a rise, but angled so they could charge down a dry streambed paved with the sparkling, rounded pebbles the meltwater had tumbled down from the mountains for age after age, polishing agate and jasper into ruby and emerald.

The gray-green hulls were light mountain tanks. The Chinese had made the mistake of training their Uighur auxiliaries on them. The whole squadron had deserted one night, coming over to ITIM.

Not the first native troops to do so, but the first to bring armor with them.

Modern machines that today he would employ for the first time. To strike a blow that would resound all the way to Beijing.

Today they were going to take down the bloody marshal.

Chagatai had been a thorn in their side since he'd arrived in the West, fresh from the massacres in Hong Kong. He'd depopulated whole regions, cramming the Uighurs behind barbed wire, then starving them. The reports from the camps were dire. Famine. Disease. Neglect.

Okay, that was how it went down in war. But you couldn't fight a guy like that with one hand tied behind your back, the way the Agency seemed to want. Or said that it wanted, though he figured they were really just preserving deniability.

Teddy had tried to kill Chagatai once before. Sucked him in with a fake IED factory, rigging it with hundreds of kilos of C-4, ready to blow a cave roof down on him. Instead his opponent had preempted with a lightning-fast spoiling attack, complete with poison gas, killing scores of rebels and hundreds of innocent townspeople.

But this time they had a source on the inside. Their informant, a junior member of Chagatai's staff, had passed their target's route and time mouth to mouth via a cutout in the bazaar.

Teddy checked his watch again. In twenty more minutes, checkpoint at Kilometer 304. The highway below, empty in both directions at the moment. The tanks would attack downhill, so any errant rounds or misses would go over the highway and into the Han compounds beyond. Which didn't bother him at all. Actually, casualties there would be a plus.

Jusuf muttered, "Kilometer 230."

Teddy did the multiplication. At forty miles an hour, the convoy would hit the checkpoint in a little over half an hour. He fidgeted, raking the valley again with the binoculars, then cleared his throat and spat. What was he doing way up here? He should be down, by the road. His hands tingled. He felt suddenly too warm, and it wasn't just the hot wind off the desert, a few miles distant.

He should stay where he was. Manage the battle.

With difficulty, he accepted that truth. But he didn't like it.

Jusuf touched his arm. "Lingxiu? Kilometer 235."

THE too-soft seat had molded itself to Andres's rump. It was almost like a La-Z-Boy. Obviously built for prolonged sessions in front of the screens. Beside him in the trailer, Major Zein seemed lost in another world. She palmed a trackball slowly, as if it were a shiatsu massager. The scene on the screen moved with the ball after about two seconds' delay.

The camera panned across a terrain familiar to him from trekking across it for months. Deeply folded, shadowed valleys. Glacial moraines. The twisting, sinuous braiding of vanished rivers, lost and sunk in desert, leaving only their outlines. Rock in a million hues of brown and gray shading to black. Serpentine streams, twisting their way down rugged valleys. And now and then, a jewellike deep blue lake, blocked by the ruler-line of a dam of earth or concrete or stone.

Finally Zein murmured, "Coming up on your coordinates. We'll drop altitude and start a close search."

The lens zoomed back, showing the rectangular gridwork of a city at one corner. The city canted and drifted left. Hills appeared, and what looked like suburbs. More rounded hills, then a highway. Then a green scablike crust on the earth, like a malignant growth, subdivided by more gridwork.

"Soybean fields," Zein murmured. She turned her head and flipped pages in a red-bound binder, then went back to observing.

Andres was finding it a little hard to breathe. He got up and let himself out of the trailer. The wind was still blowing. He looked around the compound, and saw nothing he needed. He checked for cameras, then realized: with the blowing dust, no lens would last long out here.

He unzipped and pissed in the lee of the trailer, facing away from the wind. Fighting a looseness in his bowels. The feeling that he really shouldn't be part of this.

But he was. He had his orders.

When he let himself back in and pulled the dust curtain closed behind him, Zein was discussing a terrain feature with one of the enlisted women. Cross-referencing it with a geo overlay that the computer superimposed over the video feed in a ghostly pentimento, like a shadow beneath reality. As she trackballed back and forth in minute increments the underprinting shifted, following the camera. A readout in the upper corner of the screen scrolled upward, registering the percentage of match.

"Ninety-eight percent." Zein half turned her head, probably to make sure he was back. "That's about as high as this system registers. We're in your target area."

"Oh. Can you see him?" Andres asked her.

Her right shoulder jerked, a tic or mannerism he hadn't noted before. She said, "Commencing close search. This could take a little while. Any pointers?"

"He likes a high overwatch position when he can get it." Andres looked around the interior of the van. There, a case of bottled water. He pointed. "You mind—?"

The major kept her eyes on the screen. "Help yourself."

No one said anything for a while. All three screens were lit now, with a sergeant at each of the others. Zein, in the center, trackballed from crest to crest, zooming in to examine each elevation while the enlisted flanking her studied theirs, tilting their heads and frowning. A small white square skittered here and there across the screen, nervous, flitting, dwelling only for an instant before skipping elsewhere. Nothing they did on their panels seemed to be driving the white square. Some kind of AI routine, trying to pick up whatever it had been programmed to detect.

Even as he noticed it, it hesitated, as if considering. Then darted to the side and halted, hovering over an otherwise indistinguishable dot on a sharp ridgeline.

One of the sergeants said, "Looks like a leadership element. Elevation to the north, above Road G3013."

"Let the agent see," Zein ordered.

The sergeant got up and swiveled the chair so Andres could sit in front of her screen. Its slick faux leather upholstery was warm. He cleared his throat and hitched forward, studying the display.

The view zoomed down, down, until he was looking at several figures prone amid a wilderness of slanted flattish rocks. The rocks were gray. The figures, which seemed to be wearing shaggy gray coats, blended so perfectly he had to look very closely to make them out.

"Could any of those be him?" Zein asked him.

Andres studied the image, noting details. Four—no, five, six figures. Maybe more to the rear. Packs, to the side. Definitely some kind of long thin weapon-shapes. Horses, held farther back, downhill, their backs slightly curved from above, like humped brown slugs. "Can't tell," he finally muttered. "Could we zoom in closer?"

"Sure, but we'll lose resolution." Zein demonstrated with a slow roll of the trackball. The images grew larger but blurrier, until they were just random pixelations of gray and yellow and black.

He nodded. Said, "Okay, I get it," and she pulled the camera back out. Until they seemed to hover just about where she'd originally placed them. He gnawed his lip, studying the figures again. "Could be anyone," he concluded. "How far up are we?"

"Angels five," Zein said. "Five thousand feet. Any lower and they'll hear us."

"Hey, look at this," said the other sergeant, the blonde. Zein nodded and the view lifted, panned, steadied again.

Four squarish dull green shapes were spaced out in a line at the bottom of the valley.

"Armor," the sergeant said. "Consistent with ZTQ light tank. 105-millimeter gun with laser-guided antitank missiles, kinetic penetrators, HEAT. Autoloading, IR fire-control system, crew of five."

"Chinese?" Andres said. Then thought, Damn, that was a stupid question.

"Yes, sir. Chinese," one of the sergeants said.

"What're they doing there?"

"Not sure. No movement since I picked them up, but IR shows engine heat."

Zein pulled her own screen back and panned up and down the highway, which was empty except for one truck far to the west. She panned back.

"Change," the dark-skinned sergeant to the right said.

Zein toggled to the other feed, apparently from another camera on the same drone. A cloud of exhaust, or maybe dust, was spewing out behind the armor, spreading slowly and silently across the sand. Expanding, like ink from a disturbed octopus on the ocean floor.

"Engine temp rising . . . they're on the move," the sergeant said.

On the screens, the green rectangles began rolling forward. Toward, Andres saw, an exit from the shallow depression they were hidden in. Headed down, toward the river. And the highway.

The sergeant on the left whispered something. "A-*ha*," said Zein triumphantly. She toggled back to the highway.

Seven vehicles were making what looked like good speed down the center of the previously empty four-laner. Headed east to west. Coming down the road.

Right toward where the gray-green tanks were rumbling down out of the hills.

THE man who'd once been Master Chief Teddy Oberg sat up awkwardly, shoving a leg out in front of him, tucking the other under one buttock. He held the binoculars with the tips of his fingers, peering up the valley, then down. Beside him Jusuf was intent on the radio, head cocked, listening. Finally the big muj muttered, "From Guldulla, sir. They are in sight."

"Okay, great. Get that armor moving out. And torch the car."

"It is moving, Lingxiu. Tokarev gave the order."

"*Avtomobil yonib ketganligiga ishonch hosil qiling.* Make sure they're burning the car," Teddy said again, but he felt fidgety. His hands and arms tingled. He kept wanting to spit. Wanted some more of that poppy tea. Where the fuck was Dandan? He glanced at the carbine beside him, leaned against one of the flat rocks. Shit, what was he doing up here? Then he reminded himself. Above the battle. Stay in command. Manage, don't lead.

He blew out and waggled his head. "Shit, shit, shit," he muttered.

"Are you all right, Lingxiu?" Dandan, sinking to her knees beside him. The stocky Han girl unwrapped a clay pot. "This very hot. You need to drink. Need to eat something."

He drank off the tea without looking at her, absentmindedly feeling up her butt as she stood beside him. He bolted a hard candy from his pocket, and shifted again where he sat. Finally he held up both arms. Jusuf grabbed one, Dandan the other. They hoisted him to his feet and he hobbled back toward his pony.

Jusuf followed. "Lingxiu, where are you going?"

"We're not close enough," he said in what he hoped was passable Uighur. But sometimes he'd use words he was pretty sure were right, and they just stared at him, or worse, tried to hide a smile at something stupid he'd apparently said instead. Which was why he issued orders via Jusuf when he could. "I can't see shit from up here. We need to shift our overwatch."

"The closer we get, the harder it will be to avoid the counterstroke. When their QRF arrives."

"Gotta take chances in war, amigo." Teddy grabbed the pommel and hauled on it. A sizzling hot flash of pain jolted all the way up his leg and into his spine as they rushed over to boost him, and he gasped. "Fuck. *Fuck!*"

"You are all right, Lingxiu?"

"God is great. God is great," he hissed through gritted teeth. "Let's take the battle to the enemy."

He hauled awkwardly on the reins and the pony tossed its head, wheeling reluctantly, as if affronted at his lack of riding skills. Teddy didn't like being this high off the ground, not with all these rocks, and a bum leg, and he'd never been much of a horseman. But the animal was surefooted, and when he kicked it into a downhill trot the pony picked its way without further direction.

As always before an action, he'd memorized the topography, picked routes of retreat, and set fallback points. As he climbed again on the far side, a plume of ocher dust smeared the sky ahead, where the river cut through a mountain ridge. The highway lay on the far side of that ridge. It would probably be visible now if he used the binoculars.

Yeah, he'd set up way too far back. Getting cautious in your old age, Teddy? He grinned fiercely. A mistake that could be remedied. He spurred down the slope, the pony's hooves slipping and clicking on the loose moraine, then up the next. From behind him came curses and a rattle of loose pebbles as someone went down, then the scream of a frightened or injured horse. Teddy didn't look back. He rose in the stirrups and slapped his mount's neck with the reins, urging it forward.

When they descended the last slope their armor was wheeling into position along the highway, spewing plumes of sooty high-sulfur diesel exhaust and yellow dust. Four huge machines, not quite as large as main battle tanks, but thirty tons each of steel and ordnance. Their drivers still seemed tentative, uncertain, gunning and braking to straighten the line.

Out of nowhere he remembered facing a Soviet-era BMP years before. In Afghanistan? Funny, he recalled it clearly, but not where it had taken place. The amphibious tank had suddenly burst out of a walled compound, and he'd had nothing in his hands but an RPG that wouldn't penetrate its frontal armor. Only the fact the driver had been terrible at his job had saved Teddy's ass then.

"Training, that's what wins battles!" he yelled over his shoulder to Jusuf, who was just pulling up next to him, his pony huffing, white foam dripping from its mouth.

"Truly yes, Lingxiu," he panted out, wiping his face with the colorful tie-dyed scarf most of the rebels wore, pulling them up over their faces shemagh-style when the dust blew.

Teddy half rose in the stirrups again, blinking at the blinding pain in his leg, to focus his binoculars. Then lowered them. They were close enough now he didn't need them.

Close enough to see his prey.

They were distant specks on the far highway. Descending a hill, so he could count their numbers and see what he was getting his people into. A dull green truckish thing he made as a Dongfeng, a light recon vehicle. The Chinese version of an uparmored Hummer. Maybe a second one behind it. They usually carried either machine guns or an automatic grenade launcher in a turret mount. Mine resistant, with enough armor to withstand bullets.

But not tank shells.

Behind them trailed four black SUVs, followed by another recon vehicle.

He lowered the binoculars, then lifted them again, one eyepiece to his live sight, the other to his patch, clicking to a lower power, searching the sky. For an instant he thought he glimpsed something; a tiny glint high up, very high up, very very small. But even when he switched the glasses to high magnification he couldn't find the gleam again. It couldn't be a drone; his sensor operators, spotted two miles in every direction and linked to Jusuf's radio, would have warned him.

Probably he'd imagined it, or it was merely a speck in his eye. So, no air cover? No helicopters? He grinned again. The marshal didn't expect to be bushwhacked.

Then he sobered. Either that, or Dewei Chagatai wasn't in the convoy. Far more cunning than the enemy's generals, maybe he'd learned about the ambush somehow, like last time, and prepared a devastating counterstrike.

Teddy worried about that for about a second, then shoved the doubt aside. They wouldn't know until it was too late to pull out anyway. So he'd just better be alert. Until then, he'd proceed as planned.

And anyway, whatever happened was in the hands of Allah. "Tell Guldulla: get his people out there, cut the road behind them," he told Jusuf.

His assistant murmured into the radio. Teddy hesitated again, uncertain once more as to his own role in the action. Obviously at this point he belonged up here, out of the scrum, where he could better maneuver his limited forces. Maintain situational awareness. See any threat early.

Yeah. That would be the wisest course of action. No question.

Instead, he kicked his horse in the ribs and rode forward again.

THE storm whispered and howled outside. The trailer's metal walls vibrated to the gusts. The walls thrummed and hissed, abraded by sand.

Andres took a sip from the plastic water bottle and leaned forward. The sergeant kept moving the screen, following the white square to reveal the terrain around it. From time to time she toggled to 3-D, overlaid by topo, so he could see the lay of the land. The armor had moved out of the arroyo and formed up in a rough line facing the highway.

He felt oddly remote from it all. An onlooker. Almost, a voyeur. Even though he knew many of the people who moved busily about far below. A thousand miles away, but he was looking down on them, as if he were an eagle soaring high above.

"Convoy," Zein said suddenly. "Look at that. Two light armor lead, four passenger vehicles, light armor in trail."

"HVT convoy," the sergeant said. "High-value target."

"Looks like it," the major agreed. "But who?" She spun on her chair and consulted another computer. "Intel has . . . nothing. No movement scheduled. At least that we know of."

"Chinese?"

"ITIM doesn't run convoys. They're still pretty much mountain infantry, donkey logistics, a few horses for the leadership elements."

They watched the convoy proceed steadily along the highway, smoothly as blood corpuscles flowing along an artery.

Until the other sergeant cleared her throat. "Uh, I'm picking up other activity. Two klicks to the east."

Zein put it up on the central screen. Perhaps two dozen small figures were scrambling down out of the rocky overlook above the highway. Several carried what looked like heavier weapons, though the resolution wasn't sharp enough to identify them.

"Cutting off the convoy's retreat," Andres said.

"Yeah. Nice."

The sergeant said, "Look at that. They're laying IEDs out in plain sight."

"Because the real ones are already dug in," Andres said. "If they're doing this right, they planted the live ones last night, or the night before. Those are dummies. Decoys, to channel any survivors into the kill zone."

They all three looked to him. "We could throw a wrench into the works," Zein said tentatively. "We don't have a lot of ordnance on station, but we could give that convoy a warning. Take out some of the hostiles."

Andres shook his head. "Those 'hostiles' fought the war on our side."

"ITIM? I heard they were, but . . . the armistice?"

"It's complicated," he said, and sighed. Chugged the rest of the bottle of water and set the empty aside.

The major opened her mouth as if to ask something more, then didn't, turning back to the screen instead. Obviously figuring this was Agency business and not hers.

Which was exactly right . . . He passed a hand over his hair, feeling sweat prickling his scalp, even though the air-conditioning was on full blast, the hum and whoosh fighting the sibilant sizzle of the storm outside. Yeah, sure, they could warn the convoy. Maybe save whoever was in it.

But that wasn't his mission today.

THE convoy didn't seem to be slowing, though they must have seen the smoke. A small party of mujs had set a car on fire by the side of the road. Black smoke billowed from the now fiercely burning sedan, which had been crammed with old tires. The black column braided with the white smoke from a few antitargeting grenades, rising and spreading to blanket the valley and obscure all vision. So that even with IR sights, the oncoming vehicles couldn't pick up the waiting armor.

Until it was too late.

The tanks were almost in position. Still sitting his pony, Teddy pulled his gaze from the complexly billowing smoke. He hefted the radio, which he'd taken from Jusuf. He had to get this done. But he couldn't rush it, or they'd lose everything.

If they missed this guy now, after the armistice, Chagatai would roar back with enough fresh divisions to rake these mountains with a deadly comb equipped with tungsten teeth. He'd stamp a bar code on every rock and send a teleoperated battlesnake into every hole big enough to shade a fox.

But if they could put the marshal down now, ITIM might even get a seat at the peace table.

The convoy neared. He hadn't expected it to slow for the wreck, and it didn't. Just steered over to the outside lane, and maybe speeded up a little. It came on. Closer. Closer . . .

He drew a slow deep breath and squinted up, casing the sky once more just to be sure. Still nothing but blue, and puffy white clouds, and the streamers of smoke between him and the high mountains glittering in the sun. Strange. Maybe, now that the big war was over, the Allies had imposed something like a no-fly order.

He spread his arms, overwhelmed suddenly with the beauty of

it all. The valley, the mingling smoke. The gleaming ribbon of high-way. The lush green fields beyond.

And suddenly he grasped once more, for a moment, what he'd witnessed high on a mountain that freezing night years before. Wrapped in his tatty POW blanket beside a dying fire, afraid, starving, huddled under the stars.

The very rocks had glowed from within, their component atoms milling and scintillating like clouds of fireflies.

And now, the bearded muj beside him, the stocky, faithful Dandan a few yards back—he could see into their minds. Into their souls.

Human beings were just as dazzling as the rocks and sky.

All was created, all one. All was understood, with enormous compassion.

You have always done My will.

It hadn't been an order, the command of some implacable tyrant.

The words had been said as gently as a lover's. As a parent's. As the words of the One who knew all, yet forgave all, with compassion and mercy toward all the creatures He had ordained to be, and suffer, yet be welcomed home at last.

"I do Your will again today," he said to the unknowable unimaginable he had glimpsed that night and always regretted losing. The Whole he was a tiny fragment of. One tiny colored tile, one chipped and faded cube that was still an irreplaceable part of an immense and incredibly beautiful, perfectly designed, everlasting mosaic.

"Lingxiu," Jusuf said urgently, tugging at his sleeve.

Teddy forced himself back from the beauty and the wonder to lift his binoculars again. To see that, yes, the lead vehicles were coming into range. Yet still he forced himself to say, as calmly as he could, "Wait." Counting the seconds off each by each to the hammering of his unruly heart.

Three.

Two.

One.

He lifted his radio. "This is the Lingxiu. Okay, boys, light 'em up." Then he waited. And waited . . .

"Crap," he grunted. "How the fuck long are they going to—"

The barrel of the lead tank recoiled in a flash of flame and smoke, and it rocked back on its tracks. The penetrator round lashed out arcless, flat, an instantaneous line drawn across grit and sand and scrub, ruler-straight. Dust sprang up along its track until it barreled directly over the lead vehicle, missing it by a good five yards.

Teddy opened his mouth to shout a correction but the second tank fired at that instant and the second round unzipped the desert too, the dust-trail and smoke obscuring what, if anything, had happened when it hit. No, it was a miss too; the impact burst the ground apart far downhill, half a kilometer off the highway on the other side.

"Fuck me," he groaned. Were the wheels going to come off his whole plan just because his deserters couldn't shoot straight?

Then the third and fourth tanks fired, nearly simultaneously. Those projectiles arrowed across the gravel and sand too blindingly fast to follow and both slammed directly into the trailing Donfeng, blowing it apart so violently the vehicle lifted off its wheels, spun in the air, and crashed down inverted on the far berm, where it instantly burst into flame. He couldn't make out what happened after that, the smoke was too thick, but it would be a miracle if anyone crawled out of that inferno.

The right-flank tanks fired again, bucking back as the hyper-velocity projectiles tore out, but he couldn't see. He couldn't *see*. "They've got to get in closer," he shouted, handing back the radio. "Jusuf! Tell them. Get in close, finish them off." He had another IED team up the road, but if the lead recon vehicles and the SUVs got through that way, some might well escape.

And if any got away, you could be A-fucking-sure the marshal would be in the one that made it.

The reprisals would be terrible. Chagatai didn't just shoot

hostages. He gassed whole villages, evacuated and leveled whole towns, imprisoned and starved whole provinces.

Teddy gripped his carbine, wanting to shout orders. To kick everyone into action. No. He wanted to be down there himself, riding those tanks. Pushing them forward, laying the guns, forcing them nose to nose with the enemy, even if they had to run over them and crush them under the tracks.

No, he told himself. This is your post, right here. Where you can see what's going on, as much as anyone can, anyway, in the growing haze, the blowing smoke. Nobody else was going to herd these cats.

He should. Sure. Should stay right here.

But he wasn't going to.

The leader had to lead.

He shrugged his threadbare blanket off his shoulders and pulled his carbine out of the scabbard. Seated the mag, and charged the rifle. Full mag in the well. Six more, fully loaded, in his drag bag. Gas mask to hand, check. Makarov, check. Knife, the heavy Uighur blade he'd taken off Hajji Qurban, secured in its sheath at his belt.

"What is going on? Lingxiu?" Jusuf, looking anxious.

Teddy grinned at him, and heel-kicked his pony down the hill. The big muj whirled for his own mount, looking surprised. Behind them, the others began mounting up too. Lifting rifles. Unfurling flags, the black squares with their white calligraphy rippling in the wind.

A sharp slope ahead. His pony's hooves slipped and skidded on the stones, and it lurched and nearly fell. Teddy grabbed for its mane, tensing for a spill. But it scrambled to recover and then lunged forward, gathering speed, pounding downhill at a breathtaking gallop as the rocks gave way to loose gravel and even here and there a little patch of dusty grass. He heeled it in the ribs again, and it didn't hurt, even his bad leg didn't stab him now. He yelled aloud, a formless incomprehensible howl that halfway through he modfied into *"Allahu Akbar!"* Behind him the other riders picked it up, and shots cracked out, even though he'd told them again and again never to waste ammo firing into the air.

But that was all right, they were his men, eager to follow him into battle. Foam flew back from the pony's mouth and the mane whipped at his hands. Down into a gully, out of sight of the highway. Then up, up again, over a small rise.

And there was the road, close now. There was the smoke, still rising, and the sweet battle stench of propellant and burning rubber, and the heavy ripping crack of 105 penetrators going out far above supersonic and the higher-pitched *bang bang bang* of an automatic grenade launcher firing back at them from somewhere in the milling murk. The burp-rattle of small arms. Explosions flashed amid his tanks. But even direct hits only scored the thick frontal armor, and they were growling forward again, gathering confidence, and for once, for fucking *once*, his guys had it all, surprise and fire advantage and heavier weapons than the enemy.

He plunged ahead into the bitter smoke. It stung his throat, making his eyes tear.

At the last second he veered aside out of the line of fire, and reined the pony in, one hand shading his single eye. The smoke unraveled a little just then, blown thin by a hot wind, letting tallow light bleed through from the glaring sun. Through it he could just make out the lead Dongfeng. It squatted immobile, smoking hard, with fireballs flying out the far side: ammo cooking off. The second leader was still firing at the oncoming armor with the grenade launcher, in the turret.

Then a shell from one of the tanks blew it apart in a huge detonation, white and orange, laced with the crackle of the grenades and whatever other ordnance it carried exploding too. Pieces and bodies pinwheeled through the air to crash and thud and clang off the steel siderails of the highway. When the turbulent boiling of air and fire and smoke rose it revealed a smoking, twisted chassis nearly stripped of armor.

"Hold fire!" Teddy yelled to Jusuf, hand-signaling his heavy units, and nudged the pony forward without waiting for an acknowledgment. Fortunately the tanks obeyed, ceasing their fire as he spurred in, sweeping his narrowed gaze across the black SUVs.

Some were already riddled by the machine-gun fire the tanks had been laying down along with their shells. Trapped, the convoy had herringboned out this way and that on the roadside, the correct tactic for a hasty defense. Black-uniformed Interior troops were spilling out with short-barreled personal defense weapons, propping them on the hoods to put an engine block between them and their attackers.

But Teddy and Jusuf and the other riders were on their flank, and he aimed his carbine and began firing, taking the Chinese in defilade, the little light bullpup jerking back into his shoulder with each shot. Pick up an outline, fire, watch it spin and drop. Shift to the next black uniform, a thicker upper chest area, probably some kind of body armor. A double tap into the legs and he too went down. Teddy grinned harder. Damn, he liked this optic sight.

Return fire hissed and cracked past. The pony shied, but he yanked its head around and pointed it directly at the lead vehicle and thumped its ribs again. The pony whinnied and tossed its head but obeyed, and Teddy fired again and again as they galloped in, laying a burst to finish the mag. He dropped the empty and slapped in a reload without looking, squinting through the roiling oily-tasting black smoke.

And noting, just with a microglimpse, a bulky figure clad in greens roll out of the second car back, tugging a pistol from a leather holster.

No cap, gray hair, stocky, army uniform. A patch of color on the chest. He was wearing his decorations.

Marshal Chagatai.

The troops sheltering behind the vehicles were returning aimed fire now. Gunflashes sparkled. A bullet scored Teddy's shoulder like a hot poker, breaking his aim so his next burst spanged off a bulletproof windshield. Beside him in a rough line Jusuf and the other mujahideen were firing too, some from horseback, others dismounted. One went down as his horse was hit, spilling him onto the asphalt, where he skated along, flailing and cursing, but gripping his Kalashnikov for dear life, until he could struggle up to a knee and fire again.

The seething vapor trail of a projectile from one of the tanks streaked between the second and third SUVs, deafeningly close. The blast of its passage knocked down two of the black-clad troops running forward from the rear vehicles, but it exploded far downhill, in one of the soy fields. Teddy screamed at Jusuf, "Tanks, God damn it, I said cease fire, cease fire!" He hoped they heard that, because in seconds his ragtag cavalry would be in among the SUVs.

As would he. He steered his mount around the first limo, firing more to keep heads down than to score hits. The pony's hooves slipped in the loose gravel of the berm and it almost went down again. He urged it forward, leaning to keep his own silhouette low, snap-firing as targets presented themselves. But they were getting scarcer. The hail of bullets from the rebels, plus the tank shells, had left more and more of the Interior troops lying dead or blown apart beside the vehicles, or dragging themselves crawling away, trailing blood, but still trying to escape the slaughter they knew was coming if they were overrun. Among them now Teddy made out a few civilians. Local pols, or Han intel types? He wasn't going to waste time trying to sort them out. A woman in a dark skirt tried to drag herself under the second SUV, only to be riddled by a burst from Jusuf's AK.

Howling, shooting, the rebels charged in among the vehicles. Teddy was barely keeping up. His pony seemed to be limping. Shot? Lamed? Maybe it was just tired. But the younger men were ahead of him now, firing and yipping, waving their black flags. Jusuf was in the thick of it, firing here and there, yelling as he rode down the line of cars. Teddy grinned just to see him. The kid wasn't just a technician. He was a warrior, all right.

Then a gray-haired head rose above an open door. A pistol re-coiled, and the young muj spun and toppled from his saddle. Jusuf hit the ground so hard his head rebounded. Then he lay still. His hand relaxed, and one of the shiny green Chinese grenades rolled out.

They weren't that big, but they were packed with steel balls, and Teddy was too close to avoid catching shrapnel. He ducked below his mount's back as it went off. A moment's image. Another war, and another grenade . . .

A small green spheroid. It struck the wall beside him and glanced off.

It rolled between him and Sumo Kaulukukui, and rocked to a halt midway between them. The drill was to duck or roll, but there was nowhere to go.

The big Hawaiian had said, "War's a motherfucker, ain't it?" And stepped over it, putting himself between Teddy and the gre-nade's blast.

You'd have enjoyed this fight, Sumo, he thought now. But the battle wasn't over. In fact, at this point, it might be going the wrong way. For now, as the smoke blew past, it revealed the re-maining troops safe behind the no-doubt-armored doors, firing from cover. While his rebels were being blasted off their ponies one after the other. His own began screaming, and staggered be-neath him. Glancing down, he saw the thick black blood stream-ing down its front legs. Steel shards from the grenade, or maybe a Chinese bullet.

He hauled the pony's head around, and it stumbled toward the second SUV. Where a gray-haired head showed above the door, then locked gazes with him across sixty feet of smoky hell.

Teddy aimed and squeezed the trigger, aware only when it clicked that he'd emptied the carbine. He thrust it back into its scabbard, yanked the Makarov from his shoulder holster, and fired. It recoiled, but he could tell as the sights rose that he'd missed. Snap shots usually did, especially from the back of a wounded horse. Not something they drilled at the Kill House at Dam Neck. He pulled the trigger again.

The pistol clicked, but didn't fire. Fuck, the piece of shit was jammed! And since he still held the reins, he didn't have a spare hand to clear it.

He threw it aside, and drew the blade at his belt.

The eight-inch, heavy, curved pchak, the Yengisar with the ram's-horn hilt he'd taken off Hajji Qurban after killing him in a knife fight, and carried ever since.

He urged the failing animal under him directly at the pistol Chagatai was leveling at him over the armored door of the SUV. Bending low over the saddle horn, he fixed his sight on the muzzle of the handgun. His death would emerge from that dark eye. A chance the guy would miss, but at this range, he probably wouldn't.

But then the Chinese lifted the firearm and peered down at it, face blank, then surprised. Teddy grinned. "You're out of ammo too, you old son of a bitch!" he yelled, bearing down on him. He leaned out, arm outstretched, as the dark eyes rose again to meet his own. They widened as Chagatai grasped what was coming at him, and flung his forearm up in a hasty, instinctive block.

Leaning down, Teddy swept the pchak in a wide saber-stroke that when it connected sent a shock all the way up to his shoulder and nearly knocked him out of the saddle. For a second, his arm paralyzed, he thought he'd hit the steel door. But glancing back as his mount sheered away neighing in pain, he saw the marshal sag back, gripping the top of the door with one hand. But his head lolled, nearly severed from the shoulders. Blood waterfalled down his chest, obliterating the rows of colorful ribbons with a scarlet drenching.

Then the marshal collapsed to the pavement, and the pistol spun away clattering over the asphalt.

Teddy's pony was foundering under him. Reaching down its flank, he felt the hot blood clotting on its rough coat. It sank, going down on its forelegs as its knees buckled. He clung for another second, then grabbed the mane and half slid, half rolled off as the animal collapsed and rolled onto its side.

He landed on the bad leg, and something in it snapped and tore despite the brace. The pain blinded him for a moment and he sank to a knee beside the fallen horse, gasping as his foot buckled sideways. Another weapon . . . He sheathed the pchak with shaking hands and picked up an AK one of the rebels had dropped. Racked the bolt, feeling the slight but definite resistance as it fed a live round, and propped it on the heaving flank of the dying beast.

He surveyed the aftermath of battle. Vehicles flamed and smoked. Ammunition rattled as it cooked off. From the hillside, diesels growled as his light tanks slowly rolled down the last few yards to survey their work and hose down the still-living wounded with machine guns. Rebels and Interior troops lay intermingled on the asphalt, along the berm, up the hillside. A knot of mujs were dragging terrified civilians out of the last vehicle, forcing them to their knees on the center line, and executing them with single shots to the back of the neck.

Teddy gritted his teeth and pushed himself upright, using the Kalashnikov as a cane. The pain was terrific, breaking in combers like Santa Clara surf. He panted. The mountains reeled around him. He bent, trying to force the foot back into its titanium brace, but something was bad wrong. He took one step on it, biting his lip and grunting. Then, slowly, another.

He limped toward the knot of rebels as more shots rang out.

"WHOEVER they are, they're executing the survivors," Major Zein said. Her tone was flat, without judgment. She pointed to the screen. "Is that your HVT?"

Andres bent closer, arms folded. The wind whispered outside, scratching like a million tiny claws trying to get in at them. Was it windy there? Yeah, maybe, considering the way the smoke was dissipating now. Below where the gossamer-winged drone lingered:

solar-powered, complexly lensed, an Argus eye unseen and unsus-
pected by those below.

He'd watched it all. The silent unfolding of the ambush. The
explosions, like fiery black blossoms. The silent tumbling of vehicles, and the noiseless sprawl of bodies. The smoke had obscured
the action from time to time, but sporadically cleared, at least
enough for him to follow the battle, like glimpses between passing clouds.

Far below, shimmering with magnification, a tiny figure was
limping away from a fallen horse. The animal tossed its head, obviously suffering. Red stained its side and pooled beneath it. An SUV
stood with doors flung open, slanted across the road. Bodies lay
scattered around it. He could just make out the colors of their uniforms. Black, green, gray. A few combatants looked to be of smaller
stature. Women? Boys? He couldn't be sure. And the limping figure? Probably a lot of the rebels limped, especially after a battle.

"Can we zoom in closer?" he murmured. "I know, it pixelates,
but . . ."

Zein told one of the sergeants to drop to angels four and go to
max magnification. Andres waited. The image on the screen expanded, but the larger it grew the more the details wavered, until
it boiled as if viewed through molten glass.

"Shit," the sergeant whispered. "It's the hot air off that pavement. A mini-thermal effect. Usually we can do better, but I guess
not today."

The view banked as the drone came around in a long lazy circle.
Much like, Andres imagined, a buzzard, viewing the carnage from
above. Where *were* the buzzards anyway? The V-winged scaven-
gers of the high mountains, whose effortless orbits in the sky he'd
admired so often? Well, they'd arrive soon enough, with all that
fresh meat out on the highway.

"Is that him?" Zein asked again.

Andres was about to say *I'm not sure, I can't tell,* when just
then the video steadied, just for a microsecond, and at that same
moment the lone limping figure so far below turned its face up

to the sky. As if aware it was being watched, though Andres was pretty sure that wasn't possible. The drone was far too small, far too high up.

The face was bearded, a male's, and it wore an eyepatch. He seemed to be holding some sort of rifle, or other weapon. But not in a combat stance. Was he . . . yes.

He was using it as a crutch.

With a coldness at his heart, Andres said, "That's him."

"That's your target?" Zein said. Both sergeants straightened. The leftmost one began keyboarding. "You're absolutely sure?"

"Yeah. It's him. That's SKFROG."

The sergeant on the right reached for her trackball.

"You'll need to confirm, for our records. Like I said." Zein handed him a signature pad and stylus, like what you'd use to sign for a purchase at a drugstore. He thought for a moment of asking for a printout, just to gain another few seconds, but finally resigned himself. He signed, but not with his real name, of course.

He handed it back.

"Proceed?" She avoided his eyes.

He nodded.

Zein instructed the black sergeant in a neutral tone, recentering the white box Andres had seen previously onto the individual he'd pointed out. A tap, and a set of orange brackets lit. She edged them over on the screen, then adjusted them a smidgen more, until they lined up with the white one, tracking with it. Smaller, but centered inside it.

Another click from her mouse, and crosshairs winked on. These were centered too, subdividing the orange square into quadrants. The techs discussed this in low voices, keyboarding. The orange box displaced a few yards.

Zein murmured, "What about the others down there, near him? We've got a pretty decent radius with these new warheads."

Andres touched his lips with a knuckle. On the screen, other rebels were crowding around where the second SUV stood. Looking down, apparently, at one of the bodies. The one in the green uniform. Its head lay at an unnatural angle. He couldn't make out any more detail in the boiling image.

"This heat's really distorting things," the blond sergeant complained. "Seems to be getting worse, too."

Andres cleared his throat. "What kind of radius are we talking about?"

"Kill radius? Ten meters. Wounding, fifteen."

A diameter of thirty feet would take out everyone thronging around the SUV. And any survivors inside it as well. He touched his lips again, considering. But to judge by the executions he'd just seen, the sprawl of bodies along the white centerline of the road, there probably weren't many prisoners left alive.

Once again that numbing chill touched his spine. He'd had to kill before. Sure. But never this far away, where he himself ran no risk at all—

"Sir?" The major tugged his sleeve. He flinched away.

"Sorry," she said. "But once we have a solution, it can go away at a moment's notice. The last second or two of flight guides on a laser beam. We don't turn it on until that final homing phase, so the target has no time to react once they see the illumination. But if this heat gets any worse . . . it could distort the beam. If we shoot, we don't want to miss."

"Right." He nodded. "All right . . . Take them."

"We can wait, see if he moves away from that scrum—"

"They're all hostiles. Take them." Agency orders: along with Oberg, neutralize as many of the top leadership as possible.

The sergeant murmured, "Will this be a double-tap strike?"

Andres frowned. "What? Explain?"

The major said, "We carry two missiles on these long-range missions. On underwing points. SOP on strategic-effects strikes is to place one Jagger, wait ten minutes, then place the second. To hit any responders, aid personnel, the target's senior staff, and family members. It also balances the airframe in terms of weight and drag."

Andres felt even colder. "Maybe. Let's hold off, see how the first one goes."

Zein nodded and turned back to her keyboard. She flipped open a binder and rapped several keys, a rapid, cadenced *tappa-tap-tap* she'd obviously entered many times before. The release code, he assumed. Beside her the sergeants were also busy, one monitoring the track the system was holding on the intended target, the other using a second camera to do an azimuth check, scanning around the drone's airspace. It all seemed well practiced, as if they did this every day. Which of course they probably did.

"You can put your headphones on now," she told him.

Andres settled the headset over his ears. A series of tones was sounding. The missile was initializing.

Then a separate tone, a lower, ominous hum, almost an om.

"Warhead confirmed live," Zein said. "Standing by to fire. On your command."

The agent looked down again on the scene below, remote and at the same time intimate, and shook his head slowly. *Teddy, you stupid fuck*, his lips formed, though he didn't say it aloud. You could have come home a hero. Had a nice retirement. But no, you had to be stubborn.

If only this could have ended differently.

He'd tried to make that happen. That it hadn't been enough was not his fault.

He nodded. "Do it," he said. "Do it now."

TEDDY was limping back toward the second vehicle, where his rebels were gathering around something on the pavement. Chagatai, he assumed. Off to the side his horse was groaning, lying on the hot asphalt, blood still pumping down its side. He flipped the safety off the AK and placed it against the beast's brow. It rolled tormented eyes to stare up at him. "Sorry, horse," he said, and fired. The labored breathing stopped.

He was limping toward where his men were stripping the marshal of insignia, weapons, decorations, even the uniform jacket, when he felt something strange. Sensed a sudden brightness, all around.

He caught a flash from the corner of his eye and looked about him, puzzled. A flicker.

Then he looked up.

The light was so bright he could barely squint into it. So hot it drew dazzling rings around itself in shifting colors of the rainbow, inside his eye.

He stared up, entranced, wondering. Until all at once he understood.

It was a laser.

He knew then, and let his breath ease out. His shoulders sagged. He glanced at the closest tank, maybe fifty yards away. He wouldn't reach it in time. Not if they were already illuminating. That came only in the last second or two before impact.

He started to raise a finger, a final ironical salute; then changed his mind. Instead, he lifted both hands, palms up. In the gesture of submission. Of resignation.

In that moment, a voice spoke to him from the sky once again. One of endless compassion, endless love. And endless understanding, of everything he had been and everything he had done.

There is no chance, it told him again, as it had on a mountain in the freezing dark, under the remorseless stars of the high and empty mountains. *There is no choice.*

You have always done My will.

He understood, then, that this turn of the page was all in the Plan. Had been, from the foundation of time and the universe.

He still didn't understand how he could live his life by his own decisions, yet be part of some larger design. But now he accepted that it was not for him to understand, or even to question.

All he had to do was submit.

He spread his arms wider, palms up, welcoming whatever was to be, whatever was fated to come.

The light burned hotter above him, ever more brightly, like a descending sun.

Teddy Oberg, the Lingxiu al-Amriki, watched his fate descend. As his last moment ticked away he stood immobile, offering himself, enjoying the final instants of his life. Until sound and sight and thought itself ended, in an all-obliterating flash of transcendent and transforming light.

21

The Eastern Shore, Maryland

HECTOR'S sitting in the lot, back at the VA center. It's still open, even this late in the day. There are still cars here. One has to be the counselor's. The *pendejo* who screwed him, and grinned while he did it.

The gun's on his lap. Loaded, safety off, with twelve rounds in it. And two more full mags beside him on the passenger seat, along with the bike lock. He figures that ought to be enough.

Getting hold of one wasn't hard. Three phone calls, a discreet meetup behind a long-abandoned, tumbledown barn, and the local, the redneck, had handed it over. He said it was his dad's, but Hector figured it for stolen. A heavy old pistol, the bluing worn, but he'd function-checked it and fired several shots out into the cornfield before handing over thirty of the flimsy hundred-dollar bills. All that was left of his mustering-out pay.

Which leaves him pretty much high and dry.

But he won't need money after today.

He sits in the rusty Kia with the engine ticking over, *ta pocketa, ta pocketa*, and sees himself killing them all. Imagining it unfold, like a movie. Sweat rolls down his face. The fan works, but the air conditioner's been busted for years. So it's just hot air blasting over his face and legs.

Yeah. All of them. The fucking whiteass counselor, who fucked him over. The snotty black bitch at the counter. *Every* bitch at every counter, and all the losers sitting in the fucking blue plastic chairs with their dicks in their hands. Shoot them fucking all. Do the world a favor.

Except for the old lady who'd let him go ahead of her in line, if she's there today. She was the only human being in the place. The rest of them, waste of oxygen.

"Let's go do this, Hector," somebody says. He's not sure who. Somebody else in the car. But there's no one else with him.

His finger flexes on the trigger. He sees the bullets hitting, the blood flying, the shocked, disbelieving faces. The screams. They're trying to get away, scrambling under desks, clawing at the door. But he's secured it behind him with the bike lock. Nobody gets out.

Only he can't see what comes after that. How the movie ends. Eating the gun, probably. Muzzle will be fucking hot, after three mags rapid-fire. Save the last round, stick the pistol in his mouth, end of story, roll the credits.

That'd send a fucking message, all right.

But a nagging thought keeps him from opening the broken door and stepping out into the sunlight. Yeah, he's pissed. And righteously so. But is he really this far gone? Far enough to kill a bunch of civilians?

Not that he hasn't killed civilians before. He blinks.

The hill was tangled jungle once. Now it's blasted-down matchstick trees and exposed rock with a coat of raw, wet, harrowed soil. The orange mud glitters with steel fragments and ammo casings.

Another wave of enemy pushes up from the ground, as if growing from the soil up through the stumps and craters of the shattered jungle. But these shadowy forms look different. Helmetless. Weaponless. Hector adjusts his Glasses.

Old men, kids, women. They stumble forward, glancing back fearfully as someone screams at them from behind.

Hector drags a sleeve across his face, wiping away blood and tears, sweat and powder-grime.

The enemy's driving Taiwanese from the villages ahead of them as shields. They emerge from the smoke holding one another's hands, families together, helping each other over fallen trees and between shell holes.

The Marines will have to machine-gun women, children, old men. Or be overrun.

In his pocket, Sergeant Hector Ramos fingers a plastic rosary. Whether they hold or not, he won't be going home.

He remembers now how sure of that he was, back then.

But now he's home after all. Yet he wishes he was back there, in a combat zone, where the world at least made some fucking sense.

He sits shaking in the old car, greasy sweat slicking his face, the musky stink of mouse piss and mold filling his nostrils. Thinks about taking another pill, then remembers: he threw them away. They didn't work anyway. He can't sleep. He feels guilty, angry, afraid, 24/7. Maybe finishing himself off, at least, isn't a bad idea.

He lays the gun aside and covers it with the towel he keeps in the car to wipe the sweat off. Sips some water from his CamelBak.

He sits there for a while longer, watching the front door of the center. Waiting for at least the fat white counselor to come out. Hector needs to take care of him at least. Even if he doesn't do the rest.

A car noses around from the back and passes him. Too late, he realizes the guy in it is the white guy. Leaving for the day. He's missed him. "Fuck," he mumbles.

He uncovers the gun, looks at it, clicks the safety off, and puts the muzzle in his mouth. Then presses it to his head. No, bad idea. Seen too many guys just blinded, wounded. You can never be sure where the bullet'll go after it hits the skull. So it's his mouth again. Yeah. Just like that. Between his teeth.

A crazy sense intrudes: he's been here before. Crouching in the dark, watching a monstrous toad . . . yeah.

In the eco center in Taiwan, the night the POWs beat Lieuten-ant Hawkshadow nearly to death. Glass glittering in the light of his flash. Bizarre shrunken forms drift in a clear fluid: reptile embryos, snakes, insects, amphibians in a fluorescent rainbow. And a jar of two-hundred-proof alcohol, or maybe ether, the la-bel's in Chinese. It sears the membranes of his throat. He chokes, gasps, snorting, barely able to breathe through the fumes.

Then he'd charged his carbine, and put the muzzle in his mouth . . . except . . . what had happened after that?

He blinks, shaking.

And yet here he is again. Ready to do it.

But he can't seem to get it up enough to actually pull the trigger.

"¡No me jodas!" he mutters. What the *fuck* is wrong with him?

The faces. Some are smiling at him. Others, mouths stretched wide, seem to be shouting. Breuer. Titcomb. Conlin. Schultz. Vin-cent. Orietta and Truss, Troy Whipkey, and Lieutenant Hern. Bleckford, who killed himself before they ever reached a war zone. Sergeant Clay. Patterson, Karamete, Ffoulk, dead on Taiwan.

Suddenly Hector goes still.

For the first time, he can make out what they're calling.

"We miss you, Hec."

"Come on. This way. We got point."

"Shit, okay. It don't matter," he mutters at last, and shoves the pistol into his pocket. Covers the spare mags with the towel. He'll only need the one anyhow.

He gets out, leaving the car unlocked, and heads out into the field beside the center. Time to walk away from Hector Ramos. Leave the bastard behind, and not look back.

It's a big empty field of some kind, that's all. Maybe part of a farm once, but deserted and overgrown now. The weeds stretch back to the woods, which begin a couple hundred meters from the road. A narrow worn path, not much more than a deer trail, leads toward the pines and cedars. He follows it, pistol dragging down his pocket, thumping against his thigh.

Back there. In the woods, in the shade. Someplace cool. There'll be ticks, of course, but he won't be around long enough to worry about them.

The wind rises, cooling his sweat-soaked scalp. It ruffles the grass, which has grown pretty high. It rustles gently around him, the seed-heavy heads nodding. This patch hasn't been mowed in a long time. There are little blooms, too, scattered amid the grass and small bushes. Wildflowers.

He walks more and more slowly. Looking down at them.

They're just weeds. Some purple, some blue, some white. A few, orangish yellow. *Amarillo y oro.*

But they're . . . he doesn't know the words. They're just . . . there.

When the wind blows, they nod and sway. The constant, gentle motion . . . he can't look away.

Somehow, they seem to sympathize with him. As if they know.

He has no idea what's happening. But when he looks at the flowers, he doesn't see the faces anymore.

He turns off the path and stops. Now he's standing among a patch of tall yellow flowers. They come up to his waist, so the nodding, swaying blossoms softly brush his outstretched fingers.

What's going on here? He stares down openmouthed at them. What the fuck, over?

But the comforting feeling grows. As if these plants *know* what's happened to him. As if they *care.*

Like they're drowning out the ghost voices. Saying, You're not so bad, *wey.*

He slides the gun out of his pocket and cocks it. Holds it to his face again, then his chest.

Only now he feels even less like doing it. And the flowers don't want him to. They're swaying in the wind, like they're dancing for him. Smiling up at him. It doesn't feel like he's so alone. Or maybe that there's more to all this than he's thought about so far.

It's hard to put into words.

And even weirder, he feels . . . *happy*. Deep down, like it was buried there. Like a Marine buried in his foxhole by a shell. But when you dig him out, he looks up and grins, and he's okay.

Finally Hector whispers, "Oh, fuck this."

He stands in the field for quite a while, holding the gun but not pointing it anymore. At last he decocks it. He thinks about throwing it away, but figures that wouldn't be a good idea. Kids might play out here, in the woods, in this vacant lot.

Back at the center, he hauls the creaking rusted door of the Kia shut again with a bang. Stuffs the gun into the glove box. Puts the car in gear, and heads back home.

The used tire he bought at M&W starts to thump. It's out of round or something. Maybe coming apart. And yet the weird joy he felt in the field persists. It's like he learned something out there. Or relearned it, something he'd lost sight of.

"Fuck," Hector whispers, but he's not really angry at the car anymore.

HE stops at Royal Farms for a twelve-pack, but remembers when he's at the counter that he's almost broke. Just enough for a quart bottle. He drinks half sitting in the car, gulping it down, looking straight ahead. Trying to get a handle on what's just happened.

The tire holds long enough to get home, so he's relieved.

But as he nears the house a car he doesn't recognize is hulking in his mother's driveway. He tenses. It's a prewar Escalade, a huge black Cadillac, with blacked-out windows that can't be legal.

Three men leaning against it straighten as he pulls in.

It's too late to turn around, but Hector steers away as he pulls in to put as much distance and time between them as he can. He flips open the glove compartment again.

One of the men waves. Hector recognizes him.

Mahmou', his old enemy from the Line.

The arrogant asshole who'd bullied him, back when he'd been young and scared.

Hector grins, remembering the last time they met. It had ended with the former bully on his knees, bleeding from nose and mouth, begging not to be hit again. On the way back from the bar Hector'd tossed Mahmou's car keys and wallet into a flooded ditch along the road.

He sobers. Tucks the pistol into the back of his trousers. Slams the door behind him.

Then he recognizes the second man. And that's an even bigger surprise.

"Hec-tor, my man. Come on over here." The heavyset Latino lifts a hand. His good hand, the one he didn't lose in an ice-crushing machine, years before at Farmer Seth's. Older than Hector remembers, his long gray hair slicked back. Today, instead of factory coveralls and a red bandanna, he wears a black suit, despite the heat, and a bright yellow sports shirt without a tie. Gold shines at his wrist, at his ears, around his neck. He looks . . . prosperous.

"José," Hector says. "How you doing, boss?"

"Come here, *mi hijo. Mi hermano*. I am so glad you have come back safe." His former foreman opens his arms wide.

Hector allows himself to be embraced. Allows the pistol to be gently taken from him and handed to Mahmou'. Who smiles, and sets it carefully on the seat of the Escalade.

José catches Hector's glance. He barks a laugh. "There is bad blood? I understand. You don' been friends. But I need all my friends to be good. Now the two of you, make pax." José shoves Hector and Mahmou' together.

The Arab holds out his hand. "Bygones be bygones. I don' hold no grudges, I deserved it for hittin' on your girl fren'. I did."

Mahmou' introduces the third man, a huge black whose bare arms bulge with muscle. They're scarred with the same darkened lacework that the others have, including Hector. From the spurs and beaks of the chickens. "Lebo here, he come on the Line after you left."

"We all *carnal*," José says simply. Meaning, of the same blood. "Children of the Line." He waves his hand, and Hector notes the black butt of a handgun at his belt when his jacket lifts. "You been down to the plant, Hector. I heard. You ain't thinking to go back?"

"Thinking about it," Hector says. Guarded, like.

"Army ain't got nothing for you?"

"Marines," Mahmou' corrects his boss. Getting back a glance, but no more.

José grins again and pats Hector's arm. "Marines. You done your duty, bro'. Been to *la chingada*. Now you home, but they don' do nothing for you, *wey*? I heard. Yeah, I hear everything goes on around the Shore."

"What do you need, Boss?" Hector asks, but he's pretty sure he knows. Or at least has an idea.

José hitches up his pants, a writhing gesture, since he has only the single hand. Hector remembers that habit. The foreman drove them hard in the carmine light, where the Line pulsed and whirred and droned.

It looks like these days José and his crew are into something that pays better.

"Let's get in the car," his old supervisor suggests. "It's too *pinche* hot out here, *buena onda*? You okay sitting with us, talking?"

"Sure." Hector's neck's prickling, but it seems like the least unsafe thing to do right now. And really he's not concerned. He's been in worse situations. Lebo pats him down again, not too closely, but hesitates when he feels the phone. He holds out a hand, and after a second Hector hands the cell to him. As he goes to set it carefully on the front stoop, Hector climbs in after José, into the front, while the other two take the back.

José asks about his mother, and about his brothers, and Mirielle. It doesn't sound like he's gathering intelligence, but Hector catches the meaning. It's a veiled threat. He answers carefully. These people remember him at seventeen, but he feels like he's lived a hundred years since then. He waits for what they're really here about.

And pretty soon José slides around to it. "You know, *mi hijo*, we never made much money working for Seth. It was a *negocio*, you know? A paycheck. But some people I used to know got in touch. Now we in a different line of business."

"Yeah? What're you pushing?" Hector asks him.

"*Mira, chicos,* we're not dealing with no dummy here. Hector's smarter than he looks." José dips into a side pocket of the car door. "Know what this is?"

The pale crystals are twisted into baggies. Hector regards them without emotion. He doesn't need to nod.

Mahmou' leans forward from the back seat, eager to talk. "This shit put you on Cloud Thirty. People take one hit, they can't stop. They gotta come back for more."

Lebo adds, wiping his nose, "Yeah, we in the D. The whole Shore up to Delaware. We don' deal, yo? We the middleman. Shit come in, we break it down. Stretch it a little bit, then farm it out to the hitters, the ones put they asses on the street."

José looks on, smiling and nodding. Hector likes this, his willingness to let his squad have their say. There's more of a team feeling here. The kind you have when there's a good NCO in charge. When everybody trusts everybody else to have their back.

But he remembers, too, what the foreman used to do for a joke. Catching seagulls, and hanging them up on the Line. Chuckling as they flapped and struggled, heading through the shit-smeared, blood-smeared hole in the wall that led straight to Death.

"Huh. What about the cops?" he asks.

José chuckles. "Nobody out there no more. Ain't no money left to pay cops. Don't worry about that.

"But, see, there's other boys. Bad ones, they like the money, like our product. And we need somebody to maintain discipline. Some *chingado* thinks about flipping, he got to be convinced that ain't good for his health."

He leans over and taps Hector's knee. "We need a guy can handle a tire thumper, ain't afraid to use a gun, either. It ain't easy, we all got to *chingarle mucho.* But it pays. It pays very good. *Buena onda?* An' we have fun, too." In the back seat, Lebo snickers.

"I don't know," Hector says.

José puts his one arm around him. "Veteran like you, war hero. An *hermano* we can trust. A *carnal* from the Line. You done your service. Now it's time to get on your hustle. *Wey?*"

"I don't know," Hector says again. The idea of something that pays better than Seth appeals, but he's not sure he wants to get involved in this.

The boss looks puzzled, like he's surprised Hector doesn't jump at the offer. But just pats his knee again, then sits up. Says over his shoulder to the others, "Hand that up here, let him take a look." Twisting to take it, José grunts as Lebo slides something heavy up to them between the seats. "Maybe this'll change your mind."

Hector weighs the thing in his hands, astonished.

It is black and ugly and heavy and looks exactly like what it is: a machine designed to kill as many people as quickly and cheaply as possible.

It's his old Pig. Well, not his, but from the same litter. He clears it without conscious thought, locking the bolt to the rear and putting it on safe. His hands move swift and sure. He flips up the top cover and checks the feed tray.

"Full auto, 7.62, gas-operated long-stroke piston, six hundred fifty rounds a minute," he mutters.

Behind them Lebo chuckles as Hector tilts the machine gun toward the light to inspect the bolt face. It's not just clean, it looks unfired. "Where the fuck you get this?" he breathes, but it's obvious. A painted armory number has been half obliterated from the buttstock.

"M&Ms selling off their shit." José leans back, smiling at Hector as he runs his hands over the gun. "And we got *plenty* ammo. Yeah, you like, I can see that.

"See, we goin' first-class now. With you backing us up, nobody gonna give us any shit." He makes a graceful flipping-off gesture. "Well, you take some time, think about it. We your people, *wey*? You know we will never give you up or let you down. Not too many you can say that about."

"Yeah . . . yeah, I'll think about it," Hector says.

Mahmou' reaches up and tries to give him some kind of hand-shake Hector doesn't recognize. They all laugh. Good-naturedly, as far as he can tell.

"Okay, good talk." José hands him a card. It reads *Mardelva Poultry Supplies.* Then nods regally to Lebo, who gets out and opens the door for Hector. José leans out to call after him, "We be in touch, okay."

"Here's your phone back," Lebo says. Then lowers his voice. "It's a good deal, man. He is not shitting you, it's very few people he lets in."

Hector nods. He stands by his rusted-out junker, watching as the tinted windows slide down for the three to wave a casual farewell.

The windows rise again, smoothly, soundlessly, and the Caddy backs down the drive, shells and grass crackling under the big tires.

Too late, he remembers they didn't return his pistol.

TURNS out his tire isn't actually bad. The shimmy was just loose wheel nuts. He should have torqued them down harder. That's a re-lief. Then his mother needs bread and ice and milk from the store. He takes a detour on the way to go by Mirielle's one last time be-fore he gives up.

And a gray sedan's parked in front. He pulls in, sits for a minute, then climbs the step up to the porch and knocks.

When she comes to the door he almost doesn't recognize her. She's heavier and looks tired. Her hair's cut short and she's in a stained blouse and blue pants like a nurse's scrubs. Miri stands there staring, as if he's a stranger. Her hands creep up to her mouth, then she hugs herself.

"*¿Héctor, eres tú?*"

He nods. "*Sí.* It's me."

"You're back. For good?"

"Done with the war. Yeah. I'm home now."

"I'm glad you're back safe. And how . . . how is your mother? Your sisters?"

He says they are good.

She glances at him, then away, biting her lip. Hector can't read her. A baby's crying back in the house. "How's your mom and dad?" he asks her.

"They're all right," she says. But she keeps looking away, to the side, up, not really meeting his eyes.

"Well, hey, can we talk?" he says at last.

She sighs, still hugging herself, as if she's cold. At last she glances back into the house again, then pushes the screen door open and steps out. She even walks differently, more heavily. "Let's sit on the glider. Like we used to."

He backs away to let her out, then follows her to the creaking old wooden glider. She strides sluggishly, as if burdened. He remembers how she used to bustle along the corridor at high school, confident, head up, books hugged to her chest. Yeah, and he remembers sitting here in this glider with her, like she says: the evening sky an amazing red over the bay, the smell of jasmine, the chirping music of cicadas, the manic wander of fireflies. And the kisses, how horny he used to get. But she'd guide his hands away when he got too close to the prize.

The glider creaks dangerously as it takes their weight, and he glances up at the rusty anchor bolts.

They don't say anything for a little bit. He takes her hand, but it lies limp and lifeless in his.

"We're all grown up now, aren't we, Hector," she says. She doesn't sound happy about it. But at least she's not asking if he's killed anyone.

Which he's grateful for. "Yeah. I guess so."

"Sorry I didn't answer your letters."

"You blocked my calls too."

"Yeah, I'm sorry. I didn't . . . there was a lot going on." She still doesn't meet his gaze.

"So what's going on? I heard you were down with your aunt in Virginia."

"Yeah, we . . . my mom and I were there for a while."

Hector pushes the swing into motion with a boot against the pillar, but she says no, don't, it makes her sick. So he lets it sway to a stop. He's puzzled. Can't read the situation. Finally he pulls the rosary out of his pocket. The red plastic one she sent him, after he lost the first one in the assault on Taipei. He holds it out. "You want this back?"

"No. No, you can keep it."

"It kept me safe. Like you said it would."

"That's good, Hector." She looks away.

"Mir, what's wrong? I thought you'd be glad to see me."

She shakes her head. Is she angry? Are those tears? He tries to put an arm around her, but she pushes it away.

"Maybe I better show you something," she says. "You should come in."

The front door creaks and slams. He follows her through the cramped living room. A Virgin of Guadalupe candle flickers. A smell like sour milk fills the air.

Her mother's in the kitchen, changing a baby on the bare rickety table. She gives them a sharp glance as she tapes the sides of the diaper. She thrusts the baby at Mirielle, grabs a bag of cracked corn, and goes out the back door. Excited clucking rises back there. But in the kitchen it's quiet, except for quiet snuffling from the baby, who looks eagerly about him, or her, with wide, alert brown eyes. Fastening at last on Hector, the new thing in the room.

"That your sister's kid?"

"No, Hector. He's why I din't answer your texts."

He doesn't know what to say. He's confused. Bewildered. Hers? What the fuck? He checks her hand, but there's no ring.

Finally he holds out his hands. "Can I hold it?"

"You want to?" Her voice rises, like she doesn't quite believe him.

But he wiggles his fingers, and at last, reluctantly, she slides the child into his arms. The baby doesn't seem to mind. He looks up at Hector.

And it's kind of like the same feeling he had that morning, with the wildflowers. Looking down into those eyes, which look straight at him. Straight into him. Accepting. Trusting.

Like they're saying, You're not so bad, *wey*.

Like they're saying, *It's you and me now.*

"Whose is he?" he murmurs, quietly, so as not to make the kid cry. "Not that asshole Mahmou's? Tell me it isn't fucking Mahmou'."

"What? No. No! He never touched me, after you beat him up at Porky's. No, you don't know him. He's not from here. Used to work at the Zone, but when everybody there got so sick, he didn't stay."

"He's not here?"

"No, he . . . he really didn't want a kid. Tried to make me get rid of it. I said no, I wasn't going to do that. Even if I had to raise him all by myself. At least I'd have my mom to help."

Hector feels lightheaded. He sways on his feet, and she reaches for the child. But he turns away, cradling the baby. Who's still staring up at him, gaze as steady as a targeting laser.

And something's loosening in him. Unlocking, it feels like, in his chest. It's weird, like nothing he's ever felt before. Like something hard's melting, ice in the sun, or a lead brick in a blowtorch flame. He can't look away from those eyes.

"Hey, Mirielle?" he mutters at last. "Want to get married?"

Her look turns flinty. "Don' fuck with me, Hector. I don' deserve that."

It's the first time he's ever heard her use that word. "I'm not fucking with you! I'm asking serious, do you want to get married."

"I got a baby now, Hector."

"I might not mind having a son," he says. Still looking down at the kid. Damn, he's cuter by the minute. Is that a smile? "Holy shit, he's smiling at me," he says. "Look at that."

"You are so weird, Hector. And you're playing with me now."

He goes to the screen door. Her mother's crouching in the

backyard with a chicken clamped between her knees, doing something to its beak. "Missus? Is it okay if Mirielle and I get married?"

She looks up with a hostile squint just like her daughter's. Wrinkles her nose. Speaks, not to him, but past him, to her daughter. "*¿Él tiene trabajo?*" Then goes back to what she's doing with the chicken.

"Yeah, I got work. Two job offers already," Hector tells her. "Not sure which one I'm gonna take, but don't worry about that." He turns back to Mirielle. "I'm not shitting you. You want to get married, we can. Make a *familia*." Even though half of him is standing off to the side, wondering what the fuck he's doing here. Maybe, really screwing himself. Again.

Mirielle takes his arm and leads him back into the kitchen. She's smiling now. Half disbelievingly, but still smiling. Leaning over the baby, which he's still carrying, she gives Hector a kiss. Holds his arms. Whispers up to him, eyes shining, "Are you really serious?"

"Oh yeah. Been thinking about it for a while."

"And . . . Teodoro? You're not mad?"

That must be the baby's name. It's not bad. That'd be Ted, or Teddy, in American. "I'm not mad, Mir. For a long time, I din't think I'd ever even get back. Can't blame you for thinking the same thing."

She holds his arms more tightly, smiling up, blinking back tears. "Hector, you are a saint."

"Oh, I ain't no fu—I ain't no saint. Don't say that. I been—I done things out there I'm not proud of." He chokes back saying more, afraid of scaring her. Maybe someday. Or maybe never, maybe those are the things you don't never talk to anyone about. Except maybe those who've been there.

The baby starts to fuss, and Mirielle scoops it up, so dexterously it's as if she's been a mother forever. Well, she had little sisters. He sits at the table and she brings him iced tea. It's quiet here. It's nice. He sits and drinks the tea, watching her bustle around. It's almost as if they're married already. "Want to stay for dinner?" she says brightly.

"Uh, oh. No, thanks, got to get moving. Got to get my hustle on. If we're gonna set up together."

She flashes another smile. She even looks younger now, prettier. As if he's given her some huge precious gift.

Her mother comes in, banging the screen door, and squints at him again. As if she can't believe her eyes. *"¿De verdad quieres casarte con mi hija?"* Talking to him this time.

"Oh yeah," he tells her. "Not right this second, I got to get some things straight first. But yeah. Yeah."

"Este es un hombre loco," she remarks to Mirielle, and makes an elaborate production of an uncaring shrug, an eye roll. There's even a lip curl there, like she doesn't believe a word.

Hector's pretty sure about Mirielle. He's even feeling okay about the kid. But he's not so sure about this old witch. For sure, they're going to have to get a place of their own.

HE has to drive a little ways up the neck before he gets any bars on his phone. It's a cheap fucking thing anyway. He needs to get a real one, not this piece of crap from Dollar General.

He parks by the side of the road and sits holding it for a while. Looking at the two business cards on the seat beside him. Sweat trickles down his neck. It's hot as hell out here, and the open windows don't give any relief. There's no breeze at all today. The cornstalks stand motionless, baking in the heat. At their feet, along the edge of the road, a few small blue flowers speckle the ragged grass.

Farmer Seth Industries, one of the cards reads.

The other, *Mardelva Poultry Supplies*.

He looks up at a blue enamel sky. Not even a cloud up there. As if all movement has left the world, and everything will stand still forever now.

Only the images move. They press into his mind, insistent, intrusive, pushing and elbowing. He lets them come, then pass, not dwelling on anything, just watching. Like a movie.

Birds flutter and squawk in the deep carmine light of the Hanging Room.

A dirty guy in ragged clothes hunches in a corner, playing spoons clickety-clack under his arm. His eyes dart like trapped flies. "Cigarettes is alls I needs," he says over and over. "Five bucks for cigarettes is alls I needs."

The robot cart bumps along. Then the wheels grind in plowed-up soil. Between the battered tubes of abandoned, broken mortars. The fertilizer stink of explosive. His gaze wanders among wrecked equipment, overturned, smoking boxes, piles of empty packing material, tumbled bodies.

And helmetless, dark hair unraveled in the mud. Olive skin and a hawklike nose. A severed leg lies several yards away.

Another wave pushes up from the enemy line, growing from the soil up through the stumps and craters of the shattered jungle. Old men, kids, women. They lift their arms, pleading and crying.

A flag flutters above a burning city.

Small bodies lie in ragged lines. The boys are in blue rain slickers, the girls in pink. They all have the same colorful pencil boxes.

Beside his head something chuffs and clicks. His chest rises and falls with the noise. His lungs, inflating and deflating.

A bead curtain sways in the wind. The stars glitter through the colored glass, reflected and refracted from bead to sparkling bead.

The faces. There they are again. Pale and sweaty, splattered dark with gunsoot and mud and blood. He knows their names. He was one of them. They stare back, wavery, as if they're underwater. But they aren't calling to him anymore. Just watching, eyes empty.

He rubs his face.

The images pass. Others take their place.

He understands now. They're not going to go away. They're part of him. All the dead are part of him now. Like a heavy pack he's going to have to carry, till the end of his tour.

"You just gonna have to wait a little bit," Hector mutters at last. "But I'll be along pretty soon."

Then his hand steals out, almost without him noticing, and picks up the phone.

The Afterimage

Arlington, Virginia

WHEN Dan woke the windows were still dark. The bedside clock read 0500. Blair was snoring next to him. He lay watching the light grow, and trying to think of a reason to keep breathing.

They'd won the war. Maybe that was one reason. Simple curiosity, to see what happened after.

But his daughter was gone.

He was home. He and Blair were together again. They didn't have to worry about being nuked in their beds. And that was good. But last night she'd told him what lay ahead. It would be hard, prolonged, and probably more vicious than any previous political campaign in American history.

Justin Yangerhans had declared for the nomination. Unexpectedly, out of left field. He'd asked Blair to chair his campaign, and she'd resigned from the Department of Defense. Placing her in direct opposition to the administration.

She'd need his support. Maybe, even, his personal protection. Paranoid? Maybe. But the country had changed since the war began. Edging toward some disastrous precipice.

As for his own career . . . it was pretty much over, as far as he could see. Not that it mattered, but according to Niles, he'd probably be able to retire with his rank. Yay for you, Dan, he thought sourly.

Starting with the Academy, he'd always looked ahead. The next qualification. The next warfare school. The next mission. The next command.

Now, with his war finished, there didn't seem to be any challenge left for him to face. And if the Senate *didn't* approve the flag list, he'd be out of the Navy in mere months. What then?

It left him feeling like an astronaut, beyond the reach of gravity. In search of some way to orient himself. Where was up? Where was down?

He rolled over and punched his pillow into shape, yearning for an unconsciousness that would not return.

Anyway, he'd done his part. Maybe that was all, in the end, one could really be proud of.

He lay watching the light come. Suspended. Between.

Until the alarm buzzed, and it was time.

HE got up, shaved, and dressed, but still felt tapped out, even after nine hours' sleep. A few more hairs came out in his brush. When he cut himself, it took longer to heal. Most likely, he'd picked up some rads on his trip across the Midwest. His winter blues felt loose. He forced himself to swallow cereal, though he didn't really want it. He'd been shocked by the price when he'd picked up a box at the grocery. And instead of forty choices, like there'd been before the war, there were only three brands on the nearly empty shelves. Patriot-brand ersatz raisin bran, only without raisins. Kellogg's Corn Flakes, a perennial. And some kind of oat stuff in clear plastic bags that he didn't like the looks of, but had finally steeled himself to buy.

He still didn't have an assignment. Just temporary duty, assigned to the CNO's staff. He needed something to occupy himself with. Maybe he could get in on a study. The Joint Staff and Army Futures Command were planning war games to evaluate revised battle plans and explore what a postwar force might look like. Not just with new weapons, but with far more intimate integration than the services had achieved during the war just past.

The postwar Navy would be much smaller. That was already plain. The country no longer had the resources for the huge military it had entered the conflict with, let alone to continue the massive hemorrhage of money and labor expended in the last four years. And it would be AI-enabled, with autonomous units replacing manned platforms, whether at sea, in the air, or beneath the waves.

The coffeemaker trilled the first few notes of "Camptown Races" to signal it was done. Blair came in, fully dressed in the blue suit, blouse, low heels, and what seemed to be her favorite Hermès scarf these days, the one with the little foxes. He beckoned her over for a kiss. "The power look today, huh? Very sharp," he told her. "Hair looks great too."

She brushed a lock down over her ear. "Just had it done. Got to make a good impression. And it's harder for a woman, at least, every year . . . Thanks for making coffee."

"Sure, no problem." She was stepping away when he reached out to pull her to him again. He held her for a few seconds, cheek against her tummy, her hand resting lightly on his head.

She patted him one last time and stepped away. He checked the news, flipping through it on his phone as he sipped coffee. The last Covenanter militias were being "neutralized" in Indiana. The Russians were insisting on a permanent military presence in Ukraine and Finland. Sweden and Norway were rumored to be preparing to test a jointly developed nuclear weapon in the Svalbard Islands.

She turned back from the door. "Want me to drop you off? My pass's probably still good. At least to get us into West parking."

He swallowed off the last mouthful and stacked the cup in the dishwasher. Grabbed his jacket. "If you have time."

"Our meeting's at nine. I want to sit down with Jim for a few minutes before it starts. Define my responsibilities. Especially, discuss fundraising. Without getting a lot more commitment, he's going to end up in the lower tier of prospective candidates."

Dan nodded, looked out the window at the sky, decided against an umbrella, and followed her out.

IN her car, she flipped on the autodrive. The AUTO light came on and she immersed herself in a folder of documents. "Federal reporting forms," she said, to his quizzical glance. "Form one: statement of organization. Form two: statement of candidacy. Form three: report of receipts and disbursements. Quarterly. Monthly. Cash, in-kind gifts, goods and services. Loans, guarantees, endorsements. Lobbyist contributions. This is going to be pure sheer hell."

He shifted in his seat, tensing slightly as the car sensed a slot, accelerated, and merged them into the highway traffic. Which was picking up significantly; probably a good sign for the economic recovery. "Are you really sure you want to take it on?"

"Somebody's got to, and he asked me."

He rubbed his nose as the car changed lanes. Her logic was pretty plain. Considering her unpopularity with the left wing of her party, running a presidential campaign might well be the only way she could deal herself back into the game.

The car beeped and she looked up. "Here comes the turnoff. I'll just drop you off, text you later."

He reached for the door. "That's okay. I'll probably get home before you will. I'll just take the Metro."

"We'll see." A routine, casual, everyday husband-wife peck, and he rolled out and she pulled away. He looked after her, shaking his head. She'd never stop. He had to admire it. Even when it exhausted him sometimes.

He was so fucking lucky to have her.

HE was head down at his temporary desk, down the corridor from the CNO's office, when the aide stuck her head in. "Admiral would like you to step in, sir. If you're not busy."

Actually he'd just been reading the latest *Shipmate*, having nothing much else to do. The Naval Academy alumni magazine.

Which reminded him: he had to get in touch with the guy in Seattle he'd left his ring with. Pay him and get it mailed back. You could have a new one made, fresh metal, another stone, but he'd worn the old one through so much over the years it wouldn't be the same. The gold was worn, the crisp outlines of his class seal smoothed and polished. The Academy seal was battered nearly to obliteration through thirty years of contact with handrails, bulkheads, and tools.

Yeah, couldn't forget that . . . He'd touched base with a classmate about getting in on a study for the new quad tilt-rotor, but it seemed to be fully manned already. There was an industrial base study going too, but he wasn't eager to plunge into that mindnumbing mess. He'd never been much of a bean counter.

When he tapped at the open door the chief of naval operations was at his desk. Nick Niles didn't look up as Dan came in, just waved him to a seat. "Lenson."

So they were back to last names again, Dan thought. "Admiral," he said.

Niles took a few seconds to finish whatever he was reading, during which Dan got a good look at him. He didn't look quite as ill as before. His color was better. A reprieve? Or maybe he was just bouncing back from the last chemo. His uniform still looked as if it had been made for a much bigger man, though.

Finally Niles scrawled a signature, grunted as if satisfied, and swiveled his chair away. "Okay, what'd you want to see me about," he muttered.

Dan hesitated. Finally said, "Uh, the aide said you wanted to see *me*, sir."

"Oh yeah. Right." Niles blinked, as if uncertain. The first time Dan had ever seen an unfocused look on the broad face. Then he brightened. "Oh, right. What do we have you doing right now?"

"Floater, sir. On your staff."

"Right. Right." He nodded, as if to say *I knew that.*

Dan tried a personal tack, to give him time to catch up and save face. "Your son doing okay, sir?"

Niles nodded. "Still in the Gulf. His first command. Proud of him."

"That's great." Then he remembered Niles's nephews. Missing since the attacks. He swallowed that question. Pretty much figuring he knew the answer.

The CNO gave it a beat, then rumbled, deadpan, "Speaking of kids, I have somebody waiting next door you might want to see."

He hoisted himself, with a bit of an effort, crossed to the door to an inner office, and opened it. "He's here," he said to someone inside.

A very thin young woman in a flowered headscarf stepped out.

Dan stared, dumbfounded.

She'd always been slim, but Nan was gaunt now. Wasted-looking. She limped as she ran toward him.

But it was her. It was really his daughter.

A moment later she was in his arms. They clung to each other, neither speaking. Just . . . holding each other. He buried his face in her scarf. Which smelled like . . . *her* . . . And found himself unable to speak through a thickness in his throat.

It took him a while to get words past it. "I thought you didn't make it," he muttered into her shoulder.

"I know, Dada. I guess I almost didn't."

Dada. What she'd called him so long ago he'd almost forgotten it.

Behind them Niles coughed. "I'll give you a few minutes," he suggested, and let himself out.

They caught up with each other's stories. The nuking of Seattle. Her flight across the country with the first batch of antiflu meds. His, beginning with trying to follow her, but finally losing the trail. Her captivity in the hands of the Covenanters. The battle she'd barely survived. Then the helicopter trip Niles had arranged, when the Special Action major had called him with the information she was in DHS custody.

"We both had so many close calls," she marveled.

"Sounds like yours were closer than mine."

She rolled her eyes. "You were in the *war*, Dad. Right in the middle."

So it was Dad again, fast-forward. He grinned, still unable to believe she was really here. "We were all in this together, Bear." He patted her hand. "Uh, does your mom know? That you're back safe?"

"Oh yeah. I called. She's fine. How's Blair?"

"Great. Great. She's got a new thing going, too. I'll let her tell you all about it."

He put his arm around her again, and the scarf slipped down. He glimpsed a dark fuzz, like the first regrowth of a cancer patient's hair. And a new worry gripped him. "What about radiation? Is that why—?"

She pulled the scarf back into place. "Yeah, I'm in treatment. There's actually a new protocol. They say I'll recover. But I'll still have to get checkups every year."

He was hugging her again, his face aching from the unaccustomed smiling, when someone tapped at the door. The aide. "Admiral? I'm so glad about your daughter . . . Umm, the CNO would like one more word. Before you leave."

"Excuse me, honey," he told Nan, feeling awkward all over again. "I'll just be a minute. Then we'll go home, okay? Or stop at the cafeteria. Are you hungry? They have that bean soup you used to like."

She smiled. "Sure, Dad. If you'll eat something too."

NILES was waiting in the conference room, at one end of the long table. It was bare except for four notebook computers. He looked up from one. "So. She okay? Your kid?"

"She's great, sir. Just great. I can't thank you enough—"

"Got to take care of each other these days." Niles waved it away, looking tired. "Take the rest of the day off. Take her home with you."

"Thank you, sir. Thanks again. I mean, sending a helicopter—"

"I didn't send it just for her. It was already out there on another mission." He swatted the subject away, as if embarrassed. "But I wanted to tell you a couple of other things before you go. Remember our last conversation?"

His boss sounded sharper now. As if he'd checked his schedule, looked at his notes, gotten back up to speed during Dan's reunion with Nan. "Yes, sir," Dan said.

"About the International Criminal Court. The administration's refusing to send anyone. I think it's probably the right decision, but it puts us in bad company. If we send people, it compromises our sovereignty. If we don't, the Chinese won't feel obliged to either. And so far, everybody's deadlocked. No real update, I just wanted to let you know where that stood."

Dan nodded. "I appreciate the info, sir."

"Next issue. About your twilight tour."

Dan nodded again. If he really picked up a second star, he'd be extended for two more years of active duty before mandatory retirement. And traditionally, for the final tour of duty—the "twilight tour"—Navy detailers were flexible. If at all possible, they'd give an officer, or senior enlisted, his first choice.

Which apparently was what Niles was offering. And as CNO, even outgoing CNO, he absolutely had the juice to make pretty much anything happen.

So Dan told him. Not really sure exactly when it had come to him. Maybe it had been in the back of his mind for a while.

Niles didn't answer right away. Only pursed his lips, looking back at his screen. "Huh. Interesting. You sure about that?"

"It'd be my first choice, sir. As long as you're asking."

"Uh-huh. Maybe. But the timing's awkward. Second choice?"

Dan hadn't thought about a second choice. "Uh, well, I guess, sea duty. Whatever would be commensurate with my rank."

"And consistent with the needs of the service."

"Yes sir. Exactly."

"Well. You're still on the list for two stars, Dan." Niles rubbed his nose thoughtfully, looking out toward where the Potomac glittered beyond the trees. "But maybe I can do it. *Maybe*. Your first choice, I mean.

"But . . . you'd have to agree to do something else for me first. Something kind of on the order of your second choice, actually."

Dan nodded a third time.

And without a word, Niles rotated the screen to face him.

The story of the turbulent aftermath of the war with China, and of a new and even more dangerous challenge from the north, will continue in David Poyer's *Arctic Sea*.

Acknowledgments

Ex nihilo nihil fit. I began this novel with the advantage of notes accumulated for previous books as well as my own experiences at sea and ashore. In addition to those cited earlier in the series, the following sources were helpful for this volume:

Hector's chapters benefited from earlier comments by Peter Gibbons-Neff and Katie Davis. Other useful references included: "What to Expect When Someone You Love Is on a Ventilator," *UPMC Health*, March 24, 2016. Nicole E. Jenabzadeh, RN, MS, BSN, "A Nurse's Experience Being Intubated and Receiving Mechanical Ventilation," *Critical Care Nurse* 31; no. 6 (2011): 51–54. W. J. Bowman, "Neuromuscular Block," *British Journal of Pharmacology*, January 2006. Medical passages were commented on by Dr. Frances Williams, MD.

Blair's Zurich, White House, and Pentagon scenes were mostly based on personal experience. Other references that proved useful for her chapters included: Jack Perkowski, "Negotiating in China: 10 Rules for Success," *Forbes*, March 28, 2011. Walter Lippmann, *U.S. Foreign Policy: The Shield of the Republic* (Boston: Little, Brown, 1943), 82–83. Eric Heginbotham et al., "China's Evolving Nuclear Deterrent: Major Drivers and Issues for the United States," RAND Corporation, 2017. "It's Time for China to Free Float the Yuan," *Investor's Business Daily*, August 1, 2015.

And Richard Javad Heydarian, "Can China Really Ignore International Law?," *National Interest*, August 1, 2016.

For Nan's passages: References cited in previous books, plus Joao Cabral, "Water Microbiology, Bacterial Pathogens and Water," *International Journal of Environmental Resources and Public Health*, October 2010.

For Navy passages: Previous research aboard USS *San Jacinto*, USS *George Washington*, USS *Wasp*, Strike Group One, USS *Rafael Peralta*, and M80 *Stiletto*, among others. Aaron DeMeyer, Phil Wisecup, and Matthew Stroup were especially generous with their advice. The following additional sources were valuable as background: COMNAVSURFOR Instruction 3120.1, "Zone Inspections." Naval Education and Training Command, "Navy Announces FY-20 General Military Training Requirements," *Navy News Service*, August 13, 2019. Megan Eckstein, "Navy Planning for Gray-Zone Conflict; Finalizing Distributed Maritime Operations for High-End Fight," *USNI News*, December 19, 2018. Hal M. Friedman, "Blue Versus Purple: The U.S. Naval War College, the Soviet Union, and the New Enemy in the Pacific," 1946. Naval War College Monograph no. 46, Naval War College Press, 2016. Also *Joint Training Manual for the Armed Forces of the United States*, CJCSM 3500.03E, Joint Staff, Washington, DC. "Russia's Massive New Helicopter Carriers Could Displace 35,000 Tons and Deploy Fighter Jets," *Military Watch*, July 7, 2018. And Office of Naval Intelligence, *The Russian Navy: A Historic Transition*, December 2015. Descriptions of the human aftermath of a nuclear strike benefited from Susan Southard's *Nagasaki: Life After Nuclear War* (New York: Viking, 2015) and Samuel Glasstone et al., *The Effects of Nuclear Weapons*, U.S. Dept. of Defense, 1977.

For Teddy Oberg's strand of the story, the references listed in previous volumes, plus Peter Brugger et al., "Hallucinatory Experiences in Extreme-Altitude Climbers," *Neuropsychiatry, Neuropsychology, and Behavioral Neurology* 12 (1999): 67–71. "New 105mm Light Tank for Chinese Marine Corps," *Global Defense Security*, July 20, 2018.

For overall help and encouragement along this pilgrimage, I owe recognition to the Surface Navy Association, Hampton Roads Chapter; Charle Ricci and Stacia Childers of the Eastern Shore Public Library; the ESO Writers' Workshop; with bows to Bill Doughty, James W. Neuman, Alan Smith, John T. Fusselman, Richard Enderly, and others (they know who they are), both retired and still on active duty, who put in many hours adding perspective and leading me down the path of righteousness. If I left anyone out, apologies!

Once more: these sources were consulted for the purposes of *fiction*. The specifics of tactics, units, and locales are employed as the materials of story, not reportage. Some details have been altered to protect classified capabilities and procedures.

My deepest gratitude goes to George Witte, editor and friend of over three decades, without whom this series would not exist. And Sally Richardson, Young Jin Lim, Ken Silver, Janna Dokos, Martin Quinn, Paul Hochman, Naia Poyer, Adam Goldberger, Sarah Schoof, Amelie Littell, and Kevin Reilly at St. Martin's/Macmillan.

And finally to Lenore Hart, anchor on lee shores, and my North Star when skies are clear.

As always, all errors and deficiencies are my own.